THE
KNIFE
in the
DARK

BOOK TWO OF THE SEVEN SIGNS

by

D.W. HAWKINS

The Knife in the Dark
Book Two of The Seven Signs
2nd Revised Edition

Published by Laconic Press. The publisher does not have any control over and does not assume any responsibility for author or third-party websites or their content. For all inquiries, contact *questions@laconic.press*, or visit our website at www.laconic.press.

Laconic Press
120 S. Houghton Rd., Ste. 138-145
Tucson, Arizona 85748-6731
www.laconic.press

Visit the author website: http://www.dwhawkins.com

For those who have been there and those who are still here.

WANT A FREE FANTASY BOOK?

Join the Conclave and get ***The Killings at Rockman's Ford: A Seven Signs Novella*** for **FREE**
You'll also get members-only promotions and updates right from the author's desk.
What are you waiting for?

JOIN TODAY *and* GET YOUR FREE BOOK

www.dwhawkins.com/the-conclave

THE GOLDEN MUG

"Land! Land to the west!"

Halfhearted cheers greeted the call from *Seacutter's* lookout. Dormael didn't join them. Many of *Seacutter's* crew had died on the journey. More had perished later of wounds taken in the fight. There had been a ten-day stretch which had seen a body a day given over to the care of the deep. The remaining crewmembers had managed to keep the Orrisan ship afloat, but the mood aboard ship was somber.

We're responsible for that—at least, to some degree. The Galanians had chased them for weeks prior to their departure from Cambrell, but everyone had assumed they'd be safe once they made it to sea. They had underestimated the Imperials, and the dogged lengths to which their commander—Colonel Grant—had been willing to go. After a desperate naval battle, they had escaped by the skin of their teeth, leaving the Imperial ship crippled to the mercy of the storm.

There had been a subtle change in both Shawna and Bethany since the death of Colonel Grant. They'd become closer after Shawna put her sword into Grant's skull. His death had lifted much of the darkness from Bethany's expression, though her eyes were still haunted most of the time.

Dormael and Shawna had grown closer during the trip. She tolerated him, even laughed at his jokes on occasion, and he didn't bristle at her company the way he had on the road to Borders.

1

She'd won his respect during the fight and his friendship in the following days.

Those days had been spent healing from their various wounds, continuing Bethany's lessons, and training with Shawna. She'd insisted they hold regular sparring matches, both to help their bodies heal, and to keep their skills sharp. Dormael had objected until the first three times Shawna had bested him with nothing but her footwork. After that, he had stopped complaining. The crew of *Seacutter* had took bets on the matches, and fortunes were made in the rare events Dormael or D'Jenn bested Shawna—which usually happened by luck.

Bethany had watched every match with a muted smile. Her rapport with the crew had vanished after her spectacle with the armlet. It had broken Dormael's heart to see her ostracized after they had treated her as one of their own. He'd spent days talking to them, explaining that she was a student on her way to the Conclave, and such things were to be expected of new wizards. Some of them had bought it, but most of them had kept their distance.

The sight of land on the misty horizon was welcome. Mikael had meant to head for Minsdurim, in the land of Duadan, but they had been forced to the south by increasingly dangerous weather. They had spent nearly forty days running from winter storms. Fate had brought them back to Soirus-Gamerit, in the southeastern corner of the Sevenlands—Dormael and D'Jenn's homeland.

Twin guard towers slid out of the mist on the horizon, standing on a pair of breakwaters around the harbor of Mistfall—the largest, richest city in Soirus-Gamerit. The breakwaters were curved, built outward from a natural bay to enclose Mistfall's harbor and house the guard towers. Soirus-Gamerit was in the southeastern corner of the Sevenlands, which made it vulnerable to Rashardian raiders. The guard towers housed a harbor chain which was used to close the bay to Rashardians when they came looking for slaves.

"Three more hours," came a gruff voice from behind him.

Dormael turned from his survey of the water to regard Mikael, Captain of the *Seacutter*. He had the hard-bitten look of a lifetime sailor, though he wasn't old or unkempt. His hair was plaited in a multitude of small braids, after the Orrisan fashion, and stuffed into a cravat. He wore a thick coat buttoned to the knees, and he stood holding his hands to block the wind from his pipe.

"Until we've docked, or until we pass the breakwater?" Dormael asked.

"To the wharf, I hope." Mikael sighed and regarded the distant city. "Not much traffic this time of year. We shouldn't have much trouble."

Dormael nodded. "Put in at the Chapterhouse docks."

"The Conclave Chapterhouse?" Mikael raised an eyebrow.

"Aye. As long as you're on business for us, you can put in for free."

"There is another matter." Mikael winced like he'd swallowed a sour piece of fruit. "The price Hadrick paid for your crossing was nice, but not enough to pay for the loss of sixteen crewmen. What am I to tell their wives? The ones who had 'em, anyway. Their families are promised a stipend if they die at sea, but I can't pay out sixteen at once. These boys didn't sign on to fight Imperial soldiers. Those deaths are on you and yours."

Dormael grimaced. "I understand. Listen...we didn't know they would pursue us over the sea. I'm sorry for your men."

"I've grieved for my men," Mikael said. "Right now I'm worried about their families, and how I'm going to keep this tub afloat without a mark to my name."

"I see. The Conclave offers recompense for those who have worked in its interests. It's not widely known, but I can speak to the Chapterhouse Administrator and get you a promissory note."

"Worked in its interests?" Mikael shook his head. "The Conclave hires mercenaries?"

"The Conclave does what it does. Just do your arithmetic, and I'll make sure you get paid."

"And if I add something extra for danger pay and the damage to my ship?"

"Whatever you want." Dormael shrugged. "It's not my money, but the administrator has final say on what he'll sign. Make it reasonable."

Mikael nodded and moved away to harangue a pair of sailors. Dormael turned back to regard the land sliding out of the mists on the horizon and stretched his sore muscles against the railing. His leg still ached sometimes, and it was stiff in the mornings.

"You should start doing the *Siyane*," Shawna said, coming up behind him. "It will help with your injuries."

Dormael turned at the sound of her voice and suppressed the urge to stare at the Cambrellian Baroness. Her clothing was worse for wear—they hadn't had much of a chance to restore their clothing during the chaos—but Shawna never looked shabby. The wind whipped her winter cloak around her shoulders, revealing the hilts of the twin swords at her waist.

Dormael smirked. "I wouldn't be as pretty as you, twisting my body around like that."

Shawna gave him a playful slap on the shoulder. "It would help you keep your muscles loose, you idiot."

"It's just...ah, I don't know."

She raised an eyebrow. "It's what, Dormael?"

"It's feminine."

Shawna barked a laugh and shook her head. "The *Siyane* is feminine?"

"Well, it certainly looks that way when you do it."

"My Master would laugh himself silly to hear you say that." Shawna shook her head. "You only think so because I'm the first one you've seen doing it. You have no idea how ridiculous you sound."

"Maybe I'll let you show me, then, upon a day."

Shawna rolled her eyes and looked out over the waves. "How does it feel to be coming home?"

"Good." Dormael shrugged. "It's better than the Stormy Sea. I've spent a few nights in the alehouses around Mistfall. It's an impressive place, for the most part."

"Were you born here, then?" Shawna gave him a surprised look.

"No." Dormael shook his head. "But I've been through here a good bit. I was born in the northwestern part of Soirus-Gamerit. My family has a homestead there, in the highlands."

"D'Jenn mentioned that your mother makes firewine."

"She does," D'Jenn cut in, coming up behind them. "His family owns a vineyard. They make a lot of things, but the firewine is what they're famous for."

"Famous?" Shawna raised an eyebrow at Dormael.

"Nevermind," Dormael grumbled. "Where's Bethany?"

4

"She's sleeping." D'Jenn shrugged. "I didn't want to wake her until we docked."

"I told Mikael to put in at the Chapterhouse," Dormael said, eliciting a nod from D'Jenn.

Shawna looked between them. "The Chapterhouse?"

D'Jenn nodded toward the city. "The Conclave maintains a Chapterhouse here, as it does in every major city in the Sevenlands. It has its own wharves, and no one docks there, save on Conclave business. The customs people don't bother the Conclave."

Shawna's expression was reluctant. "Will we be staying in the Chapterhouse?"

D'Jenn shrugged, gesturing to Dormael in the Hunter's Tongue—*your decision.*

They would stay for free in the Chapterhouse, and eat for free, too. Dormael couldn't remember what the food quality was like in the Mistfall Chapterhouse, though he was sure it was somewhere between 'hard dirt' and 'wet rag'. Staying there would elicit questions from the administrator—questions they weren't ready to answer.

Dormael took a deep breath and shook his head. "I'll stop in and pen a quick report for the Conclave, requisition some marks from the treasury, and meet you all somewhere else. I'd rather not stay at the Chapterhouse."

D'Jenn nodded, accepting his judgment without comment. Shawna shrugged and dismissed the idea with a wave. The three of them fell into silence as the Sevenlands came into view.

Mistfall's harbor was full of ships despite the weather—or perhaps, because of it. *Seacutter* passed close to the northernmost lighthouse and made for the Conclave docks, bypassing the normal shipping lanes. The smell of the city—a melding of dead fish, roasting meat, offal, and smoke—assailed Dormael's nose as they turned into the harbor.

Put thousands of people in a small area, and the first thing they do is start stinking up the place.

Even with the smell beating into his nostrils, Dormael smiled as lines were tossed to the wharves. Men scrambled over the deck, tying *Seacutter* to the dock. Dormael itched to get back on dry land, and it was a relief to be back home.

In the Sevenlands, he wouldn't have to hide his nature. His status as a wizard afforded him a small amount of social standing—it was even considered rude to inconvenience one of the Blessed, or the Learned. In Alderak, wizards were ostracized, hunted, and killed whenever they were found. In the Sevenlands, folks bought drinks for wizards and toasted their good health. Dormael felt an almost physical weight evaporate from his shoulders as he stepped foot on the wharf.

I'm home. Gods, it's good to be here.

A man wrapped in a blue Sevenlander cloak—vibrant against the gray mists of the morning—bustled down the quay to speak with them. He wore a thin white stole across his shoulders, signifying his position as the Conclave Chapterhouse Administrator. His hood was thrown back to the chill, revealing a neat head of graying hair.

The last time I was here, the administrator was a woman named Merris. He must have been promoted some time this year.

Shawna glanced at the administrator. "Is that someone important?"

"Chapterhouse Administrator," Dormael sighed. "He'll be the man in charge."

Shawna paled. "He's with the Conclave?"

Dormael couldn't help but smile. "Aye, evil powers and all. I'm sure he's counting up the number of child sacrifices he'll demand from us in order to tie up at the dock."

"That's not what I meant, Dormael Harlun, and you know it." She sniffed. "I'm just unsure what I should say to him. How much to reveal—does that sound so ridiculous?"

Dormael shook his head. "He's just the man who runs the Chapterhouse. He doesn't hold any real authority, Shawna—not over us."

"He's like an innkeeper who also collects information, dispenses money, that sort of thing," D'Jenn said. "No reason to worry or stand on ceremony."

As he was speaking, D'Jenn put his back to the approaching administrator and turned to Shawna, his hands moving in the Hunter's Tongue. *Say nothing to anyone about what we're doing. If anyone asks, we hired you as a mercenary, and Bethany is an orphan on her way to the Conclave.*

Understood. Shawna still had trouble forming many of the movements, but she'd practiced the silent language during the journey, and could read the gestures with confidence.

"I'll speak to him," Dormael sighed. "If you lot will take Horse to wherever we're staying tonight and care for him, I'll catch up with you afterward. I could use a long walk on my own two feet."

"Fine with me," D'Jenn grumbled. "While you're being interrogated, we'll go get some real food, maybe some bacon. I'm sure there's bacon somewhere in this city."

Dormael ignored his grumbling stomach. "Any plans for where you're putting up?"

D'Jenn nodded. "The Golden Mug, east of the Western Tradefair. Best place in Mistfall, if it's still here."

"The Golden Mug?" Dormael repeated, raising an eyebrow at his cousin. "Weren't you tossed out of there a few years back?"

"Tossed out of a tavern?" Shawna turned to smile at D'Jenn. "I thought you were better than this one." A wink at Dormael let him know exactly who 'this one' was, but softened the blow of her comments.

"I was, but that was awhile back." D'Jenn shrugged. "I doubt they even remember me."

"Oh, I'll wager the gods' own purse change they *do* remember," Dormael said.

D'Jenn scoffed. "It wasn't that serious."

"Well, now I'm interested," Shawna said.

D'Jenn waved her question away. "It's a story for another time."

"I'd say it's rather appropriate for now," Dormael smiled. D'Jenn shot him a dangerous look, but Dormael ignored it. "A few years ago, our wonderful friend of the brooding face decided to drown himself in the Mug's ale for the afternoon. The hero of the story, however, took issue with the taste and potency of the ale in question. He was a Warlock, you see, a representative of the Conclave itself! He couldn't be disrespected with such thin, tasteless horse-piss—the sort of thing one would feed to the legion of beggars in the streets."

"I wonder if your face would look better with a bruise over your right eye?" D'Jenn muttered.

Shawna laid a mollifying hand on D'Jenn's shoulder.

"No, go on, please." She shot D'Jenn a wicked smile which he returned with a flat stare.

"The proprietor of the Golden Mug took issue with the issue which had been taken by our brooding hero, and an argument between the two ensued. Harsh words were used, you understand, and our hero was tossed bodily into the street—a dishonor he simply could *not* tolerate. To demonstrate the robustness of his argument, our noble hero summoned his power and filled the proprietor's ale barrels with fish."

"Fish?" Shawna blinked. "How does that work, exactly?"

A smirk appeared on D'Jenn's face. "The bastard had the fish already. It was the catch of the day. When Dormael tells the story, I put half the bay into the man's ale barrels. Really, it was just the fish in his kitchen."

Shawna gave him a bewildered smile. "So you *did* do it."

"Oh, aye," D'Jenn said. "The smug bastard deserved it, too. It didn't go exactly as Dormael said it did."

"Oh, I'm sure that's the truth," Shawna said. "You can tell me about it on the way. Goodbye, Dormael. Try not to get mugged on the way to the tavern. Come along, Bethany."

Shawna gave him a smile and went to help with the unloading of their horses. Dormael smiled at Bethany, who had walked up during the conversation, rubbing the sleep out of her eyes. She looked at him and blinked, but that was all she offered before following Shawna.

"Do you think we should send ahead?" D'Jenn glanced at the administrator. "It might not be prudent to put anything about what's happened in writing."

"Do you really believe we need to be so cautious at home?" Dormael sighed. "Something this serious...I suspect Victus will skin us alive if we show up with the armlet in Ishamael without having warned him, given that we could have. The Deacon of Warlocks doesn't like to be blindsided, if you remember."

"Maybe you're right." D'Jenn shrugged, turning away. "Consider, though, the implications of using our powers against Imperial soldiers. Maybe that bit should be kept quiet until we make it home. Just a thought, Dormael. Be careful. I'll see you at the Mug."

With that, D'Jenn walked away.

Perhaps his cousin was right. Such a thing—Conclave wizards fighting with Galanian Imperial soldiers—would be tantamount to an act of war. Blithely talking about what had happened could cause a general uproar.

Maybe I'll just keep quiet until I can report to Victus himself.

Dormael forced a smile and turned to speak to the administrator.

**

Maarkov worked the blade of his dagger over a whetstone, listening to the creaking, rattling noises of the ship. So many people who considered themselves warriors treated their steel with shocking disregard. Success began with the small pieces, and wars were won by a series of small victories—he'd been taught that lesson years and years ago. Maarkov kept his blades sharp at all times, and that discipline bled into the rest of his life.

Life—such was not a good description of his experience with reality. He was not dead, not really, but he was certainly far from alive. His hair hadn't grown in enough years to kill most men, and he could feel a strange waning to his body, like a wet rag drying in the sun. His muscles creaked ever so slightly when he moved, and his bones ground against the pallid meat of his insides. His body sometimes felt like a temporary piece of clothing.

Maaz glared at him from behind the desk of the ship's captain. "Would you stop that infernal noise?"

Maarkov paused in his sharpening and glared at his brother. He sat huddled over a bowl of dark fluid, swaddled like an overgrown infant in a voluminous black robe. His eyes burned from within the hood, but Maarkov had long ago numbed to his brother's hatred. He had long ago returned it in equal measure.

"Stop what?"

Maaz narrowed his eyes. "It's quite difficult to use magic to communicate over a churning body of water, Maarkov."

"Am I supposed to be impressed?" Maarkov savored the flash of rage in his brother's eyes.

"You're supposed to be gods-damned *silent,*" Maaz hissed. "I can still take out your tongue."

Maarkov winked at his brother and went back to sharpening his dagger. He kept his gaze on his brother's face and drew the steel across the stone in a slow, mocking rhythm. Maaz gestured angrily to the side, and both stone and dagger were ripped from Maarkov's hands to tumble across the floor of the cabin.

Maarkov snorted in disgust and let his hands go to his lap. Tweaking his brother's nose was only a mild entertainment, anyway. It was important, after all, that Maaz knew just how deeply Maarkov loved him.

"One day I'm going to kill you, brother, or stand by and watch you die." Maarkov smiled. "I can't decide which would be more gratifying."

Maaz turned his gaze back to the bowl on the desk and went silent. Maarkov gave an obnoxious sigh. The only noises were the shifting of implements as the room rocked back and forth and the sound of the sea whispering over the ship's hull.

Maaz reached to a thong tied around his neck and fished a small leather bag from the depths of his hood. He pulled it gingerly open and plucked two tiny bones from inside. He whispered something over the bones and dropped them into the dark fluid in the bowl. Maarkov might have shuddered at the sight, knowing them to be the finger bones of his brother's apprentices. Perhaps he should have shuddered, but he felt nothing.

He and his brother were steeped in blood, swimming in it. What were a pair of tiny finger bones against a mountain of corpses? Maarkov had long ago lost the ability to rustle a single care for the disgusting things his brother did.

A covered lantern hung in the cabin, tossing wild shadows back and forth over the walls. Maaz stared over the bowl, undoubtedly using his magic, though Maarkov couldn't feel it. A pair of shadows stood from the corners of the room, as if they had been sitting there all along, and approached the desk. As they came closer, their forms deepened into something more like an actual person, though they were still indistinct.

"Master," said the shorter of the two in a female voice.

"Master," intoned the second one, a male.

"Attend, apprentices, for your Master speeds in your direction," Maaz said, causing the two shadows to stiffen. "With any luck from the gods, the two of you have managed to keep breathing from day to day. What have you learned?"

"The city is growing increasingly polarized." The male

shadow's tone was too obsequious, too eager to please, like a dog licking a boot.

Maarkov sneered in disgust.

The shadow continued, "There are whispers of discontent, mistrust in the strength of the leadership. Talk of the Conclave is rampant in the streets."

"And have you succeeded in your mission?" Maaz kept his tone light—he always did before revealing the barbs in his questions.

"I...haven't been able to see the library. The wizards only approve so many requests, Master, and—"

Maaz made a sharp gesture, and the shadow doubled over, writhing as it screamed in agony. Maarkov winced at the sound, but his brother released his apprentice before it went on for long. Maaz said nothing in the wake of his apprentice's punishment, he simply allowed the shadow to rise to its full height once more. The female shadow did not react to the suffering of her male counterpart.

Maaz sneered. "Failure is not permitted in my service, Jureus. Luckily for your pathetic, sniveling form, the gods have seen fit to throw rocks in our path. Abandon your place in Ishamael, and head south."

"South, Master?" Jureus's shadow asked.

"If I need to repeat myself, I'll remove an ear the next time I see you. If you have only one, perhaps then you will find the necessary focus to *listen* to what I gods-damned *tell* you."

Maaz leaned forward to peer at the offending shade. He let his comment hang in the air, as if daring the fool Jureus to speak again. Jureus kept his mouth shut, demonstrating good sense for the first time since the conversation began. If there was one thing Maaz's apprentices learned, it was that punishment came swiftly, and often.

Once Maaz was satisfied, he cleared his throat and went on.

"It has become necessary to shift our focus. You will go into the mountains south of Ishamael—I can't remember what they're called right now—"

"The Runemian Mountains, Master," Jureus offered.

Maarkov winced. *What a simpering little turd. That one will end under Maaz's knives, I'm sure of it.*

They all ended under his brother's knives, though, eventually.

A handful of apprentices had come and gone over the years, only living until their usefulness was outgrown by Maaz's patience. Each ended the same way—screaming while Maaz cut small, wriggly bits from their bodies.

Maaz stared daggers at the shade of his apprentice. "Jureus, you are lucky such a vast distance separates us, because I have a nagging urge to pull your innards out. Utter another word, and I remove your tongue."

Jureus, finally getting the point, offered only silence in reply.

"Head for the Runemian Mountains," Maaz continued, "and toward Soirus-Gamerit. We are hunting a red-headed woman, her belongings, and a small child traveling with her. I want the two of them alive, and the woman's property intact—and do not harm them beyond what is necessary to subdue them. They're traveling with wizards. Ensure you kill them. They'll be headed for Ishamael through Soirus-Gamerit, so begin your search in that direction. I don't care how you get it done, but I expect my instructions to be followed to the letter."

Maaz waved a dismissive hand, and Jureus's shade bowed in reply before vanishing into black smoke.

"You," Maaz said, turning his gaze on the female shadow. "What have *you* learned?"

"The location of the ancient temple, Master," she replied. "It's far in the northern Sevenlands. The locals believe it is cursed, and no one has been inside since the Second Great War."

"I've read about the curse," Maaz grumbled. "Have you been inside?"

"I entered the ground level Master, but..."

"But what?" Maaz growled.

"Master, there *is* something here. I'm camped within sight of the temple now, and I can feel it even at this distance. It's...well, whatever it is, it's old and powerful." The shadow looked at her feet. "I ventured inside, but it doesn't like interlopers."

"A great slaughter happened there," Maaz said. "The Dannons were responsible, I believe. They rounded up the priests and civilians, and they had an orgy of violence. That was what brought the Conclave into the Second Great War against Alderak. Sometimes, a thing like that leaves its mark on a place."

"I've marked the location on a map for you, Master." She stood straighter. "What am I to do next?"

"Head back to Jerrantis and send out bounties by pigeon to anyone in Soirus-Garmerit who will take them. Once you've done that, find Jureus and ensure he doesn't botch his mission. The man is a fool. When you find him, take command of the situation and see my instructions carried out. I trust you were listening and don't need a lesson in proper attention to detail?"

She shook her head. "No, Master."

"Good. You've done well in finding ancient Orm. For once, your inherent stupidity hasn't gotten in the way of the tasks I've set for you." Maaz smiled. "Here is your reward."

Maaz raised his fist, and the girl's shade bent over in surprised pain. She moaned in agony for a moment before stifling her cries, but Maaz didn't let up the pressure he wielded over her. Maarkov tightened his hands on the arms of his wooden chair.

For a moment, white-hot rage burned in Maarkov's chest. He reached for the hilt of his sword—it would take but a fleeting moment to get to him. He'd have to rise from the chair, draw his blade, and lunge straight for the heart. In the time it took Maaz to realize Maarkov was coming for him, it would be too late. In the space of a heartbeat, Maarkov's steel would decorate the spaces between his brother's ribs.

Even if I stab him again, the bastard wouldn't die.

Maaz smiled at the shadow. "This is but a tiny helping of what will happen should you fail in your new task. Let the pain serve as a reminder. Carry it with you in the coming days."

The shadow relaxed and rose to its hazy feet. Maarkov loosened the hand he'd grasped around his sword. He let out a breath he hadn't realized he'd been holding.

"Thank you, Master," the shadow croaked.

"Our quarry has a decisive lead on us. Do not dally in the execution of your tasks. You're my strongest apprentice, Inera. Do *not* betray my trust in your abilities."

"Thank you, Master," she replied.

Maaz waved his hand, and her form melted into black mist.

Maaz gestured over the bowl, and the two finger bones rose out of the liquid. He waited for them to drip themselves dry and plucked them out of the air, depositing them back into the bag tied around his neck. Once he had squared his clothing, he picked up the bowl and drank the fluid inside to the bottom.

Maarkov gagged and looked away. He remembered the whining crewman from which the blood had come. He'd taken the man in the night, while most of the crew had been asleep in their racks. They knew, though—Maarkov was sure of it. His brother reigned over this ship like some sort of demonic tyrant, a shadow that never left the captain's cabin. The only thing that kept the crew from chucking both of them in sea was terror.

My brother saw to that.

Maaz glared at Maarkov. "Bring me one of the cabin boys."

"One of the cabin boys?" Maarkov scoffed. "Why?"

"I need more information, brother mine. My power requires an...extra source of energy." Maaz smiled, showing his teeth. "You know this by now, Maarkov."

"The Lord of Bones requires blood tribute, you mean."

"Either way, Maarkov, I still need the cabin boy. Go, and hurry, for the gods' sake."

Maarkov gave his brother a disgusted look and rose from his chair. "Get your own gods-damned fodder. I'll turn my sword where you point, but I'm not one of your damned apprentices, *brother.*"

"The cabin boy will be just as dead, Maarkov. Your constant moralizing is useless."

"Fuck yourself, brother." With that, Maarkov turned to leave the cabin.

His brother's laughter chased him onto the deck and into the darkened morning. Crewmen shuffled from his path, doing their best to keep their eyes away from him. They feared drawing his attention, and rightfully so. Maarkov ignored them and went up to the aft deck to stare into the coming storm.

The sea was high this time of year, but the galleon was a tougher vessel to sink than Maarkov had realized. He knew nothing of sailing, but he was surprised at how well the ship took the water. The darkening sky would soon test his confidence.

They had been running through squalls for the entire trip, but the constant wind had provided speed. The sea made Maarkov nervous, though it wasn't as if he could drown. What frightened him was the thought of floating in the middle of the ocean, perpetually alive, being nibbled apart by toothy fish from below.

His brother's foul magic would keep him alive until most of him was gone.

Maarkov shuddered and regarded the storm clouds with trepidation. They still had a great distance to travel, but he trusted in the depths of Maaz's obsession to see them safely to their destination. He wouldn't allow anything to stand in his way.

I just hope this will be over soon, one way or the other.

**

"So, you're not going to be staying with us, Warlock Harlun?" the Administrator, an older man named Finnelan, asked.

"My compatriot prefers the ale at the Golden Mug." Dormael favored the man with a pleasant expression from across the table. "We'll be leaving Mistfall in the morning, anyway. We may as well not trouble you for more than we need."

"It's no trouble." Finnelan shrugged. "The Chapterhouse has been quiet all season. Everyone coming through Mistfall is headed back to the Conclave like horses returning to their stables. It's been me and the staff since the Winter Solstice."

"Is that odd?"

"Aye, it's a bit unusual." Finnelan regarded Dormael with a cautious eye and cleared his throat. "Listen, I'm just a salty old Philosopher who got bored with my studies. Decided to try my hand at management, and I'm not too bad, if I do say so myself."

"That's...wonderful." Dormael narrowed his eyes.

"There aren't many of us Administrators, you know. Only ten, though they may add an eleventh next year for a Chapterhouse being built in some town in the arse-end of the Teptian Mountains. We have a little meeting every season, the ten of us, to share news and such. All the Administrators say the same thing—wizards are heading back to Ishamael in droves. Save a few Warlocks—you lot are always going to far-off places. That's nothing new."

"Do you know why? We've been in Alderak since before the Solstice."

"There's been some talk. Lots of resentment for the Mekai. There are reports the Galanians are gearing up for war again. I don't know the truth of it, but rumor says they're rounding up Sevenlanders within their borders. Looking for our agents, some say." Finnelan shrugged. "Now, I'm just a salty old Philosopher, you see. I wouldn't know what sort of games you Warlocks play, but I thought you might have some insight."

Dormael kept his face bland. "No. I've been doing something else entirely. I hadn't heard anything like that."

The gods-damned Imperials again.

Finnelan's lips drew into a line. "Well, I suppose that's fair enough. You should know there's been a lot of talk about the Mekai and the lack of response from the Conclave about all the rumors going around. The city will be crawling with wizards by the time you get there." Finnelan made a huffing noise and crossed his arms. "Do you have any news to report?"

Dormael gave him a bemused look. *He thinks I'm lying.*

"Nothing of great importance." Dormael shrugged. "The Imperials move around freely in Ferolan now, though everyone moves around freely in Ferolan."

"True enough." Finnelan sighed. "Will you be needing anything?"

"I need to requisition some funds," Dormael said. "Just standard traveling money, nothing lavish."

Finnelan grimaced. "Your sea captain almost cleaned me out. I can part with a pittance, but nothing too great. The staff here doesn't work for free, you know."

"Thank you." Dormael bowed his head. "Anything you can do is appreciated."

An hour later, Dormael pushed through the front gate of the Chapterhouse gardens and into the streets of Mistfall. The conversation weighed heavily on his mind. He hadn't heard anything about Galanians rounding up his countrymen, but he had been out of touch for a while. If the Empire was imprisoning Sevenlanders, the population would be simmering.

I hope the city isn't in an uproar when we get there. I just want to enjoy being home.

Mistfall was a city alive with people. They trotted to and fro on errands and yelled happy greetings from second or third-story windows. They hawked their wares, shouted news of recent events, and shouldered past one another in the streets. Mistfall buzzed with the quiet energy to which only large cities can aspire.

The Crescent City was built of red bricks and gray stones. The outer walls were granite—dark and foreboding in the cool midday sun but free of the scars of siege engines. Mistfall had never been tested in battle, though no Sevenlander army would lay siege to another Sevenlander city. Ivy climbed the walls in many places, and the people who lived in the city did little to discourage the creeper vines from growing. Most Sevenlanders were fond of nature, and they preferred a little green to decorate the bare stone walls surrounding the city.

There were Orrisans, Runemians, Teptians, Farra-Jerrans, and even a few people from the savannas of Tasha-Mal in the streets. Mals were ever a nomadic tribe, clutching harder to their ancient traditions than the rest of their Sevenlander cousins. A strong and robust people, they hunted lions on the veldt and held some of the most famous—or infamous, depending on one's viewpoint—festivals in the entirety of the Sevenlands. Dormael greeted a few as they passed him, and the motley group of hunters raised their spears in return. They looked every bit the tattooed, nomadic people they were.

He strolled down the boulevards headed north from the Temple District, where the Conclave Chapterhouse was located, and meandered past the Conclave's docks. As he came farther north, the cries of merrymakers and merchants reached his ears as he neared the Western Tradefair. The Tradefairs were a long-standing tradition in Mistfall, as Sevenlanders from all over Soirus-Gamerit came to trade goods, stories, and to share in the company of their countrymen. They drew the attention of sharp businessmen from all over the world, who shipped anything and everything to Mistfall in order to ensure its passage under the eyes of so many possible buyers.

Tents and wooden stands carpeted Tradefair, and people of varied descent moved amongst them. There were ale tents, and Dormael could hear the sounds of mugs clinking with toasts and drunken voices rising in off-key tunes. It brought a smile to his face to hear familiar songs.

As the sun reached its noonday peak, the Golden Mug came into sight along the street. It was a large brick building, and above its open double doors hung a wooden sign with the painting of a frothy, golden mug. It was one of the most famous inns in Mistfall and a destination for many traveling musicians and storytellers. Even now, as he came within shouting distance of the door, the sound of clinking silverware and the din of conversation floated to his ears. Above the general racket, the sounds of a guitar lilted from the door like smoke from a pipe, playing something upbeat. Dormael nodded to the man at the door and pushed his way inside.

He spotted D'Jenn, Shawna, and Bethany as soon as he walked in the door. D'Jenn, as always, had picked a table near the back wall of the common room, where he would be able to see the door. Dormael waved to them as he came in, and D'Jenn's fingers waggled in the Hunter's Tongue.

Look at the stage.

Dormael checked out the stage and felt a wide smile come unbidden to his face. A woman balanced on the edge of a stool, cradling a guitar to her chest and plucking out a lively melody on the strings. Her fingers crawled over the surface of the neck like mad spiders, and she barely seemed to notice. She sang in time to the music, a sultry accompaniment to a Runemian folk song.

Her hair was a shining blonde, worn both loose and braided in different places. Odd bells and pieces of jewelry were woven into her hair after the Runemian fashion, and a multitude of bracelets decorated her delicate wrists. She wore leather pants with a loose-fitting shirt of flowing material and gilded shoes decorated with golden buckles.

It had been a while since Dormael had seen her, but the seasons had only refined her beauty. They caught eyes, and she smirked around the words she was singing. His heart beat a little faster as they acknowledged one another, and he shouldered his way to the bar to get a drink. Though it was still early in the afternoon, the Mug was packed with patrons in various states of drunkenness. By the time he had secured a pair of mugs, the music had stopped.

"You vagabond of a magus," a sultry voice said from behind him. "Where in the Six Hells have you been the last few seasons?"

"Seylia." Dormael smiled, turning to offer the woman a drink. "It's good to see you."

"I'll bet it is." She winked and took the mug from his hand. She raised her cup in answer to his, and they both took a long drink. When Dormael lowered the cup from his lips, she pulled his beard until his face was level with hers and pressed her mouth to his for a brief, passionate moment.

"Just so your woman knows who got to you first." She winked and drew back from him, favoring him with the full weight of a smile.

She's always been as infuriating as she was beautiful, damn her.

"She's not my woman, Seylia." Dormael sighed. "She's a friend."

"And the child? Did you finally get some poor maiden pregnant?"

"What a cruel fate for a child that would be." Dormael laughed. "No. She's not mine. Just follow me, I'll introduce you."

Seylia gave him an odd look, but she took his arm and allowed him to lead her back to the table.

She embraced D'Jenn as an old friend, eliciting a rare smile from him. They traded a few idle words as Dormael pulled a chair over for Seylia, and she began to go around the table making her introductions. With Bethany, she winked and produced a sweet with a flourish of her hand, tossing it to the girl from across the table. Bethany reached out with surprising agility and snatched the thing from the air, making it disappear into her own cloak in a blur of tiny hands. She beamed at Seylia, who smiled back and gave her a conspiratorial wink.

Seylia offered Shawna the traditional Sevenlander bow. "My, you're pretty for an eastern girl, aren't you?"

Shawna rose from her answering bow, her back stiffening. "I suppose."

"I tried calling on the two of you at the Conclave the last time I was in Ishamael," Seylia said, turning her back on Shawna and settling into a chair between Dormael and D'Jenn. "You were gone, though, predictably. I don't know why I continue trying to be friends with you."

D'Jenn smirked. "Because we always have the best stories for you, and Dormael has decided to pay for your drinks from now until the gods return."

Dormael opened his mouth to argue but stopped himself. He did end up paying her bill most of the time. He settled for giving his cousin a dark look, which D'Jenn ignored.

"You forgot how much I love the two of you, though you treat me so horribly. All these years and you've never deigned to take me on one of your grand adventures." Seylia smiled and tapped

Dormael's arm with a delicate finger. "One day, you're going to take me to Tauravon. I *so* want to see the Great River City."

Dormael snorted. "Our 'grand adventures' never take us to places like that. You should have seen the last place we left—a beautiful town called Borders, right on the edge of the Dannon steppes. The mud was the most pleasant brown color, and it came right up to your knees."

"Come now, it couldn't have been all that bad." Seylia favored Shawna with a considering glance. "I doubt a girl as pretty as this one came out of some mud-soaked hovel. Really, Dormael, you've got to stop picking up so many strays."

Shawna's face reddened, and Dormael winced.

"I didn't pick her up, Seylia." Dormael gave the woman a flat look.

"I'm not a cat." Shawna offered her hand over her cold, green eyes. "I'm the Baroness Shawna Llewan, from southern Cambrell."

Seylia took her hand, meeting Shawna's gaze. "I'm so pleased. You can call me Seylia, dear—we're all friends, here."

Shawna regarded the woman with a cold glare. "Of course."

Dormael raised a surprised eyebrow at Shawna. *She's changed—earlier in the winter, she probably would have demanded the respect of her station.*

"Seylia." D'Jenn cleared his throat. "Why don't you fill us in on events? We've been in the east for some time."

Both women glared at D'Jenn, but he stared them down with a blank expression.

"Well, where to start?" Seylia leaned back in her chair and pulled a knee to her chest. "The Rashardians have been restless. There are rumors of fighting in the Golden Waste."

"Rashardians fighting each other?" D'Jenn shrugged. "Good."

Seylia smiled. "Agreed—the Rashardians can kill each other until the gods return, and it would save us the trouble. They still managed to raid into Tasha-Mal, despite their little civil war. Slavers captured the son of their Kansil, though I heard he escaped."

Shawna took a sip from her drink. "The Rashardians raid the Sevenlands?"

"For as long as there have been Rashardians and Sevenlanders." Dormael nodded. "Some of our oldest stories talk about them. Rarely a year goes by when there isn't some kind of attack."

"Fighting Rashardians is every southerner's favorite sport." Seylia rolled her eyes. "The northerners are worse—Teptians, Farra-Jerrans, and Duadans. They raid into the Gathan Mountains looking for glory and the gods know what else. Only Sevenlanders worth a moment's attention are Runemians."

D'Jenn gave a derisive snort.

Shawna glanced between Dormael and D'Jenn. "I've heard stories about the Gathan Mountains. People say they're full of man-eating monsters."

Bethany, who had been laying her head on Shawna's side, opened her eyes.

"Something like that." D'Jenn nodded. "No one knows where they came from, but they've been there as long as anyone can remember. A magical barrier keeps them confined to the mountains, and that's been there as long as they have. Now and then, one of them tries to come down from the passes, but they can't pass the barrier. The magic kills them outright."

"Teptian children make a game of hunting for the corpses," Seylia said. "It doesn't always work out for them. Many have disappeared."

"Does this magical boundary not protect them?" Shawna asked. "Doesn't it keep the children away from these creatures?"

D'Jenn shook his head. "It's not a physical wall. It's an invisible boundary, and people can pass back and forth with no effect. You wouldn't even know when you'd stepped across."

Shawna raised an eyebrow. "And the children go hunting for these things?"

"Teptians are all crazy that way," Dormael said. "They believe the only way to honor the gods is to beat each other half to death, or die in some glorious fight."

Seylia grinned. "This coming from the man whose brother fights in the Gladiator's Ring?"

"My brother is a perfect example of insanity." Dormael returned her smile. "The Teptians have been made to fight their entire lives. My brother is a Gamerit—he knows better."

Shawna sighed. "I'm not following any of this."

"Oh, don't worry, dear." Seylia regarded Shawna like an errant child. "You'll learn eventually, I'm sure."

Shawna gave the woman a dangerous look. She opened her mouth to reply, but the appearance of a serving girl with a tray of drinks stilled her tongue. Seylia played at being oblivious to Shawna's expression.

"Tept is in the northwestern Sevenlands." D'Jenn helped the girl pass out the drinks. "They've always been strange. They believe the gods must be honored with blood sacrifice every solstice."

Shawna's lip curled with disgust. "That sounds archaic."

"Maybe, but they volunteer for the pleasure." Dormael shrugged. "They fight to the death in a huge spectacle. The more skilled the fighter, the greater the glory. The ones who die are worshiped like demigods. The Teptians make shrines for them."

"And your brother does this?" Shawna gave him a bewildered look. "Fights to be killed for the honor of the gods?"

"No." Dormael chuckled. "Those are just the religious festivals, and only Teptians subscribe to that old belief. My brother fights for sport."

"Tournaments are held in Tept every year." D'Jenn took a sip from his ale. "Warriors from anywhere can compete, and the prizes are substantial. The bouts are rarely to the death."

"Rarely?" Shawna said.

"Accidents happen." Dormael leaned back in his chair. "Sometimes two warriors agree to fight to the death for personal reasons. It doesn't happen often, but it *does* happen."

"I see." Shawna nodded. "Can women compete in these games?"

Seylia nodded. "Even a pretty foreign girl like yourself."

Shawna turned an empty smile on Seylia. "A pretty foreign Blademaster—don't forget that part, dear."

"Is that so?" Seylia sighed, looking Shawna up and down with a raised eyebrow. "How wonderful for you."

Shawna's answering smile was anything but warm.

Seylia rose with a smile and tossed her hair over her shoulder. "I've got to return to the stage before the innkeeper decides to keep part of my fee." She bent and gave Dormael a warm kiss on the cheek, lingering a moment longer than was proper. "Don't disappear on me."

With a final smile for Shawna, she sauntered back toward the stage.

Shawna glared at Seylia's back. "Now I know why the two of you have no idea how to treat a lady. You don't *know* any grown women."

"You'll have to ignore Seylia." D'Jenn took another pull from his cup. "She likes to stir things up. It's like a reflex for her."

"I've reflexes of my own," Shawna muttered.

Dormael sighed. "She's not so bad once you get to know her."

"How *do* you know her?" Shawna gave Dormael an unreadable look.

"We met a few years ago while I was on a mission," Dormael said. "Seylia is famous, and she knows a lot of people."

"She's highly sought after for her talents," D'Jenn added. "She gets invited to perform at a lot of parties and makes a lot of friends. Seylia's unmarried, independently wealthy...she's something of a personality."

"I'm sure it's her talents and personality that get her through life, alright." Shawna gave Dormael a meaningful look. "And I'm sure that's the only reason the two of you are so *friendly*, too."

Dormael snorted. "What's that supposed to mean?"

"I'm not an idiot, Dormael." Shawna rolled her eyes. "I saw her trying to eat your face earlier. Just when I was beginning to think you weren't all that bad, you prove me wrong."

Dormael laughed. "Do you think I'm the *only* man that she treats that way?"

"Do *you* think that makes it any better?"

"Better? Better than what?"

"Just *better*, Dormael. You know what I mean."

"I surely don't."

Shawna sighed. "Then you're an idiot."

"Idiot? All I've done today is take a long walk and tried to be pleasant. I didn't know I was being judged by some obscure, womanly standard."

"Womanly?" she laughed.

"Yes, *womanly*," he said. "You can change that out with 'irrational' if you like."

"You're on dangerous ground, Dormael Harlun."

"Am I?" Dormael took a drink of ale. "If this is all it takes to be on dangerous ground, I'll certainly find myself here again. May as well keep going."

What in the Six Hells is she so damned angry about?

Shawna laughed to herself, though the smile on her face was forced. She downed the rest of her drink and gathered her things. Rousing Bethany from her half-slumber, Shawna rose to leave.

"It's been a long voyage," she said. "We've been stuffed in a boat together for too long. I'm going to soak in a bath somewhere quieter than this."

Dormael shrugged. "Might be a good idea."

"I'll see the two of you at first light." Shawna took Bethany's hand. "Come along, Bethany."

Shawna stalked toward the stairs in the back of the common room, dragging a silent Bethany behind her. Dormael shook his head and took a long pull from his drink. His chest fluttered with unspent irritation.

Seylia makes her angry, and she takes it out on me. Bloody typical.

D'Jenn watched Shawna stomp up the stairs. "So, all that time the two of you were laid up to heal, *this* is what was happening."

Dormael scowled. "There was nothing happening."

"Of course, because you don't shamelessly flirt with every girl who crosses your path." D'Jenn snorted. "What was I thinking?"

"It's nothing like that, D'Jenn." Dormael sighed and took another drink. "We've talked a lot, but there's no flirtation. She wouldn't entertain it, anyway. She's always scolding me about the way I am with women—that's all this was. Seylia provoked her, not me."

D'Jenn narrowed his eyes and leaned forward. "Dormael, she's an eastern girl. You know what that means—she's been kept chaste so her father could marry her off to some noble lordling one day. You can't treat her the same way you treat barmaids and Sevenlander women. She's not as...worldly."

"I've only been friendly, D'Jenn, not flirtatious." Dormael held up his hands. "To the gods' ears."

D'Jenn shook his head and returned to his drink.

Seylia plucked something somber on her guitar, and the ambiance in the room calmed to a low murmur. Dormael ordered another round of drinks and settled against the back of his chair, letting the alcohol warm his limbs. Lanterns were struck as twilight came on.

Dinner was a tray of trenchers, meat, and various cooked vegetables. Once the food was settled, Dormael asked the serving girl to take something up to Shawna and Bethany. Guilt had twisted in his belly since the argument.

I'm probably just drunk.

D'Jenn dipped some food onto his plate. "Did the Administrator have anything to say?"

"He said there's been talk about Galanians imprisoning Sevenlanders, maybe searching out Conclave agents." Dormael gave a one-armed shrug at D'Jenn's questioning glance. "Also, wizards have been heading for Ishamael in droves. He said by the time we make it back to the Conclave, it will be packed with people."

"Imprisoning our agents?" D'Jenn shook his head. "The only agents we'd have in Galania would be Philosophers or Warlocks, and I doubt either would let themselves be taken."

"To be fair, he said rounding up Sevenlanders and possibly *looking* for our agents," Dormael said. "Then he tried to pump *me* for information. When I told him I didn't know anything, I'm sure he thought I was lying."

D'Jenn took a long sip of ale. "The Galanian Empire has enemies closer to home to worry about. Why would they be rounding up Sevenlanders?"

Dormael shrugged. "He also said there's grumbling about the Mekai and his lack of response. It sounded ominous."

"There's always grumbling about one thing or another." D'Jenn waved a dismissive hand. "What do people expect him to do, marshal the Conclave for war? That would be a good way to turn the whole world against us. It will blow over."

"You're probably right." Dormael sighed and leaned back in his seat. "It could be a good thing, having everyone back at the Conclave. Maybe we'll see some old friends. Victus has us all over the place all the bloody time, and our class was small enough already. I haven't seen most of them in years."

"It would be good to see some of them." D'Jenn nodded. "Some can keep their distance, as far as I'm concerned."

Dormael smirked. "Hopefully they're all still alive."

D'Jenn raised his mug. "Here's to that."

Seylia plopped into the seat between the two of them. Her face was flushed, brow rimmed with sweat, and she wore a wide grin on her face. She examined the empty cups on the table with a raised eyebrow.

"Toasting my performance, boys? You'll need something stronger than that."

D'Jenn winced. "I've already got a bellyful of that. Adding something stronger won't be good for anyone."

"I agree, for once." Dormael finished the last of his ale and put the cup on the table. "We've been at sea for weeks."

"Have you, now?" Seylia cupped Dormael's face in her hand. "Did you lose your manhood along the way? You're drinking with me."

D'Jenn chuckled.

Seylia raised an eyebrow at him. "You're not getting out of this, either."

D'Jenn sighed and leaned back in his chair. "This is not going to end well."

"It's not supposed to, dear." Seylia turned and waved at the bar. "Strong drink and regret go hand-in-hand. The gods need something to laugh at, after all."

Seylia ordered three mugs of the strongest firewine the Mug had to offer, and they settled in to drink. The alcohol pulled a pleasant curtain over Dormael's vision, blurring the harder edges of the world into softness. He ate another plate of food and lit a pipe. He laughed at Seylia's stories and relaxed for the first time in a long while.

It's great to be home again.

Seylia leaned ever closer to him as the night went on, and Dormael made no move to dissuade her. Her presence was exciting, and they had long been comfortable with one another. Even D'Jenn grew friendly with a smiling young woman who engaged him in an intense conversation. Before the firewine was gone, Dormael's limbs were heavy with its effects.

Seylia leaned against Dormael's shoulder. "D'Jenn looks to be enjoying himself."

"It's good to see." Dormael took a pull from his pipe. "He's usually got two moods—intense, and *more* intense."

"And your friend—the pretty one with the swords—what are her moods like?"

"They change like the seasons." Dormael smiled. "She was...difficult when we first met. Since then, she's become a friend. It's odd."

"What's odd about it?" Seylia raised an eyebrow.

"She's just different. Hard to anticipate." Dormael took another sip from his firewine. "She's nobility, but she starts snowball fights. She'll dress me down in one breath and tell me something in confidence the next. It's hard to figure her out."

"I see." Seylia narrowed her eyes. "What is it you like about her, then? That sounds maddening to me."

"She's genuine," Dormael said. "Whatever you're getting with her, you can be sure it's actually what she's feeling. She's trustworthy. Strong-willed."

"I think that's more than you've said about a woman in your life." Seylia slapped him on the arm.

"You, too?" Dormael chuckled. "Why is every woman turning on me today?"

"I'm not turning on you, Dormael." Seylia winked. "I *like* your simplicity."

"Simplicity?"

"I like *our* simplicity," she clarified. "Now, why don't you forget about your red-headed friend, and come do something simple with me?"

Dormael felt a smile crack his features before he could stop it. "I like our simplicity, too. Why are you so concerned with Shawna, anyway? Is the notorious Seylia Six Strings actually jealous of another woman?"

Seylia laughed. "Jealous isn't even close to the right word, magus. Forget her. D'Jenn is dragging that poor girl up the stairs as we speak, anyway. Are you two sharing a room?"

"We are." Dormael turned and looked at the stairs where D'Jenn was being led to the second floor by the woman he'd been speaking with. "He didn't even check with me."

"Looks like you're bed-less for a while." Seylia poked him in the shoulder. "Good thing I'm willing to share."

Dormael laughed. "I'd be a fool to turn down your kindness."

"Finish your drink, then." She leaned forward and pressed her

27

lips to his, smiling through the kiss. When their lips parted, she grabbed her cup from the table and drained it in one gulp. Dormael followed her example. Seylia stood, grabbed him by the arm, and allowed him to walk her upstairs.

Gods, it really is good to be home.

FLYING ROCK

Dormael woke the next morning in his own bed, having crept back into his room sometime during the night. His mouth tasted like sour firewine, and his stomach fluttered with nausea. He climbed from the bed and stumbled to the shutters, grimacing at the pounding in his skull. An orange haze glowed on the horizon, and the twilight looked chilly. Mist choked the streets, creating an odd vista of disembodied buildings and hazy outlines.

If there's an underworld, it probably looks like that.

D'Jenn coughed and roused from his blankets, prompting Dormael to turn from the window.

Dormael smirked. "Does your head feel like it's packed with stuffing?"

"More like warm, soupy shit." D'Jenn grimaced. "Why did I let that woman talk me into drinking so much?"

"She didn't do much talking." Dormael snorted. "Your resistance was token at best."

"Women like that have you going their way before you know what's good for you," D'Jenn grumbled. "I'm convinced it's another form of magic."

"Not magic," Dormael said. "Just beauty and wit."

D'Jenn rolled his eyes. "Beauty and wit, indeed. Was it her beauty and wit that kept you out until the small hours, then? That smile on your face is sickening."

Dormael shrugged.

D'Jenn made a disgusted noise. "Let's get out of this place before she wakes up. I like Seylia, but I'd rather avoid her tendency to stir up trouble. She's the last thing we need right now."

"Alright." Dormael moved to his bed and started pulling on his boots. "I'd like to hurry, in any case. If we make good time, we can stop by my family's homestead."

D'Jenn rubbed sleep from his eyes. "You really want to visit?"

"I've probably got a stack of letters from my mother waiting at the Conclave anyway, and if anyone finds out we traveled through the Red Hills and *didn't* visit, you know what an uproar there will be." Dormael stood and reached for his shirt. "The family will come after both of us."

"Aye, they probably will." D'Jenn sighed. "It's not a bad idea, anyway. Your mother will stack food on top of us, fill our saddlebags with a ton of stuff, and let us take whatever we want from the homestead, too. It's better than sleeping on the side of the road in the highlands."

"Indeed," Dormael nodded. "Maybe my brother will be there. All the tournaments are in the summer."

"Maybe." D'Jenn gave an irritated sigh and rose from the bed. "Let's get moving, then."

**

The sun was just starting to crest the horizon by the time everyone met in front of the stables. Mistfall was quiet, its streets deserted. The sounds of straps tightening and buckles clinking seemed obnoxious in the misty quiet of the dawn.

Dormael's head pounded, and his mouth was as dry as a desert. D'Jenn was silent, huddled in the depths of his cloak. Shawna shot questioning looks at both of them, disapproval clear in her expression. Bethany watched everything in silence, ignoring the weighted glances and uncomfortable coughs. Dormael tried to imitate the youngling's quiet demeanor, but he felt Shawna's eyes on him like a pair of knives tickling his back.

The shoes of their horses made loud clopping sounds on the cobblestones as they walked through the empty streets of Mistfall. The smells of the city sat thick in the mist—sea salt, fresh morning air, and pungent waste. They navigated through mist-choked avenues toward the western gate in silence.

Hoof-beats echoed from the buildings behind them—a single horse, approaching at a canter. Everyone moved their horses to the side of the road, clearing the street. Shawna put a hand to one of her blades and scowled at Dormael before turning to watch the mist.

Dormael's stomach tightened with dread.

Seylia appeared from the haze and pulled on the reins of a small black mare, smiling as she came even with them. Her guitar was strapped to her saddle atop her traveling gear, and she wore a thick leather coat. She didn't look half as hungover as Dormael and D'Jenn.

Dormael closed his eyes and took a cleansing breath. *Why do the gods do this to me?*

"Morning, boys." Seylia patted her horse's neck. "How are we feeling today?"

She balked as she caught sight of Shawna with her hand on her sword. Shawna gave her a predatory smirk and let go of her weapon, making a show of being disappointed. D'Jenn glared at Dormael, and Dormael winced under the pressure of his gaze.

"We're still recovering from our bout with you last night." D'Jenn frowned at Seylia. "What are you doing here, Seylia?"

"Well, I thought I'd tag along with you as far as Gameritus. There are Inns and Courts to be played there, and a girl alone on the road is easy pickings for bandits and the like." Seylia put a delicate hand to her chest. "You wouldn't deny me the pleasure of your company, would you? The benefit of your magical protection?"

"It must be inconvenient to be unable to protect yourself." Shawna shook her head. "I couldn't imagine being so defenseless, so dependent."

Dormael winced.

Seylia opened her mouth to reply, but D'Jenn cut her off.

"We don't mind." D'Jenn turned his frown to Dormael. "We couldn't allow anything to happen to an old friend. But this isn't a pleasure trip, Seylia—Gameritus is as far as you go."

Seylia made a conciliatory gesture. "Thank you."

"Let's be off, then." D'Jenn shook his head and turned back to the road.

Seylia offered Shawna a cold smile. Shawna ignored her, frowned at Dormael, and followed D'Jenn. Dormael sighed and nudged Horse after them, allowing Seylia to fall in beside him.

The silence deepened as they rode toward the western gate of the city. There were more people in the main streets than the lanes near the docks, and they coalesced out of the mist like ghosts. D'Jenn slowed the pace after he almost ran into a scowling old man who yelled a curse at them as they passed.

The Western Tradefair came into view around the corner of an intersection, spread out in a park in front of the gatehouse. Wooden stands stood shoulder to shoulder along a wide, impromptu avenue leading to the city gate. Behind the stands stood rows of colorful tents, most of them drawn closed against the cold, misty morning. A few traders, wrapped in thick layers of cloth against the cold, were opening their tents or placing goods on the shelves in the stands.

They passed a pair of arguing men, nudging their horses wide of the altercation, and left the Tradefair. The gatehouse towered above them, with square stone towers to each side of the road and an arched opening between. A pair of guards stood by the doors, wearing only short cudgels, and they ushered the party through without a challenge. The gigantic doors were flung wide to the cool mist of the morning, and the loamy odor of wet earth wafted through the tunnel.

D'Jenn picked up the pace once they were outside, and they left Mistfall behind.

The road meandered west, snaking over low hills on its trek inland. Soirus-Gamerit was a fertile place, and even this deep in winter, swaths of green waved amongst the swishing brown grasses. Mist clung to the low places, rolling along the saddles between gentle hilltops. The air was thick, and it smelled of farmlands and sea salt.

Dormael spent most of the day answering Bethany's questions about their surroundings, pointing out various landmarks and telling what stories he knew about the area. Seylia took over storytelling duties after Dormael grew tired. Bethany asked for darker and darker tales and seemed particularly interested in the creatures of the Gathan Mountains. Seylia obliged her, telling the story of Tirrin, a Farra-Jerran Kansil who'd been lost on an expedition—likely killed and eaten by the Garthorin in the mountains.

That's what we get for telling her about the Garthorin. Now all she'll want to hear are dark, bloody stories.

When Dormael slept, he dreamed a pair of beasts were stalking him through a dark forest.

The next few days went by with little comfort. Seylia worked at being as condescending as possible to Shawna and acted oblivious to the effects of her manner. Shawna, though she ignored Seylia's baiting, became ever more irritable as the days wore on. Fake smiles flew back and forth like arrows as the two women fenced, and Dormael could feel the tension resonating in his Kai.

For his part, Dormael made sure he did nothing to draw either woman's attention. D'Jenn's scowl deepened with each passing day, and the glances he shot Dormael said plainly where he laid the blame for the situation. Seylia was a master at making herself a nuisance, and she used her talents with gleeful abandon.

Bethany was tossed between the two women like a ball in a village square. Shawna had taken to teaching Bethany basic things about fighting, like how to move her feet and how to recognize danger. Seylia, by the third night out from Mistfall, would tempt the youngling away with lich tales and songs about heroes. Shawna pretended as if the intrusions didn't bother her, but she ground her teeth whenever she looked at Seylia. Her expression became a permanent thundercloud.

On the sixth night out from the city, they camped a good distance from the road near a sprawling field. After the meal was finished, Dormael and D'Jenn settled down to enjoy a pipe around the fire. Bethany finished her lessons and meditation, and Dormael spent a few moments enjoying the blessed silence.

Seylia regarded Shawna with a wicked smile. "Lady Shawna, why do you carry such beastly weapons?"

Dormael braced himself for the storm.

Shawna's eyes were full of cold suspicion. "They lend themselves to my style. They're light, elegant, and quick."

Shawna reached to her side and slid one of her blades from its sheath, letting the steel catch the firelight. Seylia leaned away from the sword, wrinkling her nose. Shawna showed her teeth in a wolfish grin.

"They conceal a certain brutality, though." Shawna's eyes sparkled. "The point is delicate, but the blade is weighted just right. It can pierce armor or remove a limb, often on a single swing. A Sheran short sword is often underestimated by the foolish. As I said—they suit me."

Shawna pointed the sword across the fire at Seylia, letting the flames lick over the surface of the metal. The fire's reflection sent shimmering patterns of light swimming along the blade's length. She held the sword there for a moment before pulling it back and favoring Seylia with a cool smile.

Seylia smiled back. "A bow just seems like a weapon better suited to a lady, especially a noble one like yourself. The sword is just so...*masculine*. It must be terribly disappointing for your father."

Seylia let out a titter, oblivious to the sudden stillness of the campsite.

Shawna's gaze was sharp enough to cut out her heart.

"Let me tell you something, you insufferable little harpy." Shawna got to her feet, eyes cold as she met the scandalized look on Seylia's face. She took a step closer to the fire, looming over it to glare at Seylia. Her sword was gripped tight in her hand.

Dormael got to his feet, holding up a hand for peace. "Shawna, wait—"

Shawna, eyes still locked to Seylia, elbowed him dead in the nose.

He stumbled back, his face blooming with pain. Tears filled his eyes, and he tasted blood on his lips. She hadn't hit him too hard, but her blow had landed in exactly the right spot.

That's what I get for trying to help.

Shawna didn't even look at Dormael—she had eyes only for Seylia. "I've been suffering your little snubs, your underhanded comments, and your covert disdain since we left Mistfall. I've ignored it—not because I fear the repercussions of confronting you, but because some things are beneath a *lady* with honor. I'm sure you don't understand—that's irrelevant—but there's one thing I want you to realize, Seylia."

Shawna put the tip of her blade so close to Seylia's face that she was forced to lean back.

"If this were Cambrell, I would be well within my rights to

demand satisfaction for the dishonor you have shown me—do you understand?"

Seylia looked around, uttering a nervous laugh, though her eyes were as wide as river stones. "It was only a jest, Lady Shawna. Only words."

"Words won't save you if I decide to carve up your pretty face." Shawna delivered the threat in a flat, direct tone. "Any scar across that delicate skin would just ruin things for you, wouldn't it? Would so many men want to lie with you if you were ugly? We certainly can't have that."

"Certainly." Seylia's tone was insolent, but she said nothing else.

Shawna held Seylia's gaze for a moment longer before sheathing her sword. She shot Dormael a guarded look, shook her head, and sought her blankets. Everyone sat frozen in the wake of her departure, the fire crackling into the silence.

Seylia let out a nervous breath and tried to cover it with a laugh. She looked around, as if to engender silent support, but found only the frustrated stares of the two wizards. Her mouth tightened, and she looked away.

Dormael hit D'Jenn in the shoulder. "You could have tried to help."

"That had nothing to do with me." D'Jenn shrugged and gave him a flat look.

Dormael shook his head and sat down, resting his back against his saddle. Seylia came and squatted next to him, wincing at his nose. She pulled a handkerchief from her jacket and dabbed at the blood on his face.

"That was quite the performance," she commented in a light tone. "A little barbaric, perhaps, but she made her point clear. I thought Cambrellian ladies were supposed to be poised and polite."

Shawna either didn't hear Seylia, or chose not to engage with her—a thing for which Dormael was thankful. He grunted in answer and let Seylia clean his face. The pain in his face became a slow throb in his head.

He lit another pipe and puffed blue smoke into the night air, letting his eyes fill with the stars above. The cold made the pain in his face more pronounced, and his nose tingled with each breath.

The thought of having a swollen face for the entire wintry ride to Gameritus made him simmer in quiet anger.

It was a long time before he fell asleep.

**

Dormael stood on windswept hills.

Waving, sand-colored grass stretched out in all directions, rolling gently with the lay of the land. A roiling mass of dark gray clouds stretched above him, as if a pair of storms warred for dominance of the sky. The wind whipped through his ears, carrying nothing but the sound of its passage.

I've been here before.

Dormael waved his hand through the waist-high grass, but it twisted away from his fingers like it found his touch repugnant. High, craggy mountains stretched across one horizon, and the sky was dark behind them. Their summits disappeared into the roiling haze of clouds above. As Dormael turned his head, everything rolled across his vision, leaving his senses befuddled.

This is the armlet's dream.

A nauseating wave ripped through the fabric of the dream, sending Dormael to his knees as it passed through his body like a wall of needles. He went to his knees, heaving in the grass. Dormael's stomach was empty, but his stomach still tried to empty itself.

I should have remembered the gods-damned wave.

Dormael climbed to his feet and found himself in the shadow of an ancient stone temple.

It was much as he remembered it—eight columns carved with archaic representations of the gods. The columns held up a circular slab of stone. A bowl sat on a raised dais in the center of the shrine, perched beneath an opening to the sky. Above the opening, the roiling mass of clouds spun like a top.

"Please..."

Dormael stepped around the altar, bringing the speaker into view. A man crouched in supplication before the bowl, his fist on the flagstones. A long spear was stuck into the ground outside the temple, and a round shield rested against the shaft. A blue streamer, stained with spatters of blood, fluttered in the wind from the top.

The stranger wore archaic leather-and-scale armor. He had a short, thick sword with no crossguard sheathed on his right side. His face was haggard, and a bloodied cloth was wound over his upper left arm.

"Please," the praying man said, "gods of the storm, gods of the Void, hear my call. What am I to do? Where...where is your damned *mercy*? Where's the justice?"

Dormael crept into sight, waved at the praying man. The old warrior kept his troubled eyes on the flagstones. Dormael snapped his fingers—no reaction.

The man grimaced at the floor. "My people are dying by the thousands. Entire clans have fallen to the horde. The men are slaughtered, the women...well, why am I telling you, after all? You know what's happening. You *know*!"

Something moved in Dormael's periphery, but nothing was there when he looked. The long grasses whipped in the wind, and the silent clouds roiled above. He peeked over the edge of the bowl and saw a sprig of ivy left in offering, ripe with several black berries. The leaves were a vivid green against the washed-out stone of the bowl.

"Why have you allowed this to happen?"

Dormael turned back to the praying man.

His voice was strained, face twisted with anguish. "Are we not your people? Are we no better than chattel? I've mustered the tribes against the horde, I've done everything I could to stop them! I've given you a river of blood! Why do you *still* turn your eyes from my people—from *your* people?"

A group of people appeared behind the praying man, arrayed in a semicircle around the old temple. A gray-robed man with eyes the color of the roiling sky frowned at the supplicant's back. The woman beside him had yellow hair that seemed alive in the wind and a painfully beautiful face full of pity. Beside her stood a warrior, expression exultant and eyes full of righteous anger. A motherly woman stood to the side, her dark hair shot with veins of green. She closed her eyes, sadness on her face, and looked at the ground.

"Please, just give me a sign. Give me *something*. Help us!"

Two men appeared to either side of the altar, their presence vibrating the very air around them. Dormael stumbled away, holding his hands up in a meager defense of their power. They blazed in his magical senses like the sun.

A woman struggled between them, held over the altar by her wrists and ankles. She was naked, but something about her nudity was regal and imposing, as if her skin was the vestment of a queen. She struggled against their grip, her face twisted with anger, but no sound came from her throat.

The man holding her ankles was concealed in the depths of a deep purple robe, but his hands were gnarled and wrinkled. The second man was larger by half than the first and muscled like a blacksmith. He had a dark and shaggy beard, and he held the woman's wrists in a single, meaty hand.

The old man whispered something to the bowl, his words creeping from his hood like dark smoke. The ivy in the bowl writhed and twisted in response, its creepers wiggling like fingers. It reached up and wrapped the woman in its embrace, pulling her from the hands of the two men on either side of the altar. She struggled against it, fought some of its tendrils away, but it pulled her arms to her side.

Lightning struck the bowl, Dormael screamed, and everything went white.

**

The captain of the ship wrung his hat in his hands. His eyes darted around the cabin—formerly his own dwelling—with disgust. The smell of blood was strong in the room, though no one acknowledged the fact. Maaz stared at the man from behind his own desk, hands splayed on the top like a pair of spiders.

"I mean no disrespect," the captain said, "but I can't sail this ship without a certain number of crewmen. If they keep...*disappearing*...then we're dead in the water. The next storm will take us."

Maarkov would have laughed if he had any laughter to give. The entire situation was like something from a macabre play. Maaz needed to kill in order to fuel his magic, and he needed the magic to speed their passage. The captain, however, needed the sailors to keep the vessel afloat in the first place. Everyone knew Maaz was killing the sailors, but they also knew they were powerless to stop it.

At least the captain has the guts to stand up for his men. I can respect that.

Maaz usually met dissent and criticism with one of two methods—torture or murder. Sometimes, it was one quickly followed by the other, and sometimes, it happened at the same time. It was rare, however, that anyone said a sideways word to Maaz and lived.

If you want the captain dead, you can kill him yourself. Maarkov prepared to refuse the order he knew would come. He wouldn't stab the sea captain in the back—not this time.

Maaz pinned the captain with a glare. "Your point is taken. Get out."

Maarkov turned an incredulous look on his brother as the captain left the room. The door opened to the sound of wind over the sea and slammed shut in the captain's wake. Maarkov snorted and walked to the chair across from the desk. He shook his head as he sat.

"I think that's the first time I've seen you show any mercy. Even when we were children, you twisted the heads from puppies. Is your heart thawing its cold exterior? I'm touched at the thought."

"These men will all die when we reach the Sevenlands." Maaz sighed, and looked through the porthole at the dark, rolling sea. "I will need servants, and these men are a ready crop. Better to take them than the inhabitants of a village in a foreign land. It would attract the attention of authorities."

Maarkov shuddered. "Of course. For a moment, I thought some vestige of humanity remained in that dried husk you use to slither around."

"If all you're going to do is bleat like some pained goat, find somewhere else to whine." Maaz waved him away. "I have plans to make, and your whimpering is distracting me."

"What was the name of that village we ran through when we were children?" Maarkov ignored his brother's evil look. "The one where we hid in that farmer's stables? That was so long ago, but I remember it well. All the cats in the village disappearing. You, in the middle of a pile of twisted little corpses."

Maaz scowled. "And *you*, crying while you buried them. Even then, you were a coward."

"I liked cats." Maarkov sneered. "I still like cats. What sort of bastard kills a bunch of cats? My brother—*that* kind of bastard."

"Is there a point to this drivel?" Maaz sighed. "As much as I enjoy these little fits of nostalgia, I rather prefer the room when you're not here."

"One day I'm going to pay you back for those cats." Maarkov offered his brother a smile. "Would it kill you if I twisted your neck that way? Would you just go on living? How difficult would it be to eat people if your head is facing your arse?"

"I could always test the theory on you."

"You're probably right—best to go with a tried-and-true method." Maarkov tapped the hilt of his sword. "Sharpened steel is hard to beat when it comes to killing."

Maaz rolled his eyes. "You're trying my patience. If you're just going to sit there and blather like an idiot—"

Maarkov was out of his seat in a blink, his hand going for his blade. He had always been fast, agile, and whipcord strong. He'd had a very long time to hone his skill to a fine edge, and he summoned every bit of mastery as he sought his brother's chest. His sword slid from its sheath and arced for Maaz's ribcage. Maarkov put his entire body behind the thrust.

The steel bit deep into Maaz's flesh.

Maaz let out a surprised grunt as the sword parted his ribs and pinned him to his chair. His hands sought the blade and flinched away as the edge put delicate cuts in his fingers. Maarkov always made sure to keep his steel sharp.

Maaz gave Maarkov a withering scowl. "Must we...always *do* this, brother?"

Maaz made a fist, and something unseen slammed against Maarkov, knocking him across the room. His back smacked into the door with a loud crack, sending a white flash of pain through Maarkov's head. His chest compressed as Maaz's power intensified, pinning him to the door. The breath left his lungs as he slid up the door, raised from the ground by Maaz's magic.

I got my steel in your ribs, you bastard. I got my steel in you.

Maaz wrenched the sword from his chest and flung it to the floor. The wound dripped black, putrid blood. Maaz reached to the ground beside him and put a corked bottle onto the table. Tiny points of light swirled in the water within, like stars caught in a whirlpool. Maaz uncorked the bottle, turned it up, and drank a single point of light.

His body spasmed, and Maaz put a hand to the wound in his chest. He hissed in pain as the Soulspark went to work. Having the body knit itself back together felt like a million spiders crawling around beneath the skin, and it showed in Maaz's agonized posture. His fingers clawed at the desk, drawing furrows in the wood, until the fit subsided.

Maaz took a deep breath when it was over, shuddering with fatigue. He stood from the chair, grimacing at the black bloodstains on the floor. He fingered the hole in his cloak and cursed under his breath. He scowled at Maarkov and shook his head.

With a twist of Maaz's wrist, Maarkov's entire ribcage crackled, and pain blossomed in his chest. Fluid filled his lungs, and he spat out a torrent of his own putrid blood. It tasted like ashes and sweat. He tried to growl at his brother in defiance, but all that came out was a pained gurgle.

"I know how you like to indulge your little urges, brother," Maaz said, "but this mischief, like your prattling, sours quickly. I'm going to leave the bottle here on the desk. When you reach the Soulsparks, you can have one. Perhaps crawling like the worm you are will teach you humility."

Maaz gestured again, and the bones in Maarkov's legs shattered. He screamed as best he could through the blood in his mouth. Maaz released him, and he fell to the floor on his shattered legs, his body on fire with pain. Maarkov tried to move, but all he could do was tremble.

"The next time something like this happens, it will be worse."

Maaz went to the corner of the room, sat on the floor, and went silent.

Maarkov clenched his jaw and pulled his broken body toward the desk. Every finger's width of progress cost him an eternity of pain. It was a long time before he reached the bottle.

Maaz never uttered a sound.

**

The sounds of a busy common room drifted through the floor of Dormael's room. It was dusk in Gameritus, and the quarry workers who lived in the Low City were coming to the inn for dinner. Dormael quirked a smile at the noise.

The noise is good. Distraction builds character.

Bethany squeezed her eyes shut and grimaced in concentration. She sat cross-legged in the middle of the floor, hands clasping her dress. Her brow knotted with strain.

The stone in the floor wiggled.

"Be calm." D'Jenn kept his voice quiet. "Don't squeeze your power like a branch over a cliff. Don't let it use you as a conduit for its chaos. Listen to it, draw it in with your breath—not so much, little one. A little is all you need. Let it show you the rock. Can you feel the rock through your magic? Can you see it in your mind's eye?"

Bethany nodded.

D'Jenn narrowed his eyes. "Focus on the stone."

Bethany knotted her brows. Her power stirred in the air, poised like a hand ready to catch something. The ether hummed with her song.

"Now, take the rock into the grasp of your Kai—gently, now."

The rock gave a shudder and scooted away from Bethany.

Dormael smiled. "Control it, little one. Remain calm. Work *with* your power, not against it."

Bethany's brow knotted further. The rock quivered and rose from the floor. It wobbled in the air, as if held by a shaking hand. Bethany's Kai sang a muted note of effort.

D'Jenn nodded. "There you are, girl. Hold right there. Seek stillness."

Bethany opened her eyes and gaped at the rock, which hovered in front of her face. She reached out and flicked it with one of her fingers, sending it spinning in midair. A smile cracked her features, and she gave D'Jenn a triumphant look.

The rock shot into the air and was embedded into the ceiling.

Bethany squealed in surprise, her power winking out. Dormael and D'Jenn broke down in a fit of laughter, which Bethany joined after a moment of embarrassment. Dormael reached out with his magic and plucked the rock from the ceiling, bringing it to rest once again on the floor.

"There's a lesson in this," Dormael said. "Do you realize what happened?"

"I looked away." Bethany shrugged. "I stopped paying

attention."

"That's part of it." D'Jenn nodded. "Even more important—you got excited."

Bethany's shoulders fell. "I know. I didn't mean to. I know you said my emotions affect it, but—"

D'Jenn held up a hand. "How do we keep our emotions quiet, our minds clear?"

Bethany grimaced. "Meditation."

"Get to it, then." Dormael hoisted her by the shoulders and set her on her feet. "And don't roll your eyes, love. It's rude."

Bethany hugged both of them around the neck before skipping across the hall to the room she shared with Shawna. Dormael rose to his feet, plucking the stone from the floor and dropping it on a bedside table with his Kai. His face was still swollen from Shawna's elbow, and his teeth were throbbing.

I could use a drink to dull the pain a bit.

D'Jenn nodded toward Bethany. "She's progressing well."

"Quickly, for one so young." Dormael rubbed his temples. "At her age, I could barely keep my mind clear enough to sense my Kai, let alone play Flying Rock."

"You were always a slow learner."

Dormael scowled and shot D'Jenn a rude gesture.

D'Jenn smiled. "What do you say to a drink?"

"Nothing, you drink it."

"That wasn't funny, coz."

"You'll be alright."

"I don't even want to have a drink with you now."

"You're a liar."

D'Jenn scoffed. "Come on."

They left their room and went down into the common room, which was sparsely populated with drinking patrons. The Kneeling Mare was an out-of-the-way place, and D'Jenn had chosen it mainly on that virtue. They sought a table in the corner of the room, far from other people, and sat down to have a quiet drink.

D'Jenn glanced around the common room. "Where did Seylia go? Did Shawna kill her and stuff her body down a well?"

"The gods only know." Dormael shook his head. "You know how she is. Here one moment, gone the next. I suspect she slipped away after we retired upstairs. I didn't expect we'd see her for dinner."

D'Jenn nodded and gave him a sympathetic grin. "How's your face?"

"It hurts." Dormael smiled. "I've had worse, though. It's not broken, thank the gods, just swollen to all Six Hells."

"You should talk with Shawna." D'Jenn waved a boy over from the bar. "Find out why she hit you."

Dormael snorted. "I know why she hit me. You're right, though. I need to smooth things over."

"Good luck with that, coz," D'Jenn said. "Just warn me first so I don't have to listen to it."

A young boy brought them a pitcher of ale, and they let their first round of drinks pass in silence. Dormael sat back and listened to the soft murmur of voices in the room, the tinkle of dinnerware, and scattered bits of laughter. He opened his Kai and let the song of the world speak to him through the ether. People burned in a wizard's magical senses. Any living thing was like a beacon of light, and Dormael enjoyed listening to them with his magic.

Emotions could sometimes manifest themselves in the ether. If a person was distressed, they played discordant notes back to his Kai. Young couples in love bubbled with warm tones, and the insane sounded erratic. Listening to a room full of people was like sitting in a fancy concert hall, and Dormael had enjoyed the sensation since he'd first discovered his magic.

A man entered the room who felt different from the other patrons. He was alert, watchful, and filled with suspicious energy. Dormael tracked him with his senses—a figure in a bulky winter cloak with a sword on his hip. He made his way across the other side of the common room and sat with another man. The two of them leaned together, speaking in hushed tones.

When Dormael chanced a look at their table, one of them looked away on reflex.

They're watching us.

Dormael closed his eyes and sought the men in his magical senses. He whispered through his Kai, sending a delicate thread of magic to their table. Their words vibrated the thread, bringing their voices to Dormael's ears.

"...the description."

"How do you know?"

"I'm *telling* you, I saw the girl earlier. Red-head. Real nice-looking, too."

"Very well. When did they arrive?"

"Earlier, I don't fucking know. They're here *now*. Renael said you'd pay. Was he jamming me up?"

"He wasn't. My organization always rewards those who do the work of the Clever One."

The Clever One? Gods—what are Cultists doing here?

There was a tinkling noise—money changing hands.

"Thanks."

"Thank the Clever One."

"Yes, yes, the Clever One, of course. Don't get up and walk out with me. I don't want to be seen with one of you."

"Very well."

Dormael opened his eyes and watched the second man scuttle to the door, shooting a glance over his shoulder at Dormael and D'Jenn's table. The first man—the one with the sword—still sat at his table with his back to them. Dormael caught D'Jenn's eyes as he poured himself another drink.

"We've got company."

D'Jenn finished pouring and handed Dormael the pitcher. "Company?"

"Look toward the opposite wall of the room." Dormael took the pitcher and poured himself a refill. "There's a man in a heavy cloak with his back to us. He's an Aeglar Cultist."

"A Cultist?" D'Jenn glanced at the table. "Is this some sort of joke?"

"I just listened to him pay a man for information about us," Dormael said. "He made overtures to 'the Clever One'. I'm sure you know what *that* means."

"What is the bloody Cult of Aeglar doing in Gameritus?" D'Jenn scowled at the man's back. "The local Clan Leaders must be too lenient. The Cult doesn't belong in the Sevenlands."

"I don't think they're popular." Dormael took a sip from his ale cup. "He mentioned Shawna, D'Jenn. Why in the Six Hells would a Cultist be concerned with Shawna?"

D'Jenn drew his brows together. "She's no wizard. They can't know she's important to the Conclave—the Conclave doesn't know about her yet."

"The Cult of Aeglar wouldn't do something to interfere with the Conclave directly, not here." Dormael shook his head. "They'd be obliterated. This is something else. Someone paid them to seek us out."

D'Jenn's expression darkened. "However they know about us, it isn't good."

"We'd be doing the community a service if we killed him," Dormael said. "We can't let him get back to wherever he's going with our whereabouts."

"We have to do it quiet." D'Jenn glanced around the room. "Conclave or not, we'll get arrested for murder in the streets."

"He'll probably have someone watching the inn."

"Probably."

"Let's lead them outside, then." Dormael smiled. "We can have a friendly chat in a dark alley."

D'Jenn sighed. "Let me finish my ale."

They rose and drew their cloaks around their shoulders, leaving their empty cups on the table. Dormael felt the Cultist's eyes on his back as they headed for the door, like a predator watching a herd animal cross a field. When they reached the door, Dormael turned and caught the Cultist's eyes.

He was a scowling, dark-haired man with stubble on his face. His eyes were full of hatred, and he sneered as Dormael looked at him. The candlelight glinted from armor beneath the Cultist's cloak.

Dormael smiled, offered the sneering man a wink, and slipped into the street.

Clouds kept the moon and stars behind a dark veil, and the windy streets of Gameritus were awash in shadow. The darkness was kept at bay by islands of flickering lantern-light, but those were few and far between. Rain pattered to the cobblestones, and Dormael hunched his shoulders against the cold.

Gameritus was a city of stone, built low and gray against the roaring wind of the hills. The outer districts were full of crumbling ruins where thieves and beggars crouched in abandoned corners. D'Jenn turned down an avenue headed for one of the run-down areas, where the dark silhouettes of deserted ruins beckoned.

Dormael spotted the man behind them, passing like a wraith through a bubble of orange lantern-light. He was staying far enough back to keep from arousing suspicion from passersby, few as they were, but he was definitely following them. Dormael swept the street behind them with his magical senses, but they returned only the bright form of the Aeglar Cultist.

"I only see one," Dormael muttered. "Well behind us."

D'Jenn gave an imperceptible nod. "Let's have a talk with him. Be ready."

Dormael nodded, but D'Jenn was already moving. He rushed to their right, heading down a narrow alley toward one of the ruined sections of Gameritus. Dormael sprinted after him, using his magical senses to reveal hidden obstacles during the mad rush through the darkness. They made it to an intersection, and D'Jenn cut to the left. He leapt to the wall of the building flanking their path of flight, his magic singing through the ether, and scrambled up the wall with the same spell he'd used at Ferolan Castle.

Dormael turned to the right and put his back to the wall, breathing hard from the run. He pulled the shadows around him like a dark cloak and edged away from the intersection. His heart beat into his ears as he waited for the Cultist to appear.

Running steps echoed around the corner, and Dormael tensed his magic for the confrontation. He readied a simple strike with his Kai—a smack of physical force strong enough to bowl the Cultist from his feet. The man darted through the intersection, one hand steadying the sword at his waist. Dormael punched out with his magic, slamming his Kai into the unsuspecting swordsman.

There was a sound like a thunderclap, and Dormael's magic violently unraveled.

His power rebounded as the energies came apart, flooding his mind with cold numbness. Dormael was thrown from his feet into a stack of crates. He bit his tongue in the fall and cracked pieces of wood cut into his arms and legs.

The magical energy Dormael had gathered spiraled out of control. Cracks climbed the walls on both sides of the alley, and colored lights sparkled where the magic had been Splintered. The moonlight made the shadows dance until the magical energy was expended.

The Cult member stood unharmed.

Dormael blinked and tried to rise, but he was defeated by a wave of vertigo. He reached for the dagger in his boot but fumbled the hilt with numb fingers. His sore nose tingled with pain.

Steel whispered as the Cultist drew his sword.

Dormael tossed himself to the side, rolling away from a fatal slash. He scrambled away, stumbling on his half-numbed legs. The Cultist chased him down the alley, sword raised for the kill. Dormael spun away from one slash, slipped out of another's path, and threw himself to the other side of the alley to avoid a third. The air was thick in his mouth, his body heavy with fatigue.

He reached for his Kai, but it wouldn't answer. *Fuck the gods— I'm going to die!*

Dormael threw himself into the Cultist, grabbing his arms, and aimed a heavy kick at the inside of his knee. His boot hit soft flesh with a meaty crunch. The man cried out as the joint buckled, and he fell to the ground. Dormael went down with him.

He pushed the Cultist's sword arm—still clutching the blade— above his head. The man screamed with effort and scooted to his back, trying to pull his arm free. Dormael pulled the dagger from his boot and raised it to strike, but the Cultist punched him in the eye with his free hand.

Dormael's face exploded with pain. He lost the dagger in the moment of blind agony, and the Cultist jerked his sword arm free of Dormael's grip. There was a rushing sensation, a painful impact, and a knee was pushing down on Dormael's chest. Armored hands closed around Dormael's throat, cutting off his air.

When he blinked his eyes open, the Cultist loomed over him, hatred twisting his expression.

There was a crash of splintered wood, and the man was thrown to the side. Dormael rolled away, gulping air into his injured throat, and scrambled to his feet. The Cultist lay in a heap amongst the remains of a crate. As Dormael let out a relieved breath, the debris in the alley raised from the ground and slammed into the Cultist a second time, as if to make sure he was down.

D'Jenn appeared out of the night, his hand raised toward the Cultist's inert body.

"Thanks the gods." Dormael coughed. "Something happened, D'Jenn. I think he Splintered me."

D'Jenn nodded. "I saw that. I thought he was Blessed himself— that's why I waited to attack—but he never raised power against you."

"Cultists hate magic." Dormael scowled at the unconscious man. "No one other than a trained wizard would know how to Splinter magic in the first place, so how did *he* do it?"

D'Jenn frowned and nudged the fallen man with his foot. The Cultist didn't move. D'Jenn rolled him over and looked away from his face—the eyes were vacant, and they pointed in different directions. Dormael grimaced and muttered a curse under his breath.

"He's wearing pretty armor." D'Jenn reached down and unbuckled a bracer from the man's arm. He summoned a low magical light and held it up for Dormael to examine.

The bracer was made of polished steel, and it had lines of brass inlaid in swirling patterns. The designs were flush with the surface of the metal, too perfect to have been crafted by hand. Dormael summoned his Kai and ran his senses over the piece of armor. It put off a strange echo in his Kai, and his magic recoiled from touching the steel.

"You think this Splintered my magic?" Dormael raised an eyebrow. "I've never heard of an infused item with that capability."

"And because you've never seen it, it must not exist?" D'Jenn scoffed. "I'll take this piece with me. Maybe I can learn something about it on the ride north."

Dormael nodded. "Was there another one out there? I thought he'd have someone backing him up."

"Bastard got away." D'Jenn let out an exasperated breath. "He spotted me before I saw him and scuttled away like a cockroach. I lost him in the alleys, and I didn't want to get too far from you."

"It's a good thing, too." Dormael clapped his cousin on the shoulder. "Thanks for pulling me out of the fire. How did you use magic on him without getting Splintered like me?"

D'Jenn shrugged. "It's simple. If you can't use magic *on* them, throw things *at* them. Flying Rock, Dormael—it's the first thing we learn for a reason."

Dormael couldn't help but chuckle.

"This still doesn't answer any of our questions, though." D'Jenn kicked debris over the Cultist's body and stepped away. "How would they know anything about us? About Shawna? I think the Empire is still trying to reach us."

Dormael gave a grudging nod. "It bothers me that they can do this—interfere with Conclave business right here in the Sevenlands. How did they get word ahead of us? Pigeons can't cross the fucking sea, can they?"

"Damned if I know." D'Jenn grimaced and let out an all-suffering sigh. "We're leaving tonight. Let's get back to the Kneeling Mare and pack our things."

"What about him?" Dormael nodded at the dead man.

"Leave him. The inhabitants will pick him cleaner than carrion eaters. He'll be looted and buried somewhere before we're back to the inn, and good bloody riddance."

Dormael nodded and followed his cousin into the rain-soaked darkness. Paranoia haunted him on the way back to the inn, and he found himself looking over his shoulder at every turn. Every figure trotting through the rain looked like a possible Cultist, and Dormael wondered if every lingering gaze contained an unhealthy amount of interest.

The safety of home seemed as cold and empty as the streets.

THE NATURE OF HEAT

Dormael was soaked to his bones.

Their flight from Gameritus had been tense but otherwise uneventful. D'Jenn had insisted on haste, though there were no signs of pursuit. They had stopped to camp only after the gray haze of dawn could be seen over the eastern horizon and huddled in a copse of trees far from the road. A few hours of fitful sleep later, the drizzle from the night before had grown into a cold, unforgiving downpour.

The southwestern part of Soirus-Gamerit was characterized by scrub brush and stone. The hills frequently revealed hidden caves, massive boulders peeking from the ground, or burbling creeks meandering through a maze of lowlands. The trees were low and stunted, and the wind carried a deep chill. The environment forced the companions to slow down, lest they turn the ankles of one of their mounts. The hills hid them from pursuers, but likewise hid pursuers from them.

There had been no sign of the Cult of Aeglar by the second day out from Gameritus, but D'Jenn pushed the pace as much as possible. Dormael was certain he could deal with anything the Cult could throw at him—infused armor or not—but he wondered what would happen if they got their hands on Bethany. Would they show leniency to a child? Would they kill her, regardless of her age, simply for having Eindor's Blessing?

They hate magic, but would their hatred drive them to such lengths?

They found a gigantic slab of rock sticking from the side of a hill on the fourth afternoon and decided to take advantage of the shelter it provided. The deluge showed no signs of letting up, and everyone was keen to get out of the rain. The road had become little more than a muddy stream and picking through it had tired the horses. Even Shawna's thoroughbred was showing signs of fatigue.

Dormael staked out a corner away from everyone else and removed all his clothing, save for his pants. He laid everything out on a large rock and sat down to dry out. The air was frigid, but days in this abominable weather had deadened his skin to its chill. He perched on a rock to keep his feet out of the mud and closed his eyes to meditate.

He sensed Shawna coming before she made herself known. Dormael kept his eyes closed and pretended not to notice her standing nearby. She waited for the space of three breaths before clearing her throat.

"Is there room for two?"

Dormael opened his eyes and let out a breath. "Of course."

He scooted to the side of the rock and indicated a spot beside him. Shawna picked her way over the muddy ground and sat, being careful not to slip. She rubbed against him on accident, and Dormael became aware of how tightly her wet clothing clung to her skin. She had doffed her armor, and the wetness left little to the imagination.

He concentrated on keeping his eyes above her collarbones.

"Can't you do some magic, maybe warm this rock a bit?" She offered him a nervous smile. "It's miserable."

Dormael smiled. "I suppose I could do something like that."

He closed his eyes and let his Kai sink into the rock, pouring the smallest amount of heat into the stone. It grew warm beneath him, and his body let out an involuntary shudder. He put his hands on the rock, smiling as it warmed his fingers.

Shawna let out a long sigh. "If I was a wizard, I would never be uncomfortable."

Dormael snorted. "People always say that."

"Is it not true? Couldn't you just go around being warm and cozy wherever you went?"

"I could." Dormael shrugged. "But using magic isn't easy, Shawna. It's not like I just ask the rock to be nice and heat up for me—it takes effort. You could walk everywhere on your hands if you wanted, but you don't."

Shawna chuckled. "My Master used to make me stand on my hands all the time. I think you'd be surprised at my hand-walking skills, Dormael."

"That's not the point."

"What's your point, then? How are you heating the rock?"

"Do you really want to know, or are you trying to trying to irk me?"

"Don't be like that. Tell me." Shawna nudged him with her elbow. "I want to know."

"First you have to understand something about heat."

"Understand something about heat? Done."

"Done?"

"Heat is easy to understand, Dormael."

"Is it, wise one? Please, explain it to me, then. Why is it warm? How does that work?"

"Ask the gods." Shawna shrugged. "I don't know."

"Exactly." Dormael smiled and patted the rock. "Heat is the first kind of energy we're taught to use at the Conclave. Learn to control heat—at least, to a certain degree—and you can do a lot of things. Make fire. Make ice."

"Make ice?" Shawna raised an eyebrow.

"Cold is just the absence of heat." Dormael gestured at the air. "There's no such thing as cold."

"Tell that to my arms and legs," Shawna said. "They'll call you a liar."

Dormael shrugged. "It's true, despite what your legs think."

"Are we back on the subject of my legs, Dormael Harlun?" She gave him a dangerous look.

"You're the one who brought them up!"

Shawna laughed. "Calm down, I'm only teasing. Would it be possible to learn just a bit of magic? Not the whole thing, just a little trick."

Dormael raised an eyebrow. "Like heating your bathwater?"

"Sounds like a good trick."

Dormael snorted. "I suppose, but once you learn to heat your bathwater, why stop?"

Shawna sighed. "Good point. I could move on to drying my wet clothes."

"I do that all the time." Dormael snickered.

Shawna laughed and slapped him on the shoulder. Dormael smiled and went back to staring at the rain. The haze was thick, and thunder rumbled in the sky.

Shawna winced and turned toward him. "Come here. Let me see your face."

Dormael gave her a skeptical glance, but didn't flinch away as she took his chin in her hand. She turned him gently back and forth, regarding her handiwork with a grimace. She poked a tentative finger into the side of his nose.

"I got you pretty good."

"You did." Dormael smiled around her prodding fingers. "Not the worst thing to happen to me."

She frowned. "Is it broken?"

"No," he grumbled. "No thanks to you."

She smiled. "I'd say it *was* thanks to me, actually."

"I can't tell if you're trying to apologize, or if you came over here to gloat."

"I wouldn't gloat, Dormael. Maybe I hit you a little hard, maybe I regret that. I wouldn't gloat, though."

"Maybe you did." Dormael sighed, grimaced, and forced himself to keep talking. "I can see why you were angry, though. I've had worse than a swollen nose in tavern brawls, Shawna. We're friends, right?"

"Right." She smiled.

"Good. That's the one blow you get for free, then. Next time, I'll get you back."

"You wouldn't hit me like that." Shawna slapped him on the shoulder again.

"Maybe not." He gave her a wolfish grin. "I might use magic, though. Remember what I said about the absence of heat?"

Dormael pulled warmth from the rock, bringing it to the verge of freezing. Shawna sucked in a sharp breath and stiffened, shooting him an evil look. Dormael winked and poured the heat slowly back into the stone.

"Point taken." Shawna gave him a searching glance. "Your

friend disappeared in Gameritus. Was I the reason for that?"

"Maybe." Dormael shrugged. "She comes and goes on a whim. She always has."

Shawna sniffed. "I can't say I was sad to see her go."

"Seylia can be difficult. She's like that with everyone." Dormael sighed and looked at his hands. "I know she was wrong, everyone knew she was wrong. She makes herself a nuisance for sport."

"One day that's not going to work out for her." Shawna nudged him with her elbow. "I'm sorry for hitting you. Forgive me?"

Dormael smiled. "I do. Can we sign the peace accords and stop talking about it?"

"Aye, for the love of the gods," D'Jenn called from the other side of camp.

"For the love of the gods," Bethany repeated.

The two of them chuckled like a pair of thieves.

Shawna rolled her eyes in their direction, but she settled into silence. She sat close to Dormael for a while, and they soaked up the heat of his magic together. Shawna leaned against his shoulder and stared into the rain-soaked hills, her wet hair lying over his arm. Her clothing felt thin, and Dormael was acutely aware of how supple she felt against him.

He banished those thoughts and poured more heat into the rock.

**

Maarkov stood against the aft railing of the *King's Blessing,* gazing down at the roiling wake of the ship. Sailors went about their business around him, eyes locked to the deck as much as they could manage. Since the disappearances had begun, the crew had treated them with fear. Since the afternoon, their fear had intensified.

Maarkov left the railing and made his way to the main deck. He glanced up in morbid curiosity at what everyone else was trying to ignore. The flayed cadaver of the old captain hung from the top of the mainmast by his wrists, swaying with the motion of the ship. He bounced from the sail, leaving patches of thick, drying blood on its white surface.

Symbols were drawn on the deck around the mast—twisted, curving runes in a language Maarkov didn't care to know. Square patches of the old captain's skin were nailed to the mast, one stacked atop the other in a neat column. More symbols were cut into the patches, and they smoked in the wind like embers were contained beneath.

The ship sped through the water with a great creaking of wood and rope, moving under some strange, fell power. The crewmen avoided the mast like it had the plague, stepping wide when their duties required them to go past. The rigging creaked and rattled everywhere, neglected by the frightened sailors.

I can't wait to get off this gods-damned ship.

Maarkov ducked through the gangway and entered the captain's quarters. He found his brother sitting in the chair behind the desk, leaning over a map of the Sevenlands. No evidence of the orgy of blood remained on his person. He was cold and wretchedly immaculate.

Maaz glared at Maarkov as he came into the room. "What in all Six Hells do you want?"

"When will we hit land?" Maarkov pushed the door closed behind him.

Maaz gave an irritated sigh. "Maybe a week, maybe longer, but sooner still than that pitiful captain would have gotten us there by more conventional means."

"Where do you plan to make landfall? It's going to be hard explaining all the body parts and your...artwork...to any customs officials we meet, don't you think?"

Maarkov plopped into the chair opposite his brother and put his boots on the desk—directly into Maaz's face. Water dripped onto the map, but it looked to have been treated with oil. Maaz glowered at his brother's boots. With a sigh, he leaned back in his chair.

"This mission requires a certain amount of discretion, Maarkov. Because we are not simpering fools, we will find some smuggler's cove and be done with it there. No harbors, no cities, no customs officials."

"And the ship, the crew?"

"As I said, dear brother—discretion."

"That's a lot of blood." Maarkov touched the hilt of his sword. "What happens if we just go our own way when we get to the Sevenlands? What if you let these poor bastards go home?"

Maaz gave him a blank stare.

"I'll need two of them to scry the location of our quarry. One at least to replenish ourselves—and don't look at me like that, Maarkov, you *know* you have to eat." Maaz reached to a cup at the corner of the desk and took a dainty sip. "After that, I will need servants."

"You need *strega*, you mean." Maarkov grimaced. There was nothing worse than an animated corpse. It was unfeeling, uncaring, unthinking. Maarkov could barely sleep, knowing the things were nearby.

Is it hypocritical to hate them so much? Am I not somewhat like them?

"I need what I need, brother." Maaz sighed. "Your whining is grating on my nerves. Go stare into the wind. Moralize to the gods. I don't care to hear your blathering."

Maarkov stared at his brother for a moment. How monstrous the man had become over the years, how detached from what he'd once been. What lived behind those eyes was something different now, something darker. He rose and walked to the door, pausing to glare at his brother on the way out.

One day, I'll kill him. One day.

**

The rain lightened to a drizzle the next day.

Heavier rains came and went as the party moved north. The Runemian Mountains loomed over the horizon, little more than a bluish haze through the rain. The sight of the low mountain range made Dormael smile—Ishamael lay on the other side. It would be days before they made the highlands, and more still until they passed into Runeme, but home was closer than ever.

I can almost feel the city just over the horizon.

The armlet was silent, and it sent no more dreams to trouble Dormael's sleep. He asked Bethany if she'd heard anything from it, but she only shook her head in reply. The days passed by uneventfully. The weather went from wet to wetter and back again. Suirus-Gamerit was always rainy in the south, especially in the wintertime.

Late one afternoon, the muddy trail became a wide, paved thoroughfare. The stones were old and worn smooth by time, and they stretched wide enough for a line of spearmen to march down the center. They followed the road for most of the day, watching as something tall came out of the haze in the distance. Shawna watched the growing object with a questioning look on her face, but Dormael refused to satisfy her curiosity.

Shawna gaped when they came to the base of the structure.

A deep, wide canyon ran from east to west. It cut through the terrain in a snaking line, leaving a crooked wound in the ground. Spanning the distance was an impossibly long bridge framed with curving, artistic flourishes. Twin arches made of bronze stood to either side of the bridge, hanging the road between them by an intricate web of thin metal filaments. A musical tone hummed in the air—a result of the wind passing through the web.

Shawna gave a sharp intake of breath. "What is it?"

"It's called Indalvian's Passage." D'Jenn smiled up at the bronze arches. "It's a wonder to rival anything in Lesmira."

"It was built thousands of years ago by the Founder," Dormael said.

Shawna looked at him askance.

"He was the one who established the Conclave and helped build the Sevenlands."

"Ah." Shawna put a hand to her chest and stared at the bridge. "It's beautiful."

"He built lots of things," D'Jenn said, "but this is his greatest achievement—I think so, anyway. It's a marvel of artistry, engineering, and magic. The bridge has spells woven into the very material that allow it to self-repair. It resists the cold, it drains itself of water—this thing could stand forever."

"Here we go." Dormael rolled his eyes. "You got him excited."

D'Jenn waved his comment away. "It's said Indalvian and thirty of his students constructed the pieces and had them brought here. They worked from both sides of the canyon, and the local tribesmen helped them. Before the Passage went up, Soirus-Gamerit was two lands instead of one—Soirus and Gamerit."

Shawna shook her head in wonder. "It's an amazing sight."

"Let's have a closer look." Dormael clucked to Horse and started toward the bridge.

The road sloped downward into a landing built into side of the canyon, and stone walls sat to either side of the path. A brass plaque hung against one of the walls with lines of swirling inscriptions on its face. Shawna swung down from Charlotte's saddle and strode to the metal plate, squinting at the engraved text.

"It's just like your tattoos." Shawna gestured to Dormael. "Come tell me what it says."

"It says 'look what we did' in Old Vendon."

"You're an ass, you know that?" Shawna waved him away.

"Alright." Dormael sighed and dismounted. He strode to the metal plaque and brushed raindrops from the inscription. "It says something like *'Here Indalvian healed a wounded land, he brought two worlds together. Order conquered chaos and enemies became one'*. Then it's a list of names—people who worked on the southern side of the bridge."

Shawna nodded. "That's a bit dry for an engraving. I expected more gravitas."

"It rhymes in Old Vendon." Dormael shrugged. "Maybe it was poetic for the time."

"Are any of your ancestors listed on the plaques?"

"Yes, but on the northern side." Dormael smiled. "We Harluns are Gamerits, not Soirii."

"The Pikes, too," D'Jenn said. "If you two are done, we should get going."

As they left the landing and ventured onto the bridge, the canyon yawned beneath them. The ravine stretched as far as they could see from east to west, curving with the patience of the river far below. Dormael was stiff on the ride across—he'd always had an irrational fear of a stiff breeze blowing him over the side. He'd had nightmares about it as a child.

Bethany bent far over Horse's flank to look toward the bottom of the canyon, and Dormael grabbed hold of her cloak, fearing the girl would slip. Bethany barely noticed his fretting.

They made it to the far landing, and Dormael dismounted to examine the plaque.

"Here." He pointed out a name amongst the engravings. "Ivan Harlun, journeyman stoneworker."

D'Jenn nudged his horse to the top of the landing. "And what about the Pikes?"

Dormael ran his finger down the list of names "Here it is—

Straffon Pike, wizarding apprentice."

"Look at that." D'Jenn smiled. "My side of the family was studying magic at the Conclave while yours was still stacking bricks."

"I'd rather be amongst the best than the first."

D'Jenn answered with an offensive gesture in the Hunter's Tongue.

"What does that mean?" Bethany closed her fist and extended her pinkie, trying the gesture for herself.

Dormael pushed her fist closed as he climbed back into the saddle. "Nothing you need to repeat."

"From here on out, we're in the highlands." D'Jenn nodded to the hills. "This is where Dormael and I grew up."

"Is that so?" Shawna raised an eyebrow. "I didn't think Dormael *had* grown up."

D'Jenn chuckled and led the party northward.

The rain cleared as the gloom of dusk set in, leaving huge swaths of purple and orange painted across the sky. They camped on the northern side of a low hill where a circle of stones marked an ancient waystation—one of many such places scattered through the highlands. Dormael's skin was slimy after so much time in the wet, and dirt had gathered in all his nooks. While everyone was settling around a fire, he slipped away to find a place to bathe.

There are always water sources near these waystations.

He found a pond sheltered in the space between two hills. The water was black in the fading light. It was free of scum and looked twice as frigid as the air. Dormael doffed his clothes, left them hanging over a nearby scrub bush, and stepped into the water.

Nothing shocked the body quite like a dip in freezing water. Dormael closed his eyes, controlling his body's urge to shiver, and waded out until he was waist-deep in the pond. With a deep breath, he went under.

His muscles wanted to seize as the frigid water closed in around him. Dormael forced himself to sit under the water, waving his arms in order to stay put. He held his breath as his body spasmed, closed his eyes against the needling cold.

When the initial shock was over, he relaxed in the cold, comforting darkness.

His Kai slept in his chest, rumbling at the center of his being like quiet thunder. Whenever he put his body into distress or achieved altered states of mind, he could feel his magic in its purest form. He listened to its song until he grew light-headed and his chest ached for air.

Dormael broke the surface, gasping as the frigid air touched his wet skin. He stood from the pond and ran his fingers through his hair, wiping the extra water away. He gulped deep breaths in an attempt to slow the mad beating of his heart.

"I was wondering if you were ever going to come up."

Dormael started at the sound of Shawna's voice and dropped back to chin-level in the water. He spun to scowl at the woman and found her on the shore of the pond. She regarded his discarded clothing with a raised eyebrow and a wry smirk on her face. A rolled bundle was clutched under her arm, and she had a rough cake of soap in her hand.

"Looks like we had the same idea." Dormael breathed hard against the cold. "I got here first."

Shawna smiled. "Are your nipples always blue, or is the water really so cold?"

"It's cold." Dormael snorted. "You should come in. It's refreshing."

"Come in?" Shawna shook her head. "That is *never* going to happen."

Dormael's teeth chattered. "Why not?"

"You can barely keep your eyes off me when I'm clothed." Shawna rolled her eyes. "You think I want to tempt the gods?"

"Has nothing to do with them," Dormael muttered under his breath.

"What?"

"I said I'll be a perfect gentleman, like one of your country noblemen."

Shawna sniffed. "You barely know what the term means."

Dormael shrugged. "Regardless, I got here first. If you're not coming in, you'll have to wait."

Shawna smiled. "I followed you here on purpose, Dormael."

"You did?"

"Remember how you warmed that rock for me the other day? I need a bath, and that pond needs heating before I get in."

"Ah, so you want to be my friend for the benefits of my magic?"

"Dormael, it's cold out here, and I don't want to smell like the underside of a horse." Shawna raised an eyebrow. "What other benefits are there to being your friend?"

"My charming demeanor and illuminating conversation." He favored her with a tooth-chattering smile.

"Your inflated sense of self-worth."

"My musical skills and impeccable taste."

Shawna scoffed. "You never play anything for me, and impeccable taste for what? The swill we drank in the hamlet, or the swill we drank in the mud-village?"

"What about my dashing good looks?"

"I believe I already said it—your inflated sense of self-worth."

"I'm starting to doubt our friendship."

She smiled. "No, you're not. And it's not going to cost you anything to—"

Bethany's voice rang out, high and terrified, from the direction of their camp.

Dormael shared a surprised glance with Shawna and got to his feet. He sloshed toward the shore, heedless of his nudity, as she waved for him to get out. He stumbled in the mud, but Shawna caught his arm and kept him on his feet. She shoved his breeches at him, gesturing for him to put them on.

Dormael shoved a foot into his pants. "Your swords?"

"Back at camp." Shawna grimaced at the soap in her hand. "I don't usually take them bathing, you know."

"Well, that was a good decision, wasn't it?"

"You're an ass, Dormael. Hurry up!"

"I'm trying!"

He struggled into his breeches and yanked his woolen shirt over his shoulders. Reaching into the boots he left by the shore, he grabbed the only dagger he brought and handed it to Shawna. She accepted the blade with a nod of thanks. Dormael summoned his Kai and crept up a nearby hill, headed in the direction of camp. Shawna followed him, her boots making less noise than his bare feet.

That was real fear in Bethany's voice.

Dormael neared the top of the hill and went to his belly.

Shawna crept up beside him, the dagger clutched tight in her hand. Together, they scooted high enough to look over the edge.

Six men intruders were in their camp, all wearing the strange brass-inlaid armor which had Splintered Dormael's magic. Black surcoats covered their armor, each with the symbol of Aeglar—a face, half laughing, half crying—displayed in gold on their chests. Two of the Cultists were on foot, advancing on D'Jenn and Bethany with swords drawn. The other four were mounted and pointing crossbows at D'Jenn.

The Cult is in full regalia today.

Bethany was sprawled in the grass, rubbing at her temples with a confused expression. D'Jenn stood over her with his morningstar gripped in his hand. His magic sang in the ether, reaching for stones and rocks scattered along the ground. The men with the crossbows shouted commands for D'Jenn to throw down his weapon, and the two with swords had wicked grins on their faces.

Can the crossbow bolts Splinter magic like the armor? Will they cut through D'Jenn's defenses?

Dormael shared a grave look with Shawna. He scooted back down the hill and gestured for her to follow. He raised his hands and signed in the Hunter's Tongue.

I have to cause a distraction. Don't get frightened.

Shawna nodded and backed away, crouching with his dagger ready in her fist. Dormael crouched with his hands on the ground and took a deep breath. Opening his Kai, he took a deep breath, pulling magic from the ether, and channeled power into his body.

He felt every agonizing second as his limbs changed. His hands distended, reshaping themselves into paws bigger than dinner plates. His muscles bulged, filling with powerful, thick fibers. His maw burned like fire as it lengthened, and each tooth hurt as it poked through his gums.

When it was over, Dormael crouched on the hillside in the form of a lion.

Shawna gaped at him and scooted away. Her fear sweat tickled his nose, and he could almost taste the hot rush of blood that would herald her death under his jaws. Dormael dug his paws into the dirt and crouched, ready to end her life, when he wrenched control back from the essence of the beast.

Much better meat below.

Dormael snarled and crept over the hilltop, his belly low to the ground. He made no noise, but it was hard to hide his bulk when he was outlined by the setting sun. The dirt was wet beneath his paws as he ran down the side of the hill, eyes locked to the men holding swords.

The bits in the middle are always tastiest.

One of the men screamed in terror and tossed his sword away, turning to flee. The horses bucked and scattered, crying their fear. The men atop them were either dragged along for the ride or tumbled into the dirt. Dormael's mouth watered for the taste of blood as he pumped down the hill. He leapt the child with a single bound of his legs and landed on the back of a retreating Cultist.

Pitiful screams escaped the creature as Dormael took it to the ground. He pinned the man on his face and took its neck in his mouth. With a single jerk of his head, he broke the Cultist's neck.

Your life is mine, little creature.

Dormael took a piece of the man's throat as his prize and turned to regard the running horses. The animals bolted down the trail in the opposite direction, kicking up mud in their haste to get away. One of the men who had been thrown from the saddle dove for a crossbow lying nearby.

Shawna appeared behind the Cultist and shoved one of her swords through his throat.

Dormael looked to the fleeing horses, but there was no point in chasing them. He had no interest in long sprints. The true hunter struck without warning and overpowered their prey. Dormael licked the blood from his chops and turned back to his kill. The horses would live another day—he had plenty to eat already.

Mouth watering, he rolled the corpse on its back so the belly was facing the sky. The finest parts were always in the middle, and it was much easier to go through the belly than around the spine. Best to get the organs when they were fresh, before the blood went cool.

No!

Dormael tested his will against the lion's essence and wrenched control from the beast. He shook with the effort of fighting the need to eat, but with slow determination, he held back from indulging his baser instincts. Dormael backed away from the corpse and laid his belly on the ground.

With a focused effort of will, he slid back into his own skin.

The taste of blood assaulted his mouth. He rolled over and retched into the grass, recalling the sensation of soft flesh in his teeth. He vomited so hard he grew dizzy from the effort.

D'Jenn stepped up next to him. "Thank the gods for you two."

Dormael waved his hand without looking.

"We need to go after the rest of them!" Shawna ran to her horse. "They must have been following us for days. We can't leave them to attack again."

D'Jenn nodded. "They're zealots. They'll keep on our trail until they have another opportunity to strike. Let's take them while they're still confused."

Shawna's hand squeezed Dormael's shoulder.

"Protect Bethany! We'll take care of this!"

Dormael nodded and heaved again into the grass. He retched over and over until he was out of breath from the effort. The sound of horses galloping away announced D'Jenn and Shawna's departure, but another fit of vomiting kept Dormael doubled over.

A tiny hand grasped his shoulder. "I was doing the same thing earlier, when I hit one of them with my magic. It hit me back. My lips are still numb."

Dormael chuckled until the taste of blood made him vomit again.

**

D'Jenn rose in the stirrups, leaning into a turn as Mist churned the trail to muck beneath her hooves. His right hand was tight around the hilt of his morningstar, his Kai singing with deadly intent. Shawna came behind him, ducked low in the saddle, riding with a dexterity D'Jenn could never match.

The fleeing Cultists left a wide swath of ruined earth in their wake, and D'Jenn followed it through the twists and turns of the trail. The paths through the eroded hills lay in the spaces between them, and the folds of the land hid the obstacles ahead. The twilight was fading.

If we don't run these men down before darkness falls, we'll lose them.

A pair of riderless horses came into view around a bend in the trail. D'Jenn rushed past them on the left, and Shawna went around the other side. The horses whinnied as they passed, but made no effort to follow. D'Jenn shared a glance with Shawna and urged more speed from his mount.

Two fleeing Cultists appeared around the next bend, leading a troop of empty mounts. They gestured back and forth, arguing in heated tones, oblivious to the pursuit. D'Jenn smiled and pulled magic from the ether.

The horses aren't wearing anti-magic armor.

D'Jenn reached out with a thread of will and grasped the lead horse's ankle. It screamed in pain as the joint snapped with an audible crack, tumbling horse and rider to the ground. The Cultist was thrown from the saddle with a surprised yelp. He tumbled into the bushes, rolling to a stop at the side of the trail.

The second rider veered hard to the right and avoided the horse on the ground. The man on its back screamed in fear and snapped at the reins, lying low in the saddle. Mist came to a skidding halt in front of the downed horse, skipping to the side to avoid a collision.

Shawna thundered past on the other side, her sword held to the side. "I've got him!"

"There's a third one out there somewhere!"

Shawna was gone before she could reply, and Charlotte's hoof-beats faded into the distance.

Mist whinnied and danced in a circle, moving away from the injured horse nearby. D'Jenn dismounted and went to the beast, looking over its broken ankle. D'Jenn grimaced—the leg was shattered, and the horse's side looked misshapen.

He looked into the horse's rolling eyes. "Sorry about this."

D'Jenn clenched his fist, seizing the creature's massive heart in the grip of his magic. With a whisper of power, he sent a jolt through the heart and stopped it cold. The horse sputtered, kicked, and went still.

Rocks crunched underfoot, and D'Jenn turned in time to catch the Cultist's sword on the haft of his morningstar. The blade came at him again, a flash of steel in the gloom, and D'Jenn again caught the slash on his weapon. He slipped away from the sword, using his Kai to augment his senses.

Is the sword like the armor? Will it Splinter me if I turn my power against the steel?

The Cultist hissed through his teeth every time he made an attack and favored his left leg when he advanced. His slashes were clumsy, and he attacked from weak positions. D'Jenn side-stepped toward his weakened leg, forcing him to turn.

Your sparring matches with Shawna are paying off.

D'Jenn stepped into the man's next attack, catching the edge of his blade with the haft of his morningstar. He kicked down at the Cultist's injured leg, buckling it at the knee. He screamed in pain as the leg gave out, falling to his back in the dirt.

D'Jenn stepped forward and cracked his skull, and the screams went silent.

He stood over the man's body, breathing with the exertion of the fight. He turned and walked toward Mist, dropping his morningstar into his belt. D'Jenn glanced in the direction Shawna had departed.

I've got to catch up to—

Something punched deep into D'Jenn's shoulder, sending hot pain through his arm.

D'Jenn rushed to a nearby boulder and ducked behind it, hand going to the bolt sticking from his shoulder. He closed his eyes and reached out with his magical senses, sweeping the hillside for threats. There was no sign of anything living.

I know he's out there. The armor is probably keeping him hidden.

Noises echoed from the hill behind the boulder—a scrape of boots across stone, and the noise of scree sliding downhill. The disturbance came from his right, high on the side of the knoll. D'Jenn scooted around the boulder to keep the stone between himself and the bowman. Gritting his teeth, he reached up and yanked the bolt from his arm. Hot blood leaked from the wound.

"You might as well come out, sorcerer!" a voice called. "I've got you in my sights, and my friend is taking care of your little bitch! If you come quietly, you won't be hurt!"

"Won't be hurt?" D'Jenn scoffed. "You Cultists kill wizards for sport!"

"We put them on trial before the gods, in the name of the Clever One!"

If I keep him talking, maybe he'll give away his position.

"On trial for what?" D'Jenn yelled over his shoulder. "Being born?"

"Your kind was never meant to exist!" Rocks shifted on the hillside. "You're a test for mankind—a thing to be overcome! Once you're all eradicated, the gods will return to us!"

D'Jenn chuckled. "Who told you that?"

"What?"

"Who told you that?" D'Jenn closed his eyes to listen. "Who *told* you that killing off all wizards would bring back the gods?"

There was the sound of shifting mail. "It's written!"

"Where?"

"In the Aeglari Codex!" The sound of crunching rocks announced the Cultist's footsteps. "Now, come out! Blaspheming will only reflect badly on you during your trial!"

"There won't be a trial!" D'Jenn listened hard for the man's reply.

"You will be judged and offered as a sacrifice if your sins prove—"

D'Jenn gathered his power and ripped the boulder behind him from the ground. With a grunt of effort, he sent it hurtling toward the Cultist. The stone made a whooshing noise as it flew through the air, and the Cultist screamed as he dove to the side. The boulder came down with a crash of stone and metal, and the Cultist screamed no more. The rock bounced away and tumbled down the hill, leaving the Cultist's body broken and lifeless.

D'Jenn got to his feet, favoring his injured arm.

The Cultist lay in a broken heap. His eyes were unfocused, and he made a low, unbroken groan in the back of his throat. Blood flowed freely from his head, and part of his body was crushed.

D'Jenn grimaced and fingered the hole in his shoulder. "Told you there wouldn't be a trial."

A clatter of hoof-beats sounded from behind him, and D'Jenn turned to find Shawna leading a small group of horses to the base of the hill. He rubbed the blood from his wound between two of his fingers and winced as he tried to move his shoulder back and forth. The wound had tacked into the meat of his arm, and it throbbed something awful.

At least it's not crippling. He could have split my ribs with that bolt.

"I was wondering where that third one had gone." Shawna nodded toward the body on the ground. "You're bleeding. Will you be alright?"

"Aye, I'm fine." D'Jenn sighed. "Crossbow bolt through the arm."

Shawna shook her head. "I thought I'd gather up their horses. No sense in letting them wander around out here."

"Not a bad idea." D'Jenn poked at the wound again, grimacing at the pain. "Let's take them back to camp."

"Don't forget your friend over there." Shawna wrinkled her nose at the body. "He's bubbling something from his nose."

D'Jenn winced. "Right."

He ended the man with a quick blow from his morningstar. As Shawna led the horses back down the trail, D'Jenn crouched and examined the Cultist's armor. The brass inlays—swirling, symmetrical patterns—resembled a magical equation, but they were unlike those D'Jenn had seen in the past. He already had one piece of the armor, but he ripped a greave from the man and carried it in his injured arm. The Philosophers would want at least one piece of the infused metal.

He mounted with a grunt of pain and followed Shawna back to camp.

I'll just keep one piece for myself. No reason to tell the Conclave about it.

THE OLD WITCH HERSELF

The land changed as the party rode north, going from gentle foothills to the wide plateaus of the Gamerit highlands. The Runemian Mountains loomed to the north, with disembodied summits poking through the haze. In the summer, the land would be green and ripe from east to west, with life springing from every tiny corner. Now, half the land was winter-browned and slumbering, but clumps of stubborn greenery clung to the hills where evergreens refused to surrender to the cold.

Bethany gazed over the windswept highlands, face rosy from the chill. "This is where you're from?"

"Aye." Dormael gestured in the direction of his family's homestead. "I grew up a few days north of here, and D'Jenn was born a bit farther to the northeast. These are the lands of our clan."

"What's a clan?" She glanced at Dormael over her shoulder.

"A clan is a bunch of families who live in a certain area," Dormael said. "Clans work together. They help each other, protect each other."

"Are you in a clan?"

Dormael nodded. "I am—or, I was. I'm Blessed, like you. I come from a clan, was raised in a clan, but I can no longer be *beholden* to a clan."

Bethany furrowed her brows. "What's beholdened?"

Dormael laughed. "Beholden, girl, not *beholdened*. It means I no longer have an obligation to my Clan because my responsibility is to the Conclave and the Council of Seven."

"Why?"

"Because I have Eindor's Blessing, little one. Because I have magic."

Bethany gave a thoughtful nod. "Does that mean my responsibility is to the Conclave and Council of Seven, too?"

"It can be, if you so choose."

Bethany sighed. "I didn't have a clan."

"You didn't?" Dormael raised an eyebrow. "If you didn't have a clan, what did you have?"

"Nothing." She gave him a nervous glance. "But now, I have you. Right?"

Dormael grinned. "Of course you do."

"What was your Clan?"

D'Jenn dropped back to ride even with them. "The Red Hills Clan. Dormael and I left when we were young, though. Most of our childhood was spent at the Conclave."

"Why is it called the Red Hills Clan?"

"Every summer, a red flower blooms throughout this region," Dormael said. "The hills are covered with a carpet of red, so they're called the Red Hills. The Clan takes its name from them."

Bethany nodded and went back to gazing at the waving grasses.

D'Jenn rubbed his bandaged shoulder. "Two more days, you think?"

"Day and a half, if the weather holds," Dormael said.

"Until what?" Bethany perked up.

"Until we reach my family's homestead."

"Will they have food?" Bethany smiled. "Real food?"

D'Jenn laughed.

"Trust me." Dormael squeezed Bethany's shoulder. "My mother will shove three meals down our throats at a time and load us up with so many supplies we'll need a cart to carry it out."

"Alcohol, too, don't forget," D'Jenn said.

Dormael grinned. "I haven't forgotten."

"Didn't you say your mother makes firewine?" Shawna wrinkled her nose. "I hope she has something less potent."

Dormael shrugged. "There will be plenty to drink."

"Even for four guests and all these horses?" Shawna gave him a skeptical look. "Back home, only country estates could afford such hospitality."

"Sevenlander homesteads aren't cabins on the plains," D'Jenn said. "Entire groups of families live on them."

"It's a bit like your country estate, actually." Dormael raised a musing eyebrow. "At least, where size is concerned. More than just my immediate family lives there. We have cousins, aunts, uncles. People from the surrounding villages come and work the farm, and sometimes they stay for a season."

D'Jenn smiled. "Dormael's family has grown so wealthy, their homestead is more like a compound."

"It's not that big." Dormael rolled his eyes.

"It *does* sound like a fiefdom." Shawna tapped her chin. "How much land does your family own?"

"Never mind that." Dormael waved her question away. "You'll see when we get there."

The trail became a well-traveled cart path, and on the next day, joined with a road made of hard-packed dirt. Scattered rainstorms blew over the highlands, though most of them passed wide of the road. Travelers passed with friendly waves, pulling carts or leading mules laden with gear. After another day going north on the hard-packed road, Dormael turned the companions down a narrow cart path leading east.

Tension tightened his stomach, but he forced it down with a cleansing breath.

The day was chilly, but the sun warmed Dormael's back as they rode down the path. A wide field of latticed grapes appeared on the north side of the road, enclosed by a fence made of weathered timber. They rode along the fence for an hour before Dormael spotted the entrance to the homestead.

Here we go—time to see my family.

A wooden arch stretched over the path, carved at the apex with the word *Harlun*. It was flanked on either side by runes in Old Vendon—the recorded family honors no one still living could remember. A plank hung from a pair of chains beneath the arch with the words *Family Vintners* painted in white letters. Two wreaths of woven winter grass decorated each side of the archway.

My mother still leaves offerings for Devla. Nothing ever changes around here.

A man clung to one of the pillars of the arch, hammering at the base of one of the chains. His hair was the same sandy color of Dormael's and cut just as short, but the neat beard on his face was tinged with red. He was shirtless in the cold, revealing corded muscles and a lean frame. He glanced over his shoulder when he finished with the nail and shook his head. Kicking from the arch, he hopped to the ground and slid the hammer through his tool belt.

He regarded them with a bemused grin as they approached. "Of all the things I thought might happen today, my brother coming out of the hills was not amongst them. Maybe the gods would come down and kiss me, but my brother coming home? Never."

Dormael dismounted and drew his brother into a rough embrace. "Allen—it's good to see you."

"It's always good to see me," Allen said. "Did you get uglier?"

Dormael laughed and shook his head.

Allen smiled at D'Jenn. "I see you're still as lively as mud."

"And I see you're still a mouthy little shit." D'Jenn climbed down with a smile and offered his forearm. Allen took it with a wide grin. Shawna and Bethany dismounted and came forward, sharing a nervous glance.

"This is Shawna." Dormael held his hand out to Shawna, who offered Allen a Sevenlander bow. Allen returned the bow, raising an eyebrow at Dormael.

"It's a pleasure to meet you."

Allen winked. "I know. You don't have to thank me."

Shawna narrowed her eyes and turned an unsurprised glance on Dormael.

Dormael pushed Bethany forward. "And this is Bethany."

Allen crouched down to Bethany's level, giving her a serious look in the eyes. She gazed back in confusion, but she held her ground. Allen narrowed his eyes and nodded, a thoughtful look on his face.

"I know that look," he said. "You're trouble. Trouble in a little blue cloak."

Bethany snorted. "I'm not trouble."

"You look like trouble to me." Allen smirked. "Ever been in a fight?"

Bethany crossed her arms. "Yes."

Allen raised his chin. "I see. I could tell you were dangerous. Do you want to fight me right now, so we can decide which of us is the greater warrior?"

Bethany raised her chin and matched his expression. "I'm a wizard. Wizards don't get in fights."

"Oh, I see." Allen glanced between Dormael and Bethany. "Well that makes sense, doesn't it?"

Dormael tapped his brother on the shoulder. "How's the Old Witch?"

"The same as always." Allen stood from his crouch. "She rushes around trying to do ten things at once and forgets nine of them along the way."

Dormael snorted. "Nothing ever changes."

"She's been worried about you." Allen punched Dormael in the arm. "It's been seasons since we've seen you. You know how she gets. At least once a week she brings you up and wonders aloud whether you're dead."

Dormael raised an eyebrow. "I'm not dead."

"You should tell *her* that—you know, maybe in a letter here and there." Allen shrugged. "At least then I wouldn't have to listen to it every time I'm here."

"And father?"

"The same." Allen sighed. "He makes things forges things sometimes, but he spends most of his time playing guitar and pretending to hate the puppies who follow him around. Drinks a lot of firewine."

"Things really haven't changed at all," Dormael said.

"Not much."

"Are you home for the winter, then?"

"Aye, at least for a bit. I've winnings to last me a few years. Who knows what a famous warrior can get up to?" Allen winked. "I've got options."

Dormael shared a look with D'Jenn.

Allen scowled. "What?"

"Let's get out of this cold," D'Jenn said. "We've got something we want to talk with you about."

"I've got a few questions myself." Allen turned an accusatory glare on Dormael. "Like how in the Six Hells my brother thinks he can drag home a woman and child several *years* after the deed was done and not expect our mother to set her own hair on fire. She's going to go mad."

Dormael blinked. "What did you just say?"

"Your woman and child." Allen gestured at Bethany and Shawna. "Mother's going to *kill* you. Maybe all of you. I won't stop her, either." He winked at Bethany. "Maybe I'll save you. You might be worth it."

A moment of pregnant silence passed as everyone traded bewildered glances.

D'Jenn barked a laugh. "Him, with a child?"

"I am most certainly *not* his woman," Shawna growled. "If you think for one minute that I would give myself to *him*—"

Dormael turned an injured look on Shawna. "I thought we were friends! I'm not that bad."

"You're terrible."

Allen scoffed and ruffled Bethany's hair. "And the little pig? Surely *someone* will claim her."

Bethany caught Dormael's eyes. He was on the verge of opening his mouth to explain, but the pain in her expression stilled the words in his throat. Who was she to him—who had she become to him?

"She's mine," he said. "I'm adopting her."

Everyone gaped at Dormael. Heat rose to his cheeks, but he squared his shoulders and braced himself for the barrage of objections. He met Bethany's smile, and the concerns for the opinions of his friends became a tiny thing.

Bethany reached up and took Dormael's hand.

D'Jenn regarded them with a raised eyebrow, but he gave Dormael a covert nod of approval. Shawna had the hint of a smile on her face, but her eyes were unreadable. Allen looked at them all like they were fools. Shaking his head, he crouched again to Bethany's level.

"Well then, little pig, do you want to ride back home with your uncle? I'll teach you enough trouble to keep your father pulling his hair out for years."

Bethany gave Dormael a nervous glance and held a balled fist out to Allen, her pinkie extended.

"Only if you tell me what *this* means."

**

Harlun homestead sat on a sprawling vineyard.

Dormael often forgot how much land his mother and father owned until he came home on his scattered visits and rode through it. He'd flown over it once out of pure curiosity, and had been stunned by the size of the vineyard, much less the land attached to it. The fields owned by Dormael's family extended over multiple hillsides and stretched almost to the horizon.

Allen gestured at one of the fields. "She's had to buy up four squares of field from the Caerlins."

"She's bought *more* land?" Dormael shook his head. "Can she afford it?"

"The business doubled year before last, and it doubled again last year." Allen nodded. "The Old Witch Herself thinks it will double again next year."

Shawna glanced between Allen and Dormael. "Are you calling your mother an old witch?"

Allen smiled. "Dormael, do you remember why we started calling her that?"

"I can't remember."

"Remember when she would whip us? She'd chase us out of the house—"

"—yelling at us to go tell everyone The Old Witch Herself had done it." Dormael laughed. "Now I remember."

"You should sharpen your mind." Allen snorted. "It's getting as fat as your belly."

Dormael rolled his eyes. "So, she's making money?"

"That she is." Allen smiled. "Doesn't know what to do with most of it. She's been getting orders all the way from Thardin, if you can believe it—cases of summer firewine. It's been going there for a few years. I think it's illegal."

"It's illegal in Thardin," D'Jenn said.

"Whoever it is, they pay her well." Allen shrugged. "She keeps expanding. She holds that over pop's head all the time, tells him that she's 'international' now."

Dormael chuckled. "What does he say?"

"He grumbles about all the new hands needed to work the

vineyard, the new equipment, how unmanageable the homestead is becoming—you know how he is. He does a few jobs for people in town, but mostly he writes music and talks politics with anyone who will listen. Until the next raiding cycle comes along, anyway."

"How's business for him?"

Allen sighed. "Hasn't been much work for a weaponsmith lately, and the old man refuses to leave the homestead in search of it. I've been trying to introduce him to some people from Tept— maybe he could hammer out a few weapons for the fighters, right?"

"And?"

"And he says he's got no interest in letting his operation get out of control like mother's. The old man should consider it, though. He makes good steel when he can be bothered."

Dormael nodded. "He really does."

Bethany was silent for most of the ride, but she shot Dormael covert smiles when no one was looking. He returned them, though he tried to keep his emotions bottled in his chest. Shawna kept shooting him odd looks, and the last thing he wanted was to explain his decision to adopt Bethany.

She's Blessed, like me. It only makes sense that I should look after her.

She giggled at something Allen said and gave Dormael another warm smile.

It's good to see her laughing. Who else cares about her? It has to be me.

When they rode up to the lawn before the house, Dormael's mother and father were already on the porch. There were people gathered nearby—cousins, friends of the family, distant and close relatives alike. Children ran and tumbled in the yard, and Dormael could already smell something cooking from inside the house. His mouth watered as they reined in.

Dormael's mother was a portly woman with a striking head of dark red hair. She let out a series of incoherent exclamations as she came down the stairs, gesturing for all of them to climb down and give her hugs. Dormael sighed and let her pull him into a tight embrace, returning it with genuine warmth.

"It's good to see you, old woman."

"Fuck you, it's good to see me." She wiped a tear from her

cheek. "Where in the Six Hells have you been, boy?"

She pushed Dormael away and went on a tour of his companions, embracing every one of them in turn. She surprised Shawna by foregoing the traditional bow and pulling her into a laughing hug. His mother had always been friendly to a fault.

"I'm sure my sons have told you nothing about me." She held Shawna at arm's length. "I'm Yanette."

"Shawna." A blush rose to her cheeks. "Shawna Llewan."

Yanette turned to Bethany. "And who is this lovely lady?"

"This," Allen said before Dormael could open his mouth, "is your new granddaughter."

Everyone froze.

Yanette gave Allen a sharp look, and Allen shoved an accusatory finger in Dormael's direction. She turned her glare on Dormael, then back to Bethany, and then to Shawna. Shawna shook her head, holding her hands up for peace, and the look got turned on D'Jenn. D'Jenn burst out laughing.

"I've adopted her, ma," Dormael said. "Her name is Bethany. She's got Eindor's Blessing."

Yanette gave him an astonished glance and crouched to Bethany's level. "Let me get a look at you." She took Bethany's face in her hands. "My granddaughter...my *first* granddaughter. Has anyone told you, child, that you've got eyes like a pair of emeralds? So *green*, like the grass in the middle of summer. And Blessed, too? We've so many wizards in the family, now." She gave Dormael a mischievous look and leaned close to Bethany. "Do you know what grandmothers do, child?"

Bethany gave Dormael a nervous glance. "No."

"They spoil you rotten," Allen cut in. "Don't listen to a thing The Old Witch Herself tells you, kid. Trust me."

Yanette waved Allen away. "Don't listen to him. He's always been trouble."

"She trusts me already, ma." Allen winked at Bethany. "We've bonded now. You can't corrupt her."

"Did he tell you gnomes live under the house, and they crawl through the floorboards at night to pinch your toes?"

Bethany nodded.

"Doubt the gnomes at your peril." Allen shrugged. "Let your toes get pinched."

"What grandmothers do," Yanette said, riding over Allen's comments, "is feed you until you can barely eat. Then we feed you more."

Bethany smiled. "I think I like grandmothers."

"I like you, too." Yanette turned to the porch. "Somebody get Judi down here—find my sister! She'll want to meet Bethany, too."

"Don't go passing my granddaughter around before I see her."

Dormael's father came down the steps, favoring his right leg. Saul Harlun was a tall, lean man. He had close-cropped hair and a beard of the same length, both of them long gone to gray. He favored Bethany with a wide grin and offered her his hand.

"You should know, before you get tossed between aunts and uncles, that grandfathers are the best. We tell lots of stories."

Bethany's smile widened. "I like stories, too."

The rest of the relatives closed in, and the lawn descended into shaking hands and chattering voices. Bethany was snatched away by Yanette and a squad of women, all of them gushing over the girl. Children ran in their wake, scrambling to make their introductions. Saul watched the tornado of family sweep onto the lawn and turned back to Dormael.

They clasped forearms, and Dormael's father drew him into a hug.

"Welcome home, son."

"It's good to see you, old man." Dormael smiled, taking an awkward breath. "You look terrible. Like you've got one foot in the grave already."

Saul laughed and clapped him on the shoulder.

"I can still kick the shit out of *you*, boy." He shook his head. "You and your brother forget—you're both just imperfect shadows of *me*. I came first."

"Nothing imperfect about me," Allen said. "That's how I know you're a liar, old man."

"I've been saving something for the day I had both of you here at the same time." Saul favored them with a mischievous grin. "D'Jenn—you're coming, too. You have to see this."

Dormael shared a suspicious glance with his brother. "See what?"

"Come and find out." Saul uttered an evil chuckle. "And may the gods weep for you."

**

Shawna watched Dormael's mother bustle toward the house, surrounded by a troop of laughing women. Her feet almost stepped after them—almost. What would Sevenlander customs dictate? Was it proper for her to keep her distance from the women of the household?

I have little in common with them. Is it rude to avoid their company?

With a hand on her sword to steady her anxiety, she stepped after the men.

No one protested when Shawna joined them. They walked around the side of the sprawling house and into a wide yard of trampled grass. Saul led them toward a long, low cabin tucked in the shadow of a barn. The timber looked new, as if the cabin had been built in the last season. Saul pushed open the door to the cabin and motioned everyone inside. The men ducked through the shadowed doorway, and Shawna slipped in after them.

Her nose was assaulted with a pungent, earthy smell. The scent made her mouth water, but it made her want to sneeze at the same time. Shawna shuffled in the darkness with everyone else, listening while Saul rustled around in the shadows.

"Hold on, let me find the right—ah, here's the lever."

Shutters opened along the walls of the cabin, letting in the afternoon sunlight. A beam ran down the center of the building with scores of wooden arms extending from its sides. Rows of wooden crates sat on the floor, full of what looked like dried herbs—the source of the pungent smell.

Dormael laughed. "You old bastard. I can't believe you finally did it."

Saul had a huge smile on his face. "I got that friend of yours from Tasha-Mal to bring me a bush. Jarl, Jarek—whatever his name is."

Dormael shook his head. "He would have, wouldn't he?"

"Don't tell me you're complaining, boy. The process isn't much different from the tobacco your mother sends to you, either. Uses all the same equipment." Saul gestured at the crates. "This is all from this past season, from the first test crop. Next planting, I've got a whole field of seed ready to toss out."

"You're farming now?" Dormael said.

Saul shrugged. "I'm not doing the work myself. I'll probably hire a troop of your worthless cousins to do the heavy lifting."

D'Jenn snorted.

Dormael nodded at the crates. "Is this curing, or is there something ready to smoke?"

"Did you think I'd drag you back here just to show you the process, my son?" Saul gestured to Allen, and the younger Harlun ran off to grab something. Shawna smiled at Saul as he regarded her.

"Have you ever smoked the Shaman's Leaf before, young woman?"

"Is that what this is called?" Shawna gestured at the crates. "The Shaman's Leaf?"

"Aye." Saul let out a proud sigh and looked around the hut. "The Mals—our sister tribe to the southwest—smoke the Shaman's Leaf before any important discussion. They even have a story about the Leaf."

"What's the story?"

Saul chuckled. "After Evmir forged the world, he let the other gods come down to have a look. The gods walked over every part of Eldath, so they could see his creation and give gifts to the world. The legend says Devla fell so in love with the savannas of Tasha-Mal that she cried, and from her tears sprang the first sprigs of the Shaman's Leaf."

"It's a pretty story." Shawna gave the men a questioning glance. "Is this some kind of religious practice?"

The men shared a laugh.

Allen came back with a long-stemmed pipe packed with the pungent Leaf. He handed it to Dormael, who shook his head and passed it to his father. Saul took the pipe and gave all the boys in the room a withering look.

"None of you thought to offer it to our guest first?" He shook his head. "You've been on the road too long."

He held the pipe out to Shawna, and she suddenly felt nailed to the spot. She'd never smoked anything before—tobacco or anything else. She took the pipe in delicate hands and put her mouth to the other end.

I'm going to regret this, but I can't let them scare me.

"It's going to make you cough, now," Saul said. "Keep your head, and you'll see why it's worth the trouble."

"Thank you." Shawna flinched when D'Jenn used his magic to light the pipe for her, but she didn't shy away from taking a long pull. The smoke filled her mouth, and she sucked a deep breath into her lungs.

She immediately regretted it.

The men broke down in fits of laughter while she coughed enough to rupture her lungs. Shawna heaved so long that spots appeared before her vision, and she had to hold the pipe out blindly and wait for someone to take it. Hands patted her back and helped her to straighten when she was done. She tried to hide her embarrassment at having descended into such a fit, but heat rushed to her cheeks, anyway.

Shawna cleared her throat. "Why would anyone want to do that?"

"You'll see, young lady." Saul smiled and took a hit from the pipe. "You'll see."

Every one of the men had a coughing fit, and Shawna's embarrassment lightened as the pipe went around the circle. By the time the pipe made its way back to her, the afternoon light had taken on a hazy, comfortable quality. She smiled and declined another pull, letting it go past her to Dormael's brother.

Allen caught her wrist as she passed the pipe to him. Shawna jumped, but was too stunned to pull her wrist away. Allen nodded to the tattoos on her wrists and released her with a chuckle.

"I knew it. No one carries two swords without the Mark or a massive set of balls."

Shawna snickered. "A massive set of balls?"

Allen smiled. "I'm assuming you don't have a pair of those."

"No." For some reason, she couldn't stop chuckling like a fool. "That would make it kind of hard to move around, don't you think? I couldn't imagine having to fight like that."

Allen shook his head. "It's not a problem—believe me."

Shawna barked a laugh and shook her head. "Gods, you're all the same."

"Please, no one's like me." Allen looked her over with a raised eyebrow—wrists, shoulders, ankles. "You've a real sword-fighter's build. You're not wearing those Marks just for show, are you? I've seen a few like that, you know. Seen a few pretenders, too. How long have you been Marked?"

Shawna met his eyes. "The answer to that question is only owed to someone with steel in their hands. Tradition, you understand."

"Tradition, eh?" Allen nodded toward the shutters. "The sun is still shining. Let's take advantage. How about a wager?"

D'Jenn sighed. "Here we go. Don't mind him, Shawna, he does this all the time. He's probably been itching to challenge you since he figured out you were a Blademaster."

"You're a Blademaster?" Saul's eyebrows climbed toward his hairline. "Gods be damned, boys. I think I'm in love."

Dormael blew a cloud of smoke into the center of the room. "Leave her alone, brother. We've been on the road for weeks, and the sea before that. Besides, she's never smoked the Leaf before."

All the eyes in the room turned to Shawna. She froze, snickered. Allen laughed, which made Dormael chuckle. The room filled with bubbling laughter.

D'Jenn rolled his eyes and took a hit from the pipe. "She's not fighting anyone."

"How about *you*, big brother?" Allen took the pipe from D'Jenn. "The spear circle will be drawn as soon as the meat starts cooking. Do you remember how to use a spear?"

"I'm a Gamerit." Dormael snorted. "You're gods-damned right, I remember."

"You're a Harlun." Saul thumped him on the shoulder. "You'd better remember how to use a spear, boy."

"Unless you've gotten too fat at the Conclave." Allen blew smoke in Dormael's face.

Dormael waved the smoke away. "Do I look like I'm getting fat?"

"I'll hurt your feelings if I answer that question."

Dormael chuckled. "Fine, but let me get a horn or two of ale in me first."

"D'Jenn?" Allen wiggled his eyebrows at his cousin.

"No." D'Jenn gave him a flat look. "Haven't you lot ever wondered if getting blasted and slicing at each other was the smartest idea?"

Allen rolled his eyes. "And you, old man? Think your skeleton could handle a beating?"

"I fought in a spear line before you were more than a thought, my son," Saul said. "And no—I'll be getting drunk and watching."

"It's too bad, Lady Shawna." Allen shrugged, the pipe still in his hand. "I would have expected more of a challenge from someone like yourself."

He moved to take another pull from the pipe, but Shawna snatched it from his hands before he could put it to his lips. The Leaf had filled her head with a pleasant, relaxed feeling, but she still had the quickest hands in the room. She took a dainty pull and blew a bit of smoke in Allen's face.

"Can I see your wrists?"

Allen raised an eyebrow. "My wrists?"

Shawna held up her own wrists to demonstrate. "These things. They're next to your hands."

Chuckles filled the room as Shawna passed the pipe to Saul. Allen smiled and bared his wrists so she could examine them. Shawna leaned forward and gave them a disdainful look, shaking her head.

"We couldn't fight—it wouldn't be fair, you understand. If you were Marked, it might be closer to fair, but I couldn't let you embarrass yourself. We've only just met. If you'd like instruction, though, we could arrange a time for me to show you how to fight with a real weapon. Until then, have fun playing with your...stick."

The room erupted with laughter.

Allen offered her a flourished bow, grinning ear to ear. "Until that day, then."

"Stick," D'Jenn repeated, a smile cracking his scowling face. "He's good with *sticks*, alright."

"I'm going to steal your boots when you get drunk tonight."

Shawna laughed, the muscles in her shoulders loosening. She hadn't realized they'd been so tight, but as the light took on a soft haze, her body felt more relaxed than it had for a long time. She'd been so nervous to meet these people, to be surrounded by their odd customs and attitudes.

They're not so bad, really. I could grow accustomed to this.

Through the shutters, people hauled tables and chairs onto the grass, preparing a series of small fires complete with stumps for seating Others cleared odd farming implements out of the way, or lugged crates piled with food to the tables. A troop of children ran through the yard like a tribe of barbarians, and Bethany was right in the middle of the crowd. Her hair had been transformed with braids and ribbons, and she held a pair of wooden swords over her head as she screamed a battle cry into the winter air. The kids attacked one of the men who were helping to move things. He went down, screaming in mock death, and the tribe of children moved on.

Dormael's mother appeared, sleeves rolled to her elbows in the chill, organizing the surrounding chaos. She supervised two young boys as they set up a large brick stove on the lawn, ushered a troop of frolicking toddlers toward the porch, and personally directed the seasoning of various pieces of meat. She peered across the yard, shading her eyes with one hand.

"Saul!" Yanette started toward the cabin. "Has anyone seen my husband?"

"Get down!" Saul crouched below the level of the shutters, waving for everyone else to crouch with him. "If she sees us in here, she'll put us all to work!"

Everyone crouched and moved to the windows. Shawna followed their example. Allen moved to the windows and peeked over the edge.

"She's coming this way!"

"*Saul!*"

Dormael shuffled up beside his brother. "Do you think she sees us?"

"Doesn't matter, she'll check the drying hut, anyway." Saul glanced toward the other side of the cabin. "Come on—out the back!"

D'Jenn snickered. "Stay low!"

"Saul!" Yanette's voice was closer. Her footsteps sounded through the shutters.

Allen proffered the pipe to his father. "What do you want me to do with this?"

"Bring it, of course!" Saul pushed it into Allen's hands. "Now, come on, unless you want to be conscripted into the witch's army."

Shawna followed the men through the back door of the cabin, chuckling like an adolescent girl.

**

Maarkov held tight to a slippery rope as the ship bucked beneath him, frigid water spraying in all directions. Lightning cracked across the sky, leaving a burning afterimage on Maarkov's vision. Crewmen screamed around him, calling orders through the fury of the storm. Maarkov kept his eyes in the distance, at what would be eastern Soirus-Gamerit. His eyes were full of the sea, the rain, the lightning, and—just at the edge of his sight—a dark strip of land.

Just close enough to give me hope.

He turned from the bow and picked his way hand-over-hand toward the stern. His brother was still tucked away in the captain's cabin like a spider. What was he doing while the ship was being tossed about like detritus in a flood? Munching at one of the cabin boys? A picture came to Maarkov's mind of his brother presiding over a boy's corpse, an apple stuffed in its mouth like a festival pig.

Come in and eat, he would say. *The food is so good, it's a sin.*

Despite the old captain's warnings, Maaz had culled the crewmen down to a bare minimum needed to man the ship. He'd destroyed the dinghies, cutting off the crew's only hope of escape. Maarkov suspected many had leapt into the sea in the night, braving the frigid water rather than face Maaz's magic. What few remained did what they could to keep the ship aright, but there wasn't enough to fight the storm.

If I have to swim, I'll cut his legs off. I swear it!

He fought his way into the cabin and slammed the door against the driving rain. Implements and oddities jounced around the room as the ship rocked in the swells. Water dripped from every crack, and wood shuddered under the strain. Maaz gathered a pile of his possessions in quick, desperate motions.

"Maarkov!" Maaz waved an irritated hand. "Gather your things! We're leaving this ship!"

Maarkov looked at his brother like he was insane. "And go where, Maaz? Have you noticed this fine weather? Our chances of staying afloat out there are about one in 'fuck-the-gods'. I'm not going anywhere!"

Maaz scowled. "Stay, then—follow this box to the bottom of the sea for all I care. Let the crabs pick at your swollen corpse."

"Aren't you the captain of this vessel?" Maarkov smiled.

"Shouldn't you go down with the ship? It would be less than you deserved, after the things you've done. This is *your* fault—you used up all the crewmen, and now we're floundering."

"Do you really care so much for *them*?" Maaz shook his head. "They are nothing but meat to us, Maarkov—you would do well to see them for what they are. We are gods compared to them."

"*You* are a god compared to them." Maarkov clenched his jaw. "I'm just your toy—your gods-damned experiment!"

"Now is not the time for this, brother."

"And when *is* the time, Maaz? You did this to me. You can end it."

"You don't want me to end it." Maaz grabbed the desk to steady himself as the ship lurched. "What a ridiculous thing to say!"

"Oh, my blinded brother—you have no idea what I want." Maarkov sneered. "All I want is an end. It's what I dream about when I pretend to sleep. It's what I long for."

"Then you're a fool." Maaz's glare intensified. "Go get your things. You will delay me no longer."

What if I cut off his legs now? Would the sea take him?

"My things?" Maarkov gave an evil chuckle, holding to the wall as the ship bucked again. "Oh, I don't know, I think I might have misplaced them."

"Then leave them."

"I can't—there's something I need with them."

Maaz showed his teeth. "What?"

"My whetstone."

"Your fucking *whetstone*?"

"A blade has to be sharp, Maaz." Maarkov repaid Maaz's sneer with a wide, toothy grin. "What would you do if you needed me to carve someone up for you and all I had was a dull knife? Things will get messy if I hacked at them like—"

"Brother, I swear by all the gods in the Void, I will leave you on this rickety piece of garbage if you waste one more moment of my gods-damned—"

A loud crack went through the ship, and the whole cabin shuddered.

Maaz's eyes went as wide as saucers. "Maarkov! Get—"

There was a crash, and everything went dark.

**

Dormael's room was almost as he remembered it as a child, like a memory frozen in time. His old bed still sat under the window facing the southern horizon. He'd enjoyed gazing out at the landscape as a boy, dreaming about roaming through the highlands. There was a dresser beside the bed with a few knick-knacks scattered on its surface—treasures he'd acquired as a boy.

Dormael smiled as he picked things up and turned them over, trying to recall where he'd gotten them. A pile of old arrowheads had come from a hill he and his brother had discovered. Their grandfather told them a battle was fought there between Red Hills and Pinedale Creek over a hundred years past

The old wolf always had stories to tell.

There was a rock with a piece of a strange footprint frozen in its surface. The print looked similar to something a lizard, or perhaps a bird, would have left—if a bird could have grown to the size of a small horse. Dormael's grandfather had asked him, with an ominous tone, what sort of animal he thought could leave footprints in hard stone. For the rest of that summer, Dormael and all his cousins were searching the Red Hills for this mysterious beast. They never found the creature, but those summer hunts were some of the best times in Dormael's life.

He and his cousins found a great tree that had been struck by lightning—proof, of course, that the beast could breathe fire. They found a rusted sword which led them to an ancient skeleton, half-buried in the dirt. He and the other children had decided the unknown warrior had died fighting the fire-breathing beast, and they spent the rest of the afternoon digging up his remains and preparing a pyre.

He was probably a long dead brigand, but even thieves should have their souls released to the Void.

By the following year, Dormael's Kai had awakened. He was sent off to the Conclave, and his cousins were scattered around the Red Hills. His grandfather died before Dormael could see him again.

That summer was my last as a child.

Sighing, he turned to the bed. He crouched down and reached under the frame. His hands alighted on a wooden case, and he slid it out onto the floor.

Of course it's still here. My father is more stubborn than I am.

Inside the box was a spear. It was long—it stood two heads taller than Dormael when it was upright. Its haft was made of a dark, sanded wood, which had been hardened through a process only his father knew how to explain. The base was surmounted by a steel spike, weighted to balance the blade on the other end. The head was a wide, leaf-shaped blade more than a hand long. The steel bore the stamped initials of his father.

"He comes up here once a week and oils the blade for you."

Dormael turned, clutching the spear, and found his brother standing in the entrance. Allen had a wide grin on his face and a horn of ale in his hand. He winked and leaned against the door frame.

"Just thought I'd take it out and have a look at it."

"It's a fine weapon, but it won't help you." Allen took a sip of ale. "I'm still going to win."

"Well, if I'm going to fight, I'm not going to use some crooked stick from the woods." Dormael balanced the spear on his hand, testing the center of balance. "I forgot how nice it is. The old man is a craftsman for all Six Hells."

Allen snatched the spear from his hand. "If you'd have taken this with you, he'd have made you three more by now, each better than the last. He's made *me* a lot of weapons."

"You know it's not that simple." Dormael sighed and leaned against the wall. His stomach tightened every time he thought of his father. It was like a seed had been planted when he was a boy—a malignant bundle of arguments and misunderstandings. He'd allowed it to fester, and since the day he'd been taken to the Conclave, the seed had grown into a thornbush.

I really don't see them enough. I don't come home enough.

When Dormael looked at his brother's smiling face—so strong and healthy—he was reminded of the drawbacks of Eindor's Blessing. He would outlive his family, even outlive his nephews and grand-nephews, if the magic didn't take him before his dotage. He imagined Allen's face wrinkling, his hair going gray like fabric left in the sun.

Will he look like my father? Will I look like him? Gods, watching him die will be like watching myself die.

"He made this for you as an apology, you know," Allen said, holding out the spear. "Told me so himself."

Dormael took the weapon by the haft. "I know. He left it for me to find. Didn't say a word about it, just left it here in my old room."

Allen snorted. "Your *old* room. Just try it out, let the old man see you using it. Hells, Dormael—take the damned thing with you when you leave. Things can be as simple as you want them to be."

"I'll take a few swings with it. I've got my staff, though, and I'm used to it."

"That walking stick you carry around?" Allen scoffed. "A weapon for boys and old men."

Dormael scowled. "It does its job. You forget—I have other weapons at my disposal."

"That's not something you just forget," Allen said. "Still, a walking stick is no weapon for a Gamerit, and sure as the Six Hells isn't good enough for a Harlun. Regardless of what else you are, you're still one of us. That's all the old man wants to see."

"I know. I said I'd take a few swings with it. Go bother someone else."

Allen laughed and clapped him on the shoulder. "I'll see you on the lawn, brother."

"I'll see you there."

Allen walked down the hallway and his footsteps faded down the stairs. Dormael summoned his Kai and held the spear in midair, letting his magic hum through the wood. It returned a pleasant chord to his senses, something warm and strong.

"You really put some work into it, didn't you, old man?"

With a smile, Dormael snatched the spear from the air and left for the yard.

**

It was dusk by the time Dormael faced his brother across the spear circle. Bonfires burned around the yard, keeping the gathering bright and warm. Dormael took a deep breath, goosebumps forming under his shirtsleeves despite the roaring fires. Buzzing conversation make a constant hum of noise, and the smell of roasting food was thick in the air.

Dormael bounced the spear in his hands, thrusting a few times to loosen his muscles. It had been years since he competed in a circle. He'd left home before he was old enough to fight in solstice tournaments, and his experience consisted entirely of contests fought at family gatherings with long sticks. His hands were unsure with the spear, but the pride on his father's face was worth the trouble.

Allen smiled and winked at him, drawing cheers from the crowd. Shawna watched Dormael, her eyes bleary with the haze of the Shaman's Leaf. Dormael's mother leaned over with a bottle of firewine, offering a drink to Shawna with a laugh. Saul shook his head at whatever they were saying and stood.

The crowd went quiet as Saul raised his hand. "Are you boys ready to fight, or do you want to keep blowing kisses at each other?"

"I'm ready," Allen called back. "For a fight, a kiss, either one."

The people around the circle laughed.

"Ready." Dormael smiled and thumped the base of his spear on the ground.

"Alright, hope you lads have your loins girded, the gods are watching," Saul said, turning to face Dormael and Allen. "More importantly, *I'm* watching. Whoever wins this match, remember—you're both my sons, so the glory belongs to me."

Allen hefted his spear. "Better sit down, old man, before the wind blows you over."

Saul shook his head and raised a fist to the sky. Dormael's hands tightened on the haft of his spear, digging into the unfamiliar wood. Allen's smile widened, and he stepped back into a fighting crouch.

"*Fight!*"

Allen moved forward, spear held low on his right side. Dormael stepped to the side, choking on his spear to menace his brother with a quick thrust. Allen followed him, trying to cut off his retreat around the circle. They came together, and their spears *thocked* as they traded thrust and parry.

Allen disengaged, smacking one of Dormael's attacks aside, and retreated to the edge of the circle. He blew Dormael a kiss and turned his back, waving to the crowd. Dormael shook his head—he knew better than to take Allen's bait—and tossed a clod of dirt at him with his Kai. It plopped into Allen's back, drawing a laugh from the crowd.

Allen laughed, hefted his spear, and advanced.

Dormael's spear haft vibrated with each whack as he thrust, slashed, swept, and parried. He ducked under some attacks and jumped aside from others, all while trying to find a weakness in his brother's technique. Allen flowed through the fight with ease, slipping from the path of Dormael's attacks, his spear stabbing down from angles that were increasingly hard to anticipate. Allen moved with a brutality of motion Dormael didn't know how to match.

Allen advanced, thrusting in quick, straight motions at Dormael's chest. Dormael was forced to retreat, knocking aside thrust after thrust, backing ever away from the barrage. Dormael whipped his spear in a circular parry and spun to the outside, sweeping at Allen's ankles. Allen yelped in surprise and leapt away.

Allen laughed and pointed his spear at Dormael. "You're not as fat as I thought."

"I've been practicing." Dormael winked at Shawna, who answered with a cheer.

Allen smiled. "Don't get excited—it's not going to help you *that* much."

He attacked again, thrusting and slashing, forcing Dormael to parry and retreat. Dormael tried to get the upper hand in the exchanges, but his brother was too fast, too skillful. Every time he attempted to take the initiative, he found Allen's spear already coming for him. He broke into a sweat with the effort of keeping Allen's spear at bay and retreated around the edge of the circle. The crowd went mad as Allen pressed the attack.

"Sweep! Sweep! *Sweep!*"

"Step in with your left, *no* gods-dammit, your *left*!"

"—got to stay out of his range—"

Dormael's limbs were heavy with fatigue. He made a desperate thrust at Allen's midsection, but his brother tapped the spear haft downward, forcing the blade into the dirt. Before Dormael could pull it out, Allen swiped at his fingers with the haft of his spear. Dormael sucked in a pained breath and jerked his hands from his weapon.

Allen rested his spear point on Dormael's neck, and the crowd erupted with cheers.

Dormael held his hands wide in surrender, and Allen removed his spear blade. Dormael bowed to his brother, then turned and bowed to the crowd. Allen came over and took his forearm, shaking his head.

"Not bad." Allen shrugged. "Not good enough, but not bad."

"You were always quick with the spear," Dormael said. "I never practiced as hard as you did."

"I never practiced that hard, I'm just naturally dangerous." Allen winked. "Now—bring your spear, let's go see who can drink a flagon the quickest."

"Why do I have to bring the spear?"

"I won the match, Dormael." Allen raised a challenging eyebrow. "That means you have to carry it around for the rest of the night. Winner makes the rules, and that's my rule."

"That stopped working on me when we were children," Dormael said. "Besides, I can just do this."

He snapped his fingers, and the spear leapt into the air, hovering just over his shoulder. Allen started back from the thing and gave his brother an irritated look.

"That's cheating."

"According to whom?"

"According to the gods, *whom* do you think?"

"You're lucky I didn't use it on you during the spear fight." Dormael raised a finger. "That's the real truth, you know. I fought you with one giant hand tied behind my back."

"A giant *extra* hand, you mean," Allen said. "Untie the bastard, I'll still beat you."

Dormael flicked his wrist, and two ale flagons floated over from the table nearby. A voice rose in protest from the crowd of chattering family members, but Dormael ignored it. He snatched one out of the air and floated the second one to his brother.

"How about we get drunk instead?"

Allen smiled, snatched the cup from the air, and raised it in salute.

**

As was customary at all Harlun gatherings, musical instruments appeared in the crowd. Saul came from an upstairs room with a trio of old guitars and handed them out to different people. Dormael sent one of the younglings to retrieve his own instrument, and D'Jenn appeared with his *doomba*. Songs rose into the night between the bonfires and bubbles of conversation.

The night drifted along in a warm, drunken haze for Dormael. There was music and dancing aplenty, and he found himself taking spinning turns across the lawn with Bethany, his mother, and even Shawna. When he was tired of playing instruments and kicking up his heels, he found a seat by a campfire next to D'Jenn and packed a pipe with tobacco.

Saul appeared with a trio of flagons and handed them to Dormael and D'Jenn.

"Here, boys—refreshments." Saul smiled and sat down between them. "It's damned good to have you all here. Damned good. Oh, by the way, your friend came by not too long ago."

Dormael took a sip of ale. "You mean Jarek—the Mal who brought you the Shaman's Leaf bush?"

"No." Saul shook his head. "The one with the mismatched eyes. Kendall."

D'Jenn snorted. "Evil Eye himself."

Dormael smiled. "What did he want?"

"Said he was passing through." Saul shrugged. "Asked if we'd heard from you—Jarek asked the same thing when I saw him, you know. We gave Kendall a bed for the night, filled his belly. You know how your mother likes to dote on your friends."

"Which way was he going?"

"North," Saul said. "He said there was going to be a big meeting in Ishamael soon, and the whole Conclave was headed home to be there for it. I just assumed that's why the two of you were here."

Dormael shared an interested look with D'Jenn.

"No." Dormael sat up. "We were in Alderak. Did he say anything about this big meeting?"

"Just that I'd probably hear about it later, that it was big business." Saul glanced between them. "Hells, boy—I hoped you'd be able to tell me more. It's the only reason I brought it up."

Dormael narrowed his eyes. "You've got your ear to the ground, pop. You and the other men in the Clan are always talking politics. What's been happening lately? What are the Clansmen saying?"

"Fuck all and horseshit, that's what." Saul shook his head and

94

took a drink. "Not that I've ever believed anything the Council says, mind you, but this year has been especially bad."

"How so?" D'Jenn said.

Saul huffed a frustrated breath. "Well, our taxes are going up next season. The damned Mals proposed a higher tax on the richest tribelands, and our dimwitted Kansil failed to block the motion. Berrul promised all the Clan Leaders he wouldn't allow it through, but when the time came, he voted *for* the damned motion." Saul made a disgusted gesture and downed another sip of ale. "Orris, Soirus-Gamerit, and Duadan all have to give a higher percentage on their commerce starting next spring, which means all the businesses are going to be squeezed to pay the bill. Damned Council won't even say where the money's going, just some emergency chest nonsense."

"Who proposed the motion?" Dormael asked.

"Jurillic." Saul shook his head. "Of course that old bitch voted for it. Her tribe doesn't make anything or have any business to tax. She's just fine to make decisions with other tribes' money."

"That doesn't make much sense," D'Jenn said. "What would Tasha-Mal care for taxes on commerce? They're all half-mad warrior bands out there. They only trade for what they use, most of the time. Why would they even propose such a thing?"

Dormael gave a thoughtful nod. "All they've asked for in the past is support against Rashardian raids. Never money."

"Here's the really odd bit." Saul motioned Dormael and D'Jenn closer. "Jurillic's son was captured by the Rashardians last year. I remember, because she offered a reward for anyone who would strike into the Golden Waste to take him back. Your brother almost joined some fool expedition into the desert before I talked him out of it."

"I think Seylia mentioned something about that," Dormael said. "He was some famous warrior, right? What was his name?"

"Was? Try *is*, boy—the man is still alive. Kitamin is his name."

"He's still alive?" Dormael narrowed his eyes. "Did one of those expeditions rescue him?"

Saul shook his head. "Several were lost in the attempt. The Mals were in turmoil for a while, deciding on whether Jurillic was strong enough to lead them, what with letting her son be captured in a raid. You know how the Mals are."

"They follow strength." D'Jenn shrugged. "Losing her own son would put Nyra in a tough position with her Clan Leaders."

"Well, listen to this—at the last Council meeting, the man just appears in Ishamael with his mother. No word on how he got there, no ceremony, no public hubbub at all—and he looks bad, Dormael. I sent one of your cousins to Ishamael to sell a load of your mother's firewine, and he was there when the Jurillics were. He said Kitamin looked like a corpse and had both his hands cut off." Saul leaned closer. "Tell me how he escaped with no hands, boy."

Dormael shared a confused look with D'Jenn.

"Did she say anything about it?" D'Jenn asked. "Nyra, I mean."

"Nothing I've heard." Saul leaned back in his seat, shaking his head. "Just the usual thing, you know—how happy she is to have her son back at her side. The gods only know what the Rashardians did to him, other than chopping off his meat-cuffs. After he returned, she proposed the tax raise, so everyone stopped talking about her son."

D'Jenn furrowed his brows. "Are the funds going to set up an army or to the Southern Bastion?"

"No," Saul replied. "The Council is going to collect them, and then—" Saul shrugged and waved his hands around. "They turn into smoke, apparently. It's clearly just a money grab."

"I wonder how Kitamin got home." Dormael chewed on his lip. "You can't just traipse out of the Golden Waste—or *into* it, for that matter. Rescuing him would have taken men, resources. Who brought him home?"

Saul gave a one-armed shrug. "Nyra has been silent. There's a lot of grumbling about it, though."

"What do you think happened?" Dormael asked.

"I think someone rescued Kitamin Jurillic and held it over Nyra's head. I think she was strong-armed into proposing that motion." Saul took a pull from his flagon. "Why else would she suddenly want to collect a river of silver marks? The Mals have never cared for money—someone put her up to this."

"And Berrul?" D'Jenn asked. "Why do you think he voted for it? Maybe there's a good reason. Maybe the Council just doesn't want to share the reason with the public."

"Even if there's a good reason, it doesn't explain why the

motion was proposed by the Mals." Saul held up a finger. "Why would Jurillic give two golden shits about a secret fund? Why would she be the one to establish it?"

"Let's say someone *did* pressure Jurillic into making the motion," Dormael said. "Even if everything you said was true, why would Berrul vote against his own interests?"

Saul snorted. "If this unnamed entity can rescue a man from the depths of a Rashardian slave camp and bring him back with no hands, finding a bit of leverage over Berrul would be easy. I'll bet that fat bastard has plenty of secrets a person could use to twist him."

"While that's true," Dormael said, "it's also generally true that the more complicated your explanation for any given thing becomes, the less likely it is to be the right explanation."

Saul glared at him.

"Don't start using Conclave rhetoric on me, boy. Platitudes are nice, but they don't always explain the world—that's something you have to remember, too. Sometimes the most unlikely thing is as common as you please, and political games are as common as pig shit."

Dormael laughed. "Too true, old man, too true."

Dormael went back to drinking and shrugged off his father's further attempts to discuss politics. D'Jenn, though, had a considering scowl on his face. The two of them continued to talk about the latest events, but Dormael let his attention wander.

As the night wore on, the party blurred around the edges. Dormael shared another pipe-full of the Shaman's Leaf with his father, and uncountable flagons of ale with everyone else. He sang and danced until he was sweating in the cold night air.

He spotted Bethany curled up by a fire and lifted her sleeping body from the ground. He carried her into the house and put her into one of the upstairs bedrooms. After he removed her boots and tucked her under a blanket, he left to head back outside.

In the hallway, Dormael came face to face with Shawna.

"You're not a bad dancer, you know," she said.

"I've got many skills," Dormael laughed, "but dancing isn't one of them. I'm not bad at flailing around like an idiot, though."

"Were you putting Bethany down?" Shawna asked. "I was just coming to check on her."

"She's fine." Dormael nodded. "Sleeping like a rock."

"She had a good time today." Shawna laughed and wiped an errant tear from the corner of her eye. "I don't think I've heard her laugh like that. Why would you do that? Just...decide to take the girl in that way?"

Dormael took a deep breath, unable to to summon the words. "I just couldn't imagine it any other way. I know you all probably think I'm an idiot, but I don't care what you think."

Shawna shook her head. "I don't think you're an idiot."

"No?" he chuckled. "I expected you and D'Jenn both to crawl up my arse over this, but neither of you have said anything. You don't object?"

Shawna let out a short laugh, threw her arms around his neck, and kissed him.

Dormael made a surprised noise but didn't try to back away. She smelled intoxicating, and her lips tasted of firewine. She reached up to put her fingers in his hair, and chills crawled up his spine. Before he could stop himself, he wrapped his own arms around Shawna's waist and picked her up off the floor.

She giggled into his mouth as they kissed, pawing at each other's clothing. They danced an awkward spin down the hallway, Dormael pulling her toward his old room. Shawna kissed him with enthusiasm, giggling through the spaces between their lips.

He kicked open his door and dragged her into the room, laughing with her as they kicked off their boots. Shawna clung to him when they embraced and made soft noises against him as he explored her body with his hands. Her skin was smooth, pale, and felt supple beneath his touch.

Dormael's heart pounded against his ribs.

"Nobody's going to find us?" she asked, breathing against his mouth.

"No chance," Dormael said. "Magic, remember?"

He turned and whipped a hand at his door, and it slammed shut. Shawna laughed and pulled him back into a kiss. Dormael walked her backwards until her thighs touched the bed and pushed her onto it. She went down in a fit of drunken laughter.

"Come here!" Shawna pulled him onto the bed. Dormael descended into a storm of drunken kisses, Shawna's hands pulling at his face, his hair, and running over his back. She kissed him with abandon, pulled at him with needful hands. Dormael's body was warm with desire.

He pulled her shirt out of her pants and kissed her stomach, and she sucked in a breath in reaction. He put his head into her shirt and kept exploring. She made low, pleased sounds in her throat and patted him on the head through the fabric.

Dormael laughed against her belly. "I thought you said I was terrible."

She made a noncommittal noise and squeezed his hand.

"I knew you were just pretending not to like me."

Another noncommittal noise, this time with no corresponding squeeze.

Dormael froze. He poked at her side, but she only patted his head again.

"Shawna?"

No answer.

He pulled his head out from under her shirt and looked to her face. She lay with her eyes closed, the shadow of a contented smile tickling the edges of her lips. Her chest rose and fell in a relaxed rhythm.

"Shawna." He nudged her arm.

She swatted his hand away. "What?"

"Nothing," he laughed. "I hate you. I want you to know that."

She mumbled something nonsensical in response.

Dormael put his boots back on and pulled a blanket over Shawna, tucking her in the same way he did for Bethany. Disappointment sat like a stone in his belly, but all he could do was laugh and shake his head. This had likely been nothing more than the result of the wine and the Leaf.

Will she remember cavorting with me? Even if she did, she would likely pretend she didn't. He couldn't mention this to D'Jenn, either—he would never hear the end of it.

No matter what I do, things will probably be awkward in the morning.

Earning the Knife

Dormael woke to the sounds of the homestead in bustling motion.

Feet shuffled in each direction, voices called out, pots clanged against counters, and boxes banged against the floor. The sugary smell of Sweetpenny tea floated to his nose, blended with the mouth-watering scent of sweet rolls. The shifting aromas from the kitchen drew him from his blankets in the corner of the common room floor.

He looked for his mother in the kitchen, but she wasn't there. He nabbed a piping-hot roll and dipped out a cup of Sweetpenny tea. D'Jenn was nowhere to be found. Dormael gobbled down the sweet roll and sipped the tea. Grime covered his body, and a sniff from the fabric of his shirt revealed the combined stinks of campfire and alcohol.

I need to clean up.

Harlun homestead had a high-ceilinged community bath. The floor was tiled with stone, and the entire pool was fed from copper pipes tapping a nearby stream. Though many homesteads in the Sevenlands had bathhouses, there weren't many quite as luxurious as the one upon which his mother had insisted. At the time, his father had grumbled that the woman had gone mad. Once the building had gone up, the old man had stopped complaining.

The only downside of the bathhouse was the water's seasonal temperate. A brick furnace burned in the center of the room, but it only took the sting out of the cold in the wintertime, and only worked when one stayed in the water close to it. The air inside the building was crisp with the morning chill, and the lack of fog rising from the water suggested it was even colder than the air.

Allen was in the middle of the closest pool to the furnace, working water into his hair.

Dormael tossed his clothing on a nearby bench. "A little cold, isn't it?"

"You want to help with that?" Allen sputtered through chattering teeth. Dormael opened his Kai and fed heat into the water until steam filled the room like morning mist over a river. He stepped foot into the warm water, his muscles relaxing as he submerged them.

"Is that better?"

"Aye," Allen breathed. "I swear to the gods, Dormael, it must be nice being a wizard. Warm baths wherever you go—at least, that's the way it would be if I was Blessed."

"Everyone says that." Dormael shook his head. "Listen, I've been wanting to ask you something."

"Let me guess," Allen sighed, leaning back in the water. "You'd like to know why I'm so talented and good looking. Really, it's just an accident of birth, Dormael. I think the gods smiled on me when I was in the womb."

Dormael laughed. "You know you were born with webbed feet, right? Took pop three years to cut away your toes."

Allen snorted. "I wish he'd have left them. Then I could add 'amazingly fast swimmer' to my long list of talents and achievements. What did you want?"

"I'd like you to come with us."

"To Ishamael?"

"That's right."

Allen blew out a long breath and leaned against the side of the pool.

"You know I love you, brother, and Ishamael is nice, but there's nothing for a warrior to do there—not a *real* warrior, anyway. I don't want to spend my time lounging around the Conclave with a bunch of wizards. You're all strange, and you talk on and on about mysterious, ancient, *boring* shit."

"You won't be sitting around the Conclave." Dormael rolled his eyes. "I don't need you to be my gods-damned bodyguard, you know."

"Then why do you want me to come along?" Allen gave him a curious look. "Do you have a real job? Something interesting?"

Dormael nodded. "Definitely interesting. I can count on your discretion, I assume?"

"Do you want a punch in the nose for questioning my honor? Looks like someone gave you one already." He gestured at Dormael's black eyes with a wide grin.

"Listen, brother—Shawna isn't just some woman we hired as a mercenary, and Bethany isn't just my adopted daughter," he said. Dormael started at the beginning and told his brother the entire story. He told Allen about the armlet, the Red Swords, and the mystery surrounding them. Allen listened through the whole tale, asking a few questions and nodding at the answers. The water was tepid by the tale's end.

"So...if I come with you," Allen said, "I'd get a chance to do some actual fighting?"

Dormael shrugged. "It's likely."

"There'd better be," Allen said. "I was planning on serving at the Southern Bastion for a year. I'd learn to fight in a unit, kill a few raiders. I'd be giving that up."

"Giving up the chance to chew on soldier's rations in a fortress on the edge of the Golden Waste, and all for a soldier's pay?" Dormael gave a mocking bow. "Don't let me get in the way of your little holiday."

"Are you going to pay me?"

Dormael nodded. "Of course. The Conclave keeps money around for that sort of thing. I'll requisition something. More than a soldier makes, believe me."

"Well, I suppose I could take time out of my busy schedule."

"Busy." Dormael scoffed. "You're not busy. You won enough gold to last ten years. Bored is what you are."

Allen gave him a serious look. "Alright, I'll go—on one condition."

"What condition?"

"Take the spear with you. I can't be seen with you in public if you're going to be lugging that stick around." Allen sighed. "Besides, it would make the old man happy. Time for the both of you to stop acting like idiots."

Dormael nodded. "Fine, I'll take the damned spear. I was planning on taking it in the first place."

"My puckered arse, you were planning on taking it," Allen said. "You're a horrible liar. Now—you want to get my back? My muscles are too big to get the middle."

"Get away from me." Dormael laughed and retreated to the far side of the pool.

**

Dormael held his mother in a tight embrace, weathering her sobs on his shoulder. The yard was clean—Yanette had seen to that first thing in the morning—and the sun was more than a little too bright for Dormael's eyes. The family gathered around wore knowing smiles, as Yanette was known to sniffle about almost anything. Dormael gave them a helpless look and returned his mother's fierce hugs.

Saul wrapped both of his sons in rough embraces and grasped forearms with D'Jenn. He didn't give much of a reaction upon seeing the spear tied to Dormael's saddlebags—a relaxing of the shoulders, a deepening of his smile lines—but an acknowledgment passed between Dormael and his father. A weight lifted from Dormael's shoulders, and he promised to write.

Bethany was passed from grandparent to grandparent, the victim of a storm of hugs, kisses, and hair-ruffling. She looked a little bewildered at the treatment, but weathered it with as much smiling grace as she could muster. Dormael's mother loaded her with an entire bag full of clothing, and ribbons had been braided into her hair. Luckily, the horses they'd taken from the Aeglar Cultists provided ample space for luggage.

Shawna looked terrible.

Her eyes were red around the edges, and her skin had a sallow tone. She had to be feeling nauseous, but she held herself together with a dignity that would have honored her noble station if she could stop squinting so hard into the light. Her hair was still wet from the bath she'd taken, and she kept it under the hood of a fur-lined cloak. Shawna gave a stiff traditional bow in farewell and mounted her horse with muttered goodbyes.

Does she remember last night? Doubtful. She's going to be sick all day.

Allen came trundling out of the house loaded down with weapons. Dormael might have expected such a thing, knowing his brother, but the amount of weaponry the man lugged around was ridiculous. In one trip, he carried a long spear over one shoulder and a baldric holding a curved saber over the other. On his arm was a targe—a small shield with a spike in the center—and he carried a short sword clutched in his hand. After lugging it all to his horse and tying some of it in place, he went inside for a second load.

When he appeared again, he had a pair of short bows in leather cases, complete with a quiver full of arrows. An Orrisan style hand-axe swung at his belt, which had a bearded blade and a hardwood shaft. A leather harness stocked with throwing knives was attached to the light, segmented armor he wore. His fists were covered in a type of spiked gauntlet that would turn a punch into something disfiguring. Under his arm, he carried a steel helm.

D'Jenn and Dormael snickered louder with each load of weapons.

Allen sensed they were watching him and turned. "What?"

"We were just wondering where the war is," D'Jenn said, stifling a yawn. "How many weapons do you really need? The rest of us get by with one."

"Speak for yourself," Shawna muttered.

D'Jenn gave her a bland look, and she shrugged in response.

"The rest of you can get by with one if you want," Allen said. "My level of skill, however, requires a bevy of choices. Sometimes I want to shoot things—hence, the bow. The spear is good for mounted charges, and hunting boar, too. Obviously, the sword is for stabbing people. You'd be surprised how often steel gets stuck in a body, and you have to spend precious moments wrenching it out—"

"That's enough!" Yanette threw up her hands. "I don't want to hear that shit!"

Laughter issued up from everyone standing around them, but Allen stalked over and gave her a noisy kiss on the cheek. She rolled her eyes and hugged him again, plucking at his armor as if she could straighten it.

"You know I love you, you old witch," he said.

"I know." she wiped a tear from her cheek. "You'd better get going, or I'm going to start crying again."

They mounted and rode the way they'd come, with remounts trailing behind them. Dormael turned to watch his home fade into the distance. Family members waved and called their goodbyes until the homestead was lost from sight. When they made the edge of his family's land, there was a bittersweet twinge in Dormael's chest.

I'll have to spend more time here when all this is over.

Bethany cleared her throat. "What's the Conclave going to be like?"

"What's it going to be like?" Dormael took a deep breath and tugged his cloak tight against the chill. "It will be different from anything you've ever seen."

"It's...well, it's where I'm going, isn't it?"

"That's the plan, little one." Dormael nodded. "Isn't that what you want? To learn to use your power?"

"Yes." She sighed. "At least, I think so. Are you going to be there?"

Dormael took an uncomfortable breath. He couldn't stay with her during her training or huddle over her like a mother bear. Initiates were separated from their families for a reason, and Dormael would be expected to avoid her unless she was on holiday. He would be able to visit, of course, but he also had duties as a Warlock.

"I will be able to visit you, and I will hear about everything you do. I live at the Conclave, you know, so I will be close by. The thing is, Bethany, I also have duties. Do you understand what that means?"

"Yes." She turned to look at him. "You have to take care of the armlet."

"That's part of it," he said, "but I have other duties. For you, though, the Conclave will be different. It's a school. You will learn things, be required to pass tests. You'll be put into a class—a group of children close to your age and skill level. You'll live with them, you'll become something like a family."

Bethany furrowed her brows. "But...aren't *we* family now?"

"Of course." Dormael nodded. "But your classmates will be something close, too, eventually. Nothing wrong with *more* family, right?"

She turned back around. "Maybe."

"You'll learn all sorts of things—history, mathematics, philosophy—"

"What about magic?"

"Of course," he laughed. "At the Conclave, they'll teach you the *right* way. D'Jenn and I are just improvising. You'll have real instructors."

"I want to learn to make roasts with magic." She smiled over her shoulder. "Roasts with gravy and carrots. And rolls—rolls with honey and butter. Can you do that?"

Dormael just laughed and ruffled her hair.

**

Their trek through the foothills lasted days. The weather stayed dry, which was a blessing from the gods as far as Dormael was concerned, but it was damnably cold. The wind tore at their hoods and blew dust in their eyes. Dark clouds formed over the passes, and gusts blew through the hills like icy bellows. As the days passed by, he huddled deeper into his cloak, and tried his best to get used to it.

Six days out from Harlun homestead, they began the climb into the Runemian Mountains. The road was wide and smooth at the bottom, but as they twisted higher into the mountains, it became narrower, rockier, and more eroded. They were forced to slow their pace as they went higher, and the horses had more trouble on the treacherous terrain.

The trail leveled off on the fourth day, and the road squeezed into a ravine just wide enough for three horses to ride abreast. Rocky outcroppings overlooked the road on both sides, with stunted vegetation sprouting from wherever it could take hold. The noise of a burbling creek echoed from the rocky terrain, though it was nowhere in sight from the road.

Allen led the way into the pass with D'Jenn and Shawna following close behind. Dormael had drawn remount duty for the day, and he led the train of horses they had taken from the Cultists with a long lead tied to his saddle. Bethany hummed from her spot in front of him, tapping a rhythm on her thigh.

He looked over his shoulder, taking in the view of the foothills below. The highlands were a patchwork of folded lands with brown grasses blowing in the cold wind. Ahead was nothing but craggy boulders, evergreens, and stunted bushes on all sides.

I wonder how far up the mountain we've come.

The lead rope gave a tug, and Dormael turned to see what was causing the problem. One of the horses at the rear of the train plucked at a sprig of grass at the side of the road. Dormael sighed and pulled Horse to a stop. The rest of the party disappeared around a bend in the trail, and Dormael waved for them to keep going.

May as well let the beast have his snack.

"What is that man doing?" Bethany said.

Dormael froze. "What man?"

Bethany pointed to a ridge overlooking the trail. A man was crouched behind a bush, drawing an arrow to his cheek, eyes locked in the direction D'Jenn and Shawna had ridden. Dormael's hands tightened on Bethany's shoulders, and he opened his Kai in a rush of alarm.

D'Jenn! His magic screamed a warning through the ether. *Archers!*

Dormael raised his hands, pulling magic through his Kai, and fire blossomed on the walls of the ravine. It roared across the outcroppings, pouring across the stone like liquid. The remounts screamed, reared, and tried to bolt. Dormael gripped tight to the lead, teeth clenched with the effort of holding on.

Screams of agony rose into the air, and men stumbled out of the conflagration, a few leaping down to the trail to escape the flames. Dormael pulled the heat from the flames with a fierce gesture, and the air warped as the energy dissipated, leaving nothing but smoke and charred remains. Dormael's Kai sang in his senses.

He dug his heels into Horse's flanks and screamed for Bethany to hold tight. They climbed around the narrow switchback and rejoined their friends just as chaos was taking hold. Steel whispered and rang as weapons were drawn, and the horses tossed their heads in fear. A troop of excited voices rang out, echoing from the walls of the pass on either side of them.

Gods—we're surrounded!

"*Ride!*" D'Jenn shouted, whipping his mace from his belt.

He spurred Mist down the trail at a gallop, and everyone pounded after him. Dormael yanked on the remount line and kicked Horse into a run. Like thunder, they fled down the winding trail.

Dormael rounded a bend into a clearing just in time to see his brother lean out of the saddle and stab downward with his spear, killing a man in dark leathers as he rode by. Allen abandoned the weapon and drew his saber, but was forced to pull hard on his reins and turn his horse in a circle. Shawna and D'Jenn jammed into the clearing behind him, raising a cloud of dust and crowding the rocky trail.

"A tree!" Allen pointed to the trail with his saber. "A tree across the road!"

Dormael cursed as the remounts flooded in behind him, choking the area like a holding pen. Horse swung around in a desperate circle, eyes rolling, while Dormael tried to fix his eyes on the fallen tree. He could hear D'Jenn's song playing an angry melody in the ether, though he couldn't tell if he was trying to move the tree, or defend against more assailants. Dormael spotted men here and there, but his damned horse wouldn't stop spinning. Everything was chaos.

Allen yelled and chopped down with his sword, killing a man in a spray of bright blood. More of them were coming from all sides—men dressed in cast-off leathers, all bright knives and hungry eyes. Arrows flitted through the air, and one of the horses screamed in pain.

They're closing the trap!

A wild-eyed man ran for them as Horse danced around. Dormael wrenched the bastard from the ground with his power and tossed him into the trees. He pulled ice from the air with his magic and sent it hurtling into another man who stood on a ridge above. Dust filled the clearing, obscuring everything in a chaotic haze. Screams cut through the air, and the ether warbled with angry magic.

Allen laid about with his saber, screaming and covered in blood. His horse was one of the combat-trained Cultist mounts, and it lashed out with its hooves at the men who menaced them. Allen tried to clear a space around him, but the confusion was too great.

D'Jenn picked out random men in the shifting, dusty mass, and killed them in flashes of red light. He let his horse spin and kick, and instead of trying to calm her, he concentrated on laying about with his magic. D'Jenn's Kai sang a vengeful melody, and his face was drawn in concentration.

We've got to get that tree out of the way!

He spun around until he could see the fallen tree. Seizing it in his Kai, he gestured with a fist and attempted to lift it from the ground. Horse whinnied as Dormael's weight increased—the feedback of force through his spell. He cursed and distributed the surrounding weight instead, leveraging his power against the rocks on either side of the trail. The tree shifted and cracked, uttering groaning protests as it rose from the ground, trailing a shower of dirt and pine needles. Dormael raised his hand, and the tree rose with it.

Maybe I'll drop this on some of these—

Pain exploded on the back of his head, and everything went hazy. His world toppled end over end, and he slammed into the ground. A rushing, pounding noise drowned out his hearing. Dirt filled his mouth and nose, and his magic left him like a tide receding from the shore. The tree made an awful racket as it crashed to the ground nearby, and screams lifted in its wake.

Dormael tried to rise, but pain rushed from the back of his head all the way to his legs, and his muscles gave an involuntary spasm. He dug his fingers into the dirt with a silent gasp of pain and tried again. His body responded, but his head swam with the effort. Blood ran from the top of his head into his mouth, and he spat to the side.

"Grab her!" a voice growled.

Two men had grabbed Horse's saddle, each trying to get a hand on Bethany. Horse spun, fighting to keep them away, but one of the men stepped into the beast's side and took hold of his reins. The other got a hand on Bethany's ankle.

"No!" Dormael tried to rise, but a wave of vertigo took him to the ground.

One of the men pulled Bethany from the saddle, even against the girl's flailing arms and legs. She landed on the ground in a whimpering heap and tried to scoot away. The pounding hooves and stomping boots in the chaos kept her rooted to the spot. She met Dormael's eyes and gave him a frightened look. Dormael's heart wrenched in fear as he reached for his magic, but the power eluded him, running through his mental fingers like slippery oil.

"Kill the wizard, we carry the girl back to Jureus," one of them said.

A black fear took root in Dormael's guts. His head was full of wool, and his skull throbbed like fire. His magic wouldn't respond to his frenzied commands, and Bethany was out of his reach. A hand reached down to take Bethany by the hair, and Dormael cried out. Bethany threw up her hands, shying away.

Tingles flashed over Dormael's skin, and Bethany's song lashed through the ether.

A yellow light flickered over the girl's body, down across the ground, and leapt onto the bandit like a critter made of shifting motes. He screamed and stumbled back, and Dormael watched in fascinated horror as the lights sank into his skin and crawled beneath it. His body swelled, distended, and burst like an overripe melon in a shower of gore.

Bethany saw her handiwork, and her eyes went wide with fear. Pebbles danced along the ground as her emotions climbed to a fever pitch, her magic reacting with fury and fear. Dormael fought to rise from the ground and got to a knee. Another man grabbed Bethany from behind, but she fought free of his grip and scrambled away.

Dormael saw something in her face, saw her reach a breaking point. Her expression changed between one instant and the next— from abject terror to something cold, something determined. In the space of a single heartbeat, Bethany's eyes alighted on the man pursuing her, and she concentrated. Dormael felt her magic—wild and unfocused only seconds before—move with deadly purpose.

The man was flung away from her in a spray of blood, making a wet smacking noise as if he'd been swatted by the hand of an invisible giant. His body flew into a nearby tree, cracking limbs on his way to the ground. Dormael turned a surprised glare on his newly adopted daughter. She was once again huddled into a ball.

Dormael hissed in pain as his body protested and fought down a wave of nausea as he climbed to his feet. He stumbled to where Bethany was crouched and put his arms around her, muttering assurances into her ear. All traces of the cold, determined expression were gone.

What was that?

Another gurgling scream sounded from behind them. Turning, he saw Shawna pulling one of her blades from the throat of one dying man while stepping like an eel through the space between two others. As the first man fell in a spray of blood, she slashed open the thigh of a second. The third man had enough time to attack with a desperate slash at her face, but Shawna tapped his sword aside with contempt and repaid him with a delicate cut across the eyes. He stumbled away, screaming in agony.

Dormael grabbed at Horse's reins and pulled the beast around so he could plant Bethany in the saddle. His head throbbed in time with his heartbeat, each thud coming with teeth-clenching pain. Once Bethany was perched on horseback, he struggled into the saddle behind her. His legs went weak as he climbed, and he almost pitched back into the dirt.

Dormael reached to the back of his head and probed at the wound, even as a wave of dizziness swept over him. He had a cut, and a vicious, swollen bruise, but his skull was whole. Even as the dusty chaos raged around him, Dormael breathed a sigh of relief. He closed his eyes and took a deep breath, then tried once again to summon his magic.

Shawna's scream ripped his concentration away, and he spun in her direction.

A crowd of men surrounded her, and one of them had tossed a net over her head. Shawna screamed in rage and hacked at the thing with her blades, but one of the bandits stepped forward and knocked her to the ground. Dormael tried to haul Horse around in Shawna's direction, but he was too slow. Before he could do more than pull at the reins, the men closed in and dragged Shawna into the woods.

He reached again for his magic, but the damnable power slipped from his mind, leaving nothing but a dull pain in its wake. Dormael cursed, spurring Horse after the men who had taken Shawna. He headed for the side of the road, where a trail meandered into the woods. Growling, Dormael spurred Horse up the trail, after the cloud of dust and the retreating bandits.

Flames burst from the ground in front of him, reaching three times the height of a man. Dormael felt the sensation of magic being used—a tingling along his arms and legs—but he couldn't hear the song without listening to his own power. He spent a confused moment wondering why in the Six Hells D'Jenn would prevent him from chasing their attackers before he realized the truth.

They've got a wizard amongst them!

Dormael cursed and wheeled Horse back onto the trail, holding his arm over his head. The flames dissipated as he turned away. Only his brother, D'Jenn, and corpses were left in the clearing. There were piles of them, and Dormael did a quick count.

Twenty men—what group of bandits is so strong?

Allen was covered in gore, his sword a dripping mess. He heaved out great breaths from atop his horse—a spotted chestnut he'd named Old Girl. Allen spun her in a circle, surveying the surrounding carnage. Dormael's eyes went to the man whom Bethany had burst like an overripe melon. His remains were nothing more than a splotch of blood and organs.

D'Jenn held his mace out to the side, spikes dripping onto the dirt. Dormael felt the pressure of his cousin's magic along his skin and resisted the urge to reach for his own. D'Jenn looked into everyone's faces and went rigid with concern.

"Where's—?"

"They took her." Dormael gestured toward the trail. "They took Shawna."

"They got away with her horse and most of the remounts, too," Allen said. "Let's regroup, then we'll get up that fucking trail and take them back!"

"Wait." D'Jenn held up a hand. "Earlier, was that—I mean, I thought I heard—"

"Aye." Dormael gave him a grim look. "They have a wizard."

**

Maarkov watched the corpse of the sailor move about the beach, gathering up what little equipment they could salvage from the wreck. Scattered detritus had washed up throughout the day— crates, cloth, bodies—but they would find little use in any of it. Maarkov's lip curled in disgust at the sight of the *strega*, at the thought of its slimy, dead hands upon anything Maarkov might later touch. The thing moved like a person—it was capable of moving better than a person. The *strega* could run until its legs rotted away or were damaged beyond functioning. The *strega* never tired, it performed to its utmost strength, it never asked questions, nor did it give protestations. Without some aspect of his brother's will controlling it, however, it would simply stand and stare into the distance.

Disgusting, mindless bags of stinking meat.

The sailor had formerly pulled Maarkov through the surging water, dragging him to shore in the dark. If Maarkov was alive, he would have owed the man that life. When he had seen Maarkov's face in the moonlight and realized whom he had saved, he'd tried to run. Maarkov had been fine to let the man go, but Maaz was already waiting on shore. The sailor didn't get ten staggering steps through the sand before Maaz had him.

The thing on the beach, though, was just the meat leftover when the man was gone.

"Why are you barefoot?" Maaz asked from behind him.

"Because my feet are wet, you idiot," Maarkov spat. "My feet, my hands, and everything I gods-damned own is soaked. I don't have magic to dry my clothing, so I have to do it the old fashioned way. Is there something you want?"

"We've been blown farther north than I had intended," Maaz said. "We're near the easternmost foothills of the Runemian Mountains, and we've got a long way to go. Days of travel to make up. We'll need to eat before we leave."

Maarkov shuddered, his eyes shooting into the distance behind him, where trails of smoke could be seen in the fading sunlight—a village. No one had come from the village to the beach, but this didn't look like a well-traveled area. It would be a small, unnamed hamlet on the edge of nowhere.

Perfect for him. A low hanging fruit, easily plucked.

"The *strega* found your sword. It was tangled in some sailcloth, snagged on something that washed up. I thought you'd like to know. When your clothes dry out, we're leaving. I want to be off this beach before midnight."

"Too bad I don't have my whetstone," Maarkov said, a smile coming to his face before he could stop it. He felt Maaz's presence at his back, and the air was pregnant with tension. Whatever it was he wished to say, however, he elected to keep it to himself.

Maarkov didn't turn to see where his brother went, he just listened to his fading footfalls.

Like the *strega*, Maarkov didn't need to breathe, to sleep, to slow down. He could perform to the limit of his body's ability—given he partook in his brother's blood rite. If Maaz wanted to make up days of travel, he would undoubtedly be pushing them to run, non-stop, to their destination.

I hope there are horses at the village. The horses could run until their hearts gave out, then his brother could animate them with his power—which granted them all the abilities of the *strega*. They stank just as bad, but riding them was preferable to pulverized boots.

Maarkov rose to make his way down to the beach and collect his sword. He breathed a private sigh of relief at its appearance—finding a good sword was harder than finding a good pair of boots. He looked out over the surf, losing himself with the waves of the oncoming tide. The rain had passed on, and the sunset was almost idyllic.

The *strega* passed before his vision, and Maarkov spat into the dirt. Perhaps decapitating the creature would be fun—it would certainly anger Maaz. If he dispatched the corpse, though, it would be Maarkov who was relegated to carrying and hauling. Plus, one more pair of hands meant a bit less killing for his own to do.

The gods knew there was plenty of that to come.

**

"They have the high ground." Allen pointed at the trail where the bandits had escaped. "If I were them, I'd set my camp somewhere I could post archers who could draw on a target long before it got up that trail. I'm willing to bet they've got people watching it for just that sort of assault."

"How many men could they have left?" Dormael nodded at the twenty-two corpses they'd pushed to the side of the road. At least twenty-four had been killed—the one Bethany had splattered couldn't be collected with the others, and the one she had thrown from the road had disappeared. "For that matter—why attack us in the first place?"

"Long remount train," Allen said. "Makes us look like rich traders."

"Aye, but something about this doesn't make sense." Dormael frowned. "First of all, this wizard with the bandits."

"Why?"

Dormael scoffed. "A member of the Conclave would never turn to banditry. Your average Hedge Wizard is paid the least, and they enjoy a lavish lifestyle compared to your average highwayman."

"Maybe they just enjoy a bit of rape and pillage."

"Doubtful," Dormael said. "They're risking a lot doing it *here*. We're at the summit of the Runemian Mountain range, practically overlooking the city of Ishamael—well within reach of the Conclave. Whoever this person is, they're risking their lives by demonstrating their power here. As soon as the Conclave caught wind of what was happening, the response would be swift and deadly. This isn't about loot."

"They took Shawna," Allen muttered, working his jaw. "You think this was a kidnapping?"

"They tried to take Bethany, too," Dormael said. "And they made every effort to kill the rest of us."

"You think these are mercenaries more than highwaymen?"

Dormael shrugged.

"Can he set traps—magical traps, like in the old hero stories?" Allen asked.

Dormael nodded down to D'Jenn, who sat cross-legged, scouting the trail with Mind Flight.

"We'll know soon enough."

Bethany stood, clutching the hem of Dormael's cloak and staring at the spot where she'd killed the two men. Dormael had one hand grasping the girl's shoulder, trying to convey a sense of comfort. The look of cold determination on her face when she had killed the second man stuck in his memory. She had been learning rudimentary uses of her power, but to have used it to kill at such an early stage of development couldn't feel good.

I'll find time to talk with her as soon as we get Shawna back.

Dormael reached into his boot and slipped out one of his smaller daggers—a double-sided blade with rounded quillons. He turned it over in his hands, flipped the blade into his fingers, and offered the hilt to Bethany. She accepted it, holding the dagger in both hands like a miniature sword. Dormael reached down and corrected her grip.

"Here, like this," he said, pulling one of her hands away and closing her other around the hilt. "Stick the pointy end in the bad guy, got it?"

She nodded.

"Always keep good hold of that knife and don't let it fall out of your hands. Got it?"

"Got it."

"And, listen—always put the point in the softest bit you can find, right? Behind the knee, under the jaw, just over the collarbone." He pointed out each area on the girl's body with a quick little poke. "Never let your enemy see the blade coming. Savvy?"

She nodded again, keeping her eyes on the dagger.

He took her by the shoulders and looked her in the eyes, holding her gaze when she tried to look away.

"Every Sevenlander child gets a knife at thirteen," he said. "You just earned yours, no matter how old you are. Keep it hidden, keep it safe, and never part with it."

Bethany nodded and regarded the dagger with a reverent expression. The wild look of fear had left her eyes, though. It was the only thing he could dream up to take her mind from the killings. Besides—the girl *had* earned the knife, if ever a child had earned one. Perhaps now she could draw strength from this experience instead of being afraid of it.

Allen caught Dormael's eyes and nodded in approval.

D'Jenn stood, brushing the dust from his pants. Bethany clutched her knife and crowded in with the men, as if she were joining a command conference in some general's tent. The light was fading over the horizon, painting the passes in deep orange colors.

"They've got a nice little spot up there," D'Jenn said. "The trail winds a good way up the side of this peak, then turns upward onto a flat expanse of ground—that's where the bastards have made their camp. The whole thing is surrounded by trees, and the entire approach is watched by archers. They're stationed at high places along the path."

Allen nodded. "Archers—told you."

"What about the wizard?" Dormael asked.

"A Nelekan," D'Jenn said. "The men all look like hire-outs—

bounty hunters, back-stabbers, and sell-swords. They're following his orders, but things are a little tense between them."

"A Nelekan?" Dormael raised an eyebrow. "He's a long way from home. What in the Six Hells is a Nelekan wizard doing out here?"

Allen shrugged. "Maybe the Empire has different ideas about magic than the rest of Alderak."

"No—using magic is a hanging offense in the Galanian Empire," Dormael said. "Things keep getting stranger. Do you think he's trained?"

"Not well," D'Jenn said. "He had wards at different points along the road, but he set them up like a fool. I unraveled them one by one, and he doesn't even know it's been done. His workings are no better than a third-year Initiate at the Conclave."

"And Shawna?"

"They're tying her to a post in their camp. She's out cold, so nothing's happened to her—yet," D'Jenn said. "The quicker we get up there, the better."

"You've seen the terrain." Allen tapped D'Jenn on the chest. "Got a plan?"

D'Jenn gave Allen a crooked smile. "Can you still stalk a deer?"

"Close enough to kiss."

"Good. Dormael—your magic?"

"Hurts, but I can use it," he grumbled. "I'll have one bastard of a headache tomorrow."

"Alright, then. Allen and I will go into the trees to either side of the trail. We'll take out the archers—knives only. I don't want to alert the wizard we're getting close. Amateur or not, he's dangerous.

"Dormael—I want you in the air. Drop in on their campsite and be ready to move. When people start dying, you go for this Nelekan wizard."

"What about me?" Bethany's voice shook.

"I need you to find a good hiding spot," D'Jenn said. "Somewhere on the other side of the pass where you can see this trail. Watch for anyone leaving and don't make a sound. We'll need to know if anyone gets away."

"And keep your knife close, don't forget." Dormael gave her a short, one-armed hug.

"I won't," she promised.

When night fell, they put the plan into motion.

Dormael poured his magic inward and took his favorite form—the gyrfalcon. He pulled his way into the sky, fighting against the tough currents of mountain air. The wind howled through the passes, but once Dormael climbed out of the pass and spiraled over the trail, he stayed aloft with little effort.

Spotting the camp from the air was easy. Crawling on the ground like some low-bellied lizard blinded one to the world around them. The raptor, able to soar on the wind, saw everything. Even in the fading light, he picked out the campsite in stunning detail.

The camp was spread out over several hillsides, though one of them was full of tents and rigged shelters with only a few men milling about between them. The large, central clearing was home to a raging bonfire, blaring its indifference to the night sky. A single, thin man stood before the flames, his narrow shoulders outlined by the glow. He stared away from the bonfire, scowling at three men who loitered around a large post driven into the ground.

Shawna was bound to the post.

She was slumped over with her hair covering her face. Her hands were secured above her head, tied to a nail driven into the post. Another rope ran around her waist, holding her back flat against the pole. The firelight reflected from her hair like molten copper.

Dormael was careful to keep from silhouetting himself against the moonlight as he swung around for a landing. The bonfire would have blinded most of the fools in the clearing anyway, but it was always better to be thorough. Dormael found a suitable tree on the edge of the clearing and clutched to a branch near the top, flapping his wings to stay upright.

He could go down there now. He could use the bonfire to roast the Nelekan—the short man standing next to it, Dormael guessed—and then kill the others with simple force. He'd have to hold off anyone else while he waited for D'Jenn and his brother to appear, but it might be possible. He itched to run to Shawna's rescue.

Don't be stupid. Wait for the bloody signal.

The three men standing around Shawna's inert form were examining things in turn. One of them turned her swords around in his hands, staring open-mouthed at the craftsmanship. The second was snickering as he watched the third grope at Shawna's breasts like an overeager adolescent. Indignation rose in Dormael's chest, but forced himself to stay put.

"Karv!" the slim man by the bonfire said.

Karv, who was four hands taller and twice as thick as the shorter man, straightened from his fondling with a baleful look on his face.

"The fuck you want, Jureus?"

Jureus—a Nelekan name.

"Leave the girl be," Jureus snarled. "My Master wants her unharmed, and that means unsoiled by the likes of you. Stay away from her. You can bugger anything else you find out here, but not her."

"That's the thing, Jureus." Karv flicked his meaty thumb along the blade of an axe tucked into his belt. "There hasn't been much come through here, has there? You promised us all a case full of silver marks and all the pillage we wanted. Taking the cunny from what we catch is part of the deal. You haven't paid us that case of silver marks yet, and the way I see it, I'm owed a piece."

Grumbles of agreement issued from around the camp.

"You had a girl three nights back," Jureus said, his voice cracking in the upper registers. "The drover's daughter. I had to get rid of the body because you left it lying about, like a dog with its favorite chew toy. Like a fucking beast."

Jureus sounds like a teenage boy in the middle of puberty. Karv's attitude toward him, the slight frame, the cracking voice—how did a boy with Eindor's Blessing get involved with this lot? The kid had balls, challenging a man like Karv, but he looked to be in over his head. *And who is this Master he's talking about?*

Scattered laughter bubbled from the shadows at Jureus's comments, and Karv shot a mistrustful glare around the camp. His hand tightened on the haft of his axe, but he paused just on the edge of drawing it. Kid or not, Jureus must have shown these men something in the way of dominance, else they wouldn't follow his orders.

"The drover's daughter was a bore," Karv spat. "Just laid there the whole time, grunting like a pig."

"That was you!" one of the men behind Karv said, and laughter burst out in the camp.

"Point is," Karv shouted over the laughter, bringing the noise to a low murmur, "you ain't paid us, kid. You owe us—you owe *me*, by the gods. This girl, she's pretty. Noble. A man gets one chance all his life to fuck a girl like that, and I'm taking it."

"No," Jureus said, his voice shaking, "you're *not*."

Roiling balls of liquid blossomed from the fire and hovered behind Jureus, casting a flickering reflection in Karv's eyes. Jureus took a step forward, hands clenched into fists. Tension filled the air, and the balls of flame hovered like a scorpion's tail.

Karv spat in the dirt. "Fuck the girl, and fuck you, kid. I want my gods-damned money!"

He stalked to the other side of the camp, and Jureus turned to the men gathered at the edge of the firelight. He glared into the shadows, drawing himself up. He held his hands wide.

"All of you!" His voice cracked. "If you've got any bright ideas about slitting my throat, or making a bold stand like our friend here, do it now! The fire needs blood before I can do my work, and yours will work as well as mine!"

Only silence answered him.

"Good!" Jureus spun back to the bonfire. "Then keep your bloody mouths shut!"

The fire needs blood before I can do my work?

Dormael was transfixed as Jureus scrawled symbols in the dirt. They were sharp, ugly runes enclosed with bastardized forms taught by the Conclave—a Greater Circle with the lifelines reversed was just one example. His Kai sang into the night—a rough, unfocused melody that spoke of forced confidence and deep sorrow.

Jureus whipped a long dagger from his belt and let his eyes linger on Karv, conveying a threat. When he was satisfied, he whipped the blade along his arm, drawing a bright line of blood. He flung the blood into the fire, spitting words guttural language Dormael didn't recognize. The blood hissed and sputtered when it met the flames, disappearing into wisps of oily smoke.

Is that necromancy?

Jureus went to his knees and put his face in the dirt. *"Master."*

A figure rose from a shadow and stood over Jureus. It wore a flowing black robe, and its features were obscured by shadows. The figure looked around the clearing. Wherever its gaze fell, the muttering around the camp went silent.

"Your report?" the form hissed, its voice like snakeskin over sand.

"I have the woman, Master." Jureus's voice was full of adoration. "Her belongings, too. I have succeeded in my mission, just as instructed."

"What of the child, Jureus?" the cloaked figure asked. "The wizards?"

"I...had the child, Master," Jureus said, his voice faltering. "My men had her, but one of the wizards must have saved her. I couldn't get to her in time. We had to make our escape, but we have the woman!"

The cloaked man stared at Jureus for a long moment, letting the silence fill the pregnant air between them. He turned from Jureus and paced around the camp until he found Shawna. The cloaked figure crouched, peered sideways at her, and shook his head.

"You have the right woman, but that's the only thing you managed to get right, Jureus."

"Master, I don't understand—"

"*Yes*, you fool—you don't understand. That is the problem. Your orders were to secure the girl and woman together, and to bloody make sure you killed these two wizards. Do you remember that part of your orders, Jureus? Are they still alive?"

"Master, we have the high ground. The approach is watched, it's warded! They cannot get within an arrow's shot of my sentries without my knowing."

"You demonstrate your folly with each word from your idiot mouth." The figure shook its head.

"Master, I—"

"*Silence!*" The cloaked figure stalked to Jureus and loomed over him. "Think, you buffoon! You've gone and stolen something precious from two Conclave-trained wizards, and then you left them at your back. You will be lucky to live out the night."

"Master, I—"

The cloaked man held up a single finger. Jureus made a

121

choking noise and went silent.

"Luckily for you, your rival is only a few days' travel from you. You will do your best to hold your position until she arrives. Because the more likely outcome will be your death, you will cast a tracking spell on that armlet. I want to be able to find it after your corpse has gone cold."

"*Yes—*" Jureus coughed. "*Yes...Master!*"

"If you somehow survive what is coming, Jureus, I will be so stunned that I won't kill you for this mistake. If not, then go to the Void knowing you're a fool and a failure."

Without a sound, the figure was gone.

Jureus continued to lie prostrate after the shade departed. When he finally climbed slowly to his knees, he had a dark look on his face. He brushed his clothing free of dust, coughing into his hands.

"Karv," he said in a quiet, dangerous tone. "Go check the sentries."

"I ain't been paid today," Karv grunted. "Fuck yourself, kid."

Jureus turned a dark scowl on Karv, his eyes flashing with anger. Power rumbled from the ether—an angry, vengeful melody. Jureus reached out a hand and made a plucking motion.

Karv cried out in pain and rose from the ground, his arms and legs outstretched. The men who had been nearby scrambled away from him, cursing as they scattered. Karv let out a noise between a squeal of pain and a scream of rage as Jureus tightened his magic down. The hulking sell-sword rose into the air and floated over the fire, close enough for the fur on his boots to curl from the heat. He struggled in tight, controlled spasms, but Jureus's magic held him like an invisible fist of iron.

Dormael spread his wings and leapt from the branch, gliding toward a patch of ground near Jureus. Everyone was distracted by the show, and Jureus's magic was employed—there was no better time to strike. His talons hit the dirt, and Dormael poured his magic back into his body. When the change was complete, he crouched in the dirt with his arms outstretched.

Jureus's eyes went wide. "To arms!"

Startled cries rang out from the direction of the trail, and the ring of steel on steel cut through the night. Men pulled their weapons and ran toward the entrance—where D'Jenn and Allen were cutting them down. Jureus glanced around, expression grim, and faced Dormael.

Dormael split his consciousness so he could work two separate spells at once. It was the only way to fight another wizard—to have at least one attack hidden, or a defense readied to counter whatever spell your enemy might employ. Some wizards, like D'Jenn, could split their minds into several compartments, each directing a separate thread of magic. Dormael could barely push four splits at once, and each of those needed to be simple. His brute strength was usually enough to compensate.

Dormael reached out and slammed a Splinter into Jureus's power, puncturing the man's magic and scattering the energy. Jureus reeled away, his hands going to his head as the magic numbed his senses in reaction. Karv, freed from Jureus's magical grip, dropped into the flames. He cried in wild agony as he scrambled out of the bonfire. Jureus shouted something through a swollen tongue, but Dormael couldn't discern his words.

He's acting like he's never been Splintered before. Gods, he's just a kid!

Dormael sensed an attack coming just before thumping boots sounded to his right. Dormael reacted with instinct, turning his attention away from Jureus and erecting a magical barrier of hardened air. A man carrying an axe slammed into the invisible wall and knocked himself to the dirt. Dormael grimaced and swatted him aside with his power, sending the fool tumbling away into the shadows.

Dormael's magic rang out in alarm, and it was the only thing that saved his life.

Another instinctive gesture brought the invisible back up, enclosing him in a sphere. A boulder the size of a horse-cart smashed into his shield, shattering into a hundred pieces with a noise like an avalanche. The force of the blow drained Dormael's magic, and his head throbbed with the effort of holding to his Kai.

He recovered from that Splintering pretty quickly.

Dormael went on the attack and threw lightning at Jureus— one, two, three jagged bolts—but the lightning met his hand and was reflected away in all directions, starting fires wherever it struck. Jureus countered him with fire, pulling a puff of flame from the bonfire and sending it toward him with a cry of desperation.

The boy was panicked, his magic unfocused—the fire fluttered out before reaching Dormael.

Something burned a hot line across Dormael's left thigh, and he turned to find three men standing at the edge of the clearing, ratcheting crossbows back into the armed position. He grimaced and erected a barrier behind him, turning his attention back to Jureus just in time to catch another large boulder. Bolts thumped into his shield from behind.

Stone after stone was pulled from the ground and flung at Dormael in quick succession, pounding ever harder against his shield. Dormael clenched his jaw tighter with each successive blow as the force was absorbed by his magic. Blocking the flying rocks with a stationary shield wasn't the most effective way to defeat them, but he was thinking fast and dividing his attention. Dormael focused and split his consciousness a third time, seizing on another thread of magic.

A sharp pain went through his skull like a lance of ice, but Dormael powered through it.

Turning his eyes to the archers behind him, he whipped out with a tendril of power and set their clothes on fire. They went up with a whooshing noise, and the archers screamed in frantic pain. They stumbled away until their bodies gave in and the fire consumed their cries.

Jureus tested his barrier, pushing hard with his Kai to test his strength against Dormael's magic.

Dormael turned his full attention on Jureus, bringing his own considerable strength to bear against the Nelekan youngster. Jureus looked desperate, and his Kai sang in frantic tones. Anything lying close enough was sucked toward the confrontation, and soon a line of shuddering, crumpled objects hovered in the air between them. Dormael could feel the boy's Kai starting to bleed as he summoned more power, the magic starting to escape his control.

He's strong, but he's not strong enough!

Dormael looked into his face—sunken eyes, sallow cheeks, and a wild expression of fear. Was there a mother waiting somewhere for this boy to come home? His hands pushed forward, fists clenched tight, and he screamed through his teeth as he turned the full force of his will against Dormael.

Dormael held the boy's power at bay, but his feet slid backwards through the gravel. The objects hanging between them vibrated like they'd been struck. Dormael shook his head, partitioned his mind again, and shoved another Splinter into the boy's magic.

Jureus hissed as his Kai rebounded, his magic rushing into the world without purpose.

The whole hillside gave a shudder. Gravel and scree rose from the ground like dust from a struck bell. The arrows, boulders, limbs and detritus hovering in the air between Dormael and Jureus caught fire all at once, and Dormael shied away from the sudden rush of heat. Screams rang out all over camp, and the sound of howling magic filled Dormael's senses.

Dormael's own power began to be sucked into the maelstrom. He tried to wrench it free, but it leaked through his mental fingers like water in a flood. Another sharp lance of pain through his head brought Dormael to his knees, and his own control over his Kai faltered. He pulled harder on his magic, trying to rein it in.

Blinding pain spread behind his eyes.

Jureus wailed as the magic took him. He rose from the ground, writhing in pain as iridescent foxfire crawled over his skin. The boy's screams cut off as his body was crushed, pounded into a globe by the weight of the power rushing back into him. Everything—the flaming detritus, the dirt, even the bonfire—was sucked toward the hovering remains of the Nelekan boy.

Blood filled Dormael's mouth, and everything went dark.

A River of Shadow

Haunted, that's what it's called.

No, that wasn't it, either. Paralyzed? Petrified?

Stunned, shocked? Maarkov chewed on his choice of words. Resigned?

The man—the father of a charming little family—stared at the altar with that look in his eyes, the one Maarkov couldn't place. It was all of those things he'd named and more. It was deeper. None of the words which came to mind—horrified, terrified, awestruck—could quite convey the depth of emotion in the man's gaze. It burned like a fire had been kindled inside him, and his eyes were the only place it could escape. The veins stood out on his forehead, and chest heaved with angry breaths. He'd ceased making noises against the gag in his mouth hours ago, but he hadn't taken those eyes from the table since Maaz had begun.

And those eyes—that look.

Despair. That's it. Despair.

His daughters—three girls with flaxen hair and narrow shoulders—huddled together, staring at the ground. Their shoulders bobbed in time with their sobs. Unlike their father, they refused to look.

It was the boy who got to Maarkov. The boy had fought, had punched the strega over and over until he realized it was useless. He had screamed, kicked, snarled and spat. Not anymore, though. Now, the boy only stared, refusing to look away from what was happening. Was he trying to prove something, to honor something? Couldn't he find somewhere else to look?

Close your damned eyes, kid. Please close your eyes.

The woman on the table lay spread-eagle with her arms and legs tied to stakes driven into the ground with his brother's magic. Maaz worked over her like a baker in a pastry shop, humming like he was patting flour into dough instead of cutting away her homespun dress. Maaz moved like a specter, running a long, thin blade from her hip to her armpit and pulling the fabric aside. He yanked her clothing aside and discarded it into the wind. Before it hit the ground, it was burned away by some trick of Maaz's magic.

The woman whimpered into her gag and jerked against the ropes. Her body showed the scars of motherhood, a record of the lives she had brought screaming into the world. Her nudity seemed a profane thing, the night air caressing her like an unwanted lover.

The father made a noise somewhere between a scream of rage and a howl of pain.

Close your eyes, kid. Close your bloody eyes!

But the boy was transfixed, and Maarkov didn't dare speak.

Maaz cut into the woman's skin. She spasmed and tried to move, but Maaz must have been holding her down with his power like a scribe holding a piece of parchment to the writing desk. She whimpered and mouthed jumbled words into the gag, but Maaz paid her protestations little attention. Trickles of blood ran down her sides and soaked into the table, and Maaz was soon bloody to the elbows from his work.

The father screamed into his own gag, the same word over and over. It was lost in the folds of the rag shoved between his teeth, but it might have been her name—Mara, Meera or Myra. Maarkov clenched his jaw and kept his hand tight on his sword.

Maarkov looked away as Maaz opened the woman's torso. The father wailed, Maaz's arms worked, and the woman just lay silent, tears streaming from her eyes. She made retching noises, but her eyes rolled back from the pain and the spasms weakened. Maaz, one hand inside her belly, chanted in his guttural language.

The boy saw everything.

Screams and banging issued up from the barn where the rest of the homesteaders had been barricaded. Maarkov turned to the barn—mostly to avert his eyes from the ritual—and watched the double doors shaking back and forth in their sockets. Maaz had twisted a piece of steel around the doors to hold them closed, using his magic to see the job done. Maarkov wouldn't move to stop them if they won free, but he doubted the country villagers could get out. Maaz was too thorough when it came to killing.

"Brother," Maaz hissed.

Maarkov turned, but he kept his eyes away from the woman.

"You must eat."

Maarkov grimaced. "Must I?"

The words were a reflex more than an actual question. Without taking part in the ritual, his flesh would slowly rot away. The eldritch energies keeping the ravages of time at bay would flee his body, and it would ripen like a melon left in the sun.

He would, of course, experience every agonizing second.

"You know the answer to that question," Maaz said in an all-suffering tone. "Eat."

He held out something pink, wriggly, and wet.

Maarkov took it, cupping his hands in order to keep the thing—whatever it was—from slipping into the dirt. He would chew on the rubbery meat, he would let the blood dribble down his chin, even suck the fibers from between his teeth afterward—but a little dirt would ruin everything. The thought almost made him laugh.

Maarkov raised his eyes and caught the boy looking at him.

He paused, mouth poised to bite into the bloody piece of the boy's mother. Maaz gave him an insistent look, indicating the woman's labored breathing. The meal had to be finished before she died, otherwise the magic wouldn't work—at least, that's the way Maaz explained it to him. He grimaced at the boy and shoved the warm, soft flesh into his mouth.

He'd told the boy to look away, gods damn him—or at least, he'd prayed for it. For that matter, where were the fucking gods when the boy had needed them? If ever there was divine intervention needed in a young boy's life, it was when people like Maarkov and his brother came calling.

Where were the gods when the boy had been yanked from the dirt by his hair and hauled before this makeshift altar? Had the gods cared when Maaz had rounded up all the homesteaders—

men, women and children from infants to lanky adolescents—and barricaded them in the barn? Were they watching this mother being carved up and nibbled like a festival roast, even as she struggled to heave out her last breaths?

Maarkov swallowed, his stomach giving the familiar, reflexive heave. He fought it down. The woman's struggles ceased, and her life fled the altar.

"Now," Maaz sighed, turning toward the family and wiping blood from his chin. "Let's see to the rest of you."

He gestured, and the barn went up in a roaring conflagration. Screams rose from the blaze as the flames cracked the wood and split the darkness of the night, but the family only stared in horror at the woman on the table. Except for the boy—the boy was staring right at Maarkov, his eyes empty.

Maarkov scowled at the kid. He wanted to yell at him, to tell him there was no reason for that look on his face, that the gods didn't give two golden shits about what happened to him or his family. He wanted to rail about how the world was cruel, and it would crush the weak under the heels of the strong. Before the anger made him open his mouth, though, he stopped.

By the look in the boy's eyes, he already knew.

**

The Conclave was packed, just as the Administrator had warned.

Political tension brought wizards back to Ishamael like flies to old meat, though the proper analogy might have been one involving a beehive—that's the way it felt to D'Jenn. All the hallways in the Conclave Proper were full of bustling wizards conversing with old friends they hadn't seen since their days as Initiates. Out on the Green, beside the white stone colonnade leading to the front entrance, a group of Hedge Wizards were having a meeting entirely for the purposes of discussing the best methods for brewing ale.

The Conclave had two sprawling campuses, each located to either side of the river Ishamael. The main compound, located on the eastern side of the river, was full of marble, white stone, and manicured parks. There were various buildings on the grounds, each with their own purpose and each displaying a simple, severe beauty. There was the Conclave Proper—the main tower where wizards lived and worked and where the majority of classes were held for those in their First Four. Two large greenhouses, given the affectionate monikers Plantings One and Two, stood near the Conclave Proper. On the other side was a paved section of yard where students were instructed in the basic use of chosen weapons. It was called the Bruising Stretch—this term more often used in a not-so-affectionate tone of voice.

Wizards strolled through the Conclave's wide expanse of lawns and parks, which were referred to on the whole as the Green. Most of it was open to the public, and there was a minority of people who came to enjoy the Conclave's quiet beauty. There were always troops of children in the parks, as Hedge Wizards were wont to give out free classes on subjects ranging from reading to history for any child willing to listen—it was good practice for their future profession. Parents were known to send their children down to the Conclave for the day, to see what sort of knowledge they could soak up. It was also one of the safest places for children in the entire city. Criminals didn't dare risk the ire of Conclave Wizards.

D'Jenn allowed his senses to flit about the Conclave grounds, taking in the various pockets of conversation, argument, or laughter. Despite the tense atmosphere, wizards were using this excuse to spend time socializing. Dormael would have smiled to see it.

Dormael, though, had been unconscious for days.

They had taken a mule-cart from the bandits' campsite and used it to haul his inert body down the mountain. Shawna, though she pretended disinterest, had spent every free moment hovering over him. She tried to say it was because Dormael had done the same for her, and maybe there was some truth to that, but D'Jenn could see the fear in the woman's eyes when she looked at him. Bethany had been silent since the night of the attack.

The Death Sleep was a real danger for wizards who drew too much of their power. The depth of any wizard's strength was tied to their Kai, and the Kai was somehow tied to the body. Spend too much power, draw in too much magic, and it could be harmful. Take it further—the way his idiot cousin sometimes did—and it could be fatal.

Sometimes D'Jenn wanted to punch Dormael for his carelessness.

It had been days since he'd gone under, and not a peep had come from him since. Every day he didn't wake was a day he risked falling into the darkness. D'Jenn had always known how strong his cousin could be—how damned stubborn—but it was no comfort. Since he'd gone under after his fight with Jureus, everyone had been chewing on their nails and waiting for him to wake.

D'Jenn had finally taken the afternoon to spend some time to himself. Shawna hadn't left Dormael's side, and Bethany had disappeared into the halls somewhere. Dormael's rooms at the Conclave were pleasant, but the presence of an inert body made any room feel oppressive. D'Jenn had needed to get out.

His own rooms were tidy, with artistic choices that lent themselves to his subdued tastes. There was no reason to decorate everything in sight with garish tapestries full of people stabbing each other or paintings of the gods. Form and function were much more favorable.

D'Jenn sat with his eyes closed, his magic reaching out to a stand sitting a few links away from him. The two pieces of armor he had taken from the Aeglar Cultists—a greave and a bracer—sat next to each other, humming their discordant notes through the ether. They were made of steel and decorated with swirling patterns in brass. D'Jenn's eyes traced the knotted patterns, which turned in on themselves and seemed to twist away into nothingness—though observation revealed it to be a trick of the eye. There was a mathematical function to the pattern, a solution he wasn't seeing. D'Jenn was certain, but he wasn't sure how yet to go about the formula's deconstruction.

There were a few tests one could do on pieces such as this to determine their basic nature. The first was simply to toss magic at them—which Dormael had tried, earning himself the effect of being Splintered. The second was to delve them with the senses and poke them with the barest stream of formless magical energy. In very small amounts, magic did almost nothing—it did, however, highlight the armor's reactions.

The brass pattern in the steel was definitely a spell. No armor D'Jenn had ever seen was joined so perfectly together, the brass laid into the steel in intricate, recessed patterns with no apparent seam between them. The most startling thing, though, was the effect.

The armor created a dissonance which would scatter magical energies. Splintering was the use of one's magic to pierce the power of another. It worked like a needle piercing a bubble, if the bubble was the spell and inside the bubble was magical energy. Burst the bubble, and one released the magic.

The armor, though, looked to create a surface that was, as far as D'Jenn could tell, carpeted with magical needles. Any direct use of power against the armor would result in a Splintering, but only if the armor's dissonance was at a sufficient level to scramble the magic. The two pieces before him uttered a low, irritating tone when placed side-by-side. However, when D'Jenn removed one of them to the other side of the room, the dissonance from either became less bothersome.

The things must work as greater parts of a whole.

If D'Jenn were to wear one of them, it may not afford any protection against magic. Both of them might fend off benign magic, but in order to achieve the Splintering effect, it appeared an entire suit was required. Where would an anti-magic brotherhood like the Cult of Aeglar get magical armor—and high quality magical armor, at that? How did such a thing fit into their religious framework? D'Jenn had always assumed the Cult hated all wizards and wanted the eradication of magic. No one had ever spoken of the Cult possessing infused armor, and such a thing would have been told from the hills to the valleys if it was known. Whoever made this armor knew what they were doing—it was expert craftsmanship.

Only a trained Infuser could have made these.

The problem of the armor could wait until later. His eyes were crossing, and it was time to get out of his rooms. Perhaps it was time D'Jenn called on some of his old classmates. Warlocks worked either in pairs or alone and were always on the move. Such a lifestyle didn't lend itself to friendly visits, and it had been too long since he had traded words.

He hid the Cultist armor beneath his bed and left his rooms in search of old friends.

**

Darkness, cool and quiet, wrapped him in a thick, syrupy embrace. At times it felt like water, holding him upon its surface with soft hands and carrying him on its current. Other times, it felt like the opposite of water—a space, wanting and hollow, pulling against the very fabric of his consciousness, threatening to drag him into silent oblivion.

He would have fought it if he knew how.

"Dormael," said the red-head.

Gods, she's gorgeous.

"You have to drink, you fool," she grumbled. The sky above her was a bright gray hole of roiling clouds—or was that someone else's dream? The answers fled from him like a squad of babbling children, taunting him as he chased them down. The questions, though, remained like scowling hags.

"Drink what?" he said. "There's nothing here to drink."

The woman came with the headaches. Deep, pounding drums in his head made of bright copper, each beat threatening to pop his eyes from their sockets. He would groan and cover them when the world intruded, trying to hold them against that terrible beat. Sometimes it felt like trying to hold his head together while his bastard skull was trying to break apart. Soothing hands held to him, struggling against his efforts. The hands couldn't understand the pain.

The darkness would come again when the drums shattered his head. It came on like a promise, a soothing companion too long kept from his embrace. With her arms around his chest, things were easier, warmer, silent. The trick was not to go too deep—he'd heard that somewhere—so he resisted when she whispered her promises and tried to pull him deeper.

"Oh no, I know your tricks," he said. "It's cold down there. We're not supposed to go."

"Go where?" the red-head asked. "Where are we going?"

"You tell me," he grumbled, angry as the sky intruded on his sight. "You *fucking* tell me!"

Drums, choking water over his chin, and agony against the inside of his skull.

Sometimes things moved in the darkness—skittering, slimy things he could hear in the distance. The blackness made it impossible to tell if the things could sense him, so he huddled, floating along this disembodied river of shadow, and hoped nothing could swim by and take a bite from him. Sometimes he could hear wailing cries from the dark, calling and answering each other in a mournful conversation.

"You've taken me too deep," he said. "There are things in here with me."

Only silence answered him.

Once, he awoke to the beating of the drums and no one was there. His head was a series of bright explosions, each one building upon the one before. Above him, the stars stretched as far as he could see, like a thousand candles in the black river that carried him on the other side. No one came, but the stars comforted him until the darkness pulled him back into its embrace.

More and more, between the warm periods of darkness and the cutting light, something would keep him company in the shadow. He could feel it beside him, feel its silent regard as it slid its attention over him, along him, and through him. It crouched beside him in the darkness like a mountain, like something so massive that its breadth was beyond comprehension. It didn't breathe so much as wax and wane with an ancient, terrible rhythm.

"Who are you?" he asked. "I can feel you there."

"You know who I am," she sighed. "You've been unconscious, you fool. Are you alright? You make a lot of noise in your sleep." Her hair was like fire, the gray sky igniting it from behind.

"I wasn't talking to you," he grumbled.

"Well, just let me know when you've got something to say."

She patted his chest, kissed his forehead, and filled his mouth with cold water.

He knew the thing would be there when he went under again. It waited in the darkness like an old lizard, watching from a hole for its prey to wander by. He could feel its attention. If he had eyes in this place, he might be gazing at the thing from behind some thin, tenuous barrier—man and thing, wondering what to say to each other through the veil.

The thought made him laugh, but the feeling flew from him like a bird from his hand.

He reached toward it. He knew it was there, could feel it

looking at him. He was tired of waiting for the thing to eat him, to pull him beyond the veil, or whatever the thing planned on doing to him. Some mad urge pushed him to act, so he pushed at the veil, poked at it, and reached toward that alien presence just beyond it.

The thing reached back.

In a blink, the pressure keeping them apart popped like a bubble, and the thing was touching him, grasping his mind like a branch in a flood. He held to it, grasping the thing just as hard in return, as if it was a game between the two of them. The darkness seemed to spiral around them, though such a thought was senseless.

The thing entered his mind like a creature burrowing into the ground. He thrashed, fought, screamed into the darkness, but nothing he did could keep it out. It felt alien, vast, and ancient. It rooted around in his thoughts, sifting through them as if they were documents stacked on a desk. He balked at such an intrusion, but there was nothing he could do.

"You can't just root around in my *thoughts* like that!" he grumbled. "They're mine!"

"I think you're actually getting crazier as the swelling goes down," she said. "Nothing in your thoughts I want to see—believe me." She sighed, her eyes welling with pity. "You're scaring the girl, you know. You need to get better."

More drums, always the drums. He didn't know what the woman was talking about, but guilt gnawed at him like a starving dog. He held his eyes against the beat of those gods-damned drums.

"Tell her I'm sorry."

Tell whom you are...sorry?

The thing shifted in the darkness, turning its vast, terrible eye upon him.

For what are you sorry?

"I...I don't know."

Odd. The ancient thing spoke the word to him as if it was unsure of the meaning.

"What are you?" he whispered, the darkness around them pressing him into quietude.

I am...I am one, the thing replied, tasting the words as if they were an old coat that didn't fit. *I am one where once there was two.*

I am one.

"One?" he whispered back, unsure what the thing meant.

Yes. One. Only.

"Alone," he nodded, understanding. "You are alone."

Alone, the thing repeated, the word drawing out in his mind. *Yes. Alone.*

Then, with more anger, *ALONE.*

The word punched into his consciousness like a fist, vibrating everything that made him who he was. He held to the fabric of his soul, trying to keep the intrusive thing from destroying him. The being only sat in his mind, though, like a rock in a pond—or a piece of it did. The darkness continued to spin around them, the peaceful river of black becoming a storm.

"Where do you come from?" he asked, his mind going blank of anything else.

Not this place. This is not your place.

"No," he said, "this is not my place."

You must go, before they come.

His mind gave an involuntary shudder at the thing's words. The black continued to whirl out of control, as if the presence of the thing were sending the darkness into chaos.

"Before what comes?"

The thing released him, leaving his mind like a flash of lightning. He reeled, the darkness around him shuddering with the pounding of drums. Something wailed in the darkness—something close. Its voice was like the screech of a predator bird, if a bird could grow to the size of a horse cart. The blackness undulated around him, vibrating with the anticipation of violence.

You must go.

"How?" he asked, but the thing was gone before he could get a reply. The darkness, once teeming with that ancient presence, was now empty around him. He floated inside, exposed to whatever beast was making that awful wailing. It was coming closer, as if it was casting around in the darkness, and it sounded angry. Its cries evoked a primitive response within him, the need to burrow into a hole until the beast passed him.

Something struck him in the chest, pushing him through the darkness. The surrounding blackness erupted with angry wailing. He felt the distinct sensation of being flung through some kind of barrier.

Agony turned his world white.

**

"Dormael!"

Shawna restrained his shoulders, her hands cool against his fevered skin. She stared down into his eyes, and a worried look passed between them. Dormael realized he was clutching her wrists in a death-grip and loosened his fingers. Sweat coated his naked skin beneath a multitude of blankets, and his eyes hurt with every painful beat of his heart. His head was a throbbing jumble of pain.

"Shawna?" he croaked. His throat was dry, too.

Fuck the gods.

"Do you know any other red-heads who would be taking care of you?" she asked. Dormael started to answer, but she held up a finger. "No—I shouldn't have asked. I don't want to know." Her expression softened into a tentative smile. "Are you alright?"

"I hurt," he mumbled. "Water?"

She went for a decanter on a bedside table, and Dormael blinked as his eyes absorbed the low candlelight in the room. His muscles felt sore and watery. Shawna pressed a wooden cup into his hands, and Dormael gave her the most grateful look he could muster. He'd have kissed her for that water.

He'd have kissed her anyway, truth be told.

A large fireplace dominated the room, all granite bricks and dark iron bars in flowing patterns. A roaring fire burned inside, filling the room with pleasant heat. Two tapestries hung from either side of the fireplace, adding large swaths of color to the dark wood paneling on the walls.

The first was a large depiction of a man in resplendent armor being pulled from his horse by a horde of angry beast-men. It was called *The Fall of Tirrin* and depicted the foolish Farra-Jerran Kansil who had been lost in the Gathan Mountains. Dormael had always liked it because of the moral behind the story of Tirrin— not to fall to hubris—and the mastery of this particular depiction. The amount of detail, even down to the teeth in the beastly Garthorin, was astounding.

The tapestry on the right side of the fireplace was half again as large as the first and depicted two men facing off across the yellow-brown sands of a desert. The first man was wild, wearing flowing black robes and holding a large, curving scimitar. The second man was smaller and wore simple traveling clothes. Fire, lightning, and ice erupted between the two of them—a magical battle depicted at an impasse. The tapestry was called *Gimmael Facing Morvlund the Mad.*

Gimmael was a folk hero amongst the wizards of the Conclave—to the Warlocks especially. Morvlund the Mad was a Rashardian mystic who had used his power to make a bid on the Holy Throne. Morvlund had committed a number of atrocities and used his power to kill innocents. The Conclave had dispatched four other wizards to kill Morvlund, all of whom he defeated. Gimmael had been the least favorite wizard to take Morvlund down, as he was neither the most powerful, nor most skilled Warlock the Conclave had sent. It was Gimmael, though, who would finally end Morvlund's reign of terror.

We're in my rooms. Dormael sighed with relief. *We're home.*

He took a long sip of water and cleared his throat. "When did we make it here?"

"A couple of days ago," she said. "You've been out cold since the mountain. D'Jenn thought you might not wake at all. Everyone has been worried."

"The Death Sleep," Dormael said. "He thought I had entered the Death Sleep."

"The Death Sleep?"

"It happens sometimes," he said around a cough, "when a wizard draws too much power. They let things get away from them, let the energies spiral out of control. Sometimes having that much power running through you just...breaks the body. You fall asleep, you don't wake. Your body just rots away while you sleep."

"Bethany will be so happy," Shawna sighed. "She's been silent again since you've been asleep. Won't even laugh at your brother anymore."

"Things are bad, then." Dormael managed a smile despite the pain in his skull.

Shawna rose. "Should I go get them?"

"Just give me a moment or two," he said, catching her hand before she could leave. "My head feels like Evmir himself is beating my skull into shape."

She smiled and sat back on the bed beside him.

"Alright," she said. "I suppose it can wait for a moment. They're all scattered, anyway."

Dormael narrowed his eyes. "And you stayed here with me?"

"It was my turn," Shawna replied, raising a challenging eyebrow at his look. "Your brother took lunch, and D'Jenn, breakfast."

Dormael felt a regretful sting, but hid it behind it a long sigh.

"How did you get me here? Drag me in a litter?"

"There was a cart left from the bandits' camp. We tossed you in the back. Thank you, by the way," she said.

"For what?"

"For coming after me, you fool." She smiled and wiped a bit of sweat from his brow.

Dormael let out a breath. "I'd say we could call it even. You've been giving me water every day. At least, I think that was you."

"It was." She coughed, and her cheeks turned pink. "I didn't mind so much. You *were* a bit cranky, though. You're a horrible patient."

"Sorry," he said, "I'll do better next time."

She slapped him on the arm, and they shared a smile. He reached his hand up and prodded at the back of his head, relieved to find no soft spots. It still hurt, but the evidence of the blow he'd taken was gone. His chest throbbed beneath the blankets, and his whole damned body was sore.

"So," he said. "What do you think of the Conclave? Is it the haven of evil you always imagined?"

"No, actually." She smiled. "Everyone has been friendly. Someone important met us here—Victus, I think his name was?"

"He's the Deacon of our Order."

"The what?"

"The head Warlock," Dormael clarified. "He's in charge of all the Warlocks. He answers only to the Mekai, who is the head of the entire Conclave."

"I see," Shawna said. "Things have been quiet since we arrived. I think your head Warlock has been keeping information about us a secret. No one has asked any questions, come calling, or caused any trouble. I think they're waiting to see if you will come around, too. I don't know what they've said to D'Jenn, though."

"It's time to find out." Dormael levered himself to a seated position. "First, though, let's get some food. I could use the walk down to the dining hall, in any case."

"Dormael, you've been asleep for days," Shawna said, putting a restraining hand on his leg. "Your legs will buckle halfway down the stairs, and I'll be carrying you. I'll sit here with you, give you water, but I won't carry you down a flight of stairs."

"You wouldn't do that for me?"

Shawna winked. "It's not ladylike to be seen kicking a man down a flight of stairs."

"You're a terrible person, Shawna Llewan," he said, a laugh making the muscles over his ribs and chest ache with every tug. "Fine. Just yell out the door for an Initiate."

"An Initiate?"

"The kids wearing the blue tunics," he clarified. "They're students in their first four years of study. They have classes, duties, that sort of thing. They'll do everything a full wizard tells them to do."

"Sounds wonderful."

"Just tell them Warlock Harlun needs two plates of food up here, and he needs them yesterday. They'll run to see it done, believe me. If you want, make it harder on them and tell them to bring some milk, too. I've a taste for milk, for some reason."

"Adversity *does* build character." Shawna grinned, but her expression changed, and she moved back from him in alarm. "Dormael! Your...your chest. What *is* that?"

Dormael furrowed his brows and followed her pointing hand. Across his chest, from his neck to his lower ribcage, was a giant bruise in the shape of a three-fingered hand. Cold sweat blossomed on Dormael's brow, and he poked at the painful bruise with one finger. It hurt to the touch just as any other bruise would.

The memories of the black, of the ancient voice, of the creature who had pushed him from the darkness came flooding back in a moment of clarity.

"Shawna," he breathed, "call for D'Jenn. Send an Initiate for him."

"What is that thing, Dormael?" she asked, staring at the bruise in horror.

"I don't know."

**

D'Jenn walked the halls of the Conclave Proper, nodding to people he knew in passing. He saw a few faces he recognized from his First Four, in the days before he had been selected for Warlock training. Those people, though familiar, may as well have been strangers to him now. The years had dimmed his emotional connection to the memories of his early childhood.

When an Initiate completed his First Four in the Conclave—which was full of classes on nature, philosophy, magical theory, literature and mathematics—they were given a choice as to which Discipline they wanted to pursue. There was only one Discipline that was not open for choice—the Warlocks. Instead, the Warlocks chose their recruits from the most promising students. Once a child was offered a position in the Warlocks, they had one chance to make that choice. If a child declined, they were never offered a position again. Many declined.

When an Initiate was accepted into the Warlocks, their training was intensified. While other students were perfecting crafts, or deepening their understanding of the world, Warlocks were trained to kill. Every day of training was a test. The children were organized into classes by their generation, and the classes were always small. In D'Jenn's generation, there were only twenty-four students to be accepted. Only fifteen had completed the training.

Students were pitted against each other in elaborate war-games. Other tests revolved around cunning, or strategy. Competition was the theme behind every situation—Victus believed that only adversity could hone his students' abilities.

Alliances and close friendships always developed as a result. D'Jenn often wondered, in quiet moments, whether Victus had designed things that way. Was the form of his training something the Conclave had always done, or was the entire thing the brainchild of Victus Tiranan? D'Jenn smiled as he remembered times when he had cursed his Deacon, cursed the Warlocks, cursed ever having come to the Conclave for one reason or another. Warlock training was not easy. Looking back, though, he often felt as if those were the best times in his life.

The first person D'Jenn went looking for was Vera.

Even as he thought of her name, a smile came to his lips. She would shit two golden marks to hear the story of the past winter, and he knew she would want to meet Shawna and Bethany. There was no one whose insight he would value more than hers.

Her door, though, was cold and silent. He knew as soon as he knocked that no one was behind the door, and could feel the stillness of the room beyond. His magic fluttered in and sniffed about, but he could tell from the sound of the dusty air that she hadn't been there in a while. Disappointment rose in his guts.

"D'Jenn," said a voice behind him.

D'Jenn turned to find Mataez, one of his classmates, standing in the hallway behind him. Mataez was a Runemian with short, dark hair. He was a stocky fellow but agile in his way. D'Jenn smiled, but the look on Mataez's face made the expression die on his lips.

"What's with that look, brother?"

"You were...looking for Vera?" Mataez gestured at the door.

"I was," D'Jenn said. "Why are you looking at me that way?"

Mataez's expression fell. "No one's told you, I guess."

"Told me what, Mataez?" A cold feeling crawled into D'Jenn's stomach.

"Vera," Mataez said. "I'm sorry, but she died, brother. She's dead."

D'Jenn's eyes went to the door. A spike of confused emotion went through his chest before he could stop it. It was there and gone in a flash, like a sword made of ice.

"She's dead," D'Jenn repeated.

"I'm sorry, brother," Mataez sighed. "Gods, somebody should have fucking told you. How long have you been back?"

"A couple of days." His voice felt empty.

"Eindor's blighted eye." Mataez came up and clasped arms with D'Jenn, pulling him into a one-armed embrace. "I'm sorry you've got to hear it like this, mate. From me, too—I'm the worst with this sort of thing, you know?"

"When did it happen? *How* did it happen?" His head still felt a bit cloudy as he tried to make sense of what he'd just heard. How could the woman have died? She was one of the most resourceful people D'Jenn knew.

That I used to know, he corrected. The voice in his head was angry.

Mataez shook his head. "Let's go down to the dining hall, brother. You're going to want a drink in your hand to hear this story."

"Why?"

"It's not just Vera, brother. It's Taglion, Jastom, and Kirael, too."

D'Jenn scoffed. That was nearly a third of their entire class, all dead. How could such a thing be true?

"What? That doesn't make sense," he said. "Why wasn't I told of this?"

"Did you check your missives, brother?"

"Of course I checked my fucking missives, Mataez," D'Jenn snapped before he could stop himself. He took a breath and held up his hand in apology. "I'm sorry. This is just...surprising."

Mataez waved off his apology. "I understand. We all know how you felt about her. She was family, you know. There's so few of us, mate. We all loved her."

"I know," D'Jenn sighed. "And the others? How did this happen?"

"Lost at sea," Mataez said. His voice was flat, wooden. "No one really knows, mate. But the speculation on the ship was paid out to the families of the crew—that much we do know. I looked into it myself. It's been a rough year, D'Jenn. You and your cousin just disappeared on us. Where is he? Is he alright?"

"He's in his rooms," D'Jenn muttered. How could so many of them have died at once? It didn't seem possible. "You should go and see him. He's hurt."

"Is it bad?"

"We don't know anything yet," D'Jenn shrugged. His eyes wouldn't leave Vera's door. No wonder the room beyond had felt so cold to his senses. "Go, look in on him. I'm going to take a walk."

"I'm sorry you had to hear it like this, D'Jenn," Mataez said, a grimace on his face. "The Deacon will tell you what happened, I'm sure. He's been busy all season. All of Eldath is going crazy, brother. The gods are shitting on us all."

"Looks that way," D'Jenn said.

Mataez offered him a pained smile and walked in the direction of Dormael's rooms. D'Jenn let out a long sigh and sat back against the wall. The reunion he had been hoping for would never happen. So many of his friends were dead. How was such a thing possible?

D'Jenn's eyes went to the door once again, and he contemplated going inside. The smell of Vera's hair came to mind, a spicy scent she bought from a vendor in the East Market. The memory drove another cold spike into his heart, and he had to turn his eyes away from the door.

There was no way he could go inside. The sight of the room, bare of her presence, would stick with him forever. He didn't want to remember that sight, so he decided not to expose himself to it.

Did she write before the end?

D'Jenn had been passing letters with Vera for years. The Warlocks maintained a mail office in the Conclave Proper, a drop where classmates could leave communications with one another. Vera and D'Jenn, though, had established their own drop site after their first year in training, and had continued to use it in the years since.

D'Jenn rose and walked down the hall. He found one of the narrow stairways that Initiates and servants used to move about the tower and slipped into the darkened passageway. A few twists and turns took him to the ground level, and he rushed out through a side passage and onto the Green.

The Conclave had a large campus, and there were places tucked away in the corners of the grounds that people rarely traveled. Such places were perfect for a pair of amorous youths looking for a bit of privacy to paw away at one another. D'Jenn and Vera had set up their letter-drop near the place where they had spent so much exploratory time together.

He would have run across the damp grass, but attracting attention went against his instincts. Even if Vera was dead, he wanted this little secret between them preserved. There were many people strolling through the Conclave grounds, and D'Jenn didn't want to deal with their interested gazes.

He followed a stone path to the southeastern corner of the campus. There, in a little-used park, was a bronze fountain that hadn't spewed water in years. A patio surrounded the fountain, and it had a small, weathered shrine to Neesa, Goddess of Love and Music. The little stone statue had a space hollowed beneath it—

one that D'Jenn and Vera had created. They had written a ward into the base of the shrine that would allow no one but the two of them to open it. Even as he approached the fountain, he could feel the magic resonating from the statue.

He reached out with his Kai and unlocked the magical ward. The statue of the goddess felt gritty beneath his hands, and the stone was cold. Lifting the statue from its base, he looked into the space beneath it. There, tucked into the leather folder they had used, sat a single letter, folded and sealed with a dollop of wax. D'Jenn stared at the thing.

Part of him wanted to rip it open and devour the words contained within like a dying man eating his last meal. Still, another part wished to preserve it, to hold on to the missive until his last dying day. They were, after all, Vera's last words to him.

The letter felt like a terrible weight as he pulled it out.

The wax was sealed with a blank stamp, yellow and gummy from the moisture in the air. D'Jenn held it for a moment, unable to open it and unable to put it away. It lingered in his grasp like a prophecy. Should he read it and know the secret of Vera's last message? If he did, he would crouch over the thing every night for weeks, trying to derive meaning from every single word, every turn of phrase. He would agonize over those words. If he didn't read it, though, the letter would weigh in his pocket like a lodestone, a constant reminder that she was gone.

Grimacing, D'Jenn tucked the letter away.

He sat staring at the fountain for a long time, the message weighing his pocket to the spot. Finally he rose and turned away from the Conclave Proper. The campus was large, after all, and a walk would clear his thoughts.

He resolved never to visit the fountain again.

**

"The only possible explanation is Mind Flight," said Victus Tiranan, Deacon of the Warlocks.

Victus was a large man, and he was built more like a blacksmith than a wizard. He had a wild mass of pitch-black hair and a beard just as unruly as his hair. He was swathed in a heavy, dark blue robe—which Dormael was sure concealed a knife or two—and his meaty hands tapped a nervous rhythm on the table's surface. His single golden ring of office, two sinuous bands woven together, practically shone against the skin of his sun-browned hands. Dormael had always thought he seemed out of place at the Conclave, like some beastly nomad dressed in a robe and taught pleasantries he barely understood.

Despite his wild appearance, Victus was one of the smartest people Dormael had ever known and was widely regarded as the next in line for the office of Mekai. Unlike most of his colleagues—the Deacons of the other disciplines in the Conclave—Victus had an almost military bearing and a deep dedication to his mission. Dormael held an unshakable respect for the man, who had overseen not only his training, but the training of all the Warlocks.

Victus was loved by the Warlocks, and he was hated by the other Deacons.

"Mind Flight is not the *only* possible explanation," a woman said from down the table. "We have to consider the possibility that young Dormael's mind was in an advanced state of sleep, and the entire episode was created by his Kai."

Lacelle—the Deacon of Philosophers—was among the other Deacons who hated Victus.

She was everything Victus was not—willowy, graceful, and light. Lacelle had the sort of icy beauty one might find on a statue of an ancient queen. Her hair was straight, and it was a shade of blond so light that it was almost silver. Her eyes were the color of a wintry sky. She stared at Victus with undisguised disdain and tapped her own ring of office against the table to illustrate her points.

"Physical manifestations of magic are a known phenomenon, Victus, as are descents into madness," she clipped. "Why must you complicate this—something that could endanger the people around your Warlock—with talk of Mind Flight? Where did Dormael's consciousness go, Victus? Into the Void? Maybe to the place where the faeries live?"

"Don't mock me, woman," Victus grumbled. "Just once, I'd like to have a discussion where you were acting like a Deacon instead of a petulant child."

"*Child*?" Lacelle sneered, a laugh bubbling from the edges of the word. "Let's talk about who's being childish. You have a mistaken urge to protect your Warlocks—like a child with his favorite toy who's unable to admit when one of them is broken."

Dormael winced. Lacelle could indeed be right, but her comment made him feel somehow guilty, as if he was lying about what he'd seen, or that he had misunderstood. He had a sudden urge to speak up and counter her arguments, but he disciplined himself to silence.

What's the gods-damned point?

The argument had been going on for almost an hour.

The large room—lovingly referred to as the War Room by Warlocks—was paneled in white plaster and hung with multiple tapestries that depicted victories by Warlocks of the past. There was a larger and more detailed version of *Gimmael Facing Morvlund the Mad* than the one hanging in his room. He spent a few moments following the lines of the artwork. Though the argument between the two Deacons concerned him, they were already to the point of the conversation where they were repeating themselves and hurling insults.

"I know my Warlocks, Lacelle," Victus said, slapping the table for emphasis, "and Dormael's head is as fine as it ever was. You tested his lucidity yourself. The simple fact that he woke up discounts the theory that his mind was broken, or that his magic was wild. There were no occurrences of wild magic reported either by him or his companions on the road here. It *must* be something else, and I just don't see why his testimony is considered suspect."

"His companions are not reliable witnesses. One of them is his cousin, the other his brother, and another his *concubine*," Lacelle replied, the disdain clear in her voice. "Do you really wish to posit those three as examples of objectivity?"

Dormael made to object, but Victus gestured for him to be silent.

"What exactly is your problem, Lacelle?" Victus snarled, leaning forward in his seat as if he meant to take a bite out of the woman. "The Baroness Llewan is not his concubine, and even if she was, that's no business of anyone else in this room."

Why did the Mekai invite Lacelle in the first place?

If the woman was going to be hostile, and on such a personal level, he didn't see what value she would add to the conversation. Philosophers didn't understand the world outside the Conclave in the way the Warlocks did. They knew the natural world, the sciences, and philosophies, but people were beyond them.

Lacelle was never objective when it came to the Warlocks. It was rumored that Victus and Lacelle had once been lovers, and they'd only become enemies after having a vicious row. Lacelle went out of her way to make things difficult for Victus, and Victus always repaid her in kind. Their rivalry was legendary amongst members of both Orders.

"My problem," Lacelle continued, "is that you Warlocks always watch out for your own. If it were a Philosopher who suddenly came down with a case of temporary insanity, he would be doubted and rigorously scrutinized. But, since Dormael is one of your Warlocks, he *must* be telling the truth. This is nothing but favoritism. He should be submitted for testing."

"I'm simply looking at the problem from an objective point of view instead of dismissing it because I don't like where it's coming from," Victus said. "He's been tested—*you* tested him, woman!"

"I did a quick delving to see if anything was amiss," she said. "That's not the same thing as a round of rigorous inquiry. He needs to be observed over time, questioned, and tested for a thousand other things. Those things take time, Victus. He should be removed from duty until I clear him for release. Until then, he's a danger."

Dormael shared a stealthy, astonished look with D'Jenn.

"The day I let *you* determine the readiness of *my* Warlocks is the day the gods fucking return. Look at Dormael's chest! Did his Kai cause the bruising? Did he hallucinate *that*?"

"It is possible, my dear Victus. There have been documented cases of magic causing physical harm to those who've wielded it with negligence, or of strange manifestations of power where mental instability was a concern. I could show you the records sometime if you'd like to come to the Philosopher's Tower—you'd have to learn to read first, of course," Lacelle said, her tone dripping acid.

"If you were a man," Victus snarled, "I would have hit you ten times over."

"If *you* were a man," she spat back, "you might have tried and been taught a lesson. Perhaps you'd like to try your hand in a duel?"

"Silence," said a voice from the doorway, bringing the room to immediate stillness.

An older man stood in the opening. He appeared to be somewhere in his seventies, with hunched shoulders and lines of wisdom etched over his features. He had flowing white hair and a beard that rivaled it in both length and color. Intricate silver wire was wound around his beard, cradling it like an eastern lady's headpiece. He was dressed in a simple white robe with black trim and wore a large amulet shaped like the Eye of Eindor woven around a tower—the symbol of the office of the Mekai.

His magic filled the room like mist, its presence more alive than anything Dormael had ever felt. Every wizard's power grew over the years—not only in strength but also in clarity. Arian Hilrath had served as Mekai for longer than Dormael had been alive, and his Kai was formidable.

The Mekai waved a hand as everyone made to rise from their seats, dismissing the custom as he entered the room. Two secretaries entered behind him, and his magic shut the door in their wake with a casual flick. He moved around to the head of the table and sat, acting as if he hadn't noticed the argument. Embarrassed glances went around the table.

"First, let us dispense with greetings." The Mekai turned to Dormael and D'Jenn. "It is good to have you two home again. I'll want to hear of your travels so far. You'll take supper with me?"

"Of course, Honored Mekai," Dormael replied, inclining his head in respect. The Mekai smiled, and Victus appeared to lose some of his anger. Lacelle, however, looked at Dormael as if her sky-blue eyes could stab him through the chest. He did his best to ignore her furious glare.

"Very good, very good, indeed," the Mekai said. "Let us discuss this armlet. Everything else, no matter how strongly we might feel about it, is secondary to this problem. We can discuss other matters at a more appropriate time. For now, I am willing to trust Deacon Victus and his assessment of Dormael's capabilities."

Lacelle straightened. "Honored One—"

"If something odd happens again, we shall revisit your tests," he said. "For now, let us move on."

"Yes, Honored Mekai," she said, nodding her head in respect.

"Good." The Mekai cleared his throat. "Now, Victus has already filled me in on most of the specifics of your tale, boys—finding the

Baroness Llewan, recovering her artifact, and the flight from these Galanians. That should be the first topic of our discussion here—the Galanian Empire."

"The men we fought were led by a man named Grant," D'Jenn said.

"Rengard Grant?" Victus asked.

"I'm not sure if we ever learned his first name," Dormael said. "Shawna put a sword in his skull. His soul has gone to the Void."

"Rengard Grant was the commander of the Red Swords—the Emperor's elite squad of knights. According to my agents, he's been absent from the field for the entire season. No one has seen him in Old Galan or any of the conquered cities under the Imperial flag." Victus nodded his head as if running through facts in his mind. "Now I know where he's been the past winter."

"These Red Swords—to what capacity do they operate within the Empire?" the Mekai said.

"They serve as his elite guard, and he also sends them on special missions, where the fighting is toughest on the field," Victus said. "Emperor Dargorin established the order after winning his war of succession, and it's been a point of honor for Galanian warriors ever since. Serving in the Red Swords earns a man a knighthood, and anyone who completes the training can join their ranks."

"The Emperor's personal involvement in this is troubling," the Mekai said. "How did he know about this armlet in the first place? He'd have to have advisers of a magical nature to care about such a thing. This necromancer you encountered in the Runemian Mountains could be the one behind it. Victus, we'll have to speak about how one of them was moving around within spitting distance of our city."

"I will see to that, Honored One, you have my word," Victus growled. "As for the shade in the fire—it's possible. It's also possible that Dargorin himself is Blessed, and we didn't know. I would think my agents might have reported anything strange about him, but his Blessing could have gone unnoticed. Whoever it was Jureus spoke to in the flames—and whatever his position in the Empire—he's a threat we need to deal with. If Jureus was the apprentice, the master would be much more dangerous. Perhaps we're dealing with a full-fledged *vilth.*"

Everyone went quiet at the ancient word.

Some necromancers only dabbled in the art, as Dormael suspected Jureus had, without steeping to the deeper levels of corruption. The worst of them could do terrible things with their powers. Thankfully they were few and far between, and there had only been a handful in the past few hundred years. Their names were memorized and recited at the Conclave, and their atrocities stayed burned into its memory.

Victor the Unfeeling, who had butchered an entire nomadic tribe in Dannon and used his powers to enslave their dead bodies, was one such name. Stragen Child-Eater, whose favorite activity had earned him his title, and Saarn of the Thorn, who'd used his powers to subvert the king of Shera. Warlocks had hunted them all down.

Vilthinum—that's the word for the worst of them. The corpse-makers, the flesh-eaters.

"Even more troubling," the Mekai said, "is this connection between the Galanians and the *vilth*. If the Galanian Empire is keeping a necromancer in its pocket, it's certainly something we should deal with."

"That line of thought brings up a new set of questions," Lacelle said, leaning back in her chair. "If this *vilth* is indeed powerful enough to have gained apprentices of his own, such as Jureus, then why have we not discovered him? I would think we'd have heard something."

"Perhaps he's stayed quiet, out of sight," D'Jenn said. "Eldath is vast. He could have stayed hidden for years if he didn't let things get out of control. All the *vilthinum* we've studied are the ones whom we've destroyed. They were dumb enough to try to eat entire villages, or take over kingdoms. Maybe this one has played a smarter game."

"But if he is connected to the Emperor—and logic does seem to suggest that—then he's moving within the corridors of power," Lacelle said. "Perhaps the most powerful corridors in all of Eldath, in point of fact. Why would someone with power like this *vilth* serve the ruler of a nation that makes magic a hanging offense? Dargorin must have some sort of leverage over him."

"Stranger things have happened," Victus said. "He could be the Emperor's slave, for all we know."

Lacelle narrowed her eyes. "Yes, but what possible thing could be held against a *vilth*? History shows us that they sever ties to everything that makes them human. The only thing Dargorin could give him would be power, and that's something their dark god already grants them. Why serve the Emperor?"

Victus shrugged. "Maybe it's the *vilth* using Dargorin."

The Mekai nodded. "This warrants an investigation. I suspect you already have agents inside the Empire?"

"Of course, Wise One," Victus said.

"Good. Have them dig for answers." The Mekai turned to the willowy Deacon of Philosophers. "Lacelle, send a word to our friends at the School of Magical Arts. Ask them to search through their records for anything regarding rogue wizards cast out of the Tower within the last fifty years."

"The last fifty years, Wise One?" Lacelle asked.

"Indeed. *Vilthinum* can sometimes prolong their lives through the use of their art. It never hurts to be thorough. In fact, go back seventy years."

Lacelle bowed her head. "It will be done, Honored Mekai."

"Very well," the Mekai said. "Also, have a team look through the Archives to see if they can find any mention of a relic with power such as this armlet. I will study the thing itself. Dormael, can you inform the Baroness Llewan that I wish to call upon her? Any information she can give would be of greatest assistance."

Dormael nodded. "Of course, Wise One."

"Good. Then let us adjourn this meeting and rest a bit before dinner. I am ever tired, these days," the Mekai said, favoring them with a warm smile. "My old bones, you understand."

Victus placed his hands on the table. "Honored Mekai, there is another matter that needs discussing."

"Do go on then, Deacon Victus." The Mekai sighed and settled back into his seat.

"I've received reports that the Galanians are rounding up Sevenlanders within their borders."

Dormael and D'Jenn shared a covert glance. Dormael had heard rumors of this from the Administrator in Mistfall, but they had sounded far-fetched to both him and D'Jenn. To hear it now, coming from the mouth of someone he respected, was odd. If Victus was saying it, maybe it was true.

"Yes," the Mekai said. "I've heard rumors of this, though I thought it nothing more than idle street-talk. Do you have more information?"

Something in the eyes of the Mekai piqued Dormael's interest. He had been trained to read people, to perceive when they were emotionally distressed or being duplicitous. He couldn't help but watch the expressions of the others, trying to measure their emotional state. Lacelle, of course, was irritable. Victus had the same training, so his features were schooled to blandness. The Mekai's face, though, was telling a different story. The tightening around the eyes, the slight rise in the chin—the Mekai was suspicious.

"I do." Victus nodded. "Most of it has come in recent reports. I was going to gather more information before I brought this to your attention, Honored One, but the story Dormael and D'Jenn told us makes this ever more poignant. It's not just Sevenlanders they're rounding up—it's wizards from the Mage Tower in Lesmira, too. I've received missives from friends in Tauravon, and they're concerned about the encroachment of the Empire. Neleka was on their southern border, and now they have the Empire in its place."

"Neleka was hostile to the Blessed," the Mekai pointed out. "They were no great friends of the School of Magical Arts. In fact, the Empire only hangs the Blessed it finds—Neleka used to drag them through the streets, stone them, and burn them at the stake. One would think things on Lesmira's southern border would be calm. I've received no letters that suggest otherwise. Blessed could not go openly into Neleka before, and they cannot do so now. You've confirmed these reports?"

Victus gave a grim nod. "I have, Honored One. I ask your permission to authorize a rescue operation. We should not allow the Empire to detain our people in camps."

The Mekai considered his words in silence. Dormael could tell the old man was torn. The rest of the room waited for his answer as the silence drew out. Finally, the Mekai stood and shook his head.

"I cannot authorize you to do that, Victus."

"Wise One?" Victus asked, his expression surprised.

"We cannot destroy these camps just yet. Such a thing would not only swing public attitudes against us, but would also put more of our people in danger over the course of the next few years. If we use magic against the Galanians, we'd be tearing down the laws made in the wake of the Second Great War."

"So we let our people suffer for politics? Wise One, I implore you to reconsider!"

"Not politics, Deacon Victus, but the law and good sense. We will send them what aid we are able, but until we can somehow get our people released without violence, I cannot allow it to happen."

"But Mekai, our people are dying in those camps!" Victus growled.

Dormael was appalled. He'd never seen anyone—much less Victus—speak to the Mekai in such a way. The words of the Administrator of Mistfall danced around his memory.

There's a lot of anger for the Mekai...

The Mekai's eyes hardened. "Our people die every day, Deacon Victus. People die of disease, of starvation, of murder. People die of old age. Someday, if you come to be in my position, you will be forced into the unenviable task of making decisions not only for your Warlocks but *all* members of the Conclave. What you ask is to take action on behalf of civil matters—and that's *not* the mandate of your Order."

"Honored One, I *must* insist—"

"Must you?" the Mekai asked, raising his voice the tiniest amount. His magic roiled in anger, thrashing around the room like an invisible flame. "The Warlocks were founded to deal with *magical* threats, Deacon, not to go to war on behalf of the Sevenlands. If this *vilth* shows his face, I will gladly send you and all your people screaming for his blood. I will *not*, however, bend the laws put in place after the Second Great War so we can swoop in like misguided saviors!"

The room rang with his exclamation.

Taking a deep breath, the Mekai went on in a more measured tone. "I know the urge to do something is great—do you think I do not feel it? We should lay them low with our power, teach them never to shake their swords in our direction—correct? That is exactly the thinking that brought the Conclave into the Second Great War. It is exactly the kind of thinking that saw entire armies and whole cities destroyed with magic. Every Mekai since then has endeavored to preserve those edicts written during the

Atonement, when we learned the responsibility inherent in Eindor's Blessing. What you're seeking requires their complete disregard, and I will *never* allow that. I will bring this matter to the attention of the Tal-Kansil and the Council of Seven. Until then, you have your orders, and you are all dismissed."

The Mekai strode from the room, ignoring the muttered platitudes offered to his back. The secretaries looked horrified as they scurried in his wake. The old man's power crawled down the hallway after him like a living spider made of invisible mist.

Will my power be so potent, so alive, when I'm his age?

Dormael's power was already vast, and as he'd aged, he'd felt it sharpening in some indescribable way, deepening by tiny degrees. It was rare that a wizard got to be the Mekai's age without killing himself or retreating from society in order to better commune with their own power. From what Dormael understood, it became harder and harder to control magic as one got older, and it intruded more into everyday life.

Dormael had never seen the Mekai without his Kai singing. The old man had once told him that as he aged, it grew more difficult to hold the power inside. He said it was something like holding an unruly dog to a leash—if that dog could toss lightning or set things aflame. Things like closing doors, lighting candles, or reaching for a cup happened automatically, as if the magic knew what he wanted.

The bruise on Dormael's chest hummed against his skin.

"Dormael—are you going soft in the head, boy?" Victus asked.

Dormael blinked—Lacelle was gone, leaving Dormael and D'Jenn alone with Victus. The room felt cavernous in the absence of so many wizards and their angry magic. Dormael let out a long sigh, stretching his shoulders.

"Aye, sorry," Dormael said. "Just...thinking, I guess. I must've dozed off."

"Open your ears, boy. The three of us need to talk." Victus ran his hands through his wild hair, narrowing his eyes at the table in thought. Dormael and D'Jenn shared another meaningful look as he gathered himself. Victus had always been gruff, but never so openly disrespectful, and never so outwardly angry.

The suspicion on the Mekai's face stuck out in Dormael's mind. *Why would the old man be suspicious of Victus Tiranan, of all people?*

"First, I'm glad you boys are home again," Victus said. "I know I've said it before, but it's true, and for more reasons than one. My Warlocks are like family to me, you know that. It's good to have two of my best back in one piece—though I know you were taking an unauthorized vacation, Dormael. We'll talk about that soon enough, but for now, just know I'm glad you boys are alive. Galanian Red Swords...the world is going mad, boys. It's going fucking mad."

"Deacon," D'Jenn began, his words coming in a slow, careful manner, "that bit about the Galanians rounding up Sevenlanders. Are you sure of those reports?"

"As sure as I am about anything. Why do you ask?"

"Just sounds unlikely." Dormael massaged the soreness in his chest. "Why would the Galanians care about the Sevenlands? They'd have to cross the sea to get here, and they have a war of conquest going at home. Begging trouble from us would be a crazy."

"Ah, that's the word, isn't it?" Victus said. "Insane. Think on what the Galanian Emperor has done so far. He moved against and annexed Neleka, then he took Shundovia before the ink was dry on the treaties. He massed his forces on the southern border of his Empire to move against Moravia—which seems like a sound strategy, considering Moravia owns the other half of Solace Isle with Shundovia."

D'Jenn nodded. "He would get the fertile lands Moravia offers and the goldmines on Solace Isle."

"Aye, but that's not what he did," Victus pointed out. "He's moved north, for Thardin."

"Thardin?" Dormael and D'Jenn said in unison, sharing an incredulous look.

"Aye—the frozen, mountainous home of bearded killers itself." Victus rapped his fist on the table. "He moved his forces to his northern border during the autumn, and there's been fighting in Thardin all winter."

"It's madness to attack Thardin in the middle of winter," Dormael said.

D'Jenn snorted. "It's madness to attack Thardin at all. No foreign army has ever conquered Thardin, but to enter the passes when they're locked with ice? He's going to lose half his army just to frostbite and disease."

"Exactly," Victus said. "So why, do you think, would he risk such a thing?"

"Whatever it is, it must be important." Dormael leaned back in his seat. "We should probably reconsider his actions in light of what we know about the armlet and this *vilth* who was speaking with Jureus."

"I knew you'd shake something loose in there, eventually." Victus gestured at Dormael's head. "You're right. What doesn't make sense?"

D'Jenn stroked his goatee in thought, looking out the window. Dormael ran through things in his mind, ticking them off one by one and trying to place them into some meaningful context. Dormael thought back to what he knew of the Galanian conquests.

"First," Dormael said, "the massacre at Old Shundov. Why would Dargorin have killed the entire Royal family when he hadn't done anything of the sort before or since? One of the things I found surprising during my time in Neleka was how bloody lenient the Galanians were. None of the sort of thing you might expect—orgies of blood, political purges, rapes. The war was bloody, but the transition to Imperial leadership was as smooth as it could have been."

D'Jenn nodded. "Also, this bit about the camps. Why round up Sevenlanders at all? Why borrow trouble from us? Sure, westerners are hated in the east, but no more than taxes. It doesn't fit the rest of the picture."

"And now, Thardin," Dormael said. "Instead of going after the gold and fighting a winter campaign on the sun-browned hills of Moravia, he leads his men into the snowy passes of the north in the worst part of the year for a campaign."

"Somehow, this *vilth* is involved," Victus grumbled. "The massacre I cannot explain—yet. The camps, though...think on this, boys. If you were a maniac who had designs on ruling the world, what would be one of the first things you would do?"

"Identify the greatest threats, figure out how to take them down," Dormael said without hesitation—a force of habit from his days as Victus's student.

Victus gave him an approving nod. "And there are only two

centers of magical power in the world—the Conclave and the School of Magical Arts. Military might is well and good, but he'll never take Lesmira or the Sevenlands that way, and he knows it. We know he wants the armlet, and we know he's working with this *vilth*. He must know that dabbling with magic would draw our attention. Perhaps he's looking for weaknesses, planning an operation we're too blind to see coming. Our distance from Galania may protect us, but it won't protect Lesmira. I'm telling you, boys—something big is happening. I can taste it on the gods-damned wind."

Dormael had echoed those feelings since the Stormy Sea, when he'd watched the Galanian ship fade into the distance, its sails burning against the dark waves. If the Galanian Emperor was seeking weapons of such immense power, there was trouble enough to worry about. Victus was rarely wrong in his assessments.

"What about Thardin?" D'Jenn said.

"There must be something there that would motivate him to spend so many lives in pursuit," Victus said. "Can you think of something worth more than thousands of fighting men?"

"The throne itself?" Dormael shrugged.

Victus shook his head. "No. It would have to be something more valuable. Something more useful. More powerful."

"Infused items," D'Jenn said. "Maybe he wants Ice Shard, the sword of Thardish Kings."

"Why else would he risk so much?" Victus said. "He has gold already. Armies?—He's got those. Thrones? Hells, the Galanian Empire has *three* of them. Whatever he's after in the frozen passes of Thardin must be important. And mark my words, boys—it won't be good for us."

"Or anyone," Dormael agreed.

Victus looked to the door and waved a hand. His Kai whispered out and weaved a quick ward around the room, barring anyone from listening to their conversation. Dormael and D'Jenn shared another covert, suspicious glance.

Victus put his hands on the table. "I know I can count on your discretion—right, boys?"

"Of course," Dormael said. "We would never betray the Conclave."

D'Jenn nodded his agreement.

Victus leaned forward. "Listen, boys—I don't think the Mekai realizes the danger this poses. The Deacons are just as blind. They're not trained to see the patterns, they don't recognize the knife waiting in the dark."

"We can investigate, then." D'Jenn shrugged. "Gather the evidence to convince him."

Victus sighed. "We all know things are bad—we can see it. It isn't just *this*, you know. There's violence in the south, some war between the Rashardians. The Galanian Empire is on the march again, and now this *vilth* has appeared—and mark my words, boys, Jureus probably wasn't his only apprentice. The Sheran Oligarchy is deteriorating, and there are rumors of a horde of Dannon horsemen massing on the steppe. All of Eldath is going to shit, boys. Things are going to get bad in the next few years."

Dormael hadn't heard the news about the Dannon. He thought back to their flight into the Darkroot, on the southern edge of the steppe, and the sight of the grasslands spread out to the north. There had been no campfires, no tribes massing for war.

One thing that was always certain, though, was the speed at which things could go to shit.

Victus continued. "Lots of people—myself included—don't think the Mekai is up to this challenge. He's old, boys. We've had relative peace with the rest of the world for a long time, and he's not ready to deal with the coming wars."

Dormael furrowed his brows, but couldn't find the words to reply.

"He serves for life," D'Jenn said. "Unless he steps down. Is he planning on stepping down?"

Victus smiled. "I don't think so, that's not what I meant. I mean that we need to convince him of the danger, to make our points known and understood. Didn't you see how he rushed out of here when the issue was put to him? He doesn't have the stomach for war, boys, and war is what's coming. What if he can't *be* convinced? We may be forced to act on our own."

Dormael shifted in his seat, his eyes glancing to the door. "War is the Tal-Kansil's area of responsibility. The Mekai doesn't lead the Sevenlands to war, and the Warlocks don't fight them."

Victus leaned forward and looked into Dormael's eyes. "What

if the war comes with *vilthinum* and an arsenal of infused weapons? Does that sound like something you'd trust the Tal-Kansil, the Council of Seven, or the Mekai to deal with? Look me in the face, Dormael, and tell me you trust them to see us through a crisis of that magnitude."

Dormael opened his mouth to reply, but stopped the lie before it could escape.

"It won't be just them, though," D'Jenn said. "We'll *all* meet them, if it comes to that. The Council, the Mekai, everyone—we're all on the same side."

And then Dormael saw it. He'd been trained to look for the tiny inflections of voice, the tightening around the eyes, the lips going thin. He didn't believe it at first, not coming from a man like Victus.

But there it was.

"Of course we are," Victus said, his eyes tight and his lips drawing flat. "I just wanted to be sure I could count on you boys to be there, to do what's right when the time comes. To stand behind me when I make my case to him. I would never ask more from you than that."

"Of course you can." Dormael hid his surprise behind a bland look. "We've been loyal to the Conclave since you trained us. You know that."

Victus smiled and stood from the table, hitting it a couple of times with his fist as if to adjourn the meeting. He clapped Dormael and D'Jenn both on the shoulder before moving for the door.

"I know," he said. "You're two of my best Warlocks, boys. It's good to have you home."

With that, he exited the room, leaving Dormael and D'Jenn alone at the huge, dark table.

"Did you catch that?" D'Jenn asked, turning a troubled eye on Dormael.

"Aye." Dormael glanced toward the door. "He was lying."

**

Inera stared over the scene where the camp had once stood, taking stock of the damage. She could feel the power that had been used here undulating over the ground like a misty shadow. It was difficult to sense the residue of power, but she could just manage it.

Jureus had been here—that much she had known already. A large mass grave had been dug on the hill—with magic, of course—and somewhere around thirty bodies were dumped inside. Inera had picked through them, but the corpse of Jureus was nowhere to be found.

The boy was a fool. His death was inevitable.

The Red Swords loitered nearby, shooting Inera nervous glances. They had been with her for long enough to learn the cost of her displeasure. The first man to voice a complaint to her had been killed and made *strega*. No one else had complained.

She delved the grave with her Kai, trying to tease out the melody that clung to the remains like dust on a boot. Magical residue faded with time, but if one got to it fast enough, it was possible to hear the song of the wizard responsible. The wind blew through the passes, filling her ears with noise. Inera took a deep breath and listened harder to the song her Kai was sensing.

It was a charming melody—fast and aggressive, but also pleasant. Inera closed her eyes as she heard it, the song bringing back a flood of memories that almost brought her to her knees. She stood against the tide of emotion welling in her throat and concentrated on keeping her feelings in check.

It couldn't be.

The first time she had heard that song, she had been a different woman. That had been before the invasion. It had been before her capture.

It had been before *him*.

It could not be!

Your feelings are irrelevant, her shadow said, flitting up behind her in the odd way it moved about. *The facts are before you. If you wish to grovel and cry like a sheep, then slit our throat and be done with it.*

"I'm not groveling, nor crying," she said under her breath, hoping the Galanians couldn't hear. Others couldn't see her shadow—not even her Master. He had one of his own, of course. All necromancers did.

You are distressed because you recognize the song of this one. Because you have lain with him, mated with him. This sentiment is weak. You should rid yourself of it as I have been telling you. Only then will our power be enough to take us down the path.

"I'm fine," she hissed.

If anything, this is better than we expected. Use this to our advantage.

Inera kept her answers to herself. She didn't need to talk to the thing, she knew that. It could see into her mind, feel her emotions, experience her life through her senses. The shadow was her connection to the Lord of the Void, her conduit to his power. It was part of her and part of him at the same time.

Even as she turned from the grave, the shadow flew from her in misty fits and spurts, appearing over the shoulders of the different Red Swords in turn. It enjoyed whispering to them, twisting them with slow inevitability. Over the last season, the men had become hers. They had belonged to the Emperor once, but now they enjoyed the tasks to which she employed them.

Turning from the grave, she walked onto a ledge where she could look down upon the valley below. Ishamael stood like a scattering of stones around both sides of the river which was also named for the old Sevenlander chieftain. She could almost feel Dormael there, pulsing like a beacon in the distance. It was nothing more than her fancy, but her memory played her the notes of his Kai as if he were standing next to her. She took a deep breath and drew her cloak around her shoulders again, leaving the ledge behind.

"Let's go!" she snapped at the Red Swords. "I aim to be in Ishamael by tomorrow."

THE TRUTH ABOUT KITAMIN JURILLIC

Wizards strolled the Conclave grounds, filling the air with chattering conversation.

Dormael dodged past them on his way to the river. He tried his best not to favor anyone with a sour look when they searched his face, but it was a difficult thing. His body hurt, his head was killing him, and the constant pall of political turmoil was getting under his skin.

Dormael tried his best to keep his breathing steady. The hand-shaped bruise on his chest throbbed in time with his steps. His body felt like it had been dragged behind a mad horse and trampled for good measure. He knew it was healing—his lucidity was evidence of that—but he wished the damned process would hurry itself along.

He'd woke irritable and restless. Even during his morning meditation, when he'd let his magical senses commune with his environment, he could feel the buzz of tension vibrating in the very stones of the Conclave Proper. It sounded like insects scratching at something just out of sight, a constant burr on the back of his mind.

Warlocks and Philosophers, Hedge Wizards and Scouts—everyone had something to say about the Galanian Empire and whether the Mekai's response was appropriate. Dormael had been surprised to overhear how many of his fellows and friends were angry with the Mekai, as if he had betrayed their people to a foreign enemy. Political discussions in the Conclave were known to be hyperbolic and emotionally charged, but over the last few days, things had taken a darker turn.

The entire feeling of the place was like a simmering pot.

Or the calm before the gods-damned storm.

The Council of Seven had called a meeting two days past—a closed meeting, which was rare in the Sevenlands. Meetings of the Council were open forum by tradition, and any Sevenlander could attend and listen in on the proceedings. This time, however, the Council had closed the great doors of the Hall of Kansils and posted guards around the building to ensure privacy. In all the time he'd been alive, Dormael could count the number of closed meetings of the Council on one hand. The Conclave had held its breath for the outcome.

There had been nothing—no announcements from the heralds, no official proclamations plastered to walls, no meetings of the Conclave Orders or assignments issued to the Warlocks. By the next day, there were open arguments in the hallways of the Conclave Proper, and even Initiates were taking sides. Dormael had stopped an Initiate in the hallway during the evening, asking about a red band he'd tied over his blue tunic. The boy had informed him it was to show solidarity with the prisoners of Galanian death camps, and the color was red for the blood on the Mekai's hands. Dormael had almost smacked the boy. He had commanded the child to remove the band from his uniform and informed him that an Initiate's place was to clean and learn.

He then gave the boy a magic lesson while the lad swept his rooms.

There were two factions in the Conclave. One faction called for patience, diplomacy and faith in the Mekai's judgment, while the other screamed for Galanian blood and the Mekai's immediate resignation from his seat. Various friends had called upon Dormael to ask after which faction he supported. All the Warlocks, of course, spouted Victus's lines as if they'd all read a book he'd written on the subject.

Dormael was conflicted. He felt a deep respect for Victus, but every time he felt his sympathies shifting toward him, he remembered Victus's face during the meeting with the Mekai. He remembered the Mekai's suspicion and Victus's talk of action.

Between the political tension and the unwelcome news of the death of a third of his classmates, Dormael had needed to get out.

Bethany had found him in the morning, wishing to go down to the Bruising Stretch and learn to use her knife. Dormael had sent her there with an Initiate and instructions regarding where she was allowed to go within the Conclave without supervision. Shawna would be there giving impromptu instruction on the proper way to use a blade, so he told her to find Shawna if she got bored. Shawna had become a celebrity on the Bruising Stretch since the moment she stepped foot upon it, which was no surprise. The students followed her with their eyes popping from their heads and drool dropping from their mouths. Bethany would have no trouble locating her.

Dormael had slipped a few daggers into his clothing, tossed a cloak over his shoulders, and left.

He limped to the river which split the Conclave—as it did the entire city—in two. Winding down a white stone path, he descended the stairs to the Conclave Docks, where there were always enterprising citizens willing to ferry a wizard anywhere along the river. A whole troop of them waited alongside the docks, floating in a plethora of boats.

"Where to, Blessed?" asked a young man with short-cropped brown hair and a line of tattoos down one thin forearm. He sat leaning on the side of a beaten old canoe, the oars dipped into the brown water beside him.

"East Market," Dormael replied, grunting as he stepped down into the canoe and got situated, "the quicker, the better." He tossed the young man a few bronze marks. The boy snatched them out of the air, and without another word, pushed out from the Conclave Docks.

Ishamael was an expansive city. It sat in the middle of a valley just on the northern side of the Runemian Mountains, north and west of Soirus-Gamerit. There was a lot argument between Conclave historians about when the city had been founded. Some believed it was one of the first cities in the entirety of the Sevenlands. Others said it was simply the first city built after the Sevenlands had unified. Before that, they said, there was no Ishamael, only the warring city-states of the Vendon people.

Ishamael had no walls, so it had spilled out over the

countryside through the years, growing like moss on tree roots. The residents of Ishamael and the leadership of the Sevenlands had never been afraid of being attacked in their capital city. Even during the turbulent years of the Second Great War, when the Dannon armies had ravaged the Sevenlands, Ishamael had remained unspoiled. In fact, it had been given a wide berth.

No one wanted to attack a city which contained so many of the Blessed.

The day was cold, gray, and bitter. Storm clouds gathered in the mountains, threatening the city with rain. The wind whipped by in no certain direction, blowing the cowl of Dormael's cloak about his head. He ignored it. He was in no mood for storms.

The oars made sloshing noises in the river as the young man dipped them into the green, choppy water. The current was with them, and the canoe slipped through the water at a steady pace. The fishy smell of the river filled Dormael's nose, but it wasn't altogether unpleasant. There was a peacefulness to the river, and Dormael tried his best to soak it in.

The lad was skillful on the oars, and he guided them between the larger vessels crowding the harbor with ease. Ishamael didn't have the thriving coastal markets of Mistfall, but the harbors in Ishamael were abuzz with activity year-round. The boy probably earned more than a dockworker just ferrying people around, especially wizards, who usually had the money to be generous.

The young man pulled the canoe to an innocuous dock. It bumped against the posts, and the lad whipped a rope over it in one deft movement. He pulled the canoe up to the side and gave Dormael a smirk.

"Right. East Market, just like you asked, Blessed."

"Just as I asked," Dormael said, grunting in pain as a muscle in his stomach spasmed.

"I can wait here for you, for a small fee."

"Larger than I'd want to pay you. I'll be getting drunk for the foreseeable future, anyway, lad. I've no plans to come back in your direction."

"A man's got to have priorities, Blessed."

"That he does, boy. Run along, now." He climbed from the canoe and tossed the boy a silver mark—more than ten times what his ride was worth. The boy snatched it from the air and made it disappear in the space of a breath. His smile deepened, and he offered Dormael a seated bow.

"Always a pleasure serving the Conclave, Blessed," the lad said as he pushed off.

"I'm sure," Dormael muttered. He turned to head into the city.

The East Market of Ishamael was a sprawling chaos of taverns, shops, brothels, smithies and vendors who hawked their wares from covered wagons. A web of streets criss-crossed the Market, full of choking points where the sea of humanity slowed to a crawl. Men and women haggled over items of every sort, and children dragged parents to beg for the ownership of new treasures. Dormael enjoyed the press of people and the low buzz of humanity. Having been shut up in the Conclave for a few days, it was nice to be surrounded by conversation that wasn't so charged with anger.

Dormael wove through the throng of people, his pace as quick as he could manage. He shouldered his way between groups of singing drunks and slipped by mothers carrying their babes in tight bundles. He dodged carts and horses, and he smacked the hands of a few cutpurses who tried him. His body hurt, but the movement itself was making him feel better.

Thunder rumbled in the distance, the mountain stirring the coming storm to a boil. Rain began to patter onto the cobblestone streets, and various cheers issued up from the crowd. Dormael pulled his cowl over his head and shrugged deeper into his cloak. He spared a thought for using magic to stay dry, but using any sort of spell would play his melody through the ether, which would alert any nearby wizards to his presence. He wasn't in the mood for attention unless it involved a pretty girl.

Dormael made his way down clogged thoroughfares and curving avenues. He took shortcuts through alleyways full of dirty, mischievous-looking children who melted into the surroundings at the sight of him, like minnows under rocks. His hands hovered near his knives, but most criminals could smell wizards in Ishamael, and most avoided them like the plague.

The rain began in earnest as Dormael reached his destination. He hurried out of the rain and ducked into a squat, three-story building sandwiched between two others much like it. There were six windows facing the street, three of them decorated with sighing women staring at the rain. Today was a working day in Ishamael, which meant the place would be practically empty.

Dormael was fine with that.

The Headless Dancer was a combination brothel, taproom and inn. In one place, the errant traveler could find all the services he needed after a long journey—a cool drink, a soft bed and a soft body for warmth. It was an infamous establishment, and the girls had a reputation for being rowdy. The Headless Dancer's parties were almost as sophisticated as theater productions, but the parties never got started until sundown. Under the rain on an overcast working day, it was subdued.

Dormael passed his heavy cloak to a serving man at the door and limped over to the bar. The interior of the Headless Dancer was covered with velvet, cushions and lace. Vast swaths of fabric hung from everywhere, filling the room with red, purple, and gray. Smoke hung heavy in the air, creating a pleasant haze that dulled Dormael's wits as he breathed it in. He knew from experience that the owner of the place burned a narcotic in the incense to loosen the purse-strings of his proprietors.

The bar was empty save for two men sharing a long-stemmed pipe and four girls in various states of dress—or undress, depending on how one viewed it. The barmaid, a woman with lustrous black hair over pale skin, sauntered over to him as he sat.

"What's your poison?" she asked, giving him a hooded smile.

"Firewine." Dormael situated himself at the bar. "It's a good day for that."

"Aye, it's always a good day for that, if you're asking me. You look like you've been trampled by a team of horses. What kind of rough business got you so mishandled?"

Her hands stayed busy while she spoke, pouring him a drink with practiced ease.

"Nothing good," Dormael said, tipping his cup in her direction. He took a sip and offered the cup to the barmaid. "Care to join me?"

"It's not as though I have anything else to do." She smiled, all rounded features and bottomless eyes.

"Then pull that bottle up here and let's get started."

D'Jenn sat with his legs crossed, his body relaxed, and his mind as quiet as he could make it.

It was nigh impossible since the meeting with Victus. Something about all the information he had absorbed tickled at his mind, hinted at a pattern he was not seeing. Victus had said it himself during their conversation.

They're not trained to see the patterns, he'd said, *they don't recognize the knife in the dark.*

Those words tumbled over in D'Jenn's mind. Victus had been lying during the meeting—or, at least, he had been hiding something. Body language couldn't reveal a lie, but one could deduce when a subject was distressed over their words. Victus had clearly been distressed, though for what reason, D'Jenn had yet to understand.

Vera's note sat in a nearby cabinet, weighing on his mind. His sorrow at her death was coloring everything. Dormael had escaped, probably to mourn in his own way, and left D'Jenn to brood on his own. Maybe his emotions were the reason nothing seemed right to him, maybe that's why he felt so suspicious of everything. Perhaps it was simple melancholy.

The urge to read her letter was a terrible thing.

He calmed his stormy thoughts and sank into a deeper state, where his emotions were nothing but a whisper at the edge of his consciousness. His magic was roiling at the center of his being, but he let it sleep for now. At the present moment, it was his mind he needed, not his magic.

D'Jenn thought of all the players at the table. The Galanian Emperor, whose motivations, other than power for power's sake, could not be deduced with what D'Jenn knew of him. He was an incomplete picture, a puzzle with missing pieces. He might be able to tell what the man's motivations had been in *some* situations, but divining his entire strategy from those disparate events was nigh impossible. Until he could get a fuller picture of the man, he could not make any effective predictions about his intentions, except to continue pursuing the armlet. If Victus's theory was correct, the armlet was only the beginning.

The Mekai's motivations were clear enough. D'Jenn had sensed something from him in the War Room during the meeting...mistrust? Anxiety? He'd never seen the man speak with the slightest amount of anger. On the subject of the Galanian persecution of Sevenlanders, though, he had loosened his emotional control. The controversy over the rumor was simmering throughout the Conclave—though every time D'Jenn heard the story from a new set of lips, it became more gruesome and villainous. The Mekai saw himself as the protector of the Conclave's laws, and the conventions established by hundreds of years of tradition. His motivations were sincere and predictable.

It was Victus whom D'Jenn couldn't reconcile. He knew the man, trusted the man, yet there was something that kept bringing the problem back around in D'Jenn's mind. He had lied—but why? The Deacon of the Warlocks was one of the most powerful and dangerous men in all of Eldath. What did he have to hide? Why lie to the Mekai, to Dormael and D'Jenn—Hells, why lie at all?

Why is he so invested in the idea of an offensive against the Galanian Empire? What would such a thing gain him? What would it gain the Conclave?

D'Jenn agreed that keeping the armlets safe from Dargorin was paramount and defeating this *vilth*—whether he worked with the Emperor or not—was just as important. But an offensive by Warlocks against the Galanian Empire would be an act of war. If such an operation were found out—or even worse, defeated and captured—it would mean the descent of all the world into chaos. Other Alderakan kingdoms, when it was discovered the Conclave had attacked the Galanians, would rally around them as the victims of an unprovoked magical aggression.

And they would be the victims of a magical aggression. Provoked or not, such a thing is forbidden.

All over Eldath, swords would be polished for war. Victus would have known that, though, which made his actions all the more confusing. The man who had taught D'Jenn to see these patterns, predict these outcomes, would have come to the same conclusions. Why, then, did he advocate for this dangerous path?

There must be a reason.

Uncle Saul had mentioned something strange during their idle discussions back at Harlun homestead. The man was ever into conspiracy talk, but he wasn't as bumbling as Dormael pretended. He'd had some wild theory about the son of Nyra Jurillic and the creation of a large fund for the Council of Seven through tax revenue. D'Jenn had paid only passing attention at the time, but now the conversation hovered around the edges of his pattern, begging to find a place. He tried to smooth away his concerns and thought back to what the old man had said.

Kitamin Jurillic. The name bubbled to the surface of his mind.

Kitamin Jurillic was the son of Nyra Jurillic, Kansil of the Tasha-Mal. Kitamin had been captured in a Rashardian raid and carted away in a slave caravan. If D'Jenn remembered correctly, the old man had linked Kitamin's reappearance to the vote Nyra had proposed. At the time, D'Jenn had dismissed the story as fanciful.

Now that D'Jenn had time to consider, the old man might have been on to something. Jurillic's vote to create the fund made no sense. Even stranger was the fact that the Soirus-Gamerit Kansil, Nilliam Berrul, had voted in favor of the tax hike in direct opposition to his Clan Leaders—a move that could see him deposed by the same.

Kitamin Jurillic had been a renowned warrior. He had fought in the Gladiator's Ring and had been at war with the Rashardian raiders his entire life. Even for a man of his strength, it was unlikely he could escape from a Rashardian slaver's caravan unless he did so before they crossed the border into the desert. The Golden Waste was an ocean of sand covering half of Rashardia—a deadly landscape by any measure. If one didn't know how to navigate it, one was doomed to die under the sun.

Kitamin, however, had returned a year later, missing his hands. D'Jenn had many advantages Kitamin did not, and even he would have trouble escaping from a slaver's caravan if they took him into the Golden Waste. For a hand-less Kitamin, the task would have been impossible. The man couldn't even hold a waterskin, much less any sort of weapon.

Who, then, could affect such a rescue, and press Jurillic into a vote at the next Council meeting? It would take a vast amount of resources and skilled rescuers. Fighting men could fall right and left in an operation like that, but Warlocks were trained and experienced in such missions.

Why the fund, though? Why set up an extra trove of money for the Council? D'Jenn started to see some pieces come together. He tried to think as if he was in Victus's place.

Here I am, he thought, *decades old in my duty, and simmering at all the injustice I see. I'm the leader of a dangerous faction of wizards and in a position to do a lot of dangerous, expensive favors. I want influence in order to secure the vote for Mekai, and I need political unrest in order to muddy the waters and open the door for my ascension.*

But why the fund?

Nyra Jurillic would be in the city, as the Council of Seven wrestled with the issue of the Galanians. She was the one person who could confirm for him whether his suspicions about Victus were true. He couldn't go and request an audience, though—it would leave a trail, and Victus would learn of it. Getting to Jurillic would require finesse.

D'Jenn rose from the floor, grabbed his cloak, and headed out the door.

**

"They *do* exist, I can promise you that," Dormael said. "There's a vast swath of the Stormy Sea full of the things, and they'll suck a ship right down to the bottom. Just look on a map. It's called the Maelstrom Field."

The barmaid smiled. "Come now, that can't be true. You're just trying to impress me with all the big, amazing things you've seen. Your sort are always coming in here, trying to convince me they're handsome adventurers."

"I don't have to convince you of anything—I'm a handsome adventurer no matter what some beautiful woman thinks about it," Dormael said, taking another pull from the firewine. It burned on the way down and left a sweet taste in his mouth. The bottle was almost halfway gone, most of it into Dormael's cup. His aches and pains were fading into the background, and his vision was taking on a comfortable, hazy quality.

"So I'm a beautiful woman, am I?"

"Do you need a handsome adventurer to tell you so?"

"It's nice to hear," she laughed. "Are you going to finish the entire bottle?"

"I could be persuaded to share with a beautiful woman, especially in a more intimate setting."

"Such as one of the upstairs rooms?" she asked.

"If you prefer one of those rooms, that's fine by me. It does sound convenient." Dormael gave her a sideways wink as he took another pull from the bottle.

The barmaid let out a peal of silvery laughter. "No, honey. I'm not for sale."

"Who said I was offering to pay?"

She slapped him on the shoulder and gave him a kiss on the cheek as she rose from her seat. She moved down the bar to serve the other two patrons, leaving Dormael alone with his bottle. More customers trickled into the taproom, showing Dormael quick glances of the rainy afternoon.

He turned from the bar and walked to a velvet couch covered in garish bolts of purple and crimson. The colors were jarring to the eye, but the half-dressed women lounging around the taproom were a much more pleasant sight. He smiled at them, but indicated with his expression that he didn't want to be bothered. As much as he enjoyed flirting, when he thought of buying a whore for the evening, Shawna's voice popped into his mind.

I see, she would say. *That's exactly what I would have expected.*

His thoughts were full of the memory of her skin and the taste of her lips. She had been silent on the whole thing, and Dormael dared not press her to remember. There were times he'd searched her eyes for any recognition, any acknowledgment, any hint that the fire she had shown him was lurking beneath the surface. The woman, as always, was inscrutable.

Probably wants nothing to do with an idiot like me. She said it herself—I'm terrible.

Dormael's eyes went to the door as it opened to the rain outside, and he almost choked on his drink.

A woman stood outlined by the rain, squinting around the darkened taproom. She was diminutive, and pretty in a way that outshined buxom beauties of half again her height. She had amber eyes that gave her face a fey quality and soft, enchanting features. She was wrapped in a large Sevenlander cloak, and she had the hood drawn up to cover her raven hair. As their eyes met, Dormael felt pinned to the spot.

I thought she was dead.

"Inera?"

The word escaped before he knew he'd spoken. She looked to him, and for a moment, Dormael thought he was hallucinating. Maybe his magic was destroying his mind. Maybe Lacelle had been right about him.

Her eyes conveyed a thousand emotions in a few fleeting seconds. Longing, regret, anger, shame, and confusion all shot through her eyes like lightning. When the moment was over, her expression settled into something unreadable. As he sat with his mouth agape, she rushed back into the rain, slamming the door in her wake. His heart dropped into his stomach.

"Inera, wait!" Dormael shouted, scrambling up from his seat.

Heedless of the rain, he ran after her.

**

D'Jenn moved through the city like a ghost.

He didn't need to use his magic to blend in, he only needed ingenuity. Nondescript clothing, a bit of dirt on the face, a dejected, uninterested expression, and the deed was done—he was nothing but an everyday laborer. He flowed with the river of people through the streets of Ishamael, making his way to the official holdings of the Tasha-Mal. The pace of the crowd was slow for his taste, but he endured it with patience.

For all he knew, Victus was having him watched.

The holdings of the Tasha-Mal were on the far end of the West Market alongside the holdings of the other Sevenlander tribes. Mals were less plentiful in Ishamael than in Mistfall, where the trade was more profitable. D'Jenn spotted a few here and there, marked out by their tattoos, wild hair, and menacing appearance against the backdrop of farmers, craftsmen and artisans from other tribes. The Mals were a fierce lot.

He made the Mal district by early afternoon and ducked into an alleyway across the street. He waited for some time, watching the passersby for anyone following to make the mistake of appearing. They did not.

D'Jenn slipped out of the alley and joined a smaller throng of people entering the Mal district. There were a few shops and traders scattered inside—mostly for weapons and religious curios, which the Mals favored for charms—but the majority of the district was given over to house the tribal leadership and its retinue. As the Kansil was in attendance, there were more than a few Mal warriors walking the streets, conversing with each other in boisterous tones. D'Jenn avoided these as much as possible and made his way to the offices of the Kansil.

The building was a large one, though unadorned in comparison with others in Ishamael. It was two stories high and encircled by a low stone wall covered with white plaster. There was no gate, only two guards standing by the arched entrance to the compound. The Mals didn't live in buildings back home, and they found the walls more than a little oppressive. A large fire burned inside the walled courtyard, and the sound of muddled conversation issued from around it.

Let's see what's around back.

It was more difficult than he'd anticipated to sneak through the district of the Mals. While they were not big on subterfuge, the Mal warriors were always alert and ready to fight. They lived in a constant state of warfare with the Rashardians, and that made them more than a little jumpy. D'Jenn could handle them if a problem arose, but the last thing he wanted was to answer questions. He came close to being seen a time or two, but finally made his way around to the rear of the building.

He waited for a few minutes to see if any guards were going to walk by. When they didn't, he checked to see if anyone was looking and slipped over the edge of the wall. His feet hit the grass on the other side without a sound, and he rushed to the wall of the building.

D'Jenn opened his Kai and wove a spell into his clothing—a simple suggestion to look elsewhere. He would remain visible, so the spell was dangerous, but it should serve his purposes for getting inside. Splitting his consciousness, he used his climbing spell and started up the wall.

The entire time he was stuck to the side of the building, he felt as if a cry would raise at any moment. Perhaps some maid would glance out her window from across the way, see him climbing like a spider along the wall, and scream. Perhaps one of the Mals would come around the building and start chucking pointy things in his direction.

His climb, though, went by in silence.

Reaching a top-floor window with no glass in the frame, he

slipped over the side and into an empty room. It was dark, and the door had nothing hanging over the portal but a multitude of beads. Footsteps sounded from the hallway, and D'Jenn slipped to the wall and flattened his body, waiting for the steps to fade. He held his breath as they retreated and only relaxed after they were gone.

Now—where is Nyra Jurillic?

He closed his eyes and sent his magical senses questing through the building.

There were four other people on this floor with him—two in one room at the far end of the hall and two others in separate rooms. If he had known Jurillic, he might have been able to tell which one she was, but her presence was unknown to his senses. He would have to check them all.

Cursing, he used his magic to muffle the sound of the beads and ducked into the hallway.

The interior of the building was decorated with a surprising amount of colorful scarves. They weren't tapestries, but diaphanous bands of fabric in wild hues of red, purple, and blue. Even in the still air of the hallway, the fabric waved as if in a ghostly breeze. He crept to the room at the end of the hall and stopped short of the opening.

Scattered conversation made its way to his ears—a man and a woman.

"...the Clan Leaders will not call the Summit next year," the man was saying. "I have heard no talk of deposing you, just whispers in the wake of...well, you know."

"I know," the woman grumbled. "Lot of gods-damned ungrateful cowards they are. Two years ago they would have fought each other for the chance to join my hunting party, now they squabble over the remains of my corpse. Tell those bastards I'm not a corpse *yet*, by the gods, and they will feel every inch of my wrath for their disloyalty."

"Nyra—"

"*No*, Benten, you listen to *me*. I want to know *who*. I want to know where these whispers are coming from. I will challenge them in the circle for their words—know that for truth!"

"They will vote you down for this."

"Let them," the woman said. "If they think another is strong enough to lead, then let them. I will return to my own Clan and live happily with my family. They can have this Kansil business, the politics, *all* of it! Let another dance with the snakes on the Council and see how the venom feels."

D'Jenn had hoped to be able to get to Nyra Jurillic when she was alone, but he knew it had been a slim hope. He was loath to use his magic on the man in the room, but he couldn't see an alternative. Every moment he was in the building, the danger of discovery increased.

Apologies, friend.

Reaching out with his Kai, he brushed his magic across the mind of the man speaking to Jurillic and put him to sleep. D'Jenn had to put a bit of force behind the spell in order to send the man into unconsciousness, as his mind was alert and involved in a conversation. He'd probably wake with a headache, but that would be the worst of it. A muted thump sounded from the room.

"Benten? Benten, are you alright?"

D'Jenn ducked through the beads, using his magic to muffle the noise. Nyra Jurillic was a lithe woman, all whipcord muscles and hard expression, though her hair was going to silver. She had a knife in hand before he got all the way into the room and had put her back to a corner. Her eyes shot from D'Jenn to the slumped form of Benten.

"Kansil Jurillic," D'Jenn said, holding up his hands for peace. "I mean no harm! I only want to talk."

Jurillic had the gaze of a predator, and it was locked to D'Jenn's eyes.

"You're no dockworker—or whatever costume that's supposed to be."

"No."

"You work for the Conclave," she said, rising from her fighting crouch and spiriting the knife away. "You are Blessed."

"Aye." D'Jenn nodded. "I wanted to ask—"

"Ask?" she spat. "You wanted to ask nothing. You and your master can go to the Void. We made one deal—a *single* deal—and I have paid for it every day since. There will be no more. My son...my son is a broken creature, a whipped dog. You brought him back, and I am thankful—but we're done. Get out, unless you plan to kill me. Do not think I didn't notice the death of Berrul's brother. I am not blind to your scheming."

D'Jenn gaped. *That confirms it, then. Someone in the Conclave was doing favors.*

Jurillic had just implicated that person in a murder, as well. D'Jenn made an effort to school his expression to blandness. He felt like sitting down, but he couldn't betray his disguise.

"If you're going to do it, then say so now. I will not go peacefully," she growled.

"There will be no killing," D'Jenn said, coming back to himself. "I trust you've told no one?"

Now that she had played her hand, he had no need to reveal his own truth to her. Instead, he could use this lever to gather more information. People had a tendency to fill the gaps in their knowledge with assumptions, and if left to their own fanciful musings, would deceive themselves.

"You question *my* honor?" She sniffed. "My son knows. The two who brought him back know. Your master knows, and *you* know. My husband knew, but he went to the Void last year."

"And the Council of Seven? Who else knows on the Council?"

"I have not betrayed you to the Council," she said. "Neither have any of the others your master has manipulated. I can see his influence at work. It matters not, anyway. I will be deposed and far beyond your reach. You'll need to find another puppet to dance under your strings. If that is all you came for, then get out."

D'Jenn had everything he needed—or everything he could get and maintain his disguise. He gave the woman a tense smile and turned to leave the way he'd come.

"I will look over my shoulder for you," she said to his back. "I will not be taken in my sleep like an animal. Tell your master that. If he wants to kill me, he'd best come at me from the front!"

D'Jenn ignored her and made his way back outside. There were only two Blessed in all of Ishamael who had the resources to send other wizards on dangerous missions. One of them was the Mekai, whose involvement would make no logical sense.

That left only one possibility—Victus Tiranan.

**

Rain poured into the streets as Dormael shouldered through the people choking the East Market. The firewine had dulled his wits and slowed his reactions, so he ran into people amid shouts of protest and curses, and even once went sprawling onto the wet cobbles. He caught fleeting glances of Inera in the distance, just enough to keep him on the chase.

"Stupid, stupid, stupid...," he muttered, shaking his head as he struggled in pursuit. It had been years since he'd seen Inera, and their parting had been tumultuous. He thought she'd died, a victim of the Galanian invasion of her homeland. His heart pounded with how wrong he had been, driving the point deeper into his bones with each beat.

Guilt wracked him. He should have searched harder for her, should have torn apart occupied Neleka until he found her, and to the Six Hells with the political consequences. He'd been forbidden to do just that, even though a large part of him had wanted it. He lost something of himself after her death, escaping for a time to travel the world as a vagabond in self-imposed exile. Who knew what horrors Inera had lived through? Finding him at the Headless Dancer was a fitting end to her journey—it exposed him for the wretch he was.

"Inera! Wait!" he called.

She threw a glance over her shoulder, and he caught the slightest glimpse of pain-filled eyes before she slipped down an alleyway. Dormael rushed after her, weaving through the sea of people to reach her. Thunder rumbled overhead as he followed her into the alley.

**

D'Jenn made his way through the Conclave grounds, trying to think his way through his next move. If Victus was using Warlocks to buy votes on the Council—and possibly to kill for them—there must be a reason. What was it? Power? His fear of a coming war?

D'Jenn cursed himself for not keeping up with events in the past year. If he had some greater context of Council decisions and events at home, he might be able to piece together a more complete picture of what was going on. As it was, his scant information was just enough to lever an accusation and nothing else. He needed proof.

He chewed on the problem as he entered the Conclave Proper.

The halls of the lower level were choked with petitioners. People waited on benches, lounged against the wall, and stood amidst a low buzz of conversation. Initiates made their way through the crowd, acting as ushers. D'Jenn's footsteps tapped against the black marble floor of the Common Hall as he hurried through, trying to get to his rooms. He needed to think before he brought this to anyone.

"D'Jenn! There you are, boy!" Victus called from behind him.

D'Jenn almost gave himself away by freezing in place. Apprehension crawled over his back like a hundred spiders made of ice, and he loosened his spine with an effort of will. He used every bit of training he'd received to smooth his features and turned to face his former mentor.

"Deacon," D'Jenn said, inclining his head in respect. "Did you need something?"

"I've been looking for Dormael," Victus said, pushing through the crowd. "Have you seen him?"

"Not since the morning."

"Probably went out cavorting," Victus said. "He does that when he's troubled."

D'Jenn felt a pang of sorrow at the comment, and then hot anger on its heels. Some dark, jealous part of him rose up and wanted to punch the man. He had no right to be so close with them anymore—not when he had used his position for so much personal gain.

D'Jenn cleared his throat. "Probably."

"I'll have to straighten him out when he comes back," Victus said, letting out a long sigh. "Walk with me a bit, I'll put the idea to you, and you can pass it to your cousin." Victus walked up and put an arm on D'Jenn's shoulder, turning him back down the hallway and falling in beside him. D'Jenn wanted to squirm out from under the man's grip, but he resisted the urge.

"What did you need, Deacon?"

"It's about the girl—the child, Bethany," Victus replied.

D'Jenn felt another spike of anger. "Go on."

"It's my understanding that she will begin her training soon." Victus smiled. "Her gift is substantial. She could be the greatest wizard the Conclave has seen in generations. Quite the spunky little thing, too, isn't she?"

D'Jenn had always found Bethany to be reserved, but he agreed anyway.

Victus nodded. "You know, the Mekai and Lacelle have been talking about her connection with the artifact. How she used it, how it...talks to her. It's still strange to say that, to think it aloud." He laughed and ran his hand through his wild mass of hair. "They wish to perform a series of tests on her, to gauge her connection with the artifact."

D'Jenn stopped in his tracks. "You mean they wish to put the girl and the armlet together just to see what happens? We've done that before, on the road to Borders. It didn't work out well."

"I'm sure they want to test them separately first, but I would think putting them together would be part of the process," Victus said. "And a chance happening on the road is very different from the controlled environment of an experiment."

"The armlet doesn't much like control," D'Jenn said. "It does whatever it wants."

"Regardless, they wanted me to put the question to him. They probably hoped it would sound better from my mouth than theirs," Victus said. "It brought up another point, something else I'd wanted to speak with him about."

"Such as?"

"You boys are going to be back in the field soon, if Dormael doesn't have another episode. As I said before, the girl could be the most powerful wizard in generations. Her training is important, her guidance, even more so. I thought I would offer to watch over her while Dormael was away on missions, to take a personal hand in her training."

Something black and angry twisted in D'Jenn's stomach. "Oh?"

"Listen," Victus said, "we both know the girl's talents would be wasted as a Hedge Wizard, a Scout, or a Philosopher. She has been traveling with you for a while, and she's dealt with so much more than other Initiates of her age group. You and I both know that her place will be here, boy, with us. She should be a Warlock, like her father. I would be honored to keep an eye on her, and to take up the mantle of mentor when she is ready. I would love to teach her, as I taught all of you. You know it's the right thing, boy. The girl should be a Warlock. Anything else would fly in the face of good sense."

D'Jenn tried to read Victus's face and catch some hint of subterfuge. Even though Victus was involved in some obscure plot, part of D'Jenn wanted to believe him. A darker part of him was trying to calculate what Victus thought he could gain by controlling the girl, by getting close to her.

"The other thing," Victus said, "is that her connection with the armlet will make her a target."

"What do you mean?"

"Wizards will want to study her, will want to study the armlet. She'll be made to perform in one experiment or the other, or she'll be asked to recount her experiences with it. I can help to shield her from that. Bethany's situation here in the Conclave will be unique. She'll need a friend like me." Victus stepped closer and put a hand on D'Jenn's shoulder. "D'Jenn, us Warlocks—we're family. There's a reason we stick together. Tell Dormael what I said and tell him to come find me."

"I will, Honored Deacon."

Victus turned and threaded his way back through the mass of people. D'Jenn watched him go, feeling a whirlwind of emotions warring for dominance. Grief, guilt, anger, suspicion—they all swirled through him as he tried to make sense of events.

It was time for everyone to regroup and rethink their strategy. He needed to find Dormael and inform him of his discovery. He hurried back through the Common Hall and went outside.

Rain was falling in sheets as he left the shelter of the Conclave Proper. The grounds were emptying as people rushed to get out of the weather, and no one paid D'Jenn any mind. The clouds were a roiling mass of dark gray and white. He found a clear place on the Green and opened his Kai. Closing his eyes, he tilted his head to the sky, letting the cool water run down his face.

Mind Flight was always a strange sensation. D'Jenn could still feel his physical body and the rain wetting his clothes, but his awareness hovered over the Conclave grounds. He sent a pulse of energy skittering along the streets of Ishamael, searching out the song of Dormael's magic.

The spell was something he and Dormael had worked out years past. They had grown up together, trained together, and worked together most of their lives, and they could pick out the sounds of each other's magic from anywhere. One of the things they had done was to work out different ways to find one another when needed.

His Kai rang back with a harmony, touching upon Dormael's essence and shining like a beacon. D'Jenn focused on the signature and shot off in pursuit. The ground fell away beneath him, and he soared toward the East Market.

Ishamael was a strange-looking city when viewed from above. It was one of the oldest cities in the Sevenlands, and new construction was built beside ancient temples. People flowed through the streets like ants, moving along lines they themselves could not see. The river was brown and pockmarked by the rain. Thunder rumbled in the skies.

Even in the rain, vendors still braved the streets, exchanging things with hooded customers who huddled into their cloaks. D'Jenn could feel Dormael somewhere in that sea of people, moving along streets and back alleys. The storm interfered with his spell—moving water sometimes did that—and it was hard to get a precise idea of where Dormael was going.

What is he doing?

He'd expected to find his coz holed up in some taproom, not dragging his bruised body through the rain. He strengthened the connection and followed it into a side street, chasing the spell down an alleyway. D'Jenn spotted Dormael pushing past crates and splashing through puddles, running as if in pursuit of someone. D'Jenn zipped down to intercept him.

Pain surged through his Kai in a sudden flash, bringing a nauseating dizziness with it. D'Jenn was flung from the street, as if a great hand had swatted his awareness away. His mind sailed into the sky, and he could hear a strange dissonance in his ears, an almost deafening noise that grated in his mind like rusty steel hinges. His consciousness surged back toward his body.

D'Jenn's body was thrown backwards when his mind slammed into place. He landed on his back with a squelch and shut his eyes against the rain. His head hurt like he'd been kicked by a horse, and his stomach rebelled against a rush of sensations. He groaned, rolling over to vomit into the grass, tasting blood and bile in his mouth. His head was pounding in his ears, and his hands wouldn't stop shaking. He heaved until stars swam across his vision.

People gathered around him, and plaintive hands reached down to help him stand. D'Jenn waved them away, spitting thick, bloody effluvia on the ground. He reached up to wipe his face, and his hand came away covered with wet blood. He could feel it streaming from his nose. D'Jenn climbed to his feet with a groan, waving away the helpful hands for a second time.

What in the Six Hells was that?

For a moment, D'Jenn thought he had heard another song whistling out into the ether. Someone had sensed D'Jenn's presence and expelled him from the field with enough prejudice to serve as a warning. Whoever it was wanted Dormael alone.

This is not good.

D'Jenn leaned against the wall of the Conclave Proper, feeling the pitted rock under his hands, trying to use the sensation to ground himself and expel the nausea. He took one step forward, then another, regaining his balance. The cold rain helped to wake him, but his legs were still shaky.

There was no way he could manage another Mind Flight until his head stopped spinning, and by then, it would be too late. Spitting one last time into the grass, D'Jenn set off in search of Allen. If he and Shawna disappeared, Victus would notice. Allen, though, had spent most of his time here in leisure, ignored by the leadership. Besides—if Allen found out Dormael was missing and D'Jenn hadn't let him know, there would be a fight.

He could feel the incredulous stares of the onlookers as he walked away.

**

Dormael slipped on the wet cobblestones and slammed his right side into the corner of a wooden crate. The wind fled from his chest, and a fresh wave of coughing came upon him. For just a moment, there had been a strange resonance in the air, some sort of disorienting magical pulse. Dormael pushed himself to his feet.

You can worry about that when you catch her.

"Inera!" Dormael had meant to shout, but it came out as more of a cough. His feet barely managed to stay under him as he teetered down a side street.

The back alleys of the East Market were no place to be caught alone, drunk, and desperate, but seeing Inera again was too important to care. He was surrounded by dark, old wood, shuttered windows, lines criss-crossing the alleys, and trash in the streets. Someone shouted a curse at him from one of the windows, but Dormael ignored it. He limped around another corner after the flash of a dark cloak caught his eye.

He stopped short as he rounded the corner.

She stood facing him at a dead end. Behind her rose stacks of busted crates, rotten barrels, and piles of unnameable things. The rain came down with a vengeance, casting a hazy sheen over everything. Runnels of water falling from the rooftops splashed onto the stones of the street.

Something about her manner made Dormael stop short of relief. The hood of her cloak was pulled up, hiding the wealth of hair that he remembered, shadowing everything but the lower part of her face. The cloak wrapped her body like a funeral shroud, leaving only her diminutive hands visible. She made no move toward him—only stood, waiting for him to speak.

"Inera—Inera, that *is* you, isn't it?" he ventured, taking a step toward her.

"Dormael," she breathed, as if he'd just walked in after a trip to the market.

Her voice was light and airy, just as he remembered. Dormael felt something rush out of him at that moment, and his eyes teared up of their own accord. A vicious lump grew in his throat. He took a tentative step toward her, as if she was a wild animal who would bolt at the slightest noise.

"I searched for you," he said. "I searched everywhere. I thought you were dead."

It sounded so stupid, so banal. He had lied awake many nights fantasizing on what he would say to her if he ever discovered she was alive. He had never entertained the possibility, of course, but he had said the words in his mind over and over again. This wet, harried reunion had ripped those words away and replaced them with the diction of a fool.

"Not dead," Inera replied. "Never that."

You betrayed her. You stopped looking for her and gave her up for dead, yet here she stands. You betrayed her! You fool! You gods-damned, fucking fool!

"How?" he asked, master of words that he was. "How did you...I mean, I thought the Galanians got to you. Can we go somewhere? Maybe get some food? There's...there's just so much to say."

His legs trembled.

"Alright," she said. "Let's go somewhere more private."

Her hands, those delicate hands he remembered so fondly, moved for the hood covering her hair. She raised her chin, fixing her light brown eyes on him, and gave him an unsettling smile. With a slow, deliberate motion, she pushed the hood back from her hair.

Dormael's breath caught in his throat.

The raven hair he had so loved, a flowing ebony river she'd always refused to cut, had gone stark white. Not gray as if with old age, but white like winter snow. Those fey eyes were haunted now, bloodshot and filled with terrible wisdom, something alien and jaded, a twisted remnant of how he remembered her. There was some sort of pattern on her forehead, a sinuous scar that stretched from ear to ear. Her forearms were also covered in scars of the same fashion, lines of glyphs he didn't recognize. She regarded him like a dying pet, and her eyes shot to the side.

Dormael's Kai tense with alarm.

He dove to his right as something whooshed through the air where his head had been, pain wracking his ill-used muscles. He tried to roll, but the combination of his injured body and the firewine foiled his effort. Instead, he went over one shoulder and ended up on his back, lacking the momentum to come to his feet again. Someone piled atop him as he reached for the knife in his boot, trapping his arm and pushing his shoulders back onto the ground.

"Hurry, you fools!" Inera hissed.

Dormael was shocked into immobility.

His attacker used that moment of weakness to his advantage and got his hands around Dormael's throat. Dormael struggled against him, trying to work his chin down to shield his neck, and made a quick grab for the knife the attacker had forgotten. He felt the hilt meet his hands like salvation and yanked it from its sheath. He stabbed the man—one, two, three quick strikes—and the attacker released him. Dormael put the blade into the man's armpit and tried to slide from beneath him, but the bastard was too heavy to push away.

Was this her doing? Some kind of revenge?

Something cracked across the side of his head, sending icicles of pain through his skull. He caught sight of Inera standing over him, cold, brown eyes alight with an unknown fury. Dormael had a moment to feel a sense of betrayal.

Another crack, and he felt nothing at all.

CHASING THE BLOOD

"He was here," D'Jenn said. "I saw him come this way before I was attacked."

Allen kicked at a wooden crate lying forgotten against the side of a dun-colored building. The rain came down in a cold, steady pour, and D'Jenn was soaked to his skin. He stared over the water-logged streets, watching the runoff flow by. This was the exact spot where D'Jenn had attempted to contact Dormael and had been tossed back into his body.

Allen cursed beside him.

"Can't you just wiggle your fingers, say a few words, and find out where in the Six Hells he is?"

"It's not that simple," D'Jenn sighed. "Would that it was."

"I've seen Dormael do something like that before, cast some spell that led him to something he'd lost. Can't you just duplicate that?"

"No. I've tried to scry him out, and all I get is some sort of interference. Someone is masking his presence in the ether, and that doesn't bode well at all."

"Couldn't he be doing it himself? Maybe he's lying with a woman somewhere and doesn't want to be...scried upon...or whatever it is you call it." Allen sounded hopeful.

"No," D'Jenn replied. "I know your brother's song better than any but my own, and if he were doing this, I'd know it. There is something strange going on."

Allen grumbled a curse and adjusted his weaponry. "What do we do, then?"

"There is nothing for it," D'Jenn said. "We'll have to make our way down these alleys until we find a clue that could point us in the right direction."

D'Jenn set off down an adjacent alley, and Allen had no choice but to follow. The two of them slogged through puddles with their shoulders hunched against the downpour, searching through the maze of back alleys in the East Market District. Thunder rumbled in the sky.

D'Jenn began marking off alleys they'd already investigated. The twists and turns of the East Market were bad enough on the main roads. The back alleys and forgotten side streets were a virtual labyrinth of dead ends, stairs leading nowhere, narrow spaces between buildings, and even access tunnels for Ishamael's extensive sewer system. They searched for hours and found nothing.

Just when D'Jenn grew frustrated, they rounded a corner into a dead end and found a body.

He was propped against the wall of a building with his head slumped to the side, his eyes staring at nothing. Blood had leaked from a couple of wounds in the man's side, and the rain had washed it onto the cobblestones, turning the surrounding puddles a murky, rusted color. The corpse was wrapped in a heavy cloak, staring from a deep hood. A short sword was tangled in the sheath at his waist, thrust out of sorts by the wall behind him.

D'Jenn moved his hands aside and rummaged through his clothing, finding a few silver marks in his purse. There were three punctures in his side and a wound in his armpit. D'Jenn poked at the wounds and wiped his bloody fingers on the corpse's cloak. The man's hands had the calluses of a swordsman. A dagger lay on the ground nearby, half submerged in the bloody puddle.

Allen moved to the body and drew the short sword from its sheath.

"This is no common bruiser's weapon," he said, showing the blade to D'Jenn. "It's good steel—you can tell by the color. Unless he was a *very* highly paid bruiser, I'd say this man was some sort of rich merchant's guard."

"Aye," D'Jenn said, eyeing the dagger he'd picked up from the street. "And whoever killed him didn't bother to retrieve their dagger. A man like this doesn't get mugged by street urchins. There was a fight here, up close and personal. He never drew that sword."

Allen squatted next to the body and ripped the man's sleeves open, widening the tear until the arms were visible. Standing out against the man's pallid skin was a single tattoo on his right shoulder—a red sword hanging point down.

"Galanians," D'Jenn spat, tucking the dagger into his belt. "I knew they were going to show up again."

"You said you'd crippled their ship on the Stormy Sea."

"We crippled *one* ship. Who knows how many were sent after us? They could have made landing and bought passage here on a river boat while we traveled overland through the mountains. Or even worse, they might have had agents in the city already."

I would have agents here, were I the Galanian Emperor.

"The Red Swords are supposed to be an elite military unit," Allen said. "Why would Dargorin send them here when his war is in Thardin?"

"He sent them after Shawna's armlet, too. Maybe they're just his personal mercenaries."

"My brother was here," Allen growled.

"It's all a bit too coincidental otherwise, don't you think?"

"We have to alert the Conclave and the Guard," Allen said, his weapons clinking as he turned to hurry into the street.

"Wait!"

Allen stopped and turned back to him, a frustrated look on his face.

D'Jenn sighed. "There *is* something going on, and more than Dormael's abduction. There are things happening at the Conclave—dangerous things—and I don't know who's involved and who isn't. I don't know if this is all connected and haven't had a chance to think it through. Until we know who we can trust, we have to do this own our own. You and I."

"On our own?" Allen scoffed. "You and I could tear this entire city apart looking for Dormael and never find him in time! Meanwhile, someone with the capability to capture and hide him from you is holding him! He could be tortured, or could be dying! How in the Six Hells are you and I supposed to find him on our own?"

"We don't have to tear the city apart," D'Jenn said. "There are only so many places in Ishamael where one could go to work the kind of magic necessary to hide your brother, and even fewer where it could be done without alerting every wizard within range to their presence—not to mention keeping Dormael himself from breaking free. It takes quite a bit to suppress the power of a wizard of your brother's strength."

"Where, then?"

"They'd need a hidden place, somewhere safe from prying eyes and the senses of other wizards. Somewhere with enough space to construct a Greater Circle to suppress your brother, and strong enough walls to keep the energies contained. Magic on that scale is hard to keep hidden, especially in a city full of other wizards."

"The sewers—Indalvian's Tunnels!" Allen said, speaking the realization aloud as it came into D'Jenn's mind. They set off at a jog to find the nearest entrance to Ishamael's underground sewer systems. Thunder rumbled overhead, and the rain came down harder.

**

Dormael woke with his mind hazy, a burning agony throbbing in the back of his skull. He could feel cool, damp stone beneath his skin. He was naked. Someone was running a cold finger over his chest, tracing the bruise that had formed during his dream. He tried to say something, but all that came out of his mouth was a pitiful groan of pain.

"He's awake," someone said. "Hoist him."

There was a clinking, groaning noise, and his hands rose from his stomach. He was shackled, could feel the cold metal biting into his wrists as his weight was hoisted by his arms. His torso left the cold ground, stretching the sore, bruised muscles across his midsection. He was pulled to his feet, then higher, until only his toes could touch the ground. His legs scrambled over the wet stone, toes digging through the grit as they tried to find purchase on its slippery surface. He sputtered into the low torchlight stabbing at his eyelids.

"Wake up, my love." The voice was like silk sliding over his senses.

Dormael pushed his eyelids open, head throbbing with pain.

Inera stood before him, resting a cold hand on his cheek. She had always been diminutive and had to rise on her toes to reach him. He'd once loved that about her.

"Where—"

She shushed him with a finger to his dry, cracked lips.

"Don't worry about that, love. It will all be clear soon enough." The finger left his lips and Inera stepped away from him.

Dormael was chained to an ancient pulley system—some relic of Ishamael's construction put to new use by his captors. The noise of running water echoed all around him. The air felt heavy, wet, and cool. The stones under his feet were slick and moldy, but uniform and flat.

I'm in Indalvian's Tunnels. Gods, I'm under the city!

Ishamael had an extensive system of underground sewers, storage, and secret tunnels built by Indalvian and his wizards during the city's founding. Plans for the original construction had been lost long ago, and no one had finished mapping it since. If he was being held in some obscure corner of the tunnels, hope was thin that he would be rescued. If Inera planned to kill him, his corpse would likely rot here for all eternity.

Inera stepped across something on the ground before turning to face him, and Dormael shot his eyes to the stones underfoot. There were two curving lines of colored sand laid out in a circle around him. The inside ring was bright, almost clear—perhaps glass beads, or dust—while the outside ring, piled a little higher, was charred and black. There were runic symbols scrawled in chalk on the ground, both inside and outside the concentric rings of sand. Dormael felt another curse brewing inside as he realized what they meant.

I'm inside a Greater Circle. She's suppressing my Kai.

"You begin to see," Inera said, turning to regard something laid out on a small wooden table behind her. Dormael could hear his heart beating in his ears. He felt the slight pressure of the surrounding magic, pressing inward against his senses and his skin, holding his own magic inside.

"Why—," he coughed, his throat as dry as a desert. "Why are you doing this?"

"Oh, Dormael," she replied, turning to face him once again. "It's almost endearing, how little you know."

Her white hair fell over her shoulders, now bare since she had discarded her cloak. Inera's skin was a grayish color, something between an attractive paleness and the pallor of a dead body. She wore a leather girdle across her midsection, a mockery of something a courtesan might wear, and underneath it a simple dress of dark brown slashed with cream. The dress was tattered and ripped, almost to indecency, and her shapely, pale legs were visible beneath it. She was barefoot and seemed oblivious to the cold. She moved with grace, but her countenance made it the grace of a ghost rather than a dancer.

The strange, flowing scar across Inera's forehead was matched by another on her chest, dipping down between her breasts from one collarbone to the other. Her arms and shoulders were also covered by smaller scars—runes he didn't recognize. He was disgusted by the sight of her, and yet somehow aroused at the same time, as if her ghastly appearance still conjured the memory of the way she had been before. Her eyes locked to his, and he could feel the weight of something alien behind them.

"Things have...changed...since you left me to die," she said, looking his naked body up and down. She stretched like a cat as she regarded him, the look of fond memories playing across her face.

"I begged you to leave! I wanted you to come home with me, back to Ishamael," he coughed, his spasms sending tendrils of pain over his chest.

"And what? Become your wife? Join the Conclave? Become a slave to their machinations? No, Dormael, that life was never meant for me. But reconciliation—or revenge—is not why I'm here."

"Then why?" he asked, his heart pounding.

"Answers. If you tell me what I wish to know, this will go considerably easier for you. It ends the same way no matter what happens, my love, so don't hold to any hope of escape." Her dead eyes stared into his, unyielding.

"You mean to torture me." It was a statement. He knew it to be true, and could feel the dread creeping into his body.

"Torture is such a *narrow* word. It simply can't contain the description of what will happen to you if you resist me, dear one. You will know pain, surely, but on a completely different level than you ever have, and in the end, you will serve me still. I do not *wish* to cause you pain, love, so why don't you just make this easier on the both of us? Join me. Pledge your allegiance to me. Things can go back to the way they used to be. Do you remember the time we spent together? The nights we laid under the stars making love, talking about the future? Do you remember how it felt to be together? It could be that way again."

Dormael did remember. He remembered the way she used to be, he remembered her laugh and her carefree attitude. He remembered her determination and her independence. This creature standing before him was *not* that woman. She was a remnant, a ghost. She was a puppet made of lifeless parts, animated with darkness.

Inera is dead. He repeated that to himself over and over again.

"What happened to you?" he asked.

It came out quieter than he had intended. Something inside him was screaming with grief, with disbelief. It wanted to reach out to her, to see if anything of the woman he'd known could be inside this pale creature before him. Something inside of him hoped.

Her eyes twitched just for a second, and Dormael saw her pain in that instant. Then, the alien coldness and hardened resolve was back. Her expression never wavered.

"Where is the armlet? Where is the girl?" she asked, her eyes as wooden as a doll's.

"Fuck yourself."

Inera gave a dramatic sigh, turning her back on him and reaching onto the small table behind her. She turned back to him, holding a small, jagged knife. She looked to one of the quiet men standing behind her and tossed the blade to him.

"Cut him. Do it slowly."

**

D'Jenn placed the palm of his hand on the stones of the sewer wall. He and Allen had come to an intersection, a place where the water, flowing in the deep trenches in the center of the tunnel, met before draining into the lower levels of the sewer. He pushed his awareness into the stone, trying to sense something within the magic, anything to help the two of them find Dormael. There was nothing, just as there had been nothing since they'd entered the sewer system.

"Anything?" Allen asked, squinting into the dark tunnels around them.

"No."

"There *has* to be a better way to seek him out. We've been running around blind down here," Allen cursed, pounding his hand against the wall in frustration.

"Let me think for a bit," D'Jenn said, frustration welling through his facade. "I can't do it with you stomping around and snarling at the stones."

Allen sighed and stepped away from D'Jenn, inspecting the different intersections around them. His armor clinked as he moved, his weapons shifting and rattling in their sheaths. D'Jenn shook his head and turned his attention back to the problem at hand.

Ishamael's sewer system was a maze of tunnels cut from the ground during the city's founding. It was another of Indalvian's wonders, providing a self-sustaining system of waste disposal that no other city had—not even wondrous Tauravon. D'Jenn had studied it during his training at the Conclave.

It worked upon a basic filtering principle, powered by magic built on a scale the size of the city itself. The top level of the sewers was a collection level, where the city's waste water was washed down into giant filtering reservoirs, where magical spells kept the water spinning at great speed, keeping the heavier—and nastier—things from settling. The water was then filtered through magical barriers, sent lower, and the process repeated. Eventually, the water reached the lowest level, where it was boiled sterile, again through magic, and washed back upwards to fountains inside the city where any citizen could come and obtain clean water for their home. The waste, moved through pipes to an area outside the city, was collected and given to outlying farmers to use as fertilizer. Nothing like it had been attempted since Indalvian's time.

The problem for Allen and D'Jenn was its size. The system covered more ground than the city itself, and the sewers weren't the only tunnels under the city. They'd never been fully explored, and the dangerous magic, still not understood by many wizards, kept many people from venturing into the tunnels. One could spend seasons down here and never cross the same tunnel twice. D'Jenn cursed, trying to think of their options.

"D'Jenn!" Allen called, his voice echoing in the underground passage. "There's blood over here!"

D'Jenn rushed over to his cousin. There were blood drops on the ground, red and beginning to dry at the edges, but new enough to still be wet. The humidity had probably helped to preserve it as well. But whose blood was it? Could they take that chance?

"Prick your finger," D'Jenn told Allen.

"What? Why?"

"Just do it! Quickly! Drop a little of your blood beside the blood on the floor."

Allen cursed, but he drew a dagger from his belt and slashed it over his left forearm. Red blood welled up along the wound and pattered to the stones near the drops he'd found. D'Jenn opened his Kai to feed a tiny bit of magic into the blood and created a link between the two samples. The drying blood drops began to glow, leaking a rose-colored nimbus like fog rising from a swamp. Allen's blood responded, echoing the glow even as he was wiping the wound clean.

"It's his!" D'Jenn said, rising to his feet and gazing down the corridor. Sure enough, there were more glowing drops farther down the tunnel, leading off into the darkness.

"How do you know that?" Allen rose to his feet as well.

"Your blood and Dormael's are linked. You're brothers, so there is a slight difference between the blood that flows in your veins, but enough of a similarity to cause a reaction with my spell. He came this way, recently enough that his blood is still wet. He can't be too far."

"Then what in the Six Hells are we waiting on?" Allen asked.

They took off at a run down the tunnel, their steps echoing from the stone.

**

Dormael screamed.

He'd always heard stories of honorable men staying silent and strong through torture, never giving in to the pain of it. He'd

196

thought he could do it, that somehow he'd win out over the agony. He'd been wrong—horribly, *painfully* wrong.

Inera asked her questions. *Where is the girl*, she would ask while running cool fingers across his cheeks. *Where is the armlet*, while walking in a circle around him. *What creature made that bruise*, while tracing the edges of the same.

In the beginning, Dormael would curse at her, or threaten her, or tell her with absolute surety that someone would be looking for him. She'd gesture at the man standing beside her, and he would step inside the circle with that jagged little knife.

He started with his fists, punching Dormael until his mouth bled and his lips were too swollen to speak. He'd drive his fist into Dormael's stomach, expelling the air from his lungs. When Dormael went to suck in a breath, the man would stab him in the gut.

After that, he would go to work with the knife, lips pursed like a craftsman at a workbench. He cut Dormael across the stomach in long, slow lines. He stabbed him in the belly in quick, shallow punches. He dug the blade under Dormael's skin and flayed small sections from the tissue underneath.

He cut, beat, and kicked Dormael until he was dizzy with the loss of blood. Dormael's hands eventually went numb from the weight on his wrists. His feet lost the strength to move. His blood was splattered everywhere within the Greater Circle. It ran over his elbows and into his armpits, from his lips and eyes, from the stab wounds in his midsection.

When the torture stopped, Inera would come with her questions—all soft, cool hands, and kisses along his bloody chest. She whispered to him, rubbed him, and rubbed against him. He would have been horrified, but all he felt was pain and nausea.

When he wouldn't answer, it would start all over again.

Dormael's mind went fuzzy, his hurts fading to a buzz in the background of his thoughts. He could feel his chest filling with his own blood, making it harder and harder to breathe. He wheezed, spraying a wisp of his own blood over his lips. The world retreated behind a wall of pain.

Everything went silent. The beating, the stabbing, the cutting—it went quiet. Only the sound of running water and hushed conversation came to his ears. A cool hand touched his cheek. He squinted through vision blurry with blood.

Inera wiped blood from his face, thumbing it from under his eyes. Her expression was sad, as if he were a rabid beast she was sorry she had to put down. In her other hand she held a small glass jar filled with what he thought was water—except there were tiny lights whirling around inside.

"It hurts, doesn't it?" she asked, slipping her bloodied fingers into her mouth and smiling as she tasted them. She took a deep breath, as if his blood were the most delicious wine. "I can make it all stop. You want that, don't you? To feel no more pain, to be whole again? I know you do. Just say it—say that you'll pledge your life to me. Tell me you will serve me and be mine forever. Tell me what I wish to know. It wouldn't be so bad, you know. We could lie under the stars again. We could be together again, Dormael. I know you want that as much as I do. I know you want me again."

She pressed her mouth to his chest, started giving him light kisses as if they were going to make love. Though desire was the furthest thing from his mind, Inera's lips felt cool and wonderful against the heat of his tortured flesh. Every bit of him hurt, and her kisses stayed on his skin once her lips were gone, like cold fingerprints.

I'm dying. No one is coming, and I'm going to die here. So be it— just get it over with.

He'd gone through multiple rounds of the questioning, though he couldn't remember how many. A feeling of acceptance came over him, a strange sort of peace. He had revealed nothing to her— he'd screamed and cried and sobbed like a wounded beast, but he had told her nothing.

She could kill him, but she'd never get what she wanted out of him. Release beckoned, and he let himself go deeper, listening to his laboring heart as he went. It faded into the background.

So mote it be. No one else would say the words for him, no one would speak over his pyre. No one would get the chance.

Inera was saying something again, but her voice was hazy and indistinct. Dormael's vision faded to blackness, and suddenly, he was floating. He felt weightless, cool, and comfortable. His pains were still there, somewhere in his consciousness, but they were unimportant. He could hear his heartbeat begin to stutter, failing in his last moments.

You are here. How have you come to this place again?

The alien presence he'd met in his dreams was with him in the darkness. The power touched his mind, and he felt that strange stretching sensation in his thoughts again, as if his mind was connected with eons of awareness. His consciousness felt like a piece of fabric stretched to its limit.

I am dying, he thought, pushing the words out to the alien presence.

No. Life still beats in your flesh. I can feel it.

Then how—

He felt something yank against his consciousness, as if the presence were trying to hold on to him while something else, something far away, pulled him from its grasp. Dormael's head spun. The darkness fell away like water draining from his head.

Dormael coughed, spluttered, and choked. Pain slammed back into him as he awakened. Inera was forcing water into his mouth from a jar, spilling it over his face and into his throat. He felt something enter his mouth, like he'd swallowed a bug made of electric flame.

Dormael went rigid as every muscle in his body stiffened. The chain snapped back and forth as his muscles were wracked with spasms, the clatter filling the room. He felt as if lightning were crawling over his skin, into his wounds, leaving a tingling sensation behind. His heart beat in his ears with a vengeance.

His wounds knitted together, his skin and muscle and innards twisting back into place with an unnatural tingle. Dormael's wits cleared as he sucked in a chestful of air. He could almost taste the stench of the room—sewage, blood, sweat, and rust. His pain faded and his muscles went slack, leaving him feeling oddly refreshed.

Dormael stared open-mouthed at Inera. She smiled, one side of her mouth ticking up with a knowing expression. Turning, she glided back to the table and set the glass jar atop it. When she turned back to regard him, the triumph in her expression made him want to scream.

"Now," she said. "Where is the armlet?"

**

Bethany sighed as she watched Shawna fight on the Bruising

Stretch.

Shawna slipped in and out of her opponent's reach like a cat, easily knocking aside attacks and making attacks of her own. Bethany held her own knife, stroking the flat side of the blade with her thumb. She sat on the edge of a fountain, drawn deep within her cloak. Thunder rumbled overhead as the students on the Bruising Stretch continued their lessons—though most of them were watching Shawna.

Which was why it had been so easy to give the boy Dormael had sent with her the slip. He had been staring at Shawna, watching her spin and fight. Bethany had only turned a corner—it had been the easiest thing in the world. The boy had been nice, and she hoped he didn't get in trouble.

But it was his own stupid fault—Bethany had put forth little effort to ditch him.

Shawna had seen her earlier in the day, but Bethany had ducked out of sight not long after. She felt safer watching from a distance. Big people had so many concerns at eye level that it was easy to get lost beneath their gaze. They rarely looked down.

The Conclave grounds spread around her, with manicured rows of grass, stone, bushes and fountains. The Bruising Stretch was a vast area covered with paving stones. It had twin armories at one end and a covered gazebo for resting at the other. The Conclave Proper rose up behind her, the vast tower stark against the overcast sky. Thunder cracked the day again, and Bethany could smell the storm brewing, like a quickening in the air.

She watched a group of Initiates walk by, trailing in a single file behind an old woman. They all wore blue tunics, and lately some of them had taken to wearing bands of color on their arms. These children, though, were younger even than her. She wondered if she would be like them, in a class with others like them.

Was Dormael going to leave her alone here?

Would she make any friends? Would she still be able to steal into the dining hall whenever she wanted and grab something from the cooks? Would she be made to do scullery duty?

The thought of washing out pots wasn't pleasant, but she thought she could handle it. Grease and soap and threatening ladles were a far sight better than cold streets and an empty belly.

Besides—it would probably be easy to ditch scullery duty. After all, big people never looked down.

She closed her eyes and opened her Kai. She had been forbidden to do it when she was alone. She couldn't help it.

The world sang when she was listening through her Kai.

The grass had its own music and harmonized with the wind and the bushes. The endless clanging of steel-on-steel and clacking of practice swords filled the world with a beat. The thunder above her sounded like it would shake the entire world—maybe it did.

She had never dreamed such a thing would be possible. She never thought she would come to a place like this, where higher concerns existed than what you were going to eat the next day, or where you could sleep without someone stealing your stuff, or trying other things. Nastier things.

Here, no one did the nastier things. This was a different world. Bethany knew the slums existed in the city—she'd seen the faces on the day they had arrived, dragging Dormael in a horse cart. Hungry, distant faces hovering at waist-level, flitting like ghosts through the crowds. Shawna hadn't seen them, and neither had D'Jenn. Big people never looked down, but Bethany always knew where to look.

You learn where to look, or you starve.

She used to huddle outside a tavern during the wintertime, listening to an old blind man tell stories at the window. He probably knew she was listening to his stories, because he always sat at the window, even when it was too cold to have it open. He would leave his plate close to the edge of the sill, and he never raised a ruckus when she snatched something. He just went on telling his stories and never looked down.

He was blind, anyway—he couldn't have seen her if he'd wanted to.

One night, the old man wasn't there anymore, and he never showed up again.

The stories he told, though, were always wonderful tales of magic and monsters. He told of old heroes, pirates and adventure. In the old man's stories, there was always a cave that was home to some dreadful, man-eating creature which guarded a horde of treasure, or a magical castle full of evil spells and traps. Bethany had always thought she'd never get the chance to see a real wizard.

She never thought she'd *be* one.

Bethany was enjoying her time in the Conclave, this short period where no one knew what to do with her. She was expected to start training soon, but since they'd been here, she'd been free to roam as she pleased. Bethany took frequent advantage of her freedom.

In her time in the Conclave, she'd explored most of the upper floors looking for evil magical traps. She'd flitted past classrooms full of attentive students, the teachers either blind to her presence or unconcerned. She had found areas in the tower where huge tapestries hung, large enough for her to take fifteen steps from one end to the other. There were floors polished so black they shone like a mirror, and places where flowing script was written into the very walls, inlaid with silver, brass and gold. There were high, quiet balconies jutting out of the Conclave Proper as if they had grown from it, where wind whipped across the platform and there was nothing to hold. There were close places, places that always held a gathering of one sort or another, with students bustling back and forth through a cloud of conversation. Bethany had moved through it all unseen—or, at least, unnoticed.

Thunder cracked across the sky, this time louder than before. Bethany could smell the rain coming, and her Kai tingled with excitement at the storm. The first patters of rainfall splashed to the paving stones, filling her nose with the smell of rock and water. She pulled her hood up and sheathed her dagger, rising from the edge of the fountain. Bethany had spent a hundred nights in the rain, and she had no wish to repeat the experience today.

Shawna was occupied, and Dormael had left the Conclave to go into the city. Bethany had watched Allen and D'Jenn trot across the courtyard earlier, her uncle carrying more weapons than she could name. She took a deep breath and made for the Conclave Proper.

Maybe I can steal a sweet-cake from the dining hall.

After that, she would do more exploring. She'd overheard a few of the Initiates talking about the tunnels underneath the Conclave—a labyrinth full of magical items. Bethany had found a few ways into the Conclave basements already, but had neglected to venture into the darkened corridors. Today was a fine day to explore.

Smiling, she scampered toward the dining hall.

**

Dormael wasn't sure how long the torture had continued.

Inera had taken him to the brink of death over and over again and brought him back with the jar of swirling lights. During his lucid moments, he had the presence of mind to wonder what kind of magic she'd used on him, but soon his thoughts would again devolve to pain and despair. She was breaking him, conditioning his mind to believe she was the only person who could make the pain stop and bring him back to health. The knowledge of it didn't help—he could feel his resolve slipping away. Each time she came to him, crooning to him and placing light kisses over his body, he had to fight not to beg her for respite.

If I don't get out of here soon, I'm going to break.

"I know your will is draining, my love," Inera said, swaying toward him with the jar. "Saying the words would be so easy. Serve me, Dormael. I will *show* you the ways to true power, and together we might be strong enough to challenge him!" She ran her fingers over his chest, tracing lines in the blood on his naked skin. Her mouth was stained from the kisses she'd given him, still blazing like cold fire over his chest.

"Just kill me," he uttered, forcing the words out through the blood in his mouth. "I'll never serve you, Inera. If there's anything left of you in there, just kill me."

"You're wrong, Dormael. You *will* serve me. You will *beg* to serve me!"

"No."

Inera hissed and turned back to the table, setting the jar down on its worn, wooden surface. She took a deep breath and sighed, bowing her head. The muscles in her shoulders worked beneath her pale skin. Her back, too, was riddled with those strange scars.

"This is taking too long," she said, reaching into the jar and grasping one of those strange lights in her fist. "We'll just have to do this the other way—the *harder* way. I'd hoped to have you by my side, Dormael, instead of at my feet." She whirled toward him, stalking forward and slamming her hand against his mouth, forcing the light inside.

Dormael swallowed on reflex. The fire ran through his

muscles again, his stomach heaving as his body wove itself back together, like a scarf unraveling in reverse. It made Dormael want to empty his stomach every time, even though there had been nothing on his stomach since the firewine at the Headless Dancer.

Inera moved to the wall before him, holding what looked like a piece of thin charcoal, and began scrawling on the stone. She drew a large circle on the wall and scrawled glyphs around it. He didn't recognize the working, though he knew how to construct all the types of the Greater and Lesser Circles.

"If you won't agree to help me, love, then I'll just have to force you to do it," she said, speaking through her teeth as she drew in angry, sharp strokes. "I had hoped that you would take your rightful place, but if you insist on being obstinate, I am forced to see you turned."

Turned?

"What are you doing, Inera?"

"There are ways, dear Dormael, to force you to my will. My master taught me many things, secrets beyond the ken of what you and yours are willing to learn. Old things, ancient spells of power. You will see, my love—you will see very soon." Her eyes were alight with rage, her mouth pulled in a tight line across her pallid face.

In a flash, he understood. He was suddenly filled with cold, overpowering dread. Something inside of him had suspected. The woman he'd once loved looked like a corpse. Jureus had shown no outer signs of necromancy—no scars, no pallid skin, no white hair—and he had been the first necromancer Dormael had seen up close. Jureus, though, had been a boy.

Inera must be higher in the pecking order. Her master must be the same shadowy figure who had spoken to Jureus in the camp. A new disgust welled up inside of him as he looked at her, imagining the woman he'd shared so many close nights with eating human flesh, relishing in abhorrence. He wanted to vomit all over again.

"You've become one of them," he said. "You're working with the *vilth.*" The words had been meant as an accusation, but they sounded more like an admission of defeat as they escaped his mouth. Some part of his heart—forgotten in the years since he'd seen her—ripped open again and started to bleed.

"Yes," she replied, her eyes showing no remorse.

"You've eaten human flesh. Sacrificed people to your god."

Inera shook her head, favoring him with a silvery peal of chilling laughter.

"That, and so much more, my love," she smiled. "You're about to see."

She pulled a little black dagger from her belt and slashed her palm, squeezing the gray flesh until it bled. She chanted, speaking a language he'd never heard, and began tossing her blood over the circle on the wall. The men in the room shuffled away from her. Inera threw her arms out, raising the dagger to the ceiling, and her blood began to smoke. It hissed and turned into black vapor, wisping away into nothing.

Dormael reached down into his being and pulled his Kai awake, trying to force it to bear against the magical pressure of the Circle containing him. It was no use—summoning his magic was like trying to arm-wrestle with a giant. The Circle couldn't be circumvented by battering against it with his power. Dormael felt like an animal pacing in a cage, waiting for a predator to be locked inside with him.

He tried to move on the chain, to swing far enough in any direction to gain purchase with his feet. If he could kick something across the sand forming the Greater Circle, he could break it. He scrambled back and forth with his toes, trying to gain purchase on the stone. It was wet, filthy with his blood, and his feet only slipped back and forth as he struggled. The manacles dug into his wrists as his weight jerked back and forth. Try as he might, he could not reach the sand.

Dormael's heart pounded. His eyes shot around the room, trying to find something that might help him, might get him out of this. When he looked at the little table, he froze.

The little jagged knife lay on the wooden table, forgotten. The blade was glowing—or rather, his blood was glowing, giving off a rose-colored mist. It wafted from the blade like a strange, magical fog. Everywhere his blood lay outside the Greater Circle, it was glowing. Inera's men had their eyes locked to her, fearing whatever she was about to unleash. No one had noticed his blood.

The bastards don't know where to look.

It had to be D'Jenn. He would be following a blood trail, then. The crafty bastard might even be close. Dormael turned his gaze on Inera. He had to give D'Jenn time.

"Inera!"

She ignored him.

"Inera! Turn around and face me, you bitch!"

She kept chanting, her back to him.

"You can still walk away from this, leave the service of this *vilth*! It's not too late!"

She gave no reaction.

She spat angry, guttural words at the Circle on the wall. She tossed more blood—left, right, up and down. The blood coalesced, sliding into the cracks between bricks, and became one undulating mass. It turned a deep black color, and the surface of the Circle became a mirror of darkness.

"Inera!" he shouted. "Inera, I still love you!"

She paused, her spell caught at the apex, waiting like a headman's axe at the zenith of its swing. Inera glanced over her shoulder, keeping her body turned toward the Circle. Her eyes were sad, and there was a pained grimace on her face.

Is there anything left of her under that monstrous shell?

"It's too late, now," she said. "Much too late."

I can't die this way!

Dormael's heart skipped a beat He pulled again at his Kai, trying desperately to wrench his magic free. He raged and raged against the pressure of the Greater Circle containing him, but it was a futile struggle.

"Goodbye, Dormael. No matter what you think, I will always love you."

With that, Inera turned her head back to the blackened Circle, snarled another guttural word, and tossed another splotch of blood on its inky surface.

There was a hollow thump, and the air in the room rushed toward the dark Circle. The black fluid spun and the center of the Circle pulled away, as if it were opening into the Void itself. Everything in the room was pulled toward the portal, including Dormael. His toes were sucked toward that yawning abyss, the manacles once again biting into his wrists.

A sinuous, wet hand reached from the black, grasping the edge of the Circle where it met the wall. Its skin was a grayish color, its fingers too long, disjointed and deformed. Its head appeared next—narrow and pointed in an odd, triangular fashion. Its eyes were glowing yellow embers along the sides of its face. It didn't have a mouth, but there was a hole at the tip of its snout. A long, slippery tongue whipped out and tasted the air as the creature slithered into the room. Tendrils reached from the tongue like the feelers of a blind cave worm as it met the air.

Dormael would have screamed, but terror froze the sound in his throat.

The thing—whatever it was—plopped onto the floor with a wet squelch. It was the size of a large dog, though the similarities stopped there. It didn't have legs, but two sets of arms instead, as if a mad child had designed the thing from a nightmare. Its abdomen looked boneless, like a stomach dragging behind it. When the creature got its bearings, it pulled itself along the floor with those twitching, disjointed arms toward Dormael's Circle.

A primal instinct screamed at Dormael to run. He kicked and struggled, slipped and grunted and screamed, but he continued to hang on the chain like a worm on a hook. The manacles bit into his wrists. He struggled again for his Kai, but the pressure of the Greater Circle was too much.

Another presence, something dark and subtle, entered the room.

Something ancient, something familiar circled Dormael's consciousness like a beast from the deep, its presence unnoticed by everyone else. It reached for Dormael's mind, bypassing the Greater Circle with little trouble. Dormael reached back, grasping for the entity like a man sinking in quicksand.

Time slowed—or his perception of it sped up, he wasn't sure. The creature from the wall was moving as if the air was thick jelly, and the expressions of everyone around him were frozen. He felt the ancient thing in his mind again, sifting through his consciousness to find a way to communicate with him. Pain, concern, and fear all faded to the background.

This is an abomination.

Sounds like a fair description, Dormael replied. Humor, though, was lost on the alien presence.

The woman summoned this thing from the depths?

Yes, Dormael said. *What is it? What is it going to do to me?*

It is called a Taker. It will crawl into your body and eat your insides, then wear your skin.

Every time the entity spoke to him, Dormael's vision vibrated and his sight went wildly out of focus. He could feel its voice in his chest. Its touch on his mind was hard to endure.

Why are you here? How did you get here? Through that Gate?

I do not know. My memories are shattered, my being sundered.

Dormael tried to move back as the Taker got closer. *How did you find me?*

I can sense you. I was once two, but I am now one, and now there is you. How can I sense you? The thing sounded confused.

How am I supposed to know? Dormael wanted to shake his head. *I don't even know what you are. Do you know?* He kept his eyes on the Taker which was crawling toward him in tiny increments. His skin crawled at the sight, somehow more terrible in sluggish splendor.

I do not know. My memory is fragmented. Part of me is gone. I was two, and now I am one. But now, there is you, the ancient presence said.

I don't think I'll be here much longer. Not if that thing on the floor has its way, Dormael replied.

If you die, what will happen?

I don't know, Dormael said. *I've never died before—not all the way.* The presence was quiet for a few moments, and Dormael could feel it pondering, trying to piece something together. Sharing his head with the thing was starting to give him a headache.

I may be able to touch your world. I will try.

Time rushed back into place. The Taker squirmed, quivering toward Dormael faster than anything so ugly should be able to move. It reached the edge of the Greater Circle and stopped to gather its slimy, skinny arms beneath its body. It raised itself from the floor.

Dormael's head swam with sudden vertigo. His body tensed, as if he were falling from a great height, and his vision stretched, the far wall retreating as everything in his peripheral sight rushed closer. His mind reeled, and his vision blurred. Something moved from him, an invisible force that felt *wrong*, like it didn't belong in his world.

The presence exploded from Dormael's chest like an invisible wind. Dormael swung backwards on the chain, crying out as the manacles bit into his wrists all over again. The ancient presence slammed into the Taker, struggling against its advance with what meager energy it could muster. They fought for a moment, and Dormael could feel the struggle in his mind as he communed with the alien entity. The Taker gained the upper hand, but not before the alien wind blew the sand of the Greater Circle outward, scattering the barrier.

Dormael's magic flooded into him as the presence in his mind was pushed back to its dark prison. He threw his power at the chain above him, snapping it with pure force. His feet landed on the cold, slippery stone, and he crouched, naked, facing the ugly maw of the Taker.

Inera screamed a command, rage pouring from her voice. The Taker rose up on its hands, tongue whipping at the air. Dormael smiled and took a deep breath, pulling magic from the ether.

There was a loud crack, and people started dying.

**

D'Jenn crouched in the tunnel, listening to the noises coming from the darkness in the distance. Allen was hunkered down near him, breathing heavy with anticipation. There was some sort of antechamber beyond them, and two guards watched the entrance to yet another chamber. The noises coming from the guarded room were more than disconcerting.

There was screaming, words that D'Jenn couldn't quite hear, and a woman chanting in a strange, guttural language. D'Jenn could sense something strange in the magic—a greasy, slimy, wrongness slithering into the room beyond them. Its meaning was lost to him.

We have to go now, Allen signed to him in the Hunter's Tongue. His face had an urgent, excited expression, his jaw working as he ground his teeth.

We need to deal with the guards first. Quietly.

Leave that to me, Allen signed back.

Before D'Jenn could stop him, he was moving into the darkness toward the antechamber. D'Jenn cursed but followed his cousin down the tunnel. The water trickled around them, and every noise echoed from the stone.

Allen drew a hand-axe and a long, thick dagger. He moved like a stalking predator, his footfalls silent against the sound of the running sewage. He crept down the tunnel to the edge of the torchlight and glanced to D'Jenn for confirmation. D'Jenn gave him a quick nod.

Allen reached into a pocket and drew out a coin, placing his dagger in his teeth. He tossed the coin side-arm into the chamber. It struck the wall to the guards' right, causing both of them to look in that direction, hands going to their weapons. They turned away from the tunnel, muttering to one another.

Allen rushed forward, sending his hand-axe spinning through the darkness in an overhand throw. It sailed through the shadow and found a guard's head. The man went limp as the axe sank into his skull, body slumping against the wall. His partner went for his sword and turned in Allen's direction, but Allen was upon him before he could pull it free.

Allen rushed up against the man, trapping his sword arm against his body and ramming his dagger through the side of his neck. The guard made a gurgling hiss as his legs gave out, but Allen caught his body, and lowered easily it to the ground. When it was over, the only sounds were the noises coming from the other side of the wooden door.

D'Jenn strode out of the darkness, giving Allen a fierce nod. Allen recovered his weapons and moved to one side of the old wooden door. D'Jenn moved to the other side and put a hand to the wood.

Torchlight seeped through the cracks in the door, throwing wild shadows over D'Jenn's boots. The noises stopped in the chamber beyond, but the silence felt ominous, and the feeling was reflected in D'Jenn's Kai. There was a moment of quiet, and D'Jenn caught Allen's gaze.

On three, D'Jenn signed.

Allen nodded.

There was a sucking noise like nothing D'Jenn had ever heard. It pulled at him, as if there was a whirlpool in the next room. The door vibrated on its rusty hinges, making a loud clattering noise in its decaying frame. There was a wet sloshing, slithering noise from beyond the door, and D'Jenn shared a confused glance with Allen. A scream rose from the chamber, a high-pitched wail of rage, and D'Jenn felt Dormael's song ring out in the magic, a triumphant symphony of power.

"Three!"

D'Jenn sent a torrent of magic at the door, blowing it to pieces.

**

The tunnels beneath the Conclave were an exciting place.

Bethany had known how to get to them—she had found the servants' stairs on the first day, and the top level of the tunnels had a few rooms the cleaning staff used to store their equipment. Servants and Initiates went to the top level of the tunnels all the time. It hadn't been hard to slip by them. The tunnels were dark, and the dark was always a good place for hiding.

It hadn't taken her long to find another staircase headed down. The level beneath the first looked much like the one before, only with fewer sconces for candles on the walls and more darkness. Now and then, Bethany would find a strange design laid into the wall, like knots turning in upon themselves. Other times she found the Eye of Eindor or runes she couldn't read.

For some reason, she got angry about that—she wanted to read everything.

The corridors were peppered with old wooden doors, shut tight against the dusty hallway. She tried almost every door she came to, but most of them were locked. Where they weren't, what she found wasn't much fun—old furniture covered with sheets and dusty stacks of this-or-that. Never a magical chest, like she'd heard about in all the old man's stories.

I want to be like Leyton. Pirate-King of the Sea, Rescuer of Princesses.

In all the old man's stories, Leyton fought evil wizards for one thing or another. Bethany had never wanted to be the princess— after all, what good was just sitting in a tower, waiting to be rescued? And now, to add to the problem, she was a wizard. Who was she supposed to root for in the story?

"I'm Bethany," she said aloud, her voice echoing down the darkened hallways. "I'm here to save you—I'm a wizard, not an evil one. A girl, not a princess. I'll save you, but you can keep the kiss, thank you very much."

She skipped down the hallway, wielding a length of wood she'd found in one of the storerooms. She wanted to be on Leyton's crew and sail the seas in search of gold and plunder. She wanted to rescue Princesses from evil wizards—she could use her powers for good—and be a hero to all her friends. She wanted to explore old ruins and magical caves, to slay ghosts and goblins and dragons and trolls.

"I'm Bethany," she growled. "Pirate-Queen of the Seas!"

Her voice echoed down the darkened hallways.

Pirate-Queen of the Seas...

Brandishing her table leg, she chased her voice down the hall, further into the twisting labyrinth of corridors. She laughed the way she only could when she was alone and laughed again as she heard the echoes. Her voice bounced from the stony hallways and chased her around corners. She ran between isolated bubbles of candlelight, and the sconces began to get farther and farther away from each other.

When she paused to look, the sconce she left behind her was the only one she could see. The hallway stretched into the darkness, branching off left and right, but no light peeked from anywhere. Bethany retreated back to the puddle of candlelight, eyes drawn to the blackness beyond.

This was the sort of situation Leyton would find himself in, and he always found a way to win through. Getting lost in the tunnels was a real danger, but anything good hidden beneath the Conclave wouldn't be tucked into a storeroom, guarded by dusty furniture. It would be beyond—in the dark.

"Pirate-Queen of the Seas," she growled.

Shawna wouldn't stand here in the torchlight, afraid to go on. Dormael wouldn't be scared that monsters would come out of the dark. D'Jenn would simply ask her—*are you not a wizard, Bethany?* Leyton wouldn't be afraid to go on, and neither would Bethany.

Bethany was a wizard—a Rescuer of Princesses.

She closed her eyes, sinking once again into the trance D'Jenn had taught her. Her heart fluttered a bit, fear tickling at her mind like a ghost in the darkness. Bethany stilled her breathing and concentrated, walling away her fear.

Her magic flooded into her.

It always came like lightning. She could feel the stones around her singing with their emptiness, an endless note reverberating not just through the walls but through every part of the structure.

The heat of the candles slid over her skin like warm water, flickering in time with the unpredictable rhythm of the flame. Bethany felt like a storm.

She was supposed to refrain from using her magic when she was alone—D'Jenn had taught her that word, 'refrain'. It was a stupid word, and it sounded like something you did to a piece of armor, or a wagon wheel.

"Just going to get my wagon wheel refrained," she said aloud.

Such a stupid word—*refrain*.

But what was she supposed to do? If she took the candles from the wall, she'd have no way to measure where she was. It was like when Leyton entered the Labyrinth of Carcas and was given a string by a fair maiden to show him the way out. Bethany didn't have a string, but if she took the candle, she knew she'd get lost. The candle was her string.

If she couldn't take the candle, she had to use magic. D'Jenn was always telling her—*Bethany, there's always an option, you're only stuck if you want to be stuck.* Bethany didn't want to be stuck. She thought D'Jenn might be proud of her, come to think of it.

She was only doing what he'd taught her to do.

Besides, she wouldn't *use* her magic, not exactly. With her Kai singing to her, she could feel every speck of dust on the surrounding stone. She could see, in a way. Bethany's eyes pierced the darkness like daggers with her Kai singing, but there was little light for her eyes to see. Her magical senses helped, though she was still learning how to use them.

"Pirate-Queen of the Seas," she whispered.

With her Kai guiding her steps, she ran into the darkness.

**

For a single, impossibly long second, Dormael crouched on the ground, feeling his magic sing through him like a torrent of fire, his naked body sweating and dirty, his hands still shackled to a length of rusty chain. The Taker's ember eyes bored into his, its tongue still lashing at the air around its triangular head. Inera screamed, and he could feel her gathering her power for some sort of attack. The three guards behind him reached for their swords.

Dormael weighed his options for a split second, surrounded by enemies, completely naked—and there was just something embarrassing about that on top of everything else—but far from helpless. Would it be worse to be killed by the sword, burnt to a cinder with magic, or whatever the Taker planned to do with him?

It will crawl into your body and eat your insides, then wear your skin.

Dormael liked his skin. He'd rather keep it, given the option.

He screamed his anger at the ugly thing before him, reaching deep inside his being for the magic. Tiny fingers of iridescent lightning arced up from his body, touching the surrounding stone in quick flashes. His hair stood and his skin tingled with anticipation, his muscles tensed for the explosion of power. The lightning rushed up from his feet, through his shoulders, and down his arms as he sent his magic forth.

The bolt of lightning slammed into the Taker, lifting its wet, quivering body from the floor and sending it flying toward the yawning blackness of the gate. The Taker uttered no cry as it was hit, but it left behind the smell of acrid, burnt flesh. As Dormael's lightning slammed through the gate, pushing the Taker back to wherever it had crawled from, the black substance cracked and sputtered. The gate burst like a bubble, and the Taker was gone. The dark fluid from which the gate had been made bled into the cracks in the stone.

Inera spun on Dormael, face contorted with rage. She raised her hand, and a vengeful song warbled through the ether. The shadows in the room deepened as her power gathered.

"Kill him! Take him—"

The door burst into the room in a shower of shattered wood.

Dormael had to cover his face and turn away, shielding himself from the flying debris. Inera was blown from her feet, and she tumbled across the floor until she smacked into the far wall. She let out an angry, incoherent noise as she climbed to her feet. Dormael rose and gathered his magic for another attack. He heard D'Jenn's song ringing through his Kai, and it was the most welcome noise he'd ever heard.

D'Jenn and Allen rushed into the room and took a quick look around. Their eyes alighted on Dormael, and relief washed over their faces. In the next instant, they sprung into action.

Dormael felt Inera's song ring out with an attack, and D'Jenn's answered. The two of them squared off between warring energies, steam and flame and water flying in all directions between them. Dormael wanted Inera himself, wanted to ask her why, wanted to find out so many things. He couldn't get between them now, though—not without risking D'Jenn's life. The conflagration forced him to back away from their fight.

Dormael snarled in frustration.

Allen rushed the three guards standing nearby, ripping Dormael's attention away. He held a long dagger in one hand and his Orrisan-style axe in the other. The first man stepped forward, whipping his sword from his waist in a smooth horizontal slash. Allen rolled to the outside, putting the man between himself and the other two guards. With two vicious movements, Allen's axe chopped into the back of the man's knee, eliciting a scream of pain. It ended with a gurgle as Allen rose to his feet, shoving the dagger into his throat. Blood welled over his hands as he pushed the man into his comrades, forcing them to stumble backward.

The second guard snarled and quick-stepped to the side, whipping his own sword free of his sheath. He stepped toward Allen with a feint, testing the gladiator's reflexes. Allen returned the feint with one of his own, and then the two were dancing around each other—step, parry, thrust, and swing, steel ringing from steel. Allen fought with a wolfish grace that set him apart from the other man, his movements like a predator flowing through its natural environment. The guard looked amateurish by comparison, struggling through the steps of a dance that came natural to Allen.

The third man was the one who had taken that jagged little knife to Dormael's skin. He'd been the one who had beaten him while he hung from the chain. Anger rose in Dormael's chest, heating his blood to a boil. The Red Sword tried to step in and stab his brother in the flank.

Dormael reached out and snatched him from the ground with his power, wrenching down on his chest. The man screamed as Dormael ground his power against him, feeling the satisfying crackle of ribs stretching to their breaking point resonating through his Kai. The man floated in the air, his limbs spread out as far as they could go. He tried to scream, but nothing could come out of his mouth—Dormael crushed the air from his chest, and kept the pressure on. His eyes found Dormael's and went wide with horror.

With a flick of his wrist, Dormael sent the man hurtling through the air, smashing him against the wall with a wet thump. He grimaced, but he couldn't scream—Dormael pushed him hard into the stone, holding him high against the wall with the weight of his power. Splitting his consciousness, he sent two of the discarded short swords hurtling from the ground, and slammed them through the man's shoulders, pushing hard enough to sink them into the stone. They rang as the force behind the thrust caused them to vibrate, and the man's face was a mask of agony. Dormael took the pressure off his chest and let the man's body hang from the blades.

"You bastard." Dormael couldn't take his eyes from his torturer. "You had a lot of fun with me, didn't you? A lot of bloody fun."

He glanced to the table where the jar of lights rested beside the jagged little knife.

**

The tunnels beneath the Conclave, as it turned out, weren't so easy to navigate.

Bethany had lost sight of her candle a long time ago and had wandered down endless corridors. She'd even gone down a flight of stairs and back up when she found another, but still she was lost. She tried to think of what Leyton would do, how he would get himself out of this situation, but there was nothing in the stories to give her a clue.

Pirate-Queen of the Seas, she grumbled. *Right.*

She felt sure if she kept walking, kept looking, she would eventually find her way out. There could only be so many staircases, so many intersections, so many old doors. They all looked the same to her, though, and that was the major problem. No matter which way she turned, she got turned around. Whenever she thought to backtrack, she ended up in a new place.

Bethany had called out once. Her voice had fled from her, pealing down the halls and bouncing from the stone. Her Kai still sang, but returned nothing she knew how to use. She was awash in a world of darkness, sound, and silence all at the same time.

She was utterly lost, and she knew it.

Bethany had no idea how long she'd been in the tunnels. The shadows yawned to either side of her, darkness in both directions. Fear beat a tight rhythm against her ribcage, and her mind started to play tricks on her. Did she hear something in the dark—a boot scuffling over stone, a rat skittering through the corridor?

She remembered the men in the mountain pass, the ones who had tried to take her. Her magic remembered, too, and it flared up in defense, posturing like an angry dog protecting its master. The hallway, however, was silent and empty.

You're alone now.

No! Not again, not again, not again, not again!

The voice came to her sometimes, whispering things to her in the dark. She thought she had left it behind long ago, left it in the streets where she starved and fought to keep from freezing. She thought that voice had died.

"I'm not alone," she whispered to herself, a mantra against her fear. "I'm only stuck if I want to be stuck. Fear is just a thought like any other."

It helped, but not much.

There was nothing for it but to keep going. If she froze and stayed in the same place, she might rot down here forever. It might be a hundred years before the next person came along and found her.

She ran.

She ran down the darkened hallways, unsure of her direction. She ran down side corridors, back and forth until she had no idea where she was. There were no candles this far down. Her only company was the dust and the silence.

There were a couple of times that she thought someone might be following her. She would hear a boot scrape over stone or some random noise she felt sure had come from a person. Her Kai, though, returned no sense of anyone, and the darkness pressed in on all sides. It could have been her mind playing tricks on her, but she couldn't be sure.

There was nothing to do but keep running. After what seemed like a week, she saw a puddle of candlelight in the distance— her candle, she was sure of it! She ran for it, skidding around a corner until she saw the candle at the end of a long hallway.

When she saw the candle, she slid to a halt.

A man crouched on the ground with his back to her, examining something on the floor in the puddle of light. He wore one of those Sevenlander cloaks that Dormael and D'Jenn wore, and Bethany couldn't see what he looked like. Her heart beat so loud that she was afraid he could hear it, even as far away as he was.

Her footprints told a story in the dust, leading off into an adjacent tunnel, crisscrossing back and forth between the halls. The man was gazing at them, as if he was trying to decide which fork to take, and which tracks to follow. Bethany was so afraid that she could barely move, but she forced herself to take a step backwards, keeping her eyes on the man further down the hall. The man should have been her salvation, but something—perhaps her general mistrust of bigger people—caused her to creep back into the darkness.

Her foot made a scraping noise against the stone.

The man turned his face to her so quickly that she uttered a squeal of surprise. She felt another song in the magic, and before she could move, she was surrounded with bright, white light. It caused spots to dance across her vision, and it hurt her eyes. She froze, outlined by the magical light, too afraid to move.

He locked eyes with her, and for just a second, Bethany felt silly. Maybe he *wasn't* chasing her, maybe he was just down here for another reason that had nothing to do with her. Still, she wasn't supposed to be running around in the dark all alone. What if he got her in trouble? The expression on his face was intense, and his eyes were different colors—one brown, one blue. They bored into her like daggers.

An instinct stopped her from stepping forward and identifying herself. She wasn't sure what it was, but something about the man felt wrong. Maybe it was the way he was staring at her, like one of those hungry monsters in the old man's stories. He took a step forward.

She shuffled backward.

"Child," he said. "Come here." His tone gave her a bad feeling, like there was a spider crawling over her skin. He took another step forward.

Bethany took another step back.

"Your father is looking for you," he said. "I'm a friend of his— he sent me to find you and bring you back. He's quite worried about you, you know."

He was *lying*. She would have known it even if she didn't know Dormael had gone into the city. Sometimes she could hear people lying, and his lie rang like a bell in her ears. She was so scared, but she forced herself to be brave, like Shawna, like Leyton.

Pirate-Queen of the Sea...

"Leave me alone," she said, her voice shaking under the weight of her fear. It felt good to say it, like the very words helped to bolster her courage. The man took another step toward her, and Bethany took another step away.

"Now, now," the man chided, holding his hand out to her. "Just come along, and I'll take you back upstairs. We can go find your father together, alright? Bethany is your name, right? Don't do anything silly, Bethany. We'll go right upstairs and find your father."

"You're a liar!" She wanted to say more, but his answering scowl scared her into silence. She took another step back, this time in response to his frown. Her magic coiled like a snake around her.

"You come here, child. **Now**!" he said, and the last word hit her like a blanket being thrown over her face. Before she knew what she was doing, she had taken a step toward the man. Her mouth wouldn't work, and she didn't want to go toward him, but she took another step anyway. Her body was betraying her with every movement.

"Good...come here child, that's it," he said. His voice was like a rope dragging her down the hall. Her Kai sang to her in frantic tones, struggling against the man's song, but it wrapped around her mind tighter than a snake. Her feet took another step. She fought down a wave of dizziness.

You're just a scared little girl again, all alone.

Alone again.

There was no one to help her.

No!

She took another step forward. The man's voice rang in her ears.

NO!

Her feet kept moving, though she fought them with every muscle in her body. The man stepped toward her, his hand reaching out to take hers. She felt her song slipping away, being drowned out by *his* song.

No, no, no, NO!

Bethany screamed. She screamed with everything she could muster, pouring all her fear into it, purifying the air with raw emotion. Her voice broke through the man's Kai like a rock through a glass window.

Her magic was back, roaring through her like she'd never felt before, and it was just as angry and afraid as she was. Her screams lashed across the space separating her from the stranger, slamming into him just as his voice had slammed into her, only stronger. Dust rose from the floor in a thin cloud as her scream hit him, and he slid backward across the intervening space as he struggled against her, shouting with surprise and disbelief.

His song tried to slide back into her head, but she screamed louder, pushing against him with every bit of fear in her body. His cloak flew backwards like it was caught in a storm wind. He pushed harder against her, trying to force his magic against hers, throwing some sort of attack at her. Bethany's song was too loud in her ears, and his magic slid from her like water.

Never again, never again, never again, never again!

The stones in the hallway cracked, sending more dust flying up from the ground, and the man's feet were lifted free of the floor. He slammed into the walls—once, twice, three times—and then even harder against the floor. She *felt* his breath leave his chest in a sudden, painful expulsion.

Her magic was so *angry*.

She held him to the floor, afraid he would get up and try to hurt her. His hand reached upward, struggling with his body and his Kai against her, but she was *not* going to let him up. He shouldn't have tried to hurt her. He shouldn't have tried to lie to her. He shouldn't have tried to use his magic on her.

NEVER AGAIN!

The candle in the sconce flared to life, the fire spreading like water spilling across a table. It crept toward the man in slow increments, pushing against the edges of his magic. His eyes were wild with terror.

She could feel him struggling against her—she was much, *much* stronger than he was.

He sobbed and made pitiful noises. Bethany could hear the

spittle in his voice, could hear desperation in his tone as he cried. Something about the sound made tears well up in her eyes, too, as if that one little noise had broken the floodgate holding them back. Her fire crept closer and closer to him, and she could feel him getting weaker.

"No!" he screamed. *"No! PLEASE!"*

Bethany turned and fled into the dark, her eyes blurry with tears.

Frantic screams echoed behind her.

**

The first thing D'Jenn noticed as he rushed into the room was Dormael, crouched with fingers of unspent electricity flickering over his naked skin. The remains of a Greater Circle lay scattered around him, the sand blown outward. Upon the wall to his right was another Circle, though D'Jenn didn't recognize any of the glyphs scrawled around it. It had been broken as well, and there was some sort of black substance crawling into the cracks of the stone.

He froze as he saw who was rising from the ground across from him.

D'Jenn had never seen anything like this girl before him, this remnant of the girl he'd met. The way she'd been cut upon, weaving strange designs into her skin, was something alien and abhorrent. Her hair had somehow been leached of its color, leaving it a stark, bone-white. She was a shadow of the Inera he'd met years ago, but it was her. There was no mistaking it.

Her eyes met his, bloodshot and filled with terrible anger. She wore some sort of tattered dress and a girdle around her midsection. It gave D'Jenn the impression of an old burial shroud, decaying from years left in the ground. There was a song ringing out from her that could only be her Kai, but it was interlaced with something else, some other power that felt greasy and black.

Inera snarled, startling him by lancing out with a torrent of fire. She sent it spiraling toward his face, hungry flames reaching for his skin. D'Jenn reacted with instinct, pulling the water from the sewage trench to block the flames. Steam burst from the point of contact, filling the chamber with hissing vapor. D'Jenn backed away, keeping the burning steam from his skin.

Gritting his teeth, D'Jenn split his concentration in two. He sent the other half of his magic whirling through the room, picking up every piece of errant debris. The sand, the dust, the pieces of the door, and anything light enough to be picked up by his magic was gathered into a whirling globe, blurring with the speed of its movement. He sent the globe toward Inera, engulfing her in the flying debris while still fending off the lance of fire.

She held out a hand, and the whirlpool of flying detritus was pushed outward from her. It wavered as their magic warred against each other, but the globe was pushed steadily away as she bent her strength against him. D'Jenn raised his eyebrows.

She's stronger than I remember.

She closed her eyes, and D'Jenn could feel her stabilizing her resistance. He redoubled the force against her shield, pushing hard with the strength of his Kai. Her strength wavered, and D'Jenn smiled.

Stronger, but not strong enough.

The lance of flame wavered at the edges, sputtering as the water started to win the struggle. The fire disappeared, and D'Jenn pushed his barrier of water into the whirling cloud, combining the two spells with all the power he'd summoned for those threads. His mind slid back into one focused purpose with practiced ease, and he pushed the whirlwind of debris at Inera with all the strength he could muster.

This should rip her right apart.

Since she'd abandoned her attack, however, Inera was able to concentrate on keeping the detritus away from her body, and her shield stabilized around her. Once again, the two of them were locked in a struggle of pure magical strength, and were almost evenly matched. D'Jenn was a bit stronger than Inera, and he was able to gain a little ground, but her defense was simpler than his attack, and he had to expend more effort than she did.

She grimaced, and he felt her bend more of her will into the spell. His cloud thinned and widened, pushed away from her body. D'Jenn returned her stare and poured his magic into the spell, but could gain no more ground against her.

She snarled a word in a guttural language and tossed her hand upwards.

Blood sprayed up from her palm, whirling into the water and

debris. A black smoke-like substance spread through the cloud, whirling into his spell and obscuring D'Jenn's view of her. He felt the spell start to come apart, as if it were being eaten from the inside, corroded by that same greasy power he'd felt her using before. D'Jenn cursed and abandoned his attack, and the debris evaporated into black smoke.

The cloud roiled up from Inera, gathering above her like an angry thunderhead. She smiled and held her bleeding hand above her head, the smoke leaking from her wound. D'Jenn tensed himself for another attack.

She snarled again, and multiple tentacles whipped out from the cloud, flying at D'Jenn with deadly speed. He fended them off with flashes of his magic, but every time he forced one of them aside, another whipped at him from a different direction. He danced over the slick floor, looking for a defensible position. The cloud floated after him, chasing him around the room.

Inera cackled and disappeared through the doorway. D'Jenn cursed in frustration, but he was pinned down by the reaching tentacles. Inera's laughter echoed through the tunnel beyond.

"Dormael!" he shouted.

Dormael's magic rang out, slicing into the cloud as D'Jenn fended off the tentacles. The strange mass of oily darkness fought back, but it was no match for both of them. Even as D'Jenn sliced the tentacles to pieces, Dormael brought his magic to bear against the cloud itself. With a combined effort, the two of them crushed the thing out of existence. The destruction of the spell left an odd shriek sounding through the ether, like the echo of a dissonant chord.

In the wake of the fight, all was quiet. D'Jenn could hear his own labored breathing in his ears, his heart beating against his ribs. Dormael stood beside him, his face covered in blood.

All three of the guards were dead. Two of them lay on the ground, pools of blood spreading out beneath them. The third was pinned to the wall by swords driven through his shoulders. His innards were spilled onto the floor—grayish, slimy ropes cascading from a jagged rent in his stomach. There were multiple stab wounds in him, but some of them appeared to have been made from the inside, rather than from outside—as if something had crawled into the man's gut and then back out again from another place. Atop the pile of gore sat a single jagged knife.

D'Jenn had to bite back his gorge at the sight. Allen and Dormael ignored the body. Dormael turned and spat blood to the side. D'Jenn couldn't tell if the blood was from a wound or if it had simply run into his mouth. The man was covered in it.

"Do you see my clothes anywhere?" Dormael looked around the gore-riddled room.

Allen snapped his fingers and stepped into the antechamber. In a few moments, he returned with a pile of clothing. He nodded to his brother as he handed them over.

"Saw them in the corner before we came in here," Allen said. "Are you alright? You look like the Six Hells came over and had you for dinner."

Dormael looked down at his shackles, shaking his head. He frowned, and D'Jenn felt his song murmur as the metal snapped and fell to the stone. Dormael brushed his hands together, taking the clothes and pulling them on.

"Coz, you might want to clean up a bit," D'Jenn said, indicating Dormael's blood-spattered skin.

"Oh, right." Dormael closed his eyes, and the blood lifted from his skin and flaked away into the air. "Inera got away?"

D'Jenn gave a grudging nod.

"Eindor's bloody eye," Dormael cursed. "She's working with that...with that gods-damned *vilth*. She's one of *them*."

"Gods," Allen said. "You mean a necromancer, like the one in the mountains?"

"Worse," Dormael said. "She's more powerful than Jureus by far."

D'Jenn nodded. "I remember what her gift was like before. It's changed—it's broader, stronger, and infused with that energy, whatever it was."

"Don't they eat dead bodies, kill people right and left, that sort of thing?" Allen asked.

"All of those things, and worse, I suspect," D'Jenn said. "The Conclave doesn't know much about them. They have a strict kill-them-wherever-you-find-them policy. Most of what we know comes from eyewitness accounts of past *vilthinum* activities, and some of it is...questionable. I'm surprised to see her alive."

"Imagine how I feel," Dormael muttered. "Besides, I'm not sure she *is* totally alive."

"Who is she?" Allen asked.

"I was in love with her once," Dormael said, as if he were announcing it to himself as much as his brother. "She was...different, then."

"One would hope," Allen said.

Dormael gave him an evil look, which Allen ignored.

"I'm glad you're alright, though," Allen said. "D'Jenn was worried about you."

D'Jenn uttered a derisive snort.

"Good to see I'm so loved." Dormael smiled.

"What was she doing here?" D'Jenn said. He walked over the scene, surveying the ruins of the Greater Circle on the ground. He examined the Circle on the wall, shaking his head at the unfamiliar glyphs. "These markings—I've never seen their like."

"She was...she was torturing me for information. She wanted the armlet. She wanted Shawna," Dormael's shoulders slumped beneath the weight of the admission. "When I refused her, she summoned up a demon that would have worn my skin and taken my identity—at least, I think it was a demon. She mentioned her master. There can be no question. She's one of them, through and through."

"How do you know that—the thing about the demon taking your identity?" D'Jenn asked, suddenly interested. Little was known about the denizens of the outside planes. Where had Dormael learned about them? He loved his cousin, but if D'Jenn hadn't read about it, then Dormael certainly hadn't.

Unless one could read it from the thighs of a laughing girl.

"It's not important," Dormael said.

He said that a little too quickly. It must be the day for fucking secrets. Everyone is keeping something from me.

D'Jenn let the matter lie. After all, Dormael had just been tortured—and from the amount of blood, D'Jenn was surprised he could stand. For all the gore that covered him—and what covered the middle of the Greater Circle—he should have been bleeding from a thousand cuts. Instead, he looked whole.

Too whole.

"Dormael, wait," D'Jenn said, reaching out a hand to forestall him from pulling the shirt over his head. "That bruise you had—

it's gone!"

"I know," Dormael sighed. "She used her powers on me, D'Jenn. She...*healed* me somehow. Do you see that jar on the table?"

D'Jenn looked to where his cousin was pointing, to a glass jar with a thick cork in the top. Lights swirled around inside of it, revolving in an endless parade around the edge of the glass. They threw moving shadows over the walls.

Allen walked over to the jar, picked it up off the table, and shook it.

Dormael and D'Jenn started back in surprise.

"The little sparks didn't get shaken with the rest of the water," Allen said. "Watch."

Dormael and D'Jenn both made protesting, fearful noises, but Allen swirled the bottle in a circle, causing the water to spin. The lights continued their slow revolutions of the glass as if the water wasn't there. Dormael and D'Jenn scowled at Allen.

"What?"

"Nothing," D'Jenn said. "Just that shaking that thing around might have killed us all. Nothing to worry about."

Allen smiled.

"Like this?" he asked, shaking the bottle again.

"Give me that!" Dormael said, snatching the bottle from Allen's hands. Dormael handed the bottle to D'Jenn and went back to straightening his clothing. D'Jenn raised the bottle to his eyes.

He gazed into the water, watching the sparks of light revolve around the bottle in contented circles. It was beautiful, if one didn't take into account that it had been used by a *vilth*, and was most likely made with necromancy. The gods only knew how the things had been created. For all D'Jenn knew, they were the souls of suffering children.

Shawna would like that one—he'd have to make sure and tell her.

"What did she do with it?" D'Jenn asked, still gazing into the bottle.

"She fed the lights to me." Dormael frowned. "There were more of them before—I think they're expended with each use. When I swallowed them, they...well, they healed me. Stitched my cuts together like they'd never happened. I had no idea *vilthinum* were capable of such things."

"Why in the Six Hells did she heal you?" Allen asked.

"Because," Dormael said, "I was close to death. She did it multiple times."

The casual way Dormael said it gave D'Jenn the chills. Allen's jaw worked again, his expression becoming angry. The room was silent for a tense, uncomfortable moment.

"Let's get back to the surface," Dormael said, his tone grim. "We need to get back to the Conclave as quickly as we can."

"Indeed," D'Jenn nodded. "I needed to find you. Some new information has come to light."

"No kidding," Allen said, gesturing at the carnage.

"What new information?" Dormael asked.

"It's about Victus." The words tasted like bile even as he said them. "He's been using us. He's been using everyone."

Dormael looked as if he wanted to object, wanted to argue. After searching D'Jenn's face, though, Dormael's eyes filled with grim acceptance. He sighed, his shoulders slumping.

"Of course he has."

"We need to get back, get you looked at," D'Jenn said.

"No," Dormael grunted, shaking his head. "If Victus is using us, as you say, then whom can we trust? You and I both know the only reason we came here was for his help."

"I don't know," D'Jenn said. "I just...don't know. Something will present itself, though. We're only stuck if we let ourselves be stuck."

Dormael narrowed his eyes. "Victus used to tell me that."

"Where do you think I got it?"

"Regardless," Dormael said, "Inera wanted Shawna, wanted the armlet. If I can be taken off the streets of Ishamael, wounded or not, what else are they capable of doing? What plans are they hatching? We need to get back to the Conclave, find Bethany and Shawna, and figure out our next move."

D'Jenn nodded. "Agreed."

"This just got a lot more interesting," Allen smiled. When D'Jenn and Dormael gave him a disgusted look, he shrugged. "Don't look at me like that—I've been lounging around the Conclave for days, now. You promised excitement. I'm just glad it's finally here."

Dormael rolled his eyes. "You're an idiot."

"*You* wanted to bring me along," Allen pointed out.

"True enough," Dormael said. "Let's go. I'm ready to get out of these gods-damned tunnels. I'm never coming back here, either. I'm going to spend the rest of my life above ground."

D'Jenn made sure to take the bottle of lights with them as they left the corpse-strewn room behind.

THE CRUX

Maarkov sat on the rocky ledge, watching the storm move northward through the Runemian valley. The sun peeked from the edge of the far horizon, revealing a tiny sliver of its backside as it retreated to the west. Thunder rumbled from the storm in the distance, and rain sheeted down from the clouds.

The wind in the mountains was cold, though there was no reason for him to care other than comfort. He could wade through a snowdrift on the Sea of Moving Ice, and it would not kill him. His eyeballs could freeze, his blood could freeze, and his body would go on living—or moving, anyway. He wasn't sure if *alive* was a word he would have used to describe himself.

Could eyeballs freeze? He'd have to ask Maaz. They could burst, or squish—he'd seen that before. He'd never seen them frozen, though.

Maarkov packed a pipe full of flaky tobacco and trudged over to the fire for a burning twig. The *strega*—now a veritable troop— stood silent sentry in the clearing, staring out in all directions. The things made his skin crawl. The utter silence, the stillness, the lack of anything resembling a self behind those dead, milky eyes— there were a million reasons he hated them. The boy who had watched his family be killed in the hinterlands of Soirus-Gamcrit was among them, his lanky body now gray, his eyes empty. The whole family was here, in fact—together in life, together in un-life.

Maarkov scowled at the things. He found himself staring at

them, waiting to see if something would trigger them. They only stood, deep cloaks flapping in the cold mountain wind, like statues made of rotting flesh.

Every time the wind eddied, Maarkov was assaulted by their sour fucking stench.

"There's an old superstition in Dannon," he said, unable to stand the silence anymore.

Maaz paused in his silent brooding and looked up at his brother.

Maarkov cleared his throat. "The older tribes believe the last thing a person sees is burned onto the back of his eyes, and if you pluck them out, you can see what they saw." Maarkov stared at the boy—the *strega* that had been made from the boy, he corrected himself—and raised a brow.

"What's your point?" Maaz asked.

"The boy, Maaz," Maarkov sighed. "Do you think the sight of his family murdered, his mother being eaten—do you think that's burned on the back of his eyes?" He remembered the boy's face as his mother's blood ran hot into Maarkov's mouth. The mealy texture of her flesh, and the boy's horrified expression—the combination kept revolving in Maarkov's waking dreams.

Maaz gave him a disgusted look and turned a scowl on the boy. He spat in the general direction of the things and turned back to his brother, giving Maarkov an expression deeper than disgust—pity, maybe. Maarkov doubted it, though.

"Maarkov—why in the Six Hells do you care? The boy is gone. The *strega* is nothing but a thing."

"I was just thinking about it," Maarkov grumbled. "Do we have to sit here with the fucking things standing in the trees like a bunch of silent ghosts?"

Maaz gave him a flat look. "Do they bother you, brother?"

"They do."

The shadows grew long while Maaz stared at him. His brother's eyes were like twin beads of glass reflecting the light of the campfire with no life beneath the lenses. His cloak hid most of his face, but his posture told Maarkov what his expression would be. After all—they had spent all these long, arduous years together.

"You understand they are nothing—no thoughts, no desires.

Nothing. They are not going to come for you. In fact, if we are stumbled upon, you may be glad they are here," Maaz said.

A gust of wind fluttered the flames and brought the smell of the things again to Maarkov's nose.

"I know what they are, brother," Maarkov said. "Do you think I cannot feel the dust in my own body, the dry feeling of my flesh rubbing together as it moves? I think I can hear it sometimes—and I think I can hear theirs as well!"

"Nonsense," Maaz said. "Now you're being ridiculous."

"I will take my bedroll away from the fire," Maarkov grumbled. "I don't like to sleep with those things standing over me, rotting away into the air I breathe."

"You don't really need to breathe, it's just a reflex," Maaz said, already looking again into the flames.

"And whose *fucking* fault is that, Maaz?" Maarkov said, rising to his feet. "Why must I go on breathing, paring nails that don't grow, feeling only discomfort from the temperature? Why must I persist?"

Maaz let out an all-suffering sigh. "Maarkov—"

"Why must this go on, brother?" Maarkov growled. "I should have been dead years gone. Years and years. Each passing day, I care less about this...this *everything*. When will you release me?"

Maaz swallowed his words, but avoided meeting Maarkov's eyes. Maarkov stood above his brother, chest full of heat, waiting for him to say something. Maaz just stared into the flames, those glassy eyes of his reflecting their dancing patterns across the unfeeling lenses. The silence stretched on.

"Would you leave me, then, brother?" Maaz asked, right at the moment Maarkov was about to turn away. "Would you leave me now? Leave me to finish our quest on my own?"

Maarkov's teeth settled together, his jaw muscle clenching.

"Will you leave me now?" he said, eyes full of tears. *"Are you going to leave me here?"*

Maarkov looked down at his hands, the sword still clenched in his bloody fingers. His father's eyes stared up at him, glassy and unfeeling, the accusation frozen forever in his expression. That would be the look on his face in the Void, the one the gods would see. Maarkov's father would slip into the Void and all the gods would laugh at the look on his face.

It was all his fault—everything was always his bloody fault!

"Are you going to leave me now, brother?" Maaz asked, *clutching to his arm.*

Maarkov stared at his brother, the hunched shoulders beneath the black cloak. He opened his mouth to say something, but stopped on the precipice of speaking. The lump in his throat wouldn't budge, and the words wouldn't come out around them. Something held them in his chest with fingers of iron and ice.

Maaz suddenly sat up, looking toward the road.

The *strega* all moved at once.

Maarkov jumped, an instant of terror taking wild root in his heart. When the things ran silently into the woods, he relaxed, but screamed a few curses on the inside. They got him every single time, even though he told himself over and over again that next time he would be ready.

Every single gods-damned time.

"What's happening?" he asked.

Maaz smiled. "Why, we're going to have a few more friends over for dinner. There's a caravan coming through the pass."

With that, he rose and disappeared into the dusky blue shadows between the trees.

Disgust rose in Maarkov's stomach. More *strega* would be joining them—no doubt that was what his brother had meant. Maarkov cursed and went for his bedroll. His brother and his pets could have their fun. He wanted no part of it tonight. He dragged his blankets further into the woods, near the rocky ledge overlooking the valley.

The screams reached him an hour later.

**

Bethany had run down so many darkened corridors, through so many intersections, up and down so many flights of dusty stairs that she was completely turned around. Her magic had long since abandoned her to the dark, and her heart was racing too fast to summon it up again. The air was thick in her mouth, and her breathing refused to slow.

She sobbed, unable to get the screams of the burning man to stop echoing through her thoughts. The way he'd screamed—*No! Please!*—bounced back and forth in her ears until she tried putting her hands over them, but she couldn't keep the noise out. Even the sound of her own sobbing couldn't drown it out.

Bethany was certain she was deeper under the Conclave than she'd been before. She had run down several staircases, feeling her way along curving walls, stepping with as much grace as her pounding heart would allow. She was pretty sure she'd only run *up* once—or maybe twice, she couldn't remember. All she had known was that she needed to get away.

People could be looking for her.

That thought filled her with both elation and fear—after all, if her friends were looking for her, then the burning man's friends could be looking, too. *Always expect the worst things to happen—*that was what D'Jenn told her. If things could get worse, Bethany sure didn't know how.

She was lost. She was terrified. She was hunted.

She *had* to summon her magic again. It was the only thing left she could do. Without it, she could wander these halls for days and never get out. The corridors felt ancient, like they went on forever, right to the center of Eldath. They even smelled old. She might end up living the rest of her life like a tunnel rat, scraping together dirt to eat, gone blind from never seeing the light.

Bethany tried to calm herself. She placed her hand on the dusty wall, feeling the steady stone beneath her trembling fingers. She packed her sobs away one by one until they were tucked into the smallest part of her chest and couldn't cause more than a sharp breath. She wiped away her tears.

The stone felt cool under her hand. She ran her fingers over its surface until they alighted on a cold, swirling design laid into the stone. It had the smooth, cold feel of metal. The designs were probably runes similar to those in other places in the Conclave, swirling designs that made her eyes twist trying to follow them. Bethany followed this one with her hand.

She let the smooth contours of the metal calm her, and before she knew it, there were no more sobs. Bethany took a few deep breaths, listening to the sound echo from the surrounding stone, and closed her eyes against the dark. Bethany walled off her emotions one by one, seeking the inner silence she needed to embrace her magic.

She could feel it low in her chest, like a thunderstorm inside her ribcage.

Her Kai came to her like a scared animal, but it sang. Bethany almost cried in relief to feel it coursing through her again. She relaxed, tension fleeing her shoulders.

Now—if she could just figure out how to make light. Dormael and D'Jenn had never shown her, but even with her senses heightened by her magic, there wasn't enough light to see by—the tunnels were too deep below the ground. She would just have to figure it out on her own.

Bethany clenched her jaw and gathered her will.

Light!

Nothing happened.

She scrunched up her brows, closing her eyes tight with effort. She pictured everything she could imagine connected to light— torches, sunlight, the sun, windows, flowers, campfires, heat, wood, high noon—and fixed those images in the front of her mind. She could feel her Kai rumbling like thunder.

Shine!

The darkness stayed in place.

Her Kai continued to sing, lilting through her senses like a butterfly—which did nothing to push back the shadow. Bethany ground her teeth, trying not to let her frustration intrude on her magic. She'd been forced to practice Flying Rock hour after stupid hour, but could they have taught her to make a little light against the dark, maybe some fire for company?

No!

"I never learn anything bloody useful," she said, listening to her voice echo in the dark. There was no one to hear her curse, so she couldn't get in trouble for it.

"Bloody stupid," she said. "Bloody stupid, bloody stupid, bloody *stupid*!"

None of that helped her magic, but she had known it wouldn't.

Bethany hummed under her breath—a tune she had learned somewhere—and took steps down the dusty, black hallway. She ran her hand along the wall, letting the grit roll beneath her fingers against the smoothness of the stone. With each measured step, she got her emotions back under control.

"I'm only stuck if I want to be stuck," she said, after a long, deep breath. "Pirate-Queen of the bloody stupid Seas!" Bethany took two deep breaths, then two more. She listened to her heart, made it slow down by slowing down her breathing. Her anger began to die away.

Her Kai moved through the darkness, feeling along the walls and down the corridor. The world around her let out a constant hum, a low drone just below the edge of hearing. Bethany cleared her mind of her worries and listened.

Everything has magic in it, Dormael had told her once. *You, me, Shawna—everything. If you listen hard enough, you can hear it.* The trick was keeping all the little voices in her head quiet—that, and to stop thinking about food for one minute of the day.

Even now, she wished for a big, steaming piece of buttered bread.

"Stop it," she whispered, a smile tipping the tears on her cheeks into the corners of her mouth. "Listen. There's magic in everything—you just have to listen, girl."

Bethany was almost satisfied with her impression of Dormael's voice. She would have to show him—maybe it would make him laugh. She cleared her throat and crept forward through the hallway.

It took her a moment to hear it, but the cool metal under her fingers was pulsing with a magical tone, reacting with the song of her Kai. It was a quiet thing, easy to miss. There it was, though, ringing like a bell.

What can I do with that?

Bethany bit her upper lip and brushed her Kai across the metal. Her magic returned a note to her, something warbled and dissonant. She scrunched up her face, the sour note making her skin crawl.

When she was alone, Bethany often sang to herself. She would hum tunes she'd heard from all over and tap out the rhythms on whatever surface was available. When people were around, she just tapped. Bethany changed the note her Kai was singing, applying a force of will to her magic the same way she changed her voice when she was singing. Something about it just felt right, like a shoe that hugged perfectly to her heel.

Her Kai sang in tune with the metal, and the surface began to shine, pushing the darkness away with soft, yellow light. Bethany smiled, and she clapped her hands together in excitement. She even jumped up and down a little. She'd done it!

Pirate-Queen of the bloody Seas!

It took her eyes a moment to adjust to the warm light. The metal was shining all up and down its length, like someone had written a message in fire. The walls were made of a mottled, sand-colored stone, while the floor was colored black. There were no doorways, just a long, curving hall with the designs laid into the walls and floor. The only footprints in the dust were her own.

Bethany felt certain the runes were made to shine that way—something about the way it sang to her told her so. Why would the wizards have put the runes down here, though? What did that tell her? She could almost feel D'Jenn standing over her shoulder, arms crossed, scowling as he waited for an answer.

"They don't want people without magic coming down here," she said out loud, looking up and down the hall. "No more storerooms, no more wooden doors, no more torches on the walls. Just these runes." She ran her hand over the humming metal, listening to the tone play in her Kai. "I must be pretty deep in the tunnels."

Not bad, D'Jenn would say, *but what else? You've got a mind, girl—use it.*

"The...the runes must be connected to something, they must *lead* somewhere! Why have them here to see where you're going, unless there's somewhere to go in the first place? I just need to follow the runes!"

D'Jenn would be proud of me if he was here.

If she could use these runes to light up the hallway, then so could anyone who might be looking for her. They might be able to tell that she was using them, maybe even figure out how to find her. Was the light worth the risk of discovery?

Leyton wasn't afraid of risk. Leyton was the Pirate-King of the Seas, a Rescuer of Princesses. Bethany wasn't going to be afraid, either. She was only stuck if she let herself be stuck.

"Pirate-Queen of the Seas," she growled. "Rescuer of Princesses!"

Bethany set off at a jog, following the glowing runes down the corridor.

"How long has she been missing?" Dormael asked, unable to keep an edge out of his voice.

"Since the afternoon," Shawna said, giving him an apologetic look. "If I'd known—"

"No need for that," D'Jenn said, holding up a hand to forestall another apology. "No one expected any of this."

Dormael took a deep breath and let it out, trying to send his worries out with it. He wanted to scream. He wanted to blame someone. He'd been taken off the street in the one place it should never happen, he'd been tortured to the brink of death and back multiple times, and now his daughter was missing.

He wanted to break things.

"It's nobody's fault," is what he said. After a deep breath, he realized that he meant it.

"I saw her at the Bruising Stretch," Shawna said. "She was there, watching me spar. When I went looking for her, though, she was gone. No one had seen her, or even knew who she was."

"She's nimble," Dormael said. "I swear she could hide between shafts of sunlight if she wanted to. Where could she have gone?" The last bit came out more anguished than he had meant to sound, and Allen put a comforting hand on his shoulder.

"We'll find her, brother. The girl's too smart to get lost for long."

Everyone stood around him, crowded around a bench in his sitting room. He was plopped onto the seat, his shoulders slumped, his stomach a mess of fluttering anxiety. A fire burned in his hearth, the wood crackling with warmth. The light flickered over the walls of his room, playing over the odd implements and trophies he'd collected over the years.

"I just hope no one grabbed her," Dormael said.

"They wouldn't have any reason," Shawna said. "I killed Grant, remember? She's beyond the reach of that creature forever. Why would anyone else take her?"

"Actually," D'Jenn said, "there may be a reason."

"What do you mean?" Dormael asked, shooting his cousin a sharp look.

"It's why I came to find you in the first place," D'Jenn said. He made a sharp gesture in the air, and Dormael felt his cousin's Kai reach out into the room, sealing it away from eavesdroppers. "I had a bug in my hair about something today, so I went to dig it out."

"A bug about what?" Allen asked.

"Kitamin Jurillic," D'Jenn said, "and his miraculous rescue."

"You mean that story my Pop told you?" Dormael asked. "Was the old man on to something for once?" He didn't see what in the Six Hells this had to do with Bethany, but he waited his cousin out. D'Jenn wouldn't say anything that wasn't worth the effort.

"He's not as stupid as all that," Allen said. "The old man is on to a lot of things."

"He certainly was this time." D'Jenn nodded. "Something about our conversation with Victus bothered me all day. The thing your father said about Kitamin Jurillic—that someone powerful had been behind his rescue—kept nagging at me. I knew only one person with the kind of power to affect a rescue operation good enough to remove someone from Rashardian slavers."

"This is what you meant when you said he's been using us," Dormael said.

"Aye." D'Jenn nodded again. "Victus had him rescued, Dormael. What's more, he's been buying up influence on the Council of Seven. Nyra Jurillic believed he was murdering people, or she alluded to it, anyway. I don't know what the money is for, yet—I still don't have all the pieces—but I know one thing. Victus Tiranan is a traitor, and we cannot trust him. Jurillic said she could see his hand in the Council Meetings. He's deep into something, some operation he's been planning. I know the way his mind works, Dormael. This isn't good. I can feel it."

Dormael took a moment to soak it all in. He knew his mentor had lied during their debriefing, and he and D'Jenn had shared their suspicions of him. Victus as a traitor was hard to imagine, but D'Jenn had never led him down the wrong path.

"What would he have to gain?" Dormael asked. "Let's say he moves some pieces around on the board, gets elected Mekai. What then? The Mekai serves only an advisory position. If he reached for real power, all the Sevenlands would turn against him. Wizards are forbidden the leadership of the tribe, clan or family—it's one of our oldest laws."

"He doesn't need to be the figurehead," D'Jenn said. "Think

about it. Victus has spent an entire generation grooming a crop of Warlocks, selecting the wizards he wanted to train specifically for the characteristics he valued. He oversaw every step of the training, adopted the lot of us into his care."

"He's like a father to all of us," Dormael said, a cold spear of realization twisting in his chest.

D'Jenn nodded. "He says it all the time—*we're a family*. If he's Mekai, he might as well be choosing the next Deacon outright. Anyone who is elected to the position will be one of his disciples— as are we all."

"Any operation he wanted to push, he would get it," Dormael said. "He could sit at the center of a spider's web and pull strings that reached across the world. He'd have his own personal army of Warlocks."

"That sounds terrifying," Shawna said.

Dormael nodded in agreement.

"He'd still be breaking the old edicts," Allen said. "He'd just be hiding it."

"Still—why would he come after Bethany?" Dormael asked.

"He said it outright," D'Jenn said. "She could be the most powerful wizard the Conclave has seen in generations. He wants to train her as a Warlock. Now that I've realized what he's done, I can see the reasons behind the moves he has made. Bethany represents power, and he needs to gather as much of it to his side as possible. You heard what he asked us in the War Room."

"If we would do what was right when time comes," Dormael said, the words settling into his stomach like bricks. "He may as well have said it to us."

"He wants us on his side," D'Jenn said. "He's planning something, Dormael. I don't know if he has Bethany, but if he doesn't, we need to find her first."

"Agreed," Dormael growled. "Let's go, then."

"I'll check the dining hall," Allen said, "see if anyone has seen her stealing food. The girl can eat like three grown men. I'll come back here if I find her."

"Be careful," Dormael said. "We don't know whom we can trust."

Allen nodded, checked the axe at his hip, and ducked into the hallway.

"I'll check the grounds—on this side of the river and the west side. Maybe she hid out the storm in one of the greenhouses or ducked into a garden," D'Jenn said.

Dormael nodded, and his cousin disappeared through the door on Allen's heels.

Shawna lowered herself to sit on the bench next to him. He gave her a wan smile, and she placed a warm, comforting hand over his. Dormael paused a moment, the energy fleeing from him in the face of all that had happened. The day weighed on him like a load of bricks.

"Where should we search?" Shawna asked.

"I'm going to search through the Conclave Proper, see if I can pick up something with my Kai—a trace of her magic, perhaps, or a sense of her consciousness. If she's using her magic, maybe I'll be able to hear it," he said. "I'll be immobile. Would you mind standing guard over me? After what happened today—"

"Sure," she said, saving him from having to go on. "I'll be right here. What should I do if someone we don't trust comes through the door? How bad have things gotten?"

"Just wake me," Dormael said. "Hopefully they're not so bad we'd have to worry about violence in my apartments. If someone comes in, scowl at them and grumble about disturbing the wizard during his studies."

"You want *me* to act like *your* bodyguard?" Shawna asked, raising an eyebrow. "You're mad, Dormael Harlun. I'll do it, though. You're lucky I like you."

Dormael gave her as genuine a smile as he could muster. He sat cross-legged, straightening his back and taking deep breaths. Shawna paced across the floor, hands planted on her hips. Dormael gave her a nod and closed his eyes.

He floated through the hallways of the Conclave Proper, his Kai bringing him the world in harmonious tones. The world was a beach, each sandy pebble a tiny bell, and each bell ringing its own unique note as his consciousness rushed by. He could feel a storm of noise and impressions, deep rhythmic beats felt in his chest, and bright flashes of song as other wizards used their gifts.

The Conclave was as chaotic a place as one could find through the lens of a wizard's Kai.

Dormael flashed down the hallways of residential quarters,

listening for the resonance of Bethany's song. He floated down winding stairs, through bustling kitchens, past teams of servants who cleaned in an almost hypnotic pattern, and flitted between clouds of noisy conversation. Bethany was nowhere, and she'd been nowhere. Dormael grew worried as he searched floor by floor, finding an abundance of nothing.

He came to the Common Hall, on the ground floor of the Conclave Proper.

There was an excited, dreadful quality to the energy in the room that caught his attention. It whipped through the air in the hall like ghostly lightning, originating from somewhere just past the common areas, toward the official chambers where petitioners came to plead their cases. Dormael sent his awareness toward the confusion, following it to its source.

In back of the Common Hall, there were a series of offices where representatives of the different Orders met with the public. The Hedge Wizards, Philosophers and Scouts all had offices. The Warlocks, of course, had no office. All day, petitioners would fill the hallway, waiting in every corner of the room at their chance to sit before a desk in one of those bland little offices. The crush of bodies in the Common Hall every day was a challenge for the Conclave staff to deal with and created a mess of problems on its own.

Sometime during the Conclave's past, the wizards had seen fit to fix this problem by creating a network of staircases and passageways that would keep servants and Initiates from having to dodge through the press of the Common Hall to see to their duties. These passages—only wide enough for two—criss-crossed between rooms, floors and buildings. Some of them even went down into the tunnels beneath the Conclave, down to the archives and the Crux. Some mysterious, long-standing tradition had named those passageways the Rat Holes. No one had bothered to change it in hundreds of years, as far as Dormael knew.

Around the entrance to one of the Rat Holes, there was a commotion. A few dozen people crowded near the entrance to the corridor, trying to get a look down a winding staircase. A pair of scowling wizards held the crowd at bay, calling for 'manners and good sense' with the insistence of someone who had been placed in authority. The people obeyed them for the most part, but curiosity was a powerful force. The buzz in the room flickered through his Kai like silent lightning.

Floating closer, Dormael saw the entrance to the staircase was warded from magical intrusion as well, with a swirling wall of energy that would trap his mind if he tried to penetrate it. He could not scry past it. Something had definitely happened, and a stone settled into his guts.

Dormael withdrew his senses back into his own body and jumped up from the floor.

"Did you find her?" Shawna asked.

"No." Dormael shook his head. "But I found *something*. It may or may not have something to do with her, but it's the only lead we have right now. Come on, we're going down to the Common Hall. Bring your swords?"

Shawna gave him a fierce smile and snatched her blades from his table.

**

Bethany stared at the pair of footprints trailing through the dust of the corridor. She had no idea how to tell anything from the prints, save that someone had come this way. Were they friends of the man she had encountered in the tunnels? There was no telling how long ago they had come down the corridor, but Bethany had heard nothing but her own breathing for what felt like hours.

Should I follow them?

She might be walking right into the hands of her enemies. There might be another man waiting around the corner of a distant corridor, magic poised for an attack. Maybe they would chase her back into the darkness if they found her, and she'd never find her way out. The runes emitted warm, amber light into the hallway, humming against her Kai with a soothing tone. They seemed to await her decision.

If Bethany was careful, she could sneak up on whoever had made the prints. She would have to make sure she was more watchful than last time. If nothing else, she could hang back in the shadows and follow them to safety.

The glowing runes, though, presented a problem. They lit up as she came down the hallway, warming like a fire coaxed to life, and faded as she passed by. The runes would announce her as surely as a herald, but they were the only thing holding the darkness at bay. Narrowing her eyes, Bethany stared at the curving metal lines laid into the stone.

"I need you to be quiet now," she whispered. Bethany wasn't sure how she did it, but she could feel the magic moving into the link with the runes. She pulled power from it, decreasing the volume of her own magic, until her Kai's song was just above a whisper. The runes, in response, faded to a subdued glow. It took her eyes a moment to adjust, but once she had closed them and counted to seven—a trick for saving her night-vision Dormael had taught her—there was plenty of light by which to see.

"Pirate-Queen of the Seas," she whispered with a smile.

The footprints meandered down the corridor, turned right, wandered down that hallway, then onto a winding staircase leading deeper into the tunnels. Bethany made sure the glowing runes continued on the lower level and followed the trail the footprints left for her. Bethany took her slippers off and stuffed them into her belt—they were stupid, girly things Dormael forced her to wear, anyway. In her bare feet, she could run over the smooth stone without making a sound. The slippers squeaked and scuffed and made all kinds of noise. The hard stone was chilly on the soles of her feet, but she relished the freedom. Taking her shoes off always made her want to run.

She followed the footsteps for an eternity, taking winding turns and heading ever deeper into the ground. Her Kai sang to her in a low hum, and she could tell by the sound of the surrounding earth that she was much farther underground than she had ever been. The weight of dirt pressing against the stone felt like weight on her own shoulders, though she knew she couldn't really feel it—that was some trick of her magic.

As she went deeper, though, there was something else.

At first Bethany didn't know what to make of the sound. It was like the heartbeat of a giant beast. She could feel energy in the corridors, invisible veins of magic pulsing through the hallways, humming with the very stone of the Conclave tunnels. It seemed like she'd been swallowed by a great lizard and was listening to the inner workings of its body.

The farther she went down the passageway, the more energy she could feel. Her Kai resonated with it, reached out and touched it. Bethany felt a tingle of excitement every time it did so, as if she was tapped into a river of starlight. She had to suppress the urge to laugh and skip as she moved down the hallway, following the river of magic. The runes followed her, their subdued glow humming in her senses.

When she reached the next level down, the air was so charged with power that it buzzed against her skin. Something was gathering magic to itself, something deep within the tunnels. She could feel it pulling at her Kai, beckoning her power to dance with it. It was tempting, like an itch that needed scratching, but Bethany kept her magic to herself. Her instincts prevented her from relinquishing control.

Lines of silver were laid into the floor on this level, and she could feel them humming with the spell in the distant part of the tunnels, as if they were a part of it. Bethany was careful not to touch the curving, concentric lines of silver, nor the runes scrawled over the floor between them. Some glyphs were as tall as she was, and all of it was vibrating with magical energy. She stepped over the metal, keeping her bare feet on the stone.

As she moved farther down the tunnel, a new sound emerged from the ether.

An alien, crooning song flitted through the corridor, a ghostly echo resonating with her Kai. Bethany froze when she heard it, and she drew her magic in close. The runes that been lighting her way in subdued tones waned to the whisper of an afterglow.

It was the *fiega*—Shawna's armlet.

Despite her efforts to hide, the armlet knew she was there. She could feel it in the tone of its song, the recognition it sang with, the warmth it tried to show her. Bethany wanted to brush it away—after all, the last time she'd listened to it, very bad things happened—but it was insistent. It had sent her dream after dream in the days following the fight at sea, though she had declined to tell Dormael or D'Jenn. They were never more than scattered pictures and impressions, anyway, and they hadn't meant much of anything.

The thing was lonely. Bethany wasn't sure how she could tell. It was like the way that lies sounded different to her ears, or the way she knew what her Kai sounded like—some things a person just knew. That was why the armlet was so rough with everyone. It was like a puppy, too big to know that its tail knocked over everything in the room when it wanted to play.

Bethany wasn't supposed to talk to it. She was forbidden to listen to it, and she was under strict instruction *never* to reach out to the thing with her magic. *You know what happened last time,* she could almost hear Dormael saying to her. *Don't do anything too stupid to fix.*

Before she could stop it, though, the armlet reached out to her. Before she could stop herself, she reached back.

The whole cabin vibrated with her fear, the door slamming shut against the frame, the wood creaking around her. She could feel the storm in her chest, a constant resonance with the thunder that cracked the skies and churned the seas to chaos. The song of the armlet crooned from its place in their bags, calming her magic from the storm of fear it had become.

"Yes," she whispered. "It's me—Bethany."

The armlet sent her a feeling of warmth, of something close to friendship. Bethany could feel the heat in her arms and legs, as if she'd just crawled from a warm bath. She smiled, and sent the armlet back a jumble of feelings—the way she felt when Dormael ruffled her hair, the way she felt when Shawna fixed it, the feeling of laughter at one of Allen's jokes, or of accomplishment under D'Jenn's tutelage.

The armlet sang back.

Their enemies crawled over the deck of the ship, like ants over a rotting corpse. Men and metal and sweat and lightning, cries of anger and pain. The skies boiled, the seas churned. Their enemies would win unless they went up together and burned them from the ship. Immolate them, set them aflame, BURN EVERYTHING IN SIGHT.

"Stop it!" Bethany hissed into the hum of magical energy. The sight of the man in the tunnels, his hand reaching for help, filled her mind. She heard his screams again, and she shut them away somewhere dark, banishing them from her mind. "Just...stop."

Surprisingly, the armlet complied. Its song fell to a dull hum, the insistence gone from its tone. It sang something low, something she could understand.

Come.

Biting her lip in trepidation, Bethany followed the song of the armlet down the curving hallway. She wasn't sure what would happen once she found it, but she knew one thing—wherever it was, there was probably someone there who could help her.

Letting the *fiega* guide her, she set off toward the heart of the strange magical spell.

**

"You know I can't let you down there," Jarek said. "The Deacon would have both our arses over a spit for that, Dormael."

Jarek Suriah was a hulking beast of a man, wide-shouldered and grim-faced. He was a Mal, and he bore tattoos in swirling geometric patterns over every inch of his arms, which were thicker than many trees Dormael had seen. He stood fully three hands taller than Dormael and scowled down at the swords Shawna wore on her belt. Shawna repaid his attention with a bored, feline gaze.

Jarek was one of Dormael's own generation. They had trained together as Warlocks, and they'd completed their training as part of the same small group. Jarek Suriah looked like a tavern brawler, but he had a sharp mind and a strong sense of justice. Like all people from Tasha-Mal, Jarek could be prickly about things like honor and blood-debts.

"It's nothing about a child, though," Mataez said from beside him. "It's a body, Dormael—a grown man by the looks of him. Burnt to cinders down in the Rat Holes." Jarek turned his scowl down on Mataez, which the shorter man waved off with a scowl of his own. "The Deacon didn't mean to keep the information a secret from one of ours, Jarek. Dormael's a Warlock, too. Remove the stick from your arse, brother."

Mataez was another member of their class and of a height with Dormael. He was a Runemian with short, mud-colored hair. Mataez was a bit thicker through the shoulders and waist than Dormael, but was quicker than he looked. The man had the odd talent of being able to remember everything he read with a startling amount of accuracy. His mind was like a steel trap.

The two of them stood guarding the entrance to the Rat Holes, maintaining a ward on the doorway between them. The entranceway was nothing but an undulating dark surface.

"When did this happen?" Dormael asked, dread pooling in the

pit of his stomach.

"Sometime between now and the afternoon." Mataez shrugged. "The Deacon hasn't come up from his inspection yet, but the rumor is that one of the staff found it when she went down to check after the screaming."

"Do they know to whom the body belongs?" Shawna asked. Jarek raised an eyebrow at her, but Mataez nudged him in the side. Jarek gave Mataez an evil look and cleared his throat. It sounded like boulders rubbing together.

"We don't know anything yet," Jarek said. "From what we've heard, though, it would be hard to tell."

"First murder I can remember in the Conclave," Mataez said, shaking his head.

"You believe it was murder?" Shawna asked.

"What do you think happened? Somebody tripped and fell on a candle, then managed to burn to death in the middle of a stone hallway?" Mataez said. "Of course it was murder, and it was done with magic."

Shawna gave Mataez an evil look, and he up his hands for peace.

"I can't remember that ever happening," Jarek rumbled. "A wizard murdering someone on the Conclave grounds. They'll be talking about it for a hundred years."

"I'll bet the Initiates already have a trove of rumors," Mataez said. "Remember when we were children? We used to *start* them for fun."

"I remember," Dormael smiled. His mind, though, could focus on nothing but Bethany. "Listen, brothers—It's important that I speak to the Deacon. I wouldn't ask if it wasn't about my daughter—you've met her, right?"

"Aye," Mataez grumbled, looking away. Jarek gave Dormael a narrow look.

"I need to get down there. You know I'm not going to mess anything up. Victus won't mind you letting *me* through—you know that," Dormael said. "You know I wouldn't ask if I wasn't worried for her safety."

Mataez and Jarek shared an uncomfortable look.

"Better to ask forgiveness," Mataez shrugged. Jarek just shook his head and looked away. Mataez turned back to Dormael and took a deep breath.

"Fine," Mataez sighed. "If he catches you, though, it's on you. I don't want another tour at the Southern Bastion anytime soon. Nothing but scorpions, sand, and Mals to keep you company. Dreadful."

"You know how hard I can hit," Jarek sighed, "yet you still say things like that."

"I didn't mean *you*, of course—you're one of the good ones." Mataez smiled. "It's your women I was talking about. Mean as the underworld, dry as the desert. Nothing good about them."

"Thanks, brothers. I won't forget this," Dormael said.

Just as Mataez and Jarek stepped aside and dropped their ward, however, Victus appeared on the stairs. He noticed Dormael standing between the two men he'd left to guard the entrance and narrowed his eyes at the three of them. Mataez and Jarek acted completely natural.

"Dormael," Victus said, "I've been looking for you all day, boy. Come on—there's something you need to see."

With that, Victus turned and descended once again into the darkened tunnels. Dormael shared a look with Shawna, shrugged at his two fellow Warlocks, and stepped after Victus. Shawna followed him close behind. He had hoped to avoid Victus until he could talk to D'Jenn about the details of what he had discovered, but there was no helping it now.

Now he had to lie to the man who had taught him to lie.

"I imagine the boys filled you in?" Victus's voice echoed from further down the stairs.

"Aye, at least what they knew," Dormael replied. "A body, burnt to a crisp, as Mataez put it."

Dormael came to the bottom of the landing, where Victus waited. The man's Kai hummed into the tunnels, evoking a magical light. There were usually candles on this level, but Dormael couldn't spot any pools of light. Shawna came down the steps and fell in beside him, eyeing Victus with caution. If Victus minded her presence, he said nothing of it.

"A body, indeed," Victus said. "There's something you need to see, though."

"Something *I* need to see?" Dormael asked, the dread in his stomach deepening.

Victus nodded. "Just follow me, I'll show you."

Dormael shared a concerned look with Shawna as Victus strode away, and he turned to follow the Deacon into the tunnels. Victus led them down twisting corridors to the lower levels. Shawna gave Dormael a questioning look, but he waved off her concern.

Victus stopped walking and signaled for Dormael to do the same.

"This is where it starts," the Deacon said, motioning Dormael forward. "Have a look, boy. Let's see if you're still sharp enough to pass muster, eh?"

"I passed muster a long time ago, Deacon. Watch me."

He couldn't help but feel a pang in his guts as the smile came to his face. He trusted D'Jenn, but part of his heart was rebelling against the idea that Victus was a traitor. The smirk on the Deacon's face was proud, even as the light in his eyes was calculating. Try as Dormael might, he couldn't see an enemy when he looked at the man. Taking a deep breath, he shoved his feelings into the back of his mind and focused on the task at hand.

He opened his Kai and filled the hallway with light.

The first thing that caught his eye was the fact that the doors had been pushed open. There were three doors on each side of the hallway, and each had been pushed open and left ajar. Tiny footprints in the dust marked where someone—a child, by the look of the prints—had walked to each door and looked inside. Dormael walked further down the tunnel, following the prints as they meandered past each room. Victus and Shawna stopped some distance behind him, Victus gesturing for her to give Dormael some space. The little prints continued down the hallway and around the corner.

Dormael felt ice form in his chest and tried to keep his breathing steady.

Mataez said the body was a grown man.

Some part of him knew Victus would never set him up to discover Bethany's body, even if the man was a traitor. Still, seeing her footprints in the dust—and there was no doubt in him that the prints were hers—made him feel a spike of terror he couldn't hold down. Taking a deep breath, he turned the corner.

The smell hit him as soon as he rounded it.

Burnt corpses had a stink to them that, once known, was never forgotten. Dormael's first time catching the scent had been outside a small village in Neleka after the Galanian invasion. A major battle had been fought in a field nearby, and the residents knew their options were either leaving the bodies to rot in the sun or burning them. The smell hadn't come out of Dormael's clothes for days. It was the sort of scent that straightened the spine.

The body was lying on the stone near the intersection of a few tunnels, one crispy arm reaching to the ceiling. A sconce was driven into the wall above it—one of a few along the wall—but it was warped, drooping as if the metal had grown soft with heat. Black soot stained the stone.

Dormael forced his gorge down as it tried to rise.

He followed the prints up to the body, and past it. In fact, the body sat at an intersection, and the prints went down each tunnel where the heat hadn't scorched everything away. Unless the girl had skipped past the burning man over and over again, she must have come here before the burnt man—or woman, he supposed. Mataez was right—it was hard to tell.

Upon closer examination, though, Dormael was certain the body was male. Men always had wider shoulders and more narrow hips, and this person had been tall. There were no features left in the scorched hunk of flesh that lay on the stone, but Dormael could see teeth through a hole frozen into a rictus on its face. He shuddered, thinking of the pain.

Why lay there? Why lay on the stone while you're burning? What were you reaching for?

Dormael looked at the way the body was positioned. He hadn't been reaching for the ceiling, he'd been reaching outward—toward an intersection further down the tunnel. He'd been reaching out in supplication to someone.

Dormael felt a chill run down his spine. *You were begging for your life.*

Dormael turned a sharp look backward and caught Victus's grim expression. It was obvious what had happened here to both of them, but Victus had made sure Dormael saw it with his own eyes. A rock dropped into his stomach as the two of them regarded each other.

The man—whoever he had been—had been held down and

burned to death.

Dormael turned back to the burned remains and made his way to where the other person in this altercation had been standing. A pair of footprints had been left in the stone, but not in the dust. Two perfect, dainty outlines of bare feet were apparent in the stone, and everything else for about eight hands in all directions was cracked with millions of tiny fractures, as if a great amount of pressure had been put on the rock. Dormael knelt and touched his hand to it, sinking his senses out into the ether.

He could feel Bethany's magic, still undulating in the tunnel like an angry mist.

She used her magic here—tossing it with more instinct than direction. It bled out and cracked the stone. She must have been under attack.

"I needed you to see this for yourself," Victus said from where the body lay. "I needed you to be here, to be a part of this. We need to find her, boy. We need to know what happened here."

The bastard had known already, but Dormael resisted the urge to be angry.

"Bethany doesn't know how to use magic this way," Dormael said, rising to his feet. "This was wild, unfocused. I know you can tell."

"Bethany did this?" Shawna asked, putting a hand to her mouth.

"She didn't *mean* to do this—that's what I'm saying!" Dormael snapped.

Shawna held her hands up in surrender, and Dormael gave her an apologetic look.

"I can tell that her magic was wild, but that doesn't say anything about her intent," Victus said.

"Deacon—I'm telling you, she wouldn't have done this without a good reason."

"We don't know what happened here," Victus said. "The man could have been following her, could have been trying to hurt her. Also, maybe he just startled her, scared her and something went terribly wrong. Maybe it got away from her, boy—you know how strong the girl is."

"That's not what happened here," Dormael growled. "Look at the damned footprints! She'd been all over this hall, up and down the tunnels, looking in the doors as she came through. Her prints run in all directions, so this man was following her." Dormael cast about on the ground, intensifying his magical light. Another set of prints, marred with haste, continued down the hallway in the opposite direction of the body. Dormael pointed them out. "See? She ran from him, off in this direction. I'm telling you, Bethany must have been defending herself."

"Just because she came here *first* doesn't mean he was following her," Victus said. "You're letting your emotions get in the way of your judgment, boy. Don't look at me that way, gods-dammit—you know I'm right. All we know right now is that the girl is scared, she's alone...and she's dangerous."

"Bethany is not dangerous," Dormael said, but even as he did, he remembered her burning every Galanian on board the *Seacutter* to dust. The words tasted bitter in his mouth, and bile rose in his throat.

He was terrified for Bethany.

"Regardless, we need to find her," Victus said. "We need to find her before anyone else gets hurt—including her."

Dormael nodded, and Victus walked past him, following the prints down the hallway. Dormael let out a long breath and followed him. Shawna fell in beside Dormael. She elbowed him and signed to him in the Hunter's Tongue.

What does this mean?

Bethany is in trouble, he signed back. *That's all I know. She couldn't have done that sort of magic on purpose. She was scared, she was defending herself on instinct.*

What happens when we find her?

I don't know, Dormael replied. *But I do know one thing.*

What?

We can't let anyone hurt her. I don't know what Victus wants, and I don't trust him.

I just hope Bethany is alright.

Me too, he said. *Me too.*

**

Bethany drifted down the hallway, following the rivers of pulsing magic through the gloom. She no longer needed her Kai to sing to the brass runes—the tunnel was alive with power. There was no need for her to see. Her magical senses guided her every step, and the armlet coaxed her along.

There was something nearby, some great, pulsing heartbeat that vibrated every vein in her body. She could feel each beat of the thing, pulling at her, jarring her teeth with in a steady, humming rhythm. Even as she glided along the floor, something pulled at her magic, leaching a bit of it into the whirlpool at the center of that pulsing heartbeat. Bethany was drawn to it like a moth to a flame.

Come.

The alien song walked with her, singing to her in warm tones. It showed her images—stars spinning in a sea of blackness, flame climbing a wall of struggling men, a woman made of nothing but warm smiles and terrible fire. It beckoned.

Come.

Bethany took the woman's hand and let her float down the hallway at her side. She was surprised that touching her didn't burn her skin, but she felt nothing. Bethany had her eyes closed, looking through the sight of her magical senses. Though the hallway was dark to her eyes, in her Kai the ghostly woman burned as bright as the sun.

The alien crooning surrounded her, wrapped her in a warm embrace. The *fiega* sent more images, but they were so jumbled Bethany couldn't make sense of them. She tried to fight them off, but they grew more insistent, slamming into the walls of her consciousness with greater and greater frequency.

"Would you just be *quiet?*" Bethany asked, her voice echoing through the dark.

Surprisingly, it did. The song dwindled to a silvery thread of music that tickled her senses like an errant breeze. Bethany sighed in relief.

Thank you.

A feeling of warmth came back to her in reply. *Come.*

Eyes closed, Bethany continued down the tunnel, hand-in-hand with the woman of fire. At times she felt as if she wasn't walking at all, but floating along above the stone of the tunnel floor, her toes dragging a bit in the dust. At other times the landscape would change with the alien song, and the hallway would become a battlefield. Bodies struggled around her, men killing and hacking at each other in storms of blood and flame—none of it ever touched her or the ghostly woman. They whispered through the scene like wraiths.

The distant hum of magic—the one she had been feeling all this time—grew closer as she made her way down the corridor. The woman led her ever onward, toward the center of its beating heart. Bethany got the impression she was walking along a curve, maybe around a circle, but she couldn't be sure.

Come.

"Child?"

The voice startled Bethany from her trance. At first she thought the woman standing before her was the woman of fire, but no—the ghostly woman was gone. The song of the armlet had retreated. This woman was cold, blond, and regal. She crouched in the puddle of light created by her own Kai, willowy beauty wrapped in a blue silk dress. She was as pretty as a frozen statue.

"Child," she said again. "Child, can you hear me? Are you well?"

"I—" Bethany opened her mouth to speak, but the words froze in her throat. What if this woman was with the man she had seen before? What if she was here to hurt her, or capture her?

"It's alright, child," the woman said. She crouched and beckoned Bethany over. "Come here, dear, into the light. Wherever did you come from?"

Bethany hadn't realized she was standing in the dark. She could feel the woman's magic flitting about the edges of her own, trying to get a sense of her. On instinct, Bethany reached out to her the way she did to the armlet.

The woman gasped as their Kais brushed each other. For the barest second, Bethany got a sense of the woman—cold, logical, but kind. The woman withdrew her magic from Bethany's Kai.

"You must be Dormael's child—Bethany, isn't it?" the woman asked. "I've heard of you, little one. They were right about your strength. You've a very powerful gift. Has anyone told you that? Come here, child. I'm not going to hurt you."

"I've been lost," Bethany said, finding her voice as she stepped forward. "Someone tried to grab me, tried to hurt me. I ran away."

"Someone tried to hurt you?" the woman asked, looking her in the eyes as she came forward. "Someone in the Conclave tried to hurt you? Where are they now, child?"

"Up there," Bethany whispered, pointing to the ceiling. "I left them up there."

The woman's eyes looked past her, into the darkness from which Bethany had come. She placed a pair of delicate hands on Bethany's shoulders and looked into her eyes.

"You're alright now," the woman said. "You've stumbled on the Crux, little one. My name is Lacelle—I'm the Deacon of Philosophers. Do you know what that means?"

Bethany shook her head.

"No matter," Lacelle sighed. "No one will hurt you while you're here with me."

"They won't?" Bethany wasn't so sure.

"They wouldn't dare," Lacelle promised, squeezing her shoulder. "Now, come along. I suppose you can help carry books while you're here."

"Lacelle," called a voice from an opening beyond the Deacon of Philosophers. "Bring the girl in here, if you would. I believe she has been...summoned." The last word came out with a healthy dose of incredulity.

Lacelle gave her a strange look, like a merchant weighing her take.

"Very well, Honored One," she called. She shrugged at Bethany. "Come along, dear. You're about to see something most wizards never do."

Bethany felt a small excited flame kindle to life in her chest, though it was a mute thing. It was hidden secrets that had motivated her to come down into these dismal tunnels in the first place, and part of her felt like laughing at having found one. The memory of the man she had left in the corridors above, though, killed her enthusiasm.

Lacelle led her through a circular opening in the wall of the tunnel and into a room the likes of which Bethany had never seen. It was vast and round, like a perfect bubble made of stone. The topmost part of the ceiling was at least four levels up. Lacelle led her onto a narrow walkway which widened into a circular platform in the center of the room. The chamber extended just as far beneath the platform as it did above. Bethany peered over the edge, trying to see if there was a column holding it all up, but she couldn't find one.

Runes were scrawled in concentric lines around the walls of the vast globe, all resonating with charged magic. It hummed in Bethany's senses with a note so low it only vibrated her bones. There were designs and geometrical swirls worked over the surface of the stone as well, all humming with their own veins of power. Bethany stumbled after the willowy, blond Lacelle, trying not to go slack-jawed in wonder.

In certain places, gems hung on delicate chains of silver from the ceiling. These, too, resonated with magic. Posts made of different metals rose in intervals along the platform which hummed with subtle musical notes to her physical ears and magical ones to her Kai.

Lacelle led her onto the central platform. A table sat there, with two chairs pulled up to it. Another chair sat off to the side, facing the center of the platform. An old man waited by the chair with a pleasant smile on his face.

The armlet hung in midair behind him.

It turned in the air, revolving around swirling currents of magic. Flame misted away from the ruby set into the sinuous bands of silver, disappearing into the air like mist in the sunlight. Bethany could feel its song, humming in contented tones as it greeted her magic. She resisted the urge to reach out for it once again.

"You may leave the girl with me, Lacelle," the old man said. "Send word that the Initiates are to stay out of the Rat Holes until we can look into this matter of someone attacking young Bethany."

Bethany peered at the old man. He had long, silver and white hair and a beard that was even longer. It was wrapped in silver wire, an intricate web of thin, shining strands. Bright blue eyes regarded her with genuine warmth.

That's the Mekai—the leader of the whole Conclave!

Bethany's mouth went dry.

"Of course, Honored One," Lacelle replied. "Should I send for one of Victus's thugs to investigate?"

The Mekai raised an eyebrow. "Would you rather do it yourself?"

The blond woman tightened her lips.

"Very well," the Mekai said. "Send for one of Victus's thugs, then. And don't speak so ill of them, Lacelle. You forget that they grew up right here under my tutelage. I feel very attached to them, you understand. Some of them were your own classmates, upon a day. Try not to be so persnickety."

"Persnickety?" The woman scoffed, but it looked feigned to Bethany. "I'm not being persnickety, Honored One."

"I could use more colorful words," the Mekai said, "but our company would undoubtedly repeat them, and you're not going to have me blamed for corrupting the language of such a pretty young girl." He crouched, spry for his old age, and smiled at Bethany. "In the meantime, Bethany and I are going to talk. I'll tell you a story, dear. How does that sound?"

Bethany smiled. "I like stories. My favorite is about Leyton Likinian, Pirate-King of the Seas."

Lacelle gasped, but the Mekai just chuckled.

"Where did you hear those stories, child? The ones about Leyton?" the Mekai asked.

"An old man used to tell them, back when...," she trailed off. She suddenly didn't want to say. "A long time ago," she finished. "I heard them a long time ago."

"I've a few words for the propriety of old men," Lacelle said. "Teaching a little girl stories like that—and look at you, Honored One. Laughing about it."

"Let the girl have her stories, Lacelle," the Mekai said. He shooed her away with a gesture. "Go now, see to your duties. Bethany will be fine here with me. It's been a long time since I've had such pleasant company, anyway." He winked at Bethany. "My usual companions are always so *persnickety*."

Bethany giggled.

Lacelle sniffed and walked back into the hallway, leaving Bethany alone with the Mekai. She wasn't sure if she should apologize for exploring the tunnels looking for treasure. Dormael hadn't told her she was forbidden, exactly, so it wasn't as if she had broken a rule. Not really.

If the Mekai brought it up, she could apologize. Until he did, though, she wasn't in trouble. Better not to borrow trouble from the gods—she'd heard that somewhere before.

The Mekai turned and walked back toward the furniture on the platform. As he walked, his Kai brushed against hers in a light greeting. Bethany was amazed at the feel of his Kai. While it wasn't as vast as her own, it was sharper in some way, more potent. Even as Bethany followed the Mekai to the table, his magic slid her out a chair and adjusted the old man's robe as he sat in his own seat, and it all happened without his direction.

I can barely make a stupid magical light.

"What do you know of history, dear girl?" the Mekai asked, adjusting a small pair of spectacles on his nose. She'd seen a pair of those on a traveling merchant once. She had almost stolen them, but who would pay for such a thing?

"Not much." Bethany shrugged. "I know my letters, though, and the Hunter's Tongue. I know the epics of the gods—at least, I know some of them."

A book floated through the air and into the Mekai's hand, pages flipping as it floated by. He adjusted his glasses and peered down at the text, finding something with his finger as the book settled into his hand. He winked at her over the rim of the book.

"Soon enough you'll receive all manner of education. You do mean to train here, do you not?"

"I think so." Bethany nodded. "Don't I have to?"

"Don't you want to?"

"Maybe," Bethany said. "I don't know. I want Dormael and D'Jenn to teach me. I want to stay with them."

The Mekai lowered the book from his face and regarded her with a serious look.

"You certainly don't have to stay here," the Mekai said, shrugging his shoulders. "Once we're satisfied you can go out into the world and not kill anyone with your magic, you can leave if you wish. No one is keeping you here, little one. It's your choice—surely Dormael explained it to you."

"He did," Bethany sighed. "But I know that's what he wants—for me to come to the Conclave. I could tell."

"I'm sure he does," the Mekai said. "Why don't you?"

"It's not that I don't," Bethany said. "It's just—I don't want him to leave me here. He's going to have to leave. I know that. He goes, and I'll be here, alone again."

"Child," the Mekai said, taking a deep breath. "You understand that your father lives here. The Conclave is his home. He only leaves to go on special trips, on Conclave business. He wants you to train here, yes—but he wants you here because *this* is his home.

He wants it to be your home, too. Do you see?"

"He'll still have to leave, though," she said. "I'll still be alone."

The Mekai smiled. "Yes, he will have to leave from time to time, child, but this is the place he comes back to. When you join a class, Bethany, you'll have a whole new family. Your classmates will become closer than friends—and you'll still have Dormael and D'Jenn. The rest of the Warlocks will doubtless adopt you, too. They're a tight-knit group."

"I guess so," she said.

"Still unconvinced? Let me try something else," he said. He closed the book and stood from his chair as his Kai floated the tome back to the table. He threw his hand out to indicate the surrounding globe. "This place, Bethany, is called the Convergence Chamber. Most people who know of it, though, call it the Crux."

"The Crux?" Bethany repeated, rising to follow the old man closer to the center of the platform.

"Indeed. Would you like to know what it does?"

She nodded.

The Mekai smiled. "The Crux is used to focus magic. There are techniques one can learn with magic, dear girl, secrets that go beyond something so mundane as to summon a flame with which to light a candle, or float a book across the room. Magic can do wonderful things. Would you like to see?" He held out a hand to her, one eyebrow raised in question.

Bethany nodded again and took the Mekai's hand.

"Now—let's talk again about history, young lady."

The room faded away like mist and was replaced with something new. A map appeared on the floor, mountains rising above the ground and oceans surging with storms. It glowed with its own subtle light.

"This," the Mekai said, pointing to a city in the shadow of a low mountain range, "is where we are—the city of Ishamael. Do you know anything of its founding?"

"No," Bethany said. "Everyone's heard of it, though. The City of Magic."

"And what do people say about us, then?"

"To stay away," Bethany replied. "Lots of people tell evil stories about it. None of it's true, though—obviously."

"Obviously, indeed," the Mekai laughed. "Let me tell you, then, about the City of Magic."

The land below them dissolved, blowing away like so much dust. The room became a battlefield, with men fighting and dying in tightly packed lines, eyeballs over shields, stabbing spears, and arrows falling like rain. Bethany resisted the urge to squeal and duck, taking her cues from the Mekai, who stood with quiet poise.

"Once," he said, "the Sevenlands didn't exist, child. In the years before the founding of Ishamael, our people were separate tribes, separate city-states, separate kingdoms. Each had its own system of governance, you see, and each its own values. The only thing we all shared was a language, and the desire to kill each other over things like crops and blood-debts." The Mekai held his hands out, indicating the struggling men all dying around them. "There were a lot of blood-debts."

The Mekai waved his hand, and the scene changed once again. Now they stood in a village under attack. People ran screaming in all directions, being cut down by men with conical helmets and straight, stabbing swords. The swordsmen were all over the village, destroying everything in sight and dragging people away.

"Then came the hordes from the east," the Mekai said. "Our oldest stories talk about them—great, tall men, blond and black-headed, fearsome as they were merciless. They invaded from the north, streaming down into the Sevenlands from the Gathan Mountains. They killed, destroyed, and enslaved everything they came across. They were like locusts, eating everything in their path. Our people, fractured as they were, could not band together to face this threat. Every year, the men from the north took more ground from our people, and every year, our people grew more desperate as they watched their lands be taken, their kin enslaved."

"What happened?"

"A leader appeared," the Mekai said. "His name was Ishamael."

"Like the city," Bethany said.

"Just so," the Mekai nodded. "Ishamael was a Teptian, and had been fighting the horde for years with the help of his friend, the wizard Indalvian—the man who founded the Conclave."

"Did Indalvian burn the hordes from the east?" Bethany asked. "Did he burn them all with magic and turn the skies against them?" The song of the armlet shifted, turning over like a slumbering person in the midst of the dream. The Mekai glanced at the armlet.

"Not exactly," the Mekai said. "Ishamael and Indalvian united the tribes, and together, the horde from the east was forced back to the north and across the Sea of Moving Ice. When the war was over, this city was founded and named for the leader who saved us. That was when the Sevenlands was born, and when the Conclave was built. The first stones that make up the surrounding chamber were laid in those years. This is the first thing they made, Bethany—the Crux. The entire Conclave was built around it."

"But why?" Bethany asked, immersed in the Mekai's story. "Why did they build this first?"

The Mekai waved his hand, and the scene around them fell away into motes of light. They stood once again on the platform, the armlet still floating in midair above them.

"This room gathers and focuses magic in a way that nothing else in Eldath can do," the Mekai said. "This is something you will learn during your studies here—that many things have an effect on magic. Music, shapes, materials, even places of great natural power—to all of these things does your magic respond. This room is the center of a gigantic magical Circle. The Crux of the entire Conclave, so to speak."

"You mean the whole building is part of it?"

"Exactly," the Mekai said, smiling.

"But...what is it *for*? What does it do?"

"This place, this Convergence Chamber," he said, "can be used to do any number of things. It focuses power, pulls it from the very air, and amplifies your magic. With this, you can scry out things happening on the other side of the world, or you could speak to many people at once. You could do wondrous and terrible things, dear. Terrible things, indeed."

"Terrible things like what?"

"That's a topic for another time," the Mekai said. "Let's talk about what it's doing now. The armlet—you are familiar with it, I assume? It seems to know you, little one."

Bethany nodded, eyes going to the piece of jewelry floating in midair.

"It talks to me sometimes," she said.

"What does it say?"

"You can't hear it?" Bethany asked. She walked over to the

Mekai and took his hand in her own. His wrinkled skin felt rough against her fingers, but his hands weren't gnarled or ugly. The hand contained a strength that surprised her. "Close your eyes. Listen to it."

Bethany could feel the armlet's song lilting out through the room. She waxed and waned with its alien crooning, sinking into the warm embrace of its music. The woman of fire did not appear, but Bethany could feel her in the room.

"I can hear its song, dear girl," the Mekai said, "but any messages it might have do not fall upon my ears. I can feel its presence...but no—it keeps its secrets from me. All I can see is a wall of...a wall of flame."

"I've seen that too," she whispered. Bethany knew whispering was ridiculous—the armlet would hear her no matter what. Still, the somber feeling in the room demanded it.

"It's very protective of you," the Mekai said, opening his eyes. "I felt it tense when you came into the room. It hovers about you like a den mother. Your father told me what happened on the ship. When you donned it."

Bethany's stomach went cold. "I didn't mean to put it on. It made me do it. I didn't want to."

"I know," the Mekai said, patting her shoulder. "So your father told me. Still, it's interesting the thing would take such a liking to you. I wonder why that is."

"I don't know," Bethany sighed. "I'm not the only one, you know. It talks to Dormael, too. It talks to us both."

"So he said," the Mekai replied. He laid a hand on Bethany's shoulder and turned her back toward the chairs. As they walked, a decanter floated over from the table and poured itself into two wooden cups. The book the Mekai had been perusing floated back into his hands, pages flipping through the air. Bethany settled into her chair, watching it all happen with awe. The Mekai noticed her watching, and heat rose to her cheeks.

"Don't worry, child—I'm used to the looks people give me." He smiled. "When you're as ancient as me, your magic becomes something...different."

"What do you mean?" What would she be like when her skin got all saggy and dried up like the Mekai's? She hoped her magic was as wonderful as his, but she wasn't looking forward to looking like a dried prune.

"As a wizard gets older, dear, they grow...sharper, more focused," he said. "Your power will grow into something that's nearly alive. It will do things sometimes without your foreknowledge. I find that as I get older, I spend a great deal of time in meditation."

"Why?"

"Well, say I'm walking across the Bruising Stretch one day, and I have an idle thought that a new tree would look nice out on the Green. For anyone else, that's a fine thought to have, no problems whatsoever. For me, it's different. My magic wants to make it happen, wants to grow me a tree. You have to control that sort of thing, you see, or every errant thought could turn into an embarrassing situation."

"I think I understand," Bethany said. "Like with the book—your Kai knows you want it, so it brings it to you?"

"Very astute, Bethany," he said, beaming at her. "That's it exactly."

"Will my magic get like that?"

"If you live long enough." The Mekai smiled. "I imagine that for you, though, it will be quite worse."

"Worse? Why?"

The Mekai gave a low chuckle. "Dear, when I was a young man, do you know what I did? From which Discipline that I came?"

"No," Bethany replied. "Were you a Warlock, like my father?"

The Mekai let out a laugh.

"No, dear, not even close. I was a teacher," he said. "I taught the natural sciences to the older children. They all used to call me Master Arian. My gift was a modest one. I could manage a few more difficult things, but I was quite a lot better at research and the application of my magic to the pursuit of knowledge. I had a particular interest, dear girl, in history."

"If you were just a teacher, how did you become the Mekai?" Bethany asked. "I thought you had to be the strongest, best wizard."

"And what, do you think, constitutes being 'the best'?"

"I don't know." Bethany shrugged. "I just thought it was true, that's all."

The Mekai lifted an eyebrow and regarded her over the rim of his spectacles.

"Here's a bit of wisdom for you, dear—one of those sayings old people give you sometimes. Words like 'best', or 'strongest' are all relative. They can mean whatever you want them to mean, and they can be easily twisted to mean anything. One person says he's the best swimmer, and maybe that means he can swim very fast, or for a very long time. Another says he's the best fisherman, and maybe that means he can pull more fish out of the sea, or he knows the best spots to catch them. The thing both of those fools don't realize is that the sea doesn't give a damn about who's the best swimmer, or the best fisherman. The sea takes the strong as readily as the weak. My grandmother told me that before even your father's father was born—think on that, dear girl. That's a very old bit of wisdom."

Bethany nodded. *What is he talking about?*

"Regardless," he went on, "the Mekai is not the strongest or best wizard—if there is such a thing. The Mekai is elected by the Conclave. I was elected long before you were born. Before people older than you were born, in fact."

Bethany leaned forward. "Are you the oldest wizard, then?"

The Mekai let out another laugh, and it echoed around the chamber.

"The oldest in this building, anyway," he said, smiling. "The oldest, indeed. I've forgotten how delightful children can be."

"I've always liked old people, too," Bethany said, returning his smile. "You've got the best stories."

"That we do," he chuckled. "That we do. Would you like to hear another one?"

Bethany hugged her knees to her chest and nodded with enthusiasm. She loved stories, and she was about to get one from the oldest wizard in the Conclave. Who else in the world could say that?

The Pirate-Queen of the Seas, that's who.

"This book," the Mekai said, holding up the tome for her inspection, "is the collected writings of Sevenlander Kansils from history. You know what Kansils are, dear? Has your father explained them?"

"No," Bethany grumbled. "I guess there's a lot he hasn't told me."

"I'll speak with him about that." The Mekai winked. "In the meantime, I'll try to fill you in. You see, Sevenlander society is made up of families, right? Each family has a leader who speaks for them, chosen by the families themselves. That person is called a Patron—or a Matron, if they're a girl. Now, those Patrons then elect someone to speak for *them* from amongst their own, and those are called Clan Leaders. The Clan Leaders elect the Kansil from their own ranks, and this person leads an entire tribe. Do you understand?"

Bethany nodded.

"This book is a collection of the things they have written down," the Mekai said. "It goes back a very long time. I've found something here I think you might find familiar. Keep in mind, now—these words were written hundreds and hundreds of years ago, and we're about to read them. Think of the time that passed between the thought and its passage to us, right here, right now. Exciting, isn't it?"

Bethany nodded again, favoring him with a smile.

"Good," he said. "Now, where did I...oh. Here we are." He cleared his throat, peered through his spectacles, and started to read. "*The dreams plague me nightly. I see a field of nothing but flame, I see the night sky all around me, the Void full of stars. I see a battlefield and men struggling. Even during the daylight I can hear the noise, whispering to me as I walk the halls of my home. The others think me mad, and perhaps they are correct.*"

"The dreams," Bethany said, interrupting him. "I've had dreams like that."

"Which ones, dear?" the Mekai asked, setting the book aside.

"All of them," she said. "The battle, the fire, all of it. Who wrote that?"

"These are the writings of a man named Baristacl Neborrin. He was Kansil of the Soirus-Gamerits very long ago," the Mekai said. "These musings are from his journal. Not many ever read these, but I, as I said, have a particular interest in history."

"What does it mean?" Bethany asked. "That he could hear the *ficga*? It spoke to him, too?"

"Perhaps," the Mekai said. "This alone tells us only a few things—that he may have been in possession of the armlet, and that he may have been magic-sensitive. Also, that it was reaching out even in those days, all those years gone. If, indeed, it was this artifact which was the cause of his problems, and not madness in truth."

"What is magic-sensitive?" Bethany asked. "I thought there were only Blessed and Learned."

"If you're Blessed, you're magic-sensitive," the Mekai explained. "However, it is possible for a person to be Blessed, but only to such a degree that they can sense magic, perhaps feel it when someone is using it. Their gift, however, will never be enough to use their power. Many who are magic-sensitive don't even know it, and will never realize it. The Blessing of Eindor comes to us across a wide spectrum."

"So, Baristael had the *fiega*, and it spoke to him," Bethany said. "How did Shawna get it? It's hers now, after all."

"For the answer to that question, dear, we can again look to my favorite subject—history." The man had a pleasant voice, and he told a story with an air of mystery that drew her into his tale. He must have been a great teacher. "Now," he went on, "have you ever heard of the Treaty of Duadan?"

"No," she said. "But I'd like to hear about it."

The Mekai paused and gave her a strange look, then cleared his throat.

"Aren't you just delightful," he mumbled. "Right—the Duadan Treaty was an agreement between the Sevenlands and a few countries in Alderak hundreds of years ago, before the Second Great War. There were a few provisions to it about trade and such, but the real meat of the treaty was the intermarriage of houses. Eastern kings were to take the daughters of Sevenlander Kansils to wife in order to strengthen ties between east and west. Not all the kingdoms of Alderak signed on, but a few did. One of them, dear girl, was Cambrell."

"Why would they do that?" Bethany asked. "Why make treaties about getting married?"

The Mekai chuckled. "Entire wars have been fought over marriages, dear. Wars have also been prevented by marriage, though—and such was the point. The thinking at the time was that if the Duadan Kansil has grandchildren shared with, say, the King of Lesmira, then Lesmira and Duadan would avoid going to war with each other."

"Did that work?" Bethany asked. "Did it really keep them from fighting?"

"Not really, child," the Mekai said. "It was an older time, a different time. The practice ended hundreds of years ago. In any case, the Kansils of the Soirus-Gamerit were to send one of their daughters to wed the Princes of Cambrell. Do you see why that is significant?"

Bethany thought for a moment before the answer slapped her in the face.

"Shawna is from Cambrell," she said. "She had the *fiega*. If Shawna has the *fiega* now, and Baristael had it then...that means it came from Soirus-Gamerit?"

"Very good, dear." The Mekai smiled. "Though, we don't know it necessarily *came* from Soirus-Gamerit, just that it was there at one time and in the possession of the Kansil. Now we have something to go on, a trail to follow, clues to research. Isn't it exciting? History, dear girl, is better than any story."

"I still like Leyton's stories," Bethany said. "Leyton was Pirate-King of the Seas, Sacker of Towns, Terror of the Blue."

"You like tales of plunder and mystery, do you?"

Bethany nodded.

"You'll find more plunder and mystery in the annals of history than anywhere else, dear girl," the Mekai said. "War, murder, love, death—it's all there, and it all really happened. There are many things to be learned. So—have I convinced you to train at the Conclave? I suppose you could leave the real mysteries for other people to find, but something tells me you would rather seek them out yourself. After all—why else would you come down into the Rat Holes except to search out ancient mysteries? Does your exile to the most interesting place in all the Sevenlands still sound so terrible?"

Bethany smiled and her cheeks reddened with embarrassment.

"I didn't mean it would be terrible," Bethany said. "Just that I would be lonely. And I'm sorry about coming down into the tunnels. I didn't mean to get lost...it just...I just...," she trailed off, unable to put words to how dumb she felt.

"A girl with at least one friend can never be lonely." The Mekai smiled. "So, are we friends now? I'm certainly too old to be going anywhere, so you know you'll always have a friend here, no matter what. Is that enough to convince you?"

Bethany smiled and nodded.

"And don't worry about coming down into the Rat Holes, girl. Do you think you're the first child to go running around in the tunnels, searching for old magic swords and the like? The Conclave staff are always sweeping them up out of the corridors and sending them back to their classes. You're not the first, and certainly won't be the last. I even did so, once."

Bethany smiled. "You did?"

"Oh, yes," the Mekai said. "Believe it or not, little one, I was always in trouble when I was your age. I stole quite a bit of food from the kitchens."

"The pastries are the easiest." Bethany grinned. "They leave them right out on the tables, right where anyone can grab them. I can fit two in my mouth and three in my dress and still be out of there before anyone sees me."

"Be careful, though," the old man laughed. "If Lady Gerith catches you, you'll be scrubbing pots for an entire season. Big pots, too—the kind you have to crawl into."

"Lady Gerith?"

"She runs the Conclave kitchens," the Mekai said. "Everyone calls her Lady Gerith, the Queen of Soup. Don't let her hear you say it, though—that will get you scullery duty, too."

"Did you ever have to scrub pots?" Bethany asked. She couldn't imagine the distinguished old man on his hands and knees, scrubbing away at greasy iron.

"How do you think my hands got this wrinkled?" he asked, wiggling them in the air.

Bethany laughed. *I like him.*

"What's going to happen to me now?" she asked, coming down from her fit of laughter. She remembered the man in the tunnels, and dread crept down her spine. "Am I going to be in trouble?"

"For what, getting lost in the Rat Holes?"

"No, for hurting that man," she said. "The one who tried to grab me."

The Mekai gave her a sobering look and took a deep breath. He rose from his chair and offered Bethany his hand again. She was reluctant, but she rose and took his hand, anyway. The Mekai led her inside the concentric lines of silver, to the middle of the Crux. She felt his Kai reach out and sing with the Crux, and their surroundings once again dissolved.

"Close your eyes, dear," the Mekai said, squeezing her hand. "I need you to show me the place where this happened—take me there in your mind. Can you do that? Can you picture it?"

"I think so," Bethany said. She concentrated, trying to conjure the scene in her mind. She imagined the candle sconce on the wall, the man standing in its pool of light, examining her footprints. She imagined the dusty hallway, the smell of the stone. She saw his face as he looked at her.

She saw him burn.

Please!

"Not so strongly, girl," the Mekai said, his voice intruding on her vision. "Remember to keep hold of your emotions. An unfocused mind—"

"—yields unfocused magic," she sighed, completing the mantra D'Jenn was always making her repeat. She realized what she'd done—interrupted the Mekai—and felt her cheeks reddening again. "Sorry."

"Don't apologize, dear, just do it the right way," he said, patting the top of her hand. "Now, with more control, picture it again."

Bethany brought the image up again, fixing every detail she could muster into the front of her mind. She remembered the way the stone felt against her bare feet. She remembered the way her hands had clutched into fists, and the way his magic had felt when it attacked her.

The surrounding room swirled, shifted and reformed. The Mekai held tight to her hand, sensing her unease, and tried to comfort her. She could feel his Kai doing the same thing to her magic, singing to her power in slow, soothing tones.

The picture of the hallway formed around her. It was as if she stood again in the darkness, staring at the pool of light. The man was there, crouched under the candlelight, trying to read her footprints. His image was hazy, indistinct.

"I need you to take us further, Bethany. Can you show me what he did, how he tried to take you?" the Mekai asked. He peered at the man, but his features were no more than smeared darkness and light.

"I think so," Bethany said. She took a deep breath and clamped down on her beating heart. There was no reason to be afraid now, but she still quailed at the thought of conjuring this moment again. Summoning her strength, she brought up the memory of his magic.

The scene changed. The man now stood, hand outstretched in her direction. Light flooded the hallway—the light he'd nearly blinded her with—and his face was revealed. He had a strong chin, his jaw clenched with fierce determination. He was frozen in the instant which he'd used his magic on her, and his eyes were locked in her direction—one brown, one blue.

The Mekai hissed in surprise, and the scene dissolved so quickly it made Bethany dizzy. He turned to her and crouched down to her level, taking her head in his hands. His Kai was tense, and his sudden change in behavior put her on the defensive.

"Are you certain that was the man, Bethany? Are you certain that was him, and it wasn't some mistake, some face from your memory that you put there by accident? Think hard, girl—the memory is fallible."

"No," she said. "That was him. I remember his eyes. That was *him*."

The Mekai took a deep breath, his shoulders rising as his chest filled with air. He rose and turned from her, gesturing to the armlet. It floated down from its place and deposited itself into its silver box, which had been sitting on the table. Once the armlet was secure, he turned back to her.

"Let's make a promise between friends. Can we do that?"

Bethany nodded.

"I need you to keep quiet about this, alright? Don't tell anyone about the man in the tunnel, about what he looked like. This is very important—no one but me. Do you understand?" he said. He got down to her level and took her shoulders in his hands. "This is a secret between you and the Mekai."

A commotion rang in the hallway. Voices echoed down the corridor, coming in their direction. Bethany thought she heard Dormael's voice, and she felt a wild surge of relief.

"Bethany," the Mekai said, shaking her back to reality. "Promise me!"

"I promise," she nodded. "Just me and you."

The Mekai smiled and ruffled her hair, not unlike the way

Dormael did.

"Smart girl," he said. "From now on, when someone asks about it, you just keep quiet. I'll do the talking, alright?"

"Alright," she said.

A group of people burst through the door and onto the platform.

**

"Bethany!" Dormael said, a barrel's worth of air escaping his chest. She ran down the walkway toward him, and Dormael pushed his way ahead of the rest of the group. He caught the girl in a fierce hug. "Are you all right?"

He pushed her out to arms' length and ran a critical eye over her. She didn't have any bruises or apparent injuries, though a haunted look hovered in her eyes. He pulled her into another hug and rose to his feet. Bethany sidled close to his leg, putting herself between him and Shawna as the rest of the group strode up to them.

Victus approached, scowling at the entire scene—or perhaps because Lacelle hovered just at his arm, directing as much cold disdain in his direction as was possible. The two of them had been trading barbed niceties since the woman had met them in the tunnels, bringing the already stressful situation to a boiling point.

"Hello, little one," Victus said, crouching down to her level. "My name is Deacon Victus—I'm a friend of your father's. I need to ask you something about what happened in the tunnels. Is that alright?"

Bethany sidled further behind Dormael's leg, peering at Victus with a wary eye.

"Can't it wait, Deacon?" Dormael asked. "She's been down here all day. Hasn't eaten, and she lost her shoes again." He said that last over the girl's head with enough emphasis to show that he'd noticed her bare feet. The color that rose to her cheeks made him feel a bit of relief—the haunted look in her eyes wasn't a return to the way she had been after they took her from Colonel Grant. The Bethany they'd coaxed out during the last season was still there. "Let me get some food in her. I'll bring her report to you myself."

"Dormael, you know it's important to ask these things when they're still fresh in the mind," Victus said. "I'm not going to hurt the girl, for the gods' sake, I just want to know what happened."

"I think your Warlock has a point," Lacelle said. "The poor dear is frightened—look at her. It couldn't hurt to act like a person for once, Victus. She's a little girl."

"And I think you should pay more attention to matters that concern you," Victus said, turning an angry eye in her direction. "This is Warlock business. Don't you have some old tome to be studying, something about the way ancient people shat in the bushes, or something?"

Lacelle narrowed her eyes.

"Oh, I'd much rather stand here and watch you scare little girls. What a *big* man you are, Victus Tiranan," she clipped. Dormael thought he heard Shawna utter a chuckle under her breath, but he couldn't be sure. Victus stared daggers at Lacelle, but he rose from his crouch and backed away.

"Very well," he said, holding his hands up for peace. "I'm certainly not here to scare anyone, that's not what I want. I just want to catch whoever hurt her, that's all. We're all on the same side, here."

"Aren't we?" The Mekai walked over to join the conversation.

Everyone offered him a short bow. Shawna echoed the gesture after a moment's hesitation, but executed her own bow with more grace than anyone, save maybe Lacelle. The Mekai nodded in return and offered Shawna a genuine smile.

The Mekai looked at Victus. "That was a question. I said— *aren't we?*"

"Honored One?" Victus asked.

"On the same side," the Mekai replied. The skin around his eyes tightened.

"Of course." Victus nodded. "I can wait until the girl is seen to. Have you been filled in, Honored One?"

"I've learned a very great deal," the Mekai said. "Bethany and I have had quite the long conversation—haven't we, dear?" The girl smiled up at the Mekai and nodded, and the old man winked at her. "Such a delightful child. As bright as any I've ever taught. I remember all of their faces, you know. Every one of them." He turned an opaque look on Victus. "I remember every one of them."

"So, you know of the body in the tunnels?" Victus asked in a cautious tone.

Is the Mekai suspicious, or am I overreacting? Am I reading my own suspicion into it?

"I know," the Mekai nodded. "It saddens me. This is the first killing in the Conclave in over fifty years. The one responsible for this should be ashamed of themselves." Dormael's hand tightened on Bethany's shoulders, a surge of anger rising in his chest. Surely anyone could see that Bethany had been defending herself!

Mekai's eyes, though, stayed locked on Victus.

Maybe I'm not overreacting.

The moment stretched on for an uncomfortable second.

"I've looked into this already," the Mekai said, breaking the spell. "Interviewed the girl already. I'm satisfied with what she has told me, and the evidence she has presented. What I need from the Warlocks, Deacon, is to investigate this person who attacked her. The poor dear couldn't see his face, but he attacked her with magic. Above all, we need to keep this quiet. No one can know until you've gotten to the bottom of this. Understood?"

"I will oversee the investigation myself, Honored Mekai," Victus said with a bow.

"Good," the Mekai said. "I want a full report as soon as it's available. Fall to purpose."

Victus gave them all a tight smile, bowed to the Mekai, and strode away down the path to the opening in the wall. Dormael watched him go, unsure of what he had just witnessed. Shawna, too, was giving him an odd look. Lacelle watched everyone with interest, and Dormael tried to keep his expression bland.

Don't want to reveal anything to her. She already thinks I'm sleeping with Shawna. Who knows what else she'll think?

"Lacelle, do me the kindness of gathering the research we've been collecting and bringing it to my chambers. I'll ask all of you to dine with me tonight—in the Mekai's personal rooms, understood? We have much to discuss and very little time."

"Time, Honored One?" Lacelle asked, giving him a strange look.

The Mekai turned a serious eye in her direction. "Don't forget the scrolls in Old Vendon, Deacon Lacelle. And hurry. As I said—very little time."

"Of course, Honored One," Lacelle said, bowing at the waist. She shared a confused look with Dormael as she turned to leave—

the first human emotion the woman had ever shown him—and glided from the room. Dormael and Shawna shared a confused look.

"Dormael," the Mekai said, turning toward him, "when you come tonight, make sure to bring everyone. D'Jenn, your brother, little Bethany, and you, of course, Baroness Llewan. I regret that my hospitality needs to to be so rushed, but the gods give us a strange world in which to live, do they not?"

"They do," Shawna said, giving him a confused smile. "I will be honored to receive your hospitality, Honored Mekai, in any case."

"Very good, very good, indeed," the Mekai said. He took a few steps toward the exit, then turned back to them as if he had forgotten something. "One more thing, Dormael. Don't forget to wear a clean shirt—that one is ripped, and there's quite a bit of blood on it. What happened to you, dear boy?"

His hands, though, were spinning in the Hunter's Tongue, his back to the two Deacons who had yet to reach the exit.

Pack for a long journey, you all leave tonight. Say nothing.

It took Dormael a stunned moment to separate the messages in his mind, but he stammered out a reply.

"Ah—of course, Honored Mekai. Apologies, I'll fill you in at dinner."

"Very good, Warlock Harlun. Very good," the Mekai said. "Also, don't forget to take the armlet with you when you leave this room. I've completed my study of the thing. We shall speak about it over dinner." He offered them a smile that never touched his eyes, gave Bethany another conspiratorial wink, and strode off in the wake of his Deacons.

What in the Six Hells is happening?

"Did you catch that?" Shawna whispered. "Did you see what he said?"

"Aye," Dormael replied. "I saw."

"Me too," Bethany said.

Dormael reached down and hugged her tight against his side. He'd been so afraid they would find her body in the tunnels or never find her at all. He clutched to her like a lucky charm, and she pulled just as tightly against him. Shawna strode over and grabbed the box with her mother's armlet, and the three of them made their way back into the Rat Holes.

Bethany held Dormael's hand the entire way.

UNSANCTIONED OPERATIVES

The Mekai's private residence was its own separate building on the Green. Wizards long ago had built spells into the place that warded it from scrying, intrusion, or magical tampering. More power was sunk into the very stones of this building than any other in the Conclave, save the center of the Crux. Given the number of defensive spells, it was the most secure place in the entire city of Ishamael.

Dormael ate without gusto, his stomach unable to accept much more than dread for its fuel. His thoughts were racing, trying to piece together everything that had happened in the past day. Inera, Bethany, Victus—his whole world was unraveling. He tried to feel something, anything else about it, but his emotions had fallen into a yawning pit of dread.

The hairs on the back of Dormael's neck itched through the entire meal.

He tried to keep his eyes on the decorations of the dining hall while the roast was served, taking in the expensive paintings and the rosewood paneling. The roast was delicious for two full bites before it was whisked away. During the second course, he tried to take stock of the various infused items he could count in the room—a decanter here, an ancient stylus there—but the activity failed to distract him. Try as he might, Dormael couldn't keep his mind from the issue behind the pleasant conversation being made during the meal.

Everyone's eyes reflected his concern.

Lacelle peered into her food as if some great secret were contained in the depths of her soup bowl. Shawna considered everyone at the table in turn, her eyes narrowed in thought. The Mekai made small talk with Bethany, though Dormael could feel the old man's Kai moving through the room, rooting in every empty corner in anxious spasms. D'Jenn scowled at everything, and Allen pretended not to notice the pregnant silence in the room.

Dormael felt like screaming.

By the time everyone passed around a bowl of the Shaman's Leaf, Bethany had fallen asleep on one of the benches at the edge of the room. It was late in the evening, and Dormael was beginning to feel tired himself. Though the tension kept him alert, his body had been through all Six Hells today. It begged him for a respite.

"I'm quite sorry I kept everyone waiting," the Mekai said as the pipe went around the room. "It was important they think we were up late into the night, long after anyone would do much but sleep."

"They?" Lacelle asked, raising a cold eyebrow.

"Your esteemed colleague," the Mekai replied. "Victus Tiranan, Deacon of Warlocks."

Silence filled the room like a startled intake of breath.

"So what D'Jenn said is true," Dormael said, looking to his cousin. "Victus is a traitor." The words sounded odd coming out, as if he was saying his own father was a traitor. He wanted to grab them out of the air even as they passed his lips.

"Let us all lay what we know on the table," the Mekai said. "First—what happened tonight, in the tunnels. Tell me, boys, has Bethany ever seen Kendall Induriam? Has she ever spoken with the man?"

"Not that I know of," Dormael said, shrugging his shoulders. "I thought Kendall was out of the Conclave. Haven't seen him since last year."

"You saw him earlier today," the Mekai said, "burnt to death in the Rat Holes. Bethany showed me his face in her memories, and there was no doubt in my mind. His eyes, you know."

"One brown, one blue," D'Jenn nodded. "We used to call him Evil Eye Induriam. He hated it."

"Doesn't hate anything anymore," Dormael said. The news of

Kendall's death hit him in the stomach—they'd been friends, after a fashion. "Why would Kendall try to take Bethany? She said the man attacked her. She said he tried to *take* her."

"I can't be sure," the Mekai said. "It's possible Victus wanted to speak to her, to gain her trust. It's possible he meant to kidnap her. It's possible he wanted to plant a suggestion in her mind—there are any number of possibilities."

"Bethany is linked to the armlet," D'Jenn said. "It speaks with her. If he can control her, then maybe he can control the armlet through her. He said something about how powerful she was, and how she should become a Warlock like the rest of her family. He's trying to gather up his loyal followers, counting his eggs."

"Doubtless he wants the two of you on his side," Lacelle said, narrowing her eyes at them.

"He must be planning on making a move soon," D'Jenn said. "Perhaps I can provide some context. I spent some time looking into a thing that kept bugging me. I discovered Victus has been sending Warlocks on missions as political favors. He had Kitamin Jurillic rescued from the Golden Waste, and Nyra Jurillic suspected he has something to do with the murder of Berrul's brother."

"Berrul?" Shawna asked.

"Nilliam Berrul," Dormael clarified. "He's the Kansil of Soirus-Gamerit."

"So, Victus has been dispatching his agents as his personal mercenaries?" Lacelle asked, her voice gone quiet.

D'Jenn nodded. "He had Kitamin Jurillic rescued—that I know for a fact. I met with Nyra Jurillic. She assumed I was working for Victus. She said she could sense his hand at work in the Council meetings of late, and she suspected he would try to have her killed. He has at least two Warlocks doing his dirty work, but there must be more."

"Why?" Dormael asked. *No one would go along with this. What is this nonsense?*

"Because you're all loyal to him, that's why," Lacelle said. "Say what you will about Victus Tiranan, but his Warlocks love him, one and all."

Dormael wanted to argue, but she was right.

"There have been a number of deaths recently," the Mekai said. "I hadn't thought they were much more than accidents, the natural result of the dangerous work you all do, but now I wonder if there was some sort of purge happening right under my nose. I've always allowed Deacon Victus a free hand with his people. Now I wonder at the wisdom of such a thing."

"Deaths?" Dormael asked. "You can't mean...he wouldn't. Not *that.*"

"Ragnam and Sierra," D'Jenn said. "Killed by raiders in the southern seas, apparently. Yista and Illiriam, disappeared on the Dannon Steppe. Vera, Taglion, Kirael and Jastom—all drowned on the Sea of Storms. I asked around about that, too." D'Jenn's eyes blazed brighter with each name, and Dormael felt a ball of ice forming in his stomach.

"You think he killed them? All of them?" Dormael asked, the question hollowing his chest.

"I'm sorry, boys," the Mekai said. "I blame myself for this."

"I blame Victus," D'Jenn said, a darkness entering his tone.

If there really had been a purge, if Victus had commanded such a thing, then nothing would satisfy D'Jenn other than the man's head. Those had been his friends, his family. He'd grown up with most of them and looked up to some of them. Dormael wanted retribution as well, but he hovered on the edge of anger.

Victus wouldn't do such a thing. He couldn't!

"Are we sure about this?" Dormael asked.

"I can see the way he's moving," D'Jenn said. "He's influenced the Council to set aside a large sum of money and sewed rumors about death camps overseas. He's purged anyone who might have the power to stand against him and bought up influence where it's needed. Those who have served their purposes are pulled down by those below them—at which point he'll have them killed, severing any ties for good. If he plans to depose you, Honored One, he's been methodical."

"It appears so," the Mekai nodded. "He's challenged me publicly on a number of issues and engendered support within the Conclave. I should have seen this coming."

"What he didn't count on was Bethany," D'Jenn said. "He could have used her in order to secure our loyalty, or draw us out in order to assassinate us if he felt we would turn against him. She defeated the ambush, though, and now everything is up in the air."

"Indeed," the Mekai said. "His hand has been revealed, and

he'll have to move soon if he wants his plan to succeed, whatever his goals are. We don't have much time."

"We are ready to do our duty," D'Jenn said, rising to his feet. Dormael nodded, but still felt overwhelmed. He could see the logic behind it all, and he trusted his cousin.

Garner support, maybe—but kill our friends? Not that. Would he?

A cold, logical voice inside told him it was likely true. Victus had trained him, and Dormael knew the lengths to which the man would go if he deemed it necessary. If he had decided to go down the path to power, he wouldn't stop at anything to achieve his goal. Dormael caught eyes with D'Jenn and saw the certainty in his cousin's face.

Nodding to D'Jenn, Dormael stood with him.

"If Victus is responsible for the deaths of all our friends, then we need to move now," Dormael said.

"Victus has to die." D'Jenn nodded. "We kill him tonight. If we give him a chance to make the first move, we will fail. I know the way his mind works, the way he plans an operation. We have to do it now, or we risk yielding the initiative."

"Do you think we can take him?" Dormael asked. "What if the others are near him, guarding him? Do you think they'll fight us?"

"They've killed eight of us already," D'Jenn said. "What makes you think they'll hesitate for you and I? If we don't do this tonight, Honored One, I fear we will lose our chance. I urge you to grant us his Death Coin."

As he heard the words come out of D'Jenn's mouth, Dormael gave an involuntary shudder. Death Coins were issued only against rogue wizards—dangerous Blessed who had used their powers for subjugation or harm. Once a Warlock took up a Death Coin, they couldn't return to Ishamael without having made good on its promise. Dormael once again hesitated, but looked to the intensity in D'Jenn's eyes.

It's Vera—he's been in love with her for years. That's why he's so angry.

"I cannot," the Mekai said.

The room sat for a moment in stunned silence. Even Lacelle looked at the Mekai as if he had lost his mind. Allen coughed, then held up his hands when everyone gave him an irritated look.

"Honored One, if we don't act soon, Victus will put his plans into motion. We'll be blindsided and ultimately defeated. I must insist that we end him tonight," D'Jenn said.

"I cannot—and not because I fear to act," the Mekai said. "There are greater forces at work."

"Greater forces than the integrity of the Conclave?" Dormael asked before he could stop himself. "What could be more important that that?"

"Do not forget to whom you speak," the Mekai said, his tone going flat. The room went silent, and Dormael felt his cheeks color. He'd let his anger get the best of him.

"Apologies, Honored One," Dormael said.

"No need for all that—and yes, greater forces than the integrity of the Conclave. Lacelle, did you bring that research I asked of you?"

"I did," Lacelle said. She rose from the table and walked to the edge of the room, where a leather scroll case had been left on a bookshelf. She snatched it and brought it over to the table, popped the end, and pulled a sheaf of documents out of the cylinder. The Mekai reached over and leafed through them, finally settling on a copy of something in Old Vendon.

"You see, we've been looking through old records since you boys brought back the Baroness Llewan's armlet. We believe we have discovered what it is."

**

Maarkov gnawed on a piece of dried beef as he stared into the darkness. They'd come down the mountain into Runeme, and as soon as Maaz had instructed his *strega* to set up camp, Maarkov had taken his bedroll as far from the stinking things as possible. He sat under the sheltering boughs of an evergreen, listening to the water drip from the leaves in the wake of the day's storm. Ishamael sat in the distance, a scattering of lights along the river's path.

Maarkov was uneasy being this close to it. Growing up, he had heard horror stories of Ishamael. It had been said that their altars reached hundreds of links to the sky, and every day, infants were tossed from the edge to splatter on the stones below—offerings to Eindor, the Father of Magic. Now, of course, he knew such things were ridiculous.

His brother, after all, was the real horror.

The Conclave of Wizards was down in the city. It had been the great monster of Maaz and Maarkov's life. Even in the early days, when Maaz had been little more than a lanky, awkward youth, they'd had to hide from the wizards. Now, here they stood, half a day's walk from the Conclave itself.

Maarkov wondered how they would kill his brother. What did they do to necromancers, anyway? What did they do to someone who had killed so many and with such disturbing efficiency? He could almost hear his brother's voice.

It's artistry.

Maarkov wondered for the thousandth time what his brother's plan might be. Were they to sit here until sunrise? Were they to skip through the gates of the city?

Don't mind us, just a traveling band of rotting corpses and dead-eyed killers.

Maarkov finished his dinner and packed a pipe bowl, leaning back against the tree to relax for a spell. His fingernails did not grow, nor did his hair, most wounds couldn't kill him, and he didn't need to breathe—but he still felt a release of pleasure from tobacco. The gods truly built man as a mystery.

A bird dropped from the night sky, fluttering its wings as it came in for a landing a short distance from his foot. It was a crow or maybe a raven—Maarkov had never given two shits about the difference. He almost raised his leg to kick the damned thing. He didn't want it pecking at his flesh when he went to sleep.

In the instants while he was still trying to decide, the bird rippled and changed, sliding into the form of a diminutive young woman. She rose and brushed her tattered dress straight, blinking her eyes.

"Where is your brother?" she asked.

"And a mighty fine evening to you too, Inera," Maarkov said. "He's by the fire. Where do you think?"

Inera looked in the direction of the orange light, dread painting her features. In the low echo of the firelight, her face was outlined by the shadow. She looked as if she was staring at her own death.

"I suppose things didn't work out in Ishamael," Maarkov said.

"Not that he'd go down there himself—you can tell him I said that, too."

"You know I will not."

"I know," he sighed. "You may as well get out of my fucking sight and go meet your doom. He already knows you're here—you know that." Maarkov tried to keep his distance from his brother's apprentices. They had a nasty habit of dying when they'd outlived their usefulness. Maarkov didn't want to see Inera go, though. Not that he liked her—he didn't think he was capable of that—but her company was the only pleasant thing about his existence, and she was easy on the eyes. He wanted to bed her, but the woman eluded his every advance. He had long ago stopped trying.

Another odd thing his body did—lusting.

"I do, in fact, already know," Maaz hissed, coming out of the darkness. Maarkov almost jumped out of his skin. He wanted to throw something at his brother, but the only thing in his hand was his tobacco pipe.

Inera bowed her head, keeping her eyes on the grass at Maaz's feet. Maarkov always watched these little exchanges with a wry sense of humor. He could remember when his brother had been a pleading little shit, and now he made all those who served him cower at his very gaze. It all seemed so useless and petty to Maarkov, but what did his opinion matter?

"Master," she said. "I have failed."

"A fact I have deduced, given you have neither the girl nor the artifact in your possession, as I instructed you. What explosion of idiocy resulted in your failure, Inera?" he asked.

The space between master and apprentice was loaded with tension.

"Dormael's cousin proved to be more resourceful than I'd expected," she said. "He found my hiding place before the Taker could do its work. Somehow Dormael was able to break the Circle I had constructed—it makes no sense. It held him in check right up until the end. He shouldn't have been able to break it."

Maarkov could tell by Inera's posture that she was struggling not to cower.

"If your former lover was able to break your Circle, you must have constructed it incorrectly," Maaz said. "And if his cousin found your hiding place, it was your own stupidity that led him to you. You failed and failed yet again. Why am I not surprised, Inera?"

"Because I'm a failure, Master."

Maarkov wanted to puke.

"Because you're a failure," Maaz said. He reached out his hand, fingers curling into a claw. Inera collapsed to her knees, making only the smallest noise at the pain. Maaz left the pressure on until Inera whimpered under her breath.

Maarkov reached to his side, looking for the dagger he kept at his belt.

"Explain to me why I should not just kill you now," Maaz said. "If all that lies between us in the future is failure, Inera, you would better serve as a corpse."

Inera made a coughing noise and reached a hand to her side. She cried out in pain as the movement nearly doubled her over, but then raised her hand into the air. Clutched in her fist was a piece of cloth.

Maaz let the pressure recede, and she gasped in relief. He walked forward and snatched the piece of cloth. He ran it under his nose, sniffing at it like a lady's undergarments.

Maarkov gagged.

"At least you have finally done something of value, Inera. You have earned your life tonight," Maaz said. He turned his gaze on Maarkov. "Perhaps others could learn from your example."

"I've no interest in pleasing you, brother," Maarkov sighed. "Fuck yourself."

Maaz turned from him, walking a short distance away to clear a space on the ground. Inera gave Maarkov a guarded look and turned to follow her master. Maarkov leaned back against the tree again and puffed on his pipe. He watched his brother simply because there was nothing else to look at.

Maaz gestured to the space he'd cleared, and flames burst to life. They rushed across the grass in a circle, burning shapes and sinuous lines into the ground. Maaz directed the flames, drawing his spell like a man with a paintbrush.

Maaz turned toward the camp and hissed something into the darkness. Two of the *strega* came out of the shadows, silent figures wrapped in ratty scarves and deep Sevenlander cloaks. Why did his brother even bother with making them shroud themselves so—it did nothing for the stink.

They stepped over the circle of low flame and laid side-by-side in the center, their dead eyes staring at the sky. One of them was the boy they'd captured days ago, the one who had watched Maarkov eat a piece of his mother. Maarkov couldn't keep the shudder out of his body as he looked at the thing. Maaz slashed his arm open and slung his blood around the circle, whispering in that strange, guttural language.

Each spatter of blood became a cloud of mist as it touched the spell, and each cloud of mist began to crawl through the air, congealing in smoky tendrils. Maaz continued chanting, tossing more of his black, putrid blood into the circle. Two forms coalesced out of the crackling mist.

Their bodies were translucent, like shadows pierced by moonlight. It was hard to make out much about them, but Maarkov thought their features were distended, like a strange mockery of the human body. Their arms were too long, fingers too thin, and legs too short. They had a hunched stance, and they looked around the circle in quick, jerky movements. The only thing Maarkov could see clearly about them were their eyes, which were glowing motes of red light.

Something about the look those things turned on him chilled Maarkov to the bone.

Maaz hissed something to them in that same language, and the things gazed down at the two *strega* beneath them. One of them looked up and made a sweeping gesture with one of its ghostly arms. Maaz hissed something angry and raised a fist toward the one who had replied to him. Darkness gathered around it, and it cringed in what appeared to be pain, though Maarkov could hear no sound. It went on for a few seconds before the thing flashed its eyes at Maaz in surrender.

These things are intelligent. They're communicating with him.

The two shadows looked once again to the *strega*, and one of them reached its misty arm down into the mouth of one of the corpses. It crawled down into the *strega*, twisting the corpse's shape as it wriggled down its throat. The second shadow crawled into the boy's body, and Maarkov turned his eyes away. The sound of the flesh stretching and spasming was enough to disgust him without the sight of it.

Maarkov turned back as the sound abated and watched the things rise from the ground. Though their skin was still the pallid gray of a corpse, there was something charged about it, something hard. The bodies no longer resembled anything close to human. The legs were shorter, hips somehow shifted to give the thing a more predatory stance. The arms were longer, and claws now decorated the fingers at the ends of their distended hands. The eyes burned with a red, fell light.

They rose from the ground and adjusted their clothing, wrapping scarves around their faces until nothing showed but the light from their eyes. The cloaks hugged their bodies in odd ways, but if they crouched, Maarkov supposed they might be able to pass for a man. He shivered at the thought. The things moved with a canine grace.

Maaz took the blood-covered cloth Inera had given him and ripped it in two. He said a few words and tossed each one a piece of the cloth. Maarkov gagged a second time as the things swallowed the pieces, gulping them down like a pair of snakes.

As one, their heads turned toward the city of Ishamael. They spared one last look for Maaz and bounded into the night, loping away like a pair of ghostly wolves. A howl rose up in their wake, echoing into the darkness.

They're hunters, like some kind of gods-damned bloodhound.

Like bloodhounds that could squeeze your head off, perhaps.

Strega tore after them, running through the night at full speed in complete silence. Maarkov tried to count them before they disappeared into the shadows, but the bastards were too quick. Maaz had made many new servants from the caravan in the mountains, and only a few remained in camp. They stood motionless, milky eyes looking at nothing. Maaz liked to keep a few of the rotten things around for menial labor.

"Perhaps now we shall see some results," Maaz said, brushing his hands off. "By morning the artifact and the girl will be in my possession. We'll move tomorrow."

"What is my next task, Master?" Inera asked.

"Travel to Thardin, inflict yourself upon the Emperor. Ensure everything is going according to my plan. Prepare the way for our culling," Maaz said. "And Inera—I shouldn't have to tell you that this is your last chance. Fail me again, and you will end on my table."

With that, Maaz turned and slithered away into the night.

Maarkov let out a long breath and took another pull from his pipe. Inera gave him a long, opaque glance. For a moment, Maarkov thought she might open up to him, speak to him with honesty. There was so little honesty in their little band of murderers, and Maarkov's heart momentarily ached for it. He thought he saw something in her eyes.

Maarkov offered her a weak smile.

She turned, her body sliding back into the blackbird, and fluttered away into the night.

Maarkov watched her go with a scowl. He took another pull from his pipe. Perhaps this would be over by morning. They could head back to Shundov, and he could go back to ignoring his brother.

A man needs something to look forward to, after all.

**

"This," the Mekai said, holding a scroll gingerly to the light, "is one of the oldest pieces in the archive. It's four copies down, and in Old Vendon."

"What does that mean?" Shawna asked.

"Whenever a document falls into disrepair, it is copied down into a new text," Lacelle explained, shuffling through her research. "If it's written in an old language, it's translated. This is the fourth copy of this text, and it's in a dead language—so it's very old, you see."

"I understand," Shawna said, turning a reverent eye on the ancient scroll.

"What is it?" D'Jenn asked.

"It's a history," the Mekai said. "It's in an old style, though— when the words were meant to be sung in verses. It's a poem about the founding of the Sevenlands."

"A folktale, you mean," D'Jenn said.

"Don't be so quick to judge," the Mekai replied, turning a serious gaze on D'Jenn. "Just because something is old doesn't mean you can dismiss it."

"What does this have to do with my mother's armlet?" Shawna asked.

"You're about to see," the Mekai said. He perused the document, muttering to himself. His spectacles floated up of their own accord, depositing themselves on his nose, and he cleared his throat. "Here we are—*And Ishamael went to the holy place on the hill where the gods listen.*

"He said to them 'Look upon my people, they are dying, they are enslaved. Look upon my people'.

"The gods replied to him 'Ishamael, have you not fought the invader, have you not killed him, have you not driven him before you?'

"'I have' said he.

'Then it is your lot to die, it is the lot of the Vendon to die, their bones ground to dust, their cities burned, their children wailing,' said the gods. 'If Ishamael cannot beat the invader, then it is the lot of the Vendon to be shattered.'

"Ishamael's heart was firm, though, and he challenged the gods. 'Why' said he, 'have you sent this horde upon us? You give them steel and anger, and men as numerous as the stars, yet you make the Vendon fractious and mistrustful. Are the Vendon not your people, do they not cry out, do you cower from the wailing of their children?' Ishamael shook his fists at the gods and decried their judgment. 'Cower, then' said he, 'as this horde-from-nowhere shatters the Vendon and kills the last of the Blessed of Eindor. Let the gods cower in fear'."

"I've never heard this version," Dormael said. "In the one I've read, he prays to them and they bless him with victory, or some such. Where did this version come from?"

"It is very old," Lacelle said. "One of many such scrolls in the archive, all scattered pieces of something greater. You have no idea how much I wish we had the rest of it."

The Mekai cleared his throat, and everyone went silent.

He continued, "*So the gods looked down on Orm, the Place Where the Gods Listen, and they looked down on Ishamael, and they looked down on the Vendon. They weighed Ishamael as a man and found the worth of him. Then the brothers—Evmir, whose Hammer forged the world from the Void, and Eindor, who gave the world magic—looked down on Ishamael and said 'Do you wish to drive your enemies before you, to shatter their steel, to break their anger, to kill their men as numerous as the stars?'*

"'Yes' said he, 'I wish the children of the Vendon to live.'

"Then the brothers looked down on Orm, the Place Where the Gods Listen, and said 'Give us a sacrifice'. Ishamael had brought a sprig of new ivy, fresh with berries on the stem, and he gave that to the bowl, and said 'It is life that I bring to you'.

"The gods answered him."

"Wait," Dormael said. "Did you say a sprig of new ivy?"

He recalled the armlet's dream in a sudden rush of vivid color—the stone bowl, the ivy, the kneeling man, and the woman being stretched over the altar. Dormael's blood went cold, and he tried to make sense of what he was hearing.

"I believe that was what it said, yes," the Mekai replied. "Why?"

"The armlet," Dormael said. "It showed me a scene like that in a dream." He explained the dream to everyone in the room, recalling as many details as he could. Lacelle and the Mekai listened to his tale and shared a guarded look with each other.

"I believe that's confirmation," Lacelle said. "It is as we feared."

"What?" D'Jenn asked.

"The armlet," the Mekai said, handing the scroll over to Lacelle, who put it aside. "Tell me something about it—when it acts out, what universally appears?"

"Fire," Shawna said, and Dormael nodded in agreement.

"Young Bethany refers to the thing as *'fiega,'* which you all know is the Old Vendon word for 'fire'. This is something the armlet told her, not something she produced on her own," the Mekai said. "You see, in the story, the gods answer Ishamael, and gifted a weapon to him. If I recall correctly—*'And so she shall serve you, and grant you seven signs of power over the world. Take her and hammer their bones to dust, kill their men as numerous as the stars, shatter them, and leave their children wailing. Take this hammer and drive them before you' said the gods. And Ishamael took it."*

"So you believe my mother's armlet is this weapon?" Shawna asked. She sounded skeptical, and Dormael echoed her feelings. He was as religious as the next man, but even with the dream, it sounded hard to believe.

"Only a piece of it," Lacelle said. "I know it sounds a bit rich, but hear us out. This weapon, this Nar'doroc, was used to drive the hordes back to the east. There are many old stories amongst the steppe tribes in Dannon, songs as old as this one that tell of their people being killed by a god-man who had a weapon they called '*hirminusloch*'. Many historians believe it's the source of the hatred they hold for westerners."

"By the time he had driven the horde from the lands of the Vendon, Ishamael had united the nine tribes into one," the Mekai said. "Two of them wanted him to share the power of the Nar'doroc, though, and Ishamael refused. So, seven tribes fought two, and only seven remained. He used the power of the Nar'doroc to twist the rebels and drive them into the mountains. In his shame, he sundered the Nar'doroc into seven pieces, and gave the chief of each tribe a single piece of the whole. According to the story, though, the Nar'doroc stopped working when it was sundered."

"What do you mean he twisted them and drove them into the mountains?" Allen asked, joining the conversation. "You mean the Gathan Mountains? Do you mean that Ishamael created the Garthorin with this...this thing?"

"This is just one story," Lacelle said. "We're drawing on different sources, here, and each one can be difficult to translate given many things—the assumed diction of the time, the dialect in use, the location where it was recorded, and many other things you don't care to hear about. In other words—there's no way to be certain about any of this. Don't take it for the gospel of the gods. Remember, these poems were meant to be performed for an audience. There is some embellishment."

"I see," Allen said. "But still—according to this story, Ishamael used Shawna's armlet to create the Garthorin. The bloody Garthorin." His eyes went to the silver box on the table, and he smiled. "I've been waiting for a chance to hunt the Garthrorin. That's a real test for a man."

Lacelle gave Allen a bewildered look.

"The thing Ishamael would have used to 'create' the Garthorin, as you put it, would have been completely different," Lacelle said. "The Baroness Llewan's armlet is only a single piece of a greater whole."

"Wait," Dormael said. "If Shawna's armlet is only one of seven pieces of this thing, then where in the Six Hells is the rest of them?"

"You've stumbled right onto the problem," the Mekai said.

"Where, indeed? We've already spoken of the players in this game—the Galanian Emperor, this mysterious *vilth*—but now we better understand the stakes."

"What does Victus know of this?" D'Jenn asked.

"Some of what we do," Lacelle said with a grimace. "But we can take some small solace in the fact that his knowledge doesn't run very deep. He knows the armlet is powerful, but the research the Mekai and I have been gathering is unknown to him."

"What have you been gathering, Deacon?" Dormael asked.

"Anything we could find that mentioned the thing, or something like it," Lacelle replied. "Most of it is scattered information, but there are a few pieces that point to possible locations for the other pieces of the Nar'doroc."

"The Nar'doroc?" D'Jenn asked. "The...God-hammer?" That was what the words would mean, translated directly. Dormael wasn't as adept at the ancient language as his cousin, but even he could make out what the words were intended to mean, the idea they were meant to convey.

"That is the word used for the thing in the original poem," the Mekai said. "It's a rough translation, and I've never seen the word elsewhere."

"We can bet that Victus will send agents to search for the other pieces of this thing as soon as he finds out what it is," Dormael said. "I would, were I him. The moment he is able to get his hands on the research—or anyone who performed it—he'll put operations in play to recover them. If we suddenly disappear with the thing in tow, he'll suddenly become curious about it."

"That's why we have to kill him tonight," D'Jenn growled. "It's the only way to ensure he's out of the game. Leaving him to act in our wake is dangerous."

"No," the Mekai said.

"Honored One, I must insist, everything I've been taught says that—"

"*No*, Warlock Pike. I will not repeat myself," the Mekai said, holding up a hand to forestall more argument. "The truth is that Victus has already won. I knew it the moment I saw that boy's face—Kendall—in Bethany's memories. The mysterious deaths, the machinations, the odd decisions made by the Council...all these things and more I should have seen coming. Victus has purged any

Warlock with the desire to stand against him—all except the two of you. We don't know what contingencies he has in place against an attack, but we can safely assume he would have something nasty prepared. Look me in the eye, D'Jenn, and tell me you believe the man will be unguarded."

D'Jenn let out a frustrated breath and looked away.

"Exactly," the Mekai said. "If the two of you tried to go after him tonight with no plan, no preparation, you would be killed—at which point, all hope of recovering the Nar'doroc would be lost. We cannot allow that to happen."

"Honored One," Dormael said, "he *will* move against you. If you don't kill him, he will kill you. The Mekai serves for life—death is the only way he ascends to your office."

"Do not think I go forward blindly, young Dormael." The Mekai smiled. "I can see the field as readily as anyone. I know what is waiting for me."

"Why would you sacrifice yourself willingly?" Shawna asked. Everyone grew silent, and all eyes turned to the Mekai. He offered Shawna a melancholy smile and let out a long sigh.

"He's already secured all the real power to be had," the Mekai said. "He has the only group of wizards in the Conclave who are trained to fight with their magic. If I try to command them to arrest him, they will refuse. If I come out against him publicly, he takes control by force, killing any who oppose him. The violence would be terrible—wizard against wizard, brother against sister. Such a thing might spiral out of control and tear the entire Conclave apart. Maybe the entire city."

"So you're just going to give up without a fight?" Allen asked.

The Mekai turned a sharp gaze on him.

"Not at all," he said. "With what power I have left, I will put a burr in his plans. First, the lot of you will leave here tonight, taking the entirety of this research with you. Lacelle, you and your team—the people you used to dig all this up—must also go into hiding. Anyone who worked on this will be just as important as the documents themselves, and Victus cannot be allowed to get his hands on you."

"As you say, Honored Mekai," Lacelle said, blinking in surprise. "Must we also leave tonight?"

"You must." The Mekai nodded. "Though it pains me, you must.

Take your people east, Lacelle, to Alderak. The Sevenlands will not be safe for you."

Lacelle nodded, the bewilderment contained to her cold blue eyes.

"As for the rest of you," the Mekai said, turning his gaze on Dormael and his friends, "you will be charged with recovering the rest of the Nar'doroc. Find it before the others can. I'm sure I don't have to elaborate upon the desperate nature of our situation—do everything in your power to recover the pieces. Fight, even kill, if you have to. Find the other pieces of the Nar'doroc and find a way to destroy them."

"Why destroy it?" Allen asked. "If it's such a powerful weapon, we should use it—or someone should, anyway."

"No," the Mekai said. "Though I admit, the prospect is tempting. A thing such as this is terrible. I have felt the breadth of this armlet's power, and it is truly frightening. If there are six more of these things out there—and others looking for them—their destruction is paramount. Even if we were able to control it, which I doubt, such a thing would only attract those who would seek its power. There would always be the chance that the wrong person may wield it. We must prevent that at all costs. It *must* be destroyed."

"Did you find information on the thing's destruction, Honored One?" D'Jenn asked. "We've barely been able to contain it with our magic, much less destroy it."

"There is one place we think you'll be able to find out," Lacelle said. "The Holy Place, at Orm—in the story, the Place Where the Gods Listen."

The room went silent.

Orm had been the site of a great temple in the old days, the holiest place in all the Sevenlands. Its place was significant in all the histories Dormael had ever read. The temple to the gods at Orm was built upon the stones of an older temple, built to older gods. For thousands of years, it had served as a holy place to the people of the Sevenlands.

During the Second Great War, Orm had been sacked by the Dannons.

There had been no soldiers at Orm, only priests, priestesses, their families, and the people for whom they had cared. The details of the slaughter recorded in the archives were disturbing—even to Dormael, who had a strong stomach for such stories. It was the move that pushed the Conclave into action against the coalition of Alderakan kingdoms and saw the wanton slaughter that had earned the Conclave such enmity worldwide. The event changed the history of the Conclave forever.

People believed the weight of all that blood—the innocents at Orm and all the people who died as a result of the Conclave's revenge—had laid a curse on Orm. The once holiest place in all the Sevenlands, holy stones built upon holy stones, now stood corrupted. People avoided the place with religious fervor.

Dormael had no wish to go himself, and he didn't consider himself a superstitious man.

"What will we find at Orm?" D'Jenn asked.

The Mekai got a strange gleam in his eyes.

"As you may know," the Mekai said, "I have a particular obsession with history. One of my abiding interests happens to lie in the life of the man who founded the Conclave—Indalvian himself. Amongst a small group of serious historians, there has long been a theory that Indalvian left vaults full of his lost writings and inventions scattered around the world—we call ourselves the Cabal of the Epitaph."

"Cabal of the Epitaph?" D'Jenn asked. "That sounds a bit macabre, Honored One."

"The name is from an inscription on an old obelisk, a story for another time, perhaps," the Mekai said. "I have long believed one of these vaults to be in the catacombs beneath the temple at Orm. The inscription—there's a piece of it that reads *'in the place of the dead under the house of the gods, behind a door only their hammer can open'*. I believe we now understand the significance of the word 'hammer'. I always believed its use was metaphorical, but after reading about the Nar'doroc, I'm not so sure."

"That's not a lot to go on, Honored One," Dormael said.

"Regardless, it's the one place mentioned in connection with the Nar'doroc," the Mekai said. "If this thing is truly a weapon, a gift from the gods, there must be some mention of it in the ruins of Orm. We've gathered together what information we could from the Conclave's archive, but the holes in it need to be filled. Orm is where you will find your answers."

"We'll be seen leaving," D'Jenn said. "If he's gone so far as to make an attempt on Bethany, you can bet Victus is having us watched. Getting out unseen will take planning, and we'll have to duck Conclave agents all the way to Orm—a feat Dormael and I both know is nigh to impossible. I still say we kill Victus tonight. Leaving him behind us is a mistake, Honored One. Leave him to strengthen his power base, and he becomes exponentially more dangerous."

"You may be right, Warlock Pike," the Mekai said. "But sending you boys in to kill him would more than likely result in your deaths. Like it or not, you two are my only loyal assets, and I will not allow you to waste your lives in a foolish attempt. I will spend your abilities where they are needed—and right now, they're needed to find the seven signs of the Nar'doroc."

D'Jenn's jaw tightened, but he nodded his head in assent.

"Victus will send people after us," Dormael said. "He'll send our friends after us."

"Small point," Allen said, "but they're not exactly your friends anymore if they're trying to kill you. Those are called *enemies*, brother."

Dormael gave his brother a flat look, but Allen just shrugged his shoulders in response.

"And you will not be seen leaving," the Mekai said. "There is a way, through the lowest level of the Rat Holes, to get into Ishamael's sewers. It's an old escape route only revealed to the Mekai, passed down from one to the other. It comes out north of the city, on the western side of the river. From there, you'll have to continue on your own."

The thought of going into those sewers again filled Dormael with cold anxiety. He schooled his face to a bland expression and loosened his shoulders. The last thing he wanted was for anyone to see him unmanned by the thought.

"Even if we make it out, he'll have Warlocks searching for us by morning," D'Jenn said. "And when he makes his move for power, they'll issue Death Coins for us. We'll be hunted to the ends of Eldath for all our days—that's the law. They'll name us rogue sorcerers, treat us as any Rashardian Mystic."

"Yes," the Mekai nodded. All eyes in the room turned to him. "The Conclave will hunt you. You will be forced to fight your own.

But that's not something you can change, those pigeons have flown. If you wish to join your Deacon, then say so now—it's your only guarantee for safety, after all."

Everyone at the table traded looks, but no one said a word.

"Good," the Mekai said. "Then from this night on, you will be considered unsanctioned operatives. I have faith, though, that you boys are uniquely suited to surviving such a distinction—and ladies, of course."

Shawna bowed her head in acknowledgment.

Dormael felt a small bit of warmth for the Mekai's vote of confidence, but he knew the odds were against them. Every Warlock under Victus's command had received the same training, had survived the same trials. Each one of his colleagues had their own unique strengths and weaknesses, and amongst their company, Dormael was nothing special.

"So, we escape through the tunnels under the Conclave, into the sewers under the city," Allen said. "Then we dodge hostile wizards all the way up the countryside to the most accursed place in all our histories, and from there...something. We *hope* something, anyway."

"If you wish to boil it down into absurdity, then yes," the Mekai said, turning a serious look on Dormael's brother.

Allen turned a flat look on Dormael. "Well, you did promise me a bit of excitement, didn't you?"

"You could always go home," Dormael offered. "Hope that Victus leaves you alone."

Allen snorted. "And leave you lot to stumble on without me? The best warrior amongst you is a woman, by the gods."

"Still is, even in your company," Shawna said, giving Allen a pat on the shoulder. "Don't feel too bad about it, though. I'm sure they could use you back on the homestead if you're feeling a bit light in the ankles."

"I'm not sure if you're calling me a whore or a coward," Allen said. "But there's no way I'm going anywhere. You'll have to put up with me the entire way."

"Do you think they could use *me* back on the homestead, then?" Shawna asked.

Everyone shared a laugh, but the mirth in the room was thin at best.

"The important thing is that none of you have a choice," the Mekai said. "I've taken the liberty of having your horses taken to the place where the escape route terminates. Go a different way if you wish, but you will do so on foot. I had to act quickly, you understand, and there was no time to convince you beforehand. I am the Mekai, after all—for a short while longer, anyway."

"You should go with Lacelle, Honored One," D'Jenn suggested. "Go into exile, stay out of Victus's reach."

"I will not run from him, D'Jenn," the Mekai said. "I have been Mekai for a very long time, and I will not be the first to abandon the Conclave in such a time. If Victus wants to take my seat, he'll bloody well have to take it. I am not as defenseless as he seems to think. You all have other things to worry about, however. I will worry about the Conclave, you worry about finding the Nar'doroc."

"Very well, Honored One," D'Jenn said, though Dormael could see the tension in his jaw.

"Now is the time, I'm afraid," the Mekai said. He rose and walked to one of the windows, peering out over the moonlit grass of the Green. "The moon is high, and most of the Conclave is already asleep. If you're quite ready, we should make our way down to the Crux. Gather your people, Lacelle, and meet us there."

"Yes, Honored One," Lacelle said. She organized the research into a scroll case, gathered it to her chest, and rushed from the room. Her willowy form disappeared through the door like a ghost.

"We'll need to cover our retreat somehow," Dormael said. "Even if most of the Conclave is asleep, Victus will have someone watching."

"Leave that to me," the Mekai said.

"What are you planning to do, Honored One?" D'Jenn asked.

"I am the most experienced wizard in the Conclave, with access to the most powerful magical Circle in all of Eldath," the Mekai smiled. "I'm going to do magic."

INTO THE TUNNELS

If it comes to a fight, D'Jenn thought, *we can't depend on this lot.*

Lacelle herded her people down the tunnel like a clutch of frightened children. The light hanging in the air above them was bright, cold—like the woman who had conjured it. Lacelle's Kai sang into the ether with a clear, precise note.

The scholars who the Deacon of Philosophers had jostled into the corridor were an odd bunch. D'Jenn had spent so much of his time around Warlocks that he'd forgotten what the rest of the Conclave was like. None of the three looked a day over twenty springs, and they fumbled along the hallways as if they weren't sure they were supposed to be there. D'Jenn couldn't blame them—if he had been roused from his bed in the middle of the night and ushered out of the Conclave with no warning, he would probably be just as clueless as Lacelle's three researchers.

The Mekai had ushered them all down to the Crux and sent them through a little-used tunnel that went deeper underground. He had assured them it would connect with the sewers, given them instructions on how to navigate it, and retreated back to the Convergence Chamber to use his magic to cover their escape.

The Mekai had chosen a slow, insidious sleeping spell to keep the Conclave in thrall. It would creep up on unsuspecting wizards and draw them into a slumber. They wouldn't fall asleep right away, but the closer they got, the sleepier they would become.

Those who were already out for the night would be impossible to wake until the Mekai's magic had run its course. With the power of the Crux behind him, the Mekai had whispered his spell over the entire Conclave. Anyone caught in it would be affected.

Vera's letter burned in the pocket of D'Jenn's cloak.

The Mekai's words had ignited a storm. Connections were made as everything fell into place, and the deaths of his friends had taken on a new stink as all the information was mixed together. All it had taken was the off-hand mention of a purge taking place, and everything had fallen together. Being lost at sea was such a convenient way for his friends to have disappeared, and he cursed himself for not having seen through it before.

A thousand questions came bubbling to the surface. Mataez had looked into the deaths himself, and D'Jenn had trusted his word. What reason would he have had to discount it? His brothers and sisters, his family, had never lied to him.

Never before.

His hands shook with the urge to rip Vera's letter from his cloak and tear into it, but everyone was too close. He didn't care to have anyone's eyes on him when he read it—he knew it would be trying, regardless of what he found within.

"My cat is probably hungry," said Jev, one of Lacelle's Philosophers. He made a sour face as he wrestled with his pack, the man's narrow shoulders doing little to support its weight. Jev was short, sallow, and surly in the way old women were surly—though the bags under his eyes spoke of his fatigue.

"Nobody gives two golden shits about your cat, Jev," spat Lilliane. She wiped a meaty arm across her brow, cheeks already red from the exertion of the walk. Lilliane was fat—very fat, in fact. The woman was pouring sweat already, and they had only just started. D'Jenn worried that she wouldn't make it if they had to run. For all her sweating and heavy breathing, though, she outpaced Jev with ease, and with the least amount of complaining in the group.

"Your cat," she breathed, "is going to die, Jev. Maybe a dog will get hold of its neck and shake it like a little doll. Snap it right in half, you know? You've seen what happens with dogs, I'm sure."

"You're such a bitch, Lilliane," Jev snapped.

"Maybe a street urchin will cave its little skull in with a sling, and it will end up in a stew. They'll leave its guts out in the streets, but maybe they'll make a little hat out of its skin."

"You don't have to be so mean to him," said Torins, the third of Lacelle's team. Torins, in contrast to both Jev and Lilliane, was built like a bull. He was four full hands taller than D'Jenn and had shoulders wide enough for a plow. Torins, though, jumped at every shadow, and constantly talked about the gods.

"Torins, I hope they find a cure for the fungus that ate your mind away," Lilliane huffed. "There's another thing—maybe your cat got snatched up by an apothecary. I heard they experiment on cats sometimes. Just think of little mister tickles—"

"That's not her name," Jev snapped.

"—just think of him, little legs twitching, tongue lolling out its mouth around all that bloody foam—"

"If you were a man, Lilliane, I'd smack your face right off!"

"If you were a man, Jev, you'd shut your gods-damned mouth about your cat," Lilliane huffed. "You've been muttering about your cat the whole damned way, and everyone's damned tired of hearing about it."

"Don't you think everyone's also tired of listening to your fat arse slither down the hallway?"

"Slither?!"

Bethany let out a tittering laugh. D'Jenn was tired of listening to the three of them bicker back and forth, but he stifled his own chuckle at the comment. Shawna shushed Bethany's laughter, and the walk continued in silence.

Only for a few moments, of course.

"Jev," Lilliane huffed, eyes still trained straight ahead, "does your father write you every season to tell you how disappointed he is, or is it more often? If I had a son like you, I think I'd marry him off to a real man."

"You and I both know that when you finally pass a calf, Lilliane, it will go straight to the gods-damned milking stable," Jev spat. "When is the farmer planning on putting you down, anyway? Aren't you seasoned enough yet?"

"That was mean, Jev," Torins sighed, shaking his bull head. "Just mean."

"Says the eunuch," Lilliane clipped.

Torins grew red in the face and went silent.

"All three of you need to keep your mouths shut," Lacelle snapped, stopping and turning on them. The little trio almost ran the woman down, but Lilliane was able to skid to a halt, and Torins pulled Jev up short by the scruff of his neck. Lacelle gave them all a frosty eye. "Need I remind you of the possibility that we're being watched? Do you think this is a friendly jaunt, just a little trip through the tunnels to the outskirts for an early morning picnic?"

"Deacon, we—" Lilliane started.

"Quiet!" Lacelle hissed. "I know you're all frightened, but this is no way to deal with your fear. You're endangering everyone!"

"We're sorry," Torins said.

"Take your cues from the Warlocks," Lacelle said, gesturing at D'Jenn with an angry sweep of her fingers. "If they're silent, then you keep silent!"

With that, the Deacon turned and stalked away, her back as stiff as a board.

That's a tough woman. Victus underestimates her.

At the thought of his former mentor, D'Jenn again felt warm anger twisting around in his chest. Every moment they fled through these darkened tunnels, D'Jenn could feel his revenge getting farther away. More than anything, he needed to know the man's reasons. What was so important that it had warranted the death of so many of his friends?

Dormael strode up, scowling at the three Philosophers. Jev, Lilliane, and Torins scurried away in Lacelle's wake, avoiding Dormael's frown. D'Jenn had seen that look on Dormael's face a hundred times, and it usually meant he was thinking. Dormael's 'pensive' looked a great deal more like 'angry'. D'Jenn wondered if Lacelle's researchers had been cowed by the look.

Jev and Torins, maybe—not Lilliane, though. That woman is as nasty as a snake.

Dormael carried his spear over one shoulder and stared at everything like the very shadows were going to jump out and grab him. It hadn't been a day since his last trip under the city had seen him tortured, though. Perhaps his memories were what stalked the shadows.

Shawna hovered nearby, and the two of them each rested a hand on one of Bethany's shoulders. D'Jenn wondered if either of them could see what was happening. His cousin could talk a country girl right out of her dress—and brag about it later—but he couldn't see it when a woman was stalking him in turn.

"Do you think we're being watched?" Dormael asked. "I think we're being watched."

"He hasn't stopped talking about it since we came down the ramp," Shawna sighed. Dormael gave Shawna an irritated look. Bethany looked at D'Jenn and rolled her eyes, the expression invisible to the two adults flanking her.

"I haven't felt anything." D'Jenn shrugged. "But I wouldn't take our guard down."

"I thought those three were never going to shut up," Dormael said, scowling in the direction of Lacelle's bubble of light. "I thought about saying something to them, but they're Lacelle's people. I didn't want to step on the Deacon's toes."

"Why not?" D'Jenn said. "You heard the Mekai—we're unsanctioned operatives now. Disavowed. Set free, like a pair of pigeons."

He smiled and made himself laugh, but something inside of his chest writhed at the comment. From the sour look Dormael gave him in return, his cousin felt the same way.

"I don't like it," Dormael said.

"What an eloquent way to put it," D'Jenn replied.

"I don't bloody like it."

"What are you thinking?"

Dormael took a long breath and let it out in a slow exhalation.

"I don't know. I still don't like running away."

"Do you think the Mekai was right?" D'Jenn asked. "Do you think we'd be killed if we went after him?"

"I don't know." Dormael shrugged. "All I know is that I'm not leaving Bethany's side until I'm sure she's safe. If we go after him, and he comes in behind us and steals her away—"

"Do you really think that would happen?" D'Jenn asked.

"It's possible," Dormael said. "It happened once already, don't forget."

"Maybe," D'Jenn sighed.

"Besides, you know if we want to take him out—and we do—we'll have to make a plan," Dormael said. "As much as I want to see him dead, it's just not feasible. The Mekai was right."

D'Jenn let out a chestful of air and nodded his head. "I suppose you're right."

"We'll have our chance, coz," Dormael said. "Once the rest of this is over, we'll have our chance."

"I suppose," D'Jenn said. Still, the anger didn't go away. It sat in his chest like a warm stone.

The tunnels under the Crux were wide and tall—large enough to ride a pair of horses through. D'Jenn tried to occupy his mind with wondering why the things had been made so large. What needed to be moved underground that required a tunnel big enough for a marching column of men? There were no decorations, glyphs, or candles. Everything smelled like centuries-old dust.

The Mekai had given them all the directions through his secret passageway. When Dormael had called it a 'secret passage,' though, the Mekai had pointed out that it was only a secret route through the tunnels, and nothing quite so dramatic as a passageway. D'Jenn thought of it as a secret passage, anyway.

All one had to do to follow it, however, is keep a certain location marker on one's left side. At every intersection they had to search for the marker. If it was there, they took the branch that put the marker over their left shoulder. If there was no marker, they continued forward. D'Jenn grew impatient with the pace, as they had to stop at each branch and look for the mark—an engraved Eye of Eindor no larger than D'Jenn's palm.

This was the one thing, however, that Lacelle's team was good at. The three scholars took to the task with gusto, talking in excited, hushed tones while they worked. Once they were focused on something, the bickering took a back seat to their task. They searched out markers in record time, and Jev was apparently keeping track of all the turns they made in his head. Things crept along slowly, but creep along they did.

D'Jenn's mind, however, kept returning to Victus.

The man would not get weaker if left to his own devices. Now would be the best time to strike, before the Deacon could put his plans into motion. The Mekai was a wise man, but he was no prophet, no muse. He was just a man.

A man who was soundly outmaneuvered.

He clenched his jaw together as everyone continued deeper into the tunnels. Dormael and Shawna strode ahead of him, speaking in low tones and keeping watchful eyes on Bethany. Allen walked behind them, weapons clinking all over him. D'Jenn wondered for the hundredth time why the man wouldn't just pick one or two that he liked. The bubble of light—with Lacelle and the scholars—shone ahead of them, pushing back the darkness in the ancient corridor. No one was paying attention to him.

D'Jenn couldn't stand it any longer.

He reached into his cloak and ripped Vera's letter from inside. The paper was thin but still in good condition. D'Jenn closed his eyes for a moment, steeling himself for what might lay within. His hands shook as he took a deep breath and read her last words to him.

D'Jenn—

I don't know if this will ever reach you, though I hope it will. You might hear a lot of things about me—about all of us. How we're traitors, or maybe that we had gone rogue, I don't know. None of it is true. I don't have long, and I don't know if someone is going to find this and destroy it. To the Hells with them. Victus is not who you think. He killed some of us already, I'm sure of it, though I can't prove it. I'm going to try, though. I hope it's me who tells you this, and not this letter. If not, know that I always loved you. I always will. If I'm dead and you're reading this, then get out of Ishamael, D'Jenn. Run and never come back.

There was no signature, but he recognized Vera's flowing script. There was a smudge on one of the words that made it barely legible, as if from a drop of water, or a tear. D'Jenn folded the letter carefully, placing it back in his cloak. It was more difficult than he thought it would be, with his hands shaking so much.

"Dormael!" he said. His cousin turned, a knowing look on his face.

"Somehow I knew that you were going to do this," Dormael said. "You know what the Mekai said."

"I know what he bloody well said," D'Jenn growled. "I don't agree. Since I'm now an outlaw, I think I'm going to start acting like one. He killed them, Dormael—all our friends. He killed Vera."

"I understand, coz, but what if the Mekai was right? What if you're killed?"

D'Jenn shrugged. "That's the risk we take. You know that. Give me a pebble and make sure everybody gets out of here alive."

Dormael gave him a reluctant nod of his head. He reached into his purse and drew out a pair of copper marks, opening his Kai to weave a bit of magic into the coins. D'Jenn and his cousin often performed this spell using pebbles, which would allow them to find one another. Once Dormael was done, he flipped one of the marks to D'Jenn.

"That should do the trick," Dormael said. "If you live and the mark doesn't work for some reason, just look north along the river. We'll keep an eye out for you."

"Don't die up there, Warlock," Shawna said. "You're not as bad as you pretend to be." She surprised him by wrapping him in a quick hug. Dormael gave him a silent nod which D'Jenn returned. Allen walked up and held out one of his hand-axes, proffering the hilt to D'Jenn.

"Take it," he said. "It will be better for the sort of killing you're looking to do than that big, clunky thing." Allen gestured down at D'Jenn's mace, then held out his hand to receive it.

"Thank you," D'Jenn said. He switched weapons with Allen and hefted the axe. It was light, and the head was bearded. He slipped it through the loop on his belt and clasped arms with Allen.

"Don't die," Allen said, giving his hand a firm shake.

"It's certainly not in the plan."

"How do you mean to avoid the Mekai's sleeping spell?" Dormael asked.

D'Jenn smiled.

"With a little something we picked up along the way."

**

Abdiel's feet were killing him, his heels flattened under all the weight he had carried during the day. Unloading crates at the river docks was back-breaking work, and nothing fit for a skilled man like Abdiel. Him, a talented smith, forced to move bloody crates for a pittance of bronze per week. Even the dockman—Rulan, the fat fucker—made three silver marks a week. Abdiel's pay was robbery, plain and simple.

Let's move to Ishamael, Jalien had said, *there's opportunity, and we'll live in the grandest city in the Sevenlands!* The only opportunity Abdiel had found was six bronze marks per week for listening to Rulan's voice screaming, his mouth chewing, and his chest heaving with overworked breaths if he actually had to get up from his seat at any point during the day. Three silver marks per week, and all the bastard did was yell at everyone else and shove mounds of food down his gullet.

Oh yes, the grandest city in all the Sevenlands.

Every day he came closer to kicking that fat bastard into the river.

It was all for Jalien, though. Abdiel loved her like nothing in the world—and she knew it, too. All it had taken was a batting of the eyes, a smile, and a night of pleasure the likes of which he may never see again. The next week they had been off to Ishamael, leaving Gernholdt forever behind them.

Though part of him resented the work he had found, Abdiel was a lucky bastard, and he knew it. The object of his desire actually returned his love. He could spend his days suffering under Rulan's horseshit—that was fine.

His nights would be spent curled around Jalien, and those were worth a million days with Rulan.

Jalien had been the innkeeper's daughter, and the prettiest girl in the village, too. Abdiel had always prided himself on that. The prettiest girl in all the village, and she loved him. They'd been betrothed for an entire season, but hadn't been able to keep their hands from each other. When Abdiel got Jalien pregnant, they were wed early amidst the scandal. Jalien hadn't been able to take the talk and didn't want their daughter Selah to be an outcast when she grew old enough to play with the other children. The thought of the town ostracizing their daughter had been more than she could take, even though she had taken the whispers of her former friends for almost a year by the time she wanted to leave.

The truth was, Abdiel hadn't needed much convincing. He had been a smithy's apprentice back in Gernholdt. He'd been sure he would be able to find work as a journeyman here in Ishamael, especially if anyone got a look at his work. His hands could work steel like they'd been made to do it. In Gernholdt, Abdiel would have been condemned for the rest of his life to build wagon wheels and shoe horses. He might have been able to mend one or two weapons in his life, but he'd never learn how to make them. He grimaced down at his hands, as if they were to blame for the rotten luck.

The grandest city in all the fucking Sevenlands.

The reality in Ishamael was that the Smithing Guild controlled every smithy in the capital—setting prices, making rules, and deciding whom to endorse. They'd told him there just wasn't a high demand for smiths in the city, and their positions for journeymen were all filled. They had told him with condescending smiles that since his endorsement couldn't be verified by Guild documents, he was out of luck. Unless he wanted to make a contribution to the Guild and receive the test from a Guild member—then, of course, his skills could be verified.

He didn't mind that they doubted his ability—he'd expected as much. But he'd hoped his work would speak for itself, and he'd be able to get a job on his merits instead of the weight of his purse. Abdiel hadn't had any money to give them—not after the move, or the first month's rent at a decrepit apartment building just north of the Conclave of Wizards. The Smithing Guild had given him empty smiles, pats on the shoulder, and told him to come back when he'd saved the money.

He'd heard them laughing as they slammed the door in his wake.

None of the smiths in the city would hire him under the Guild's nose, and there wasn't much work for anything but tradesmen and whores in Ishamael, unless one was a skilled worker endorsed by their Guild. The best Abdiel had been able to find was six marks a week and Rulan's displeasure. With that bloody fortune, he could just keep everybody fed if he went without food two days a week. It wasn't the best thing in Eldath, but it was what they had.

Jalien had dreams of setting up an apothecary, as her passion was for plants and such. Abdiel gave her what little money he could save so that she could buy seeds and pots and maybe sell a few herbs and such at the East Market someday. He wanted her to be happy, and he'd save the money for the test, eventually. If he worked hard enough, maybe he could even talk Rulan into giving him more coin per week.

Maybe—one could hope, after all.

The Conclave came into sight as he rounded a corner, the

towers rising into the night against a full moon. Abdiel walked these streets every night on his way home, moving north through the East Market and skirting the edge of the Conclave grounds on his way back to his own district. Though some surrounding areas were poor, the presence of the Conclave kept criminals off the streets. Abdiel wasn't sure if it was out of fear of the wizards or respect for them.

As long as he made it home safe every night, he didn't care.

The streets in this part of the city were dotted with entrances to the tunnels underground. In odd alleyways there would be a stone staircase leading downward, with an iron gate locked over the entranceway. Down the street he was walking, just on the other side of a main thoroughfare, Abdiel saw something crouched above one of the staircases.

Abdiel thought it was a man at first—just a man sitting in an odd crouch. Maybe he was a Lirium addict or a cripple. Then, the thing moved, sliding over the ground in a wolfish gait that made the hair on the back of Abdiel's neck stand on end. It prowled back and forth at the entranceway, sniffing at the air like some sort of hound. It had long, thin arms that clacked every time they struck the stones under them—the result of the claws sticking from its fingers. It was cloaked in heavy winter wool and had a scarf wrapped around its head.

Abdiel froze, his breath locked in his chest.

What in all the Six Hells is that thing?

He took a slow step backward, praying it wouldn't turn and see him. He tried to step into the shadow of the two-story building on his right, creeping backward with his eyes locked on the creature down the street. His heart pumped fear into every limb of his body, and he could hear it pounding in his ears.

He froze again as he bumped against something with the distinct feel of flesh.

Abdiel turned, fear stilling the breath in his throat as he regarded the thing behind him. It was larger than him by a good margin, its limbs long and distended. It had the distinct smell of rotting flesh hanging about it, and it twitched as it moved, with muscles spasming in random places. It was cloaked in dirty cloth much like the other one, with an old scarf wrapped around its head. Two burning pinpoints of red light shone from eyes frozen over with death.

The thing leaned forward and sniffed at him, crooning in its throat. Abdiel was frozen with terror, his limbs unresponsive to his mind's desperate calls to flee. Fire burned through him with every terrible heartbeat, but his body was paralyzed. The thing rose on its haunches and turned its head to the side, regarding Abdiel with a cold, lifeless stare.

Warm piss ran down Abdiel's leg, cold before it got to his ankles.

Cold, long fingers clamped around Abdiel's throat like thin bands of iron, and his breath cut off. The thing had moved so damned fast Abdiel hadn't had time to utter a cry before his throat was locked in its grip. He felt his feet leave the ground in the same instant, kicking the air with desperation. He struggled, but it availed him nothing. He may as well have struggled to bend metal with his bare hands.

The creature shook him—a single, violent movement that sent a hot explosion of pain rending through the back of Abdiel's neck. After that, his body was just gone. He couldn't feel it, but he could still feel its weight hanging from the creature's grip. When the thing reached its long, distended fingers into Abdiel's belly, he only felt a vague tugging sensation, and the sudden loss of weight accompanied by the sound of his guts plopping into the alley.

The creature dropped him right into his viscera and bounded across the street to join the other creature. Abdiel couldn't move, but he had happened to land in full view of the things down the street. He smelled his own guts, could feel their warmth against his cheek. He tried to suck in a breath, but no air was able to fill the hole in his chest. Abdiel lay like a discarded pile of meat on the cobblestones, struggling to keep his eyes open.

He watched the creatures bend the metal gate leading into the tunnels, and he watched them crawl into the sewers. A gang of people came into sight, sprinting for all they were worth, and followed the creatures underground. Abdiel tried to remember the face of his daughter, her laughing smile, the way Jalien felt against him. He watched his blood spread into the street and struggled against the darkness pulling at his eyelids.

Jalien will be expecting me anytime now.

His last thought was the cold acceptance that Jalien would be expecting him forever.

**

"Is there a river down here?" Bethany asked, listening to the sound of running water. It permeated the sewers with a constant whisper. She wrinkled her nose at the smell. "A stinky river."

Dormael echoed Bethany's sentiments.

Everyone sat huddled under Lacelle's magical light, taking a break from their walk through the tunnels. They had passed from the ancient corridors beneath the Conclave and into the sewers under the actual city—at least, Dormael thought they had. The tunnels beneath the city were like another world, and he had long since lost his way. One stone hallway looked much like the rest of them—a deserted tunnel, locked in perpetual shadow.

The tunnels they currently walked through were part of an access system built alongside the actual sewer, probably for maintenance purposes. There was no effluvia-filled river running through these tunnels, though he could hear it nearby—and smell it, of course. The stink was bad enough to keep his breathing shallow.

"A river of shit," Lilliane sighed between gulps from her waterskin. She favored Bethany with a smile. "Did you use any of the latrines on the Conclave grounds? Any of the public toilets in the city?"

"Well, I had to," Bethany said. "It's not nice to ask about it, though. It's gross."

Dormael held back a snicker at her serious tone.

"Well excuse me, little princess," Lilliane said. "I hadn't realized your royal bottom was so special. In any case, this is where all the shit and piss from the entire city comes. It all flows right down to this delightful place."

"Why?" Bethany asked.

"Sanitation," Lacelle said, riding over Lilliane's comment and giving the woman a warning glance.

It was odd, but Jev, Lilliane and Torins were starting to grow on him. Even Lacelle had begun to make light conversation here and there, proving that despite all previous evidence to the contrary, the woman wasn't made of ice and indignation. Bethany had begun to ask questions, and the four Philosophers couldn't help but start teaching. Dormael found himself listening in, though he pretended distraction.

"There was a time in our history when great things were achieved," Lacelle said. "This city is testament to that time—these sewers, even more so."

"How?" Bethany asked.

Lacelle smiled. "Ask any man or woman on the streets of any city in the world about wondrous things, and they'll probably mention a few different places—Tauravon, the Great River City, or the bridge between East and West Laronto in Shera. Maybe the Keep, in Thardin. No one will mention the sewers of Ishamael, though they are a feat arguably as complex and wonderful as anything in Tauravon."

"How?"

"Well," Lilliane said, "in Tauravon you'll find bridges that go underwater, architecture that seems impossible and more beauty than anywhere else in Eldath. But none of that provides a constant source of clean drinking water to the huddled, stinking masses. In Ishamael, that's what we have. It's the real benefit of living here."

The woman's expression fell in the wake of her words. The other two scholars looked at her, but none of them said anything. Dormael sympathized with them—he was feeling the loss of his home, too. The tunnels, however, were making him too anxious to pay much attention.

"Maybe we can go to Tauravon," Jev said in a hopeful tone. "Certainly the Mage Tower will take us in. They're our allies, after all."

"You can't go to Tauravon," Dormael said. All eyes turned on him. "You can't go to the Mage Tower, you can't go to your families, you can't seek refuge with any of your known acquaintances. Victus will find you there, and none of you have the skills to see him coming."

Lilliane looked sick, but Dormael could tell she was smart enough to have seen it already. Jev was smart enough, too, but the man was too hopeful by half. Dormael hated to do it, but he had to step on that hope like a cockroach and crush it under heel. It would get them killed faster than anything else.

"Where are we supposed to go, Deacon?" Jev asked. "You say we're running, then fine—but where? Don't we have a plan?"

"East, to Alderak," Lacelle said. Her expression, though, betrayed the uncertainty.

"There are lots of places in Alderak," Jev said. "Alderak could mean Lesmira, or Cambrell. It could also mean the Dannon Steppe, though, or Thardin—not to mention the Galanian Empire."

"I heard they're kidnapping wizards, using them in experiments," Torins said.

Lilliane scowled. "That's just a rumor, you drooling idiot."

"I don't want to be experimented on," Jev said. "They burn wizards at the stake in Alderak! Or hang us, or stone us to death. I've read the stories."

"We're not going to be burnt at the stake," Lacelle sighed.

"Just this morning, I'd have said there was no way I'd be stumbling through Indalvian's bloody tunnels with these two," Lilliane said. "Here I am, though. The gods and their bloody humor."

Shawna touched Dormael's shoulder, and he looked up as she spoke.

"You can go to Cambrell," she said. Lacelle gave her a sharp look, and the other three regarded her with frightened interest. "In Ferolan there's a man by the name of Alton Dersham. He's my cousin, and he'll take you in."

"Can we ask that of Alton?" Dormael whispered in her ear. "We've asked so much of him already. This will put him in direct danger."

"Alton understands what is at stake," Shawna whispered back. "And he's already in danger. Sending him four wizards sounds like a smart thing to do, don't you think? Look at them, Dormael—they don't know what to do. They're pitiful."

Shawna was right—they did look clueless. It wasn't very long ago when Shawna herself had been the clueless one, but no longer. Dormael hadn't realized just how much Shawna had changed until this moment, with the Philosophers' ineptitude on display before him.

"He's *your* cousin," Dormael said, shrugging. "It's your call."

"We wouldn't want to impose on anyone," Lacelle said. "Are you certain?"

"Alton helped us escape Ferolan when we fled the city." Shawna nodded. "He won't shy from offering our friends aid when it's needed. He's the most honorable of men."

"Thank you, Lady Baroness," Lacelle said, inclining her head. "Genuinely, thank you."

"It's nothing," Shawna said. "We're all in this fight together now, like it or not."

Lacelle narrowed her eyes at Shawna, giving her a considering look. Dormael wondered what Shawna would say if she knew that Lacelle had referred to her as his 'concubine'. He decided to keep silent, though—Lacelle would change her opinion of Shawna in time.

Dormael looked down the corridor in the direction from which they had come. He fingered the copper mark in the pocket of his cloak—the twin to the one he had spelled and given to D'Jenn. Anxiety kept gnawing at him, worrying him. D'Jenn was the most capable man Dormael knew.

The most capable except for Victus.

Dormael sighed. "We should get moving."

Shawna gave him a knowing look, glanced down the empty corridor, and pushed herself to her feet. Allen followed her, and Bethany scrambled after the gladiator, questions about his weapons rolling from her tongue. The others—except for Lacelle—all gave him reluctant expressions, making a big show of shouldering their gear and getting their feet moving. Jev had a unique gift for melodrama, uttering grunts and whines and groans with every protracted movement. It had been so long since Dormael had been confronted with such behavior that he was unsure what to do about it.

He smiled at them and walked on by, leaving them floundering behind him. Lacelle stepped off beside him, bringing the light with her. Jev, Torins and Lilliane rushed to keep up, and the complaining noises died off.

For a long time the only sounds were running water, echoing footfalls, and muttered conversation at the edge of Lacelle's magical light. The Deacon of Philosophers kept pace with him in silence, making his walk more than a bit uncomfortable. Lacelle had never liked him—or, at least, he thought that was true. Even now, being in his presence stiffened her back and chilled her expression. She stared straight ahead as they walked, jaw muscles clenched tight. Every once in a while she would glance over at him, as if she was going to say something, but then the moment would pass. Dormael didn't press her—he had no real desire to talk to her.

They passed through what Dormael imagined were maintenance tunnels and moved into an older part of the corridors that branched off from the main path. Dormael had hoped the Mekai's escape route would take them wide of the main sewer, but the constant sound of churning water hovered just at the edge of hearing. The smell also hovered, and so strong that it was almost a taste.

Dormael had studied Ishamael's sewers during his First Four. They had been built to last a thousand years, so the scholars said, and had lasted longer. The tunnels ran deep into the ground—so deep, in fact, that entire parts of the sprawling complex were beneath the river. Dormael cringed at the thought of all the water that might be overhead even now, waiting to fall through the ceiling and drown them.

After all, these tunnels have been here for over a thousand years.

"Have you ever been down here?" Lacelle asked, startling him from his reverie.

"Just today, actually," Dormael said, favoring her with an empty smile.

"I got lost down here when I was a girl," she replied, looking around at the stone. "I thought I was going to die. Do you know how I found my way out?"

"How?" he asked. Anything to get the conversation over with.

"I followed the water," she said. "I knew the water had to go somewhere—back up to the city, or out into the countryside—so I followed it until it led me back to the surface."

Dormael nodded.

"My friends had all dared me to come down here, called me a sissy," she went on. "I was too afraid back then to stand up to them, so I went into the tunnels instead. I nearly died."

"Did your friends get in trouble for daring you to go in?" Dormael asked. D'Jenn kept intruding on his thoughts. An urge to run back the way they had come and catch up to him was making his bones itch.

Lacelle smiled. "The little cowards tried to say I had dared *them* into the tunnels and got lost myself when they refused. This was a very long time ago, back when I was in my First Four...with your Deacon."

Dormael looked up at her.

"He was different when we were children," she said. "We hated each other back then—he used to throw things at me in class. Thought it was hilarity of the highest order. I was always nervous around him, because I knew every day he would irritate me until I wanted to scream."

"He was one of the kids who dared you into the tunnels?"

"No," she said, shaking her head. "That was a group of girls I thought were my closest friends—at the time, anyway."

"Some friends," Dormael said.

Lacelle smiled. "Some friends, indeed. No—Victus found out what happened from them and went to find one of the Masters. I had already made my way back into the streets only to find that a search had been organized, and the whole Conclave was in an uproar."

"What happened after?"

"We had to stand before the Mekai," she said, smiling at the memory. "All of us—the girls, Victus, and me. I'd had no idea at the time that Victus was even involved. I was so frightened."

"I can imagine," Dormael said. "If I'd had to stand before the Mekai during my First Four, I'd probably have been wetting myself."

"I would have, but I was too nervous to let anything out," Lacelle said. "Victus, though...he stood right in front of the Mekai and called every one of those girls liars. He wasn't frightened at all. He told the Mekai he'd be stupid to punish me because the fault lay with my 'bitchy friends', as he put it."

"That sounds like something he'd say," Dormael replied.

"I was in love with him for a very long time after that," she said. Dormael almost fell over in surprise. It was strange enough to learn that Lacelle was human in the first place, but hearing those words come out of her mouth made him stumble. Lacelle raised an eyebrow at him, but kept walking.

"What?" she said. "Is it such a strange thing to hear? I know you Warlocks talk. The Philosophers do, too—in that, at least, you're all alike."

"Well," he hedged, trying to recover, "there have always been rumors, but there are always rumors."

"Oh, yes—he spurned me, and that's why I hate him so much," she smiled. "Or I went behind his back with another man, and that's why he hates me so much. Stay silent on something, and people fill in the blanks you leave with their imaginations. It is the nature of things, I suppose."

"Did you ever tell him?" Dormael asked. "That you loved him, I mean."

"We were inseparable," Lacelle said, another wistful smile creeping onto her face. "After that, we sat in the back of the room together and threw things at other students. He was...I don't know. He was my first love, my first everything. The first person to stand up for me, the first to treat me with actual respect."

"What happened?"

Lacelle let out a long breath. "The Warlocks happened, of course. Victus had a strong gift, and he was wickedly smart—he was that way even then, when we were just becoming full wizards. He wanted to be a Hedge Wizard at one time, you know. He always said that he wanted to move to Orris, enjoy the beaches, and help people grow their crops and bear their children."

"What?"

That didn't sound like Victus at all.

"Oh, yes. He was very interested in communities and people," she said. "And he loved the beach. We traveled there sometimes, back in those days. Victus would have pitched a tent on the beach and stayed there for the rest of his life." Her eyes darkened. "Then, the old Deacon of the Warlocks started spending time with him. He convinced Victus to try out for the Warlocks, if only for the challenge. Victus always did love a challenge."

"It's exciting," Dormael said, eliciting a look from the Deacon of Philosophers. "It's easy to get addicted to the nature of it all. I couldn't imagine my life any other way now that I'm a Warlock— former Warlock, I guess." A black feeling twisted in his guts at the thought.

"I suppose I can understand," Lacelle said. "It was fine at first. I decided to join the Philosophers and stay in Ishamael. I couldn't imagine my life without Victus, so staying seemed to be the right choice. Victus, though...he just changed."

"How?"

"He just...I'm not sure. He started to look at things differently. He'd spend days brooding in silence, his mind somewhere else. He got angrier, sharper. The world ate away at him, like the ocean at the beaches he used to love. Then, he just disappeared for an entire season. He didn't say anything, didn't warn me, sent no letters. When he came back, he had changed. Something in him had darkened, I don't know what. And the rest of the Warlocks, they just closed ranks around him. That's the way you all are, you know—bloody insular, bloody secretive. I've always hated it."

"I'm...sorry."

"No, you're not," Lacelle sighed, giving him a sidelong glance. "I don't know why I'm telling you this, maybe just to allow some of these thoughts out of my skull. Maybe...listen, Dormael—I know how this ends. I've watched him for years, for longer than the two of you have been alive, probably. I just...I just wanted you to know that he's not evil, that he's...I don't know—"

"I know," Dormael said, cutting her off. "I understand."

"Does your cousin understand?" Lacelle asked. "I...I noticed he left. I was there, I heard what he said to the Mekai. I know where he's gone."

"He understands," Dormael said. "Nobody wanted this, Deacon. We all have to survive."

"Just call me Lacelle," she said, holding out her hand. "I'm not a Deacon anymore."

Dormael nodded and took her hand.

"I'm not happy about the circumstances, but I'm glad you're with us," he said. "It will probably take me a long time to stop calling you 'Deacon', though."

"Fair enough," Lacelle said, smiling.

They walked in silence for a while. Time meant nothing in the endless maze of tunnels, intersections and rivers of pungent slime. Bethany held her nose and made gagging noises whenever they passed through one of the sewer tunnels. The hum of magic was ever-present, and it kept the effluvia moving to its next destination while also doing something about the air circulation—though it did nothing about the smell. If Dormael had designed the thing, he would have thought to do something about the stink.

Dormael understood the way the system worked, if not the magic at play beneath the surface. The waste was collected on the upper levels, washed through a series of churning rooms that separated the waste from the water. At that point, the water would drain to a deeper level where the process was repeated. Dormael couldn't remember how many times the water was filtered, but he knew that at some point in the process, more magical filters had been slapped in place.

The lowest level was said to house giant cauldrons that boiled the filtered water on magical braziers. Dormael had never been down there, nor did he know anyone who had been, but he had heard stories about it growing up. It was supposed to be the lowest chamber built into the tunnels.

The Mekai's escape route led them deeper into the sewer. Sometimes the path followed a spiraling stairway, and sometimes a wide, curving ramp, but it always went downward. Lacelle's light held the shadows at bay, but the halls felt more ancient the deeper they went. The conversation went from hushed tones to complete silence, and each footfall echoed off the surrounding stone.

Dormael jumped at every sound. Once, he even hoisted his spear at the darkness behind them, making Lacelle jump so hard that her light flashed in reaction. There had been nothing, but Dormael couldn't shake his feeling of dread. Even Jev, Lilliane and Torins were quiet.

"Dormael!" Shawna called from ahead of them, her voice echoing from the stone. "Come see this!"

Dormael and Lacelle shared a look and rushed ahead to where Shawna and Allen had been walking with Bethany. The three of them winced at Lacelle's magical light, which the woman toned down with a muttered apology. They stood framed by a wide doorway cut into the stone, and it took Dormael a moment to see the low, orange light coming from the room beyond. He closed his eyes for a few seconds to relax them, then opened them when he could see farther into the darkness.

The room beyond the tunnel was so vast that Dormael couldn't see the other side. He walked into the enormous room onto a walkway raised above the floor. He went to the edge of the path and looked down, trying to gauge the distance to the floor below. It wasn't high enough to kill a man if he fell from the walkway, but certainly high enough to break his legs when he hit.

Spaced in even rows along the floor were pillars, and on those pillars were huge globes made of bronze. Glowing sinuous lines decorated the globes' surfaces, and they made the metal beneath them shine with heat. They stood like monoliths, their shapes disappearing into the vastness of the chamber.

They're like giant magical kettles.

"This must be the mythical boiling level," Dormael said.

"I was just thinking the same thing." Lacelle smiled. "I've never seen it before."

"Nor I."

"The boiling level," Shawna muttered, looking around at the towering globes. "I see. That's why it's so hot in here."

"This is supposed to be the lowest chamber under the city," Torins said. "We're under the river now. Amazing! The gods are good for having shown us this sight."

"I agree, and all," Lilliane huffed, "but I'm about to bloody sweat myself to death over here. Can we get moving?"

"I think the sweating is probably good for you," Jev said. "Maybe you should stay down here, Lilliane. No one would ever look for you here, and you'd make a perfect cave beast."

"Jev, do you really want me to hold you down and make you cry in front of all these people?" Lilliane asked. "I wonder what that steely eyed Warlock would think if he saw you blubbering like a fool because a fat girl twisted your nipples off."

"That's disgusting," Torins said.

"You'd have to catch me first, Lilliane," Jev shot back. "I don't know if your hooves can get enough traction on this walkway."

"Traction, is it?"

Lilliane leaned over and punched Jev in the leg. Jev squealed in pain as his leg gave out. He sprawled onto the walkway with all his gear, clutching his leg in a grand melodramatic performance.

"You are such a *bitch*, Lilliane!"

Dormael busted out laughing. He couldn't help it—the sight of Jev rolling around on the walkway hit him with just the right amount of emotional spin, and the laughter began flowing out. Before long, everyone was sharing a laugh at Jev's expense. Jev glared daggers at everyone else, but that only made it worse.

"Alright," Dormael said, gesturing for everyone to calm down. "We should get moving."

"If Jev can walk, that is," Allen said, giving Jev a wide grin. "I don't know, though—maybe we should just take the entire leg, don't you think?"

"Maybe you're right," Dormael said. "I don't think the boy will make it another step on that leg."

"We're in agreement, then?" Shawna walked up between them. "Do you two want to hold him down while I take the leg, or should Allen take the leg while Dormael and I hold him down?"

"I gave D'Jenn my only good axe," Allen said, "so it will have to be you, Shawna."

"My swords are probably the best tool to get it done, anyway."

"Lady Baroness," Lilliane asked, "would you mind if I did the honors? I've been dreaming about a day like this for so, *so* long."

"I hate all of you," Jev clipped, gathering his things and rising to his feet. Everyone snickered at his comments and helped him get his belongings together. Bethany walked up and handed him an odd piece of something from his pack, paying his leg a suspicious look. She rolled her eyes and turned away, eliciting another round of laughter from the group. Jev put himself back together and started limping down the walkway ahead of them.

Bethany trotted up and tugged at Allen's wrist. "I'll race you!"

"Race me to where, girl? You run on ahead, I'll catch up."

"Stay close," Dormael said, pushing a bit of hair from her eyes. "Don't get too far from the light."

"I won't."

Bethany took off down the walkway at a run, slapping Jev on the leg as she went by. The man made a squealing noise and swatted at the girl, but Bethany was too nimble for the awkward, limping youth. She skipped backwards in front of him, taunting as she went, before turning and gaining a good lead on him. Jev limped along like his legs were going to give out.

"Let's go find the next symbol, figure out which way to go," Lacelle said, gesturing at Lilliane and Torins. The two of them nodded and followed her down the walkway, Lilliane throwing another mock-punch at Jev as she went by. Shawna turned to Dormael and Allen as the rest of the party made their way down the path.

"Do you think D'Jenn is alright?" she asked. Dormael shared a look with Allen.

"I hope so." Dormael said. "D'Jenn is cunning, but so is Victus.

320

D'Jenn has gotten out of a hundred things worse than this. We'll see him by morning. I'm sure of it."

"Shawna!" Bethany called from down the walkway. "Come see this!"

"Calm down, I'm coming," she replied. Shawna shrugged at Allen and Dormael and jogged down the path in Bethany's direction. Allen sighed and gave Dormael a guarded look.

"Did you suspect any of this was going to happen when you recruited me?" he asked.

"No. I had a bad feeling, but this...no."

"Do you think our family is in danger? Tell me the truth. Will your Deacon go after the homestead?"

Dormael shook his head. "Victus is ruthless, but that's always been his style. It's the way he trained us. He would never hesitate to make a tough decision if it gained him something, but he's not petty. He wouldn't go after them to settle a score with us."

"What about drawing you out?"

Dormael took a deep breath and let it out in a long sigh.

"He's got more to worry about with managing things here," Dormael said. He and Allen walked toward the others but slowed their pace to allow some privacy. Even so, they passed Jev and left the man to struggle along. "If it's clear to Victus the Mekai knows his plans, he'll have to work quickly to secure his power. He may send a Warlock or two out to find us, maybe to kill us, but he won't be able to divert much attention until things have settled for him here."

"I don't even like the thought of *one* of you bastards after me," Allen said. "Dormael—do I have to look over my shoulder for the rest of my life?"

"I don't think so," Dormael said. "I'm sorry about this, brother. Truly sorry. But no—I think if you laid low for a while and got as far from us as possible, you would be fine."

"And you? Do you have to worry for the rest of your life?"

Dormael nodded. "Aye. Until I don't know when."

Allen let out a long sigh.

"Well," he said, laying a hand on Dormael's shoulder, "I hope we can stay at inns on this trip. I mean, we'll be keeping low and all, I'm sure, but I would like to bathe now and then, brother. I can't let the ladies see me in anything less than 'glorious'. It's good for enemies, too."

"Cleaning yourself is good for your enemies?"

"Not the act of bathing, no. But, if you show your enemies your best side—this is only true in my case—it gives them something to aspire to."

"And then you kill them."

"But in that short span of time, Dormael, they're inspired."

Dormael laughed. His brother had always been able to do that, ever since they were children. The laughter banished the anxious feeling—or softened it, anyway.

A beastly cry rang out behind them.

It was high-pitched and piercing, like something a giant bird of prey would utter as it snatched a baby from its mother. It touched something primal in Dormael, and before he knew it, he had dropped his pack and spun around, clutching his spear in a white-knuckled grip. Steel whispered against leather as Allen pulled his own weapons free.

A pair of odd forms crouched in the shadowy doorway. Dormael couldn't see much about them, but something about their posture marked them as predators. They moved like wolves, graceful and deadly. They were wrapped in dark, rotten cloth, with scarves over their heads revealing nothing but burning pin-points of light. The creatures looked at Dormael, and their burning eyes flashed with red light.

"Jev!" Allen shouted. "*Jev!*"

The boy stood frozen, staring behind him in shock. The sound of his name snapped him out of his trance, and he dropped his packs and shuffled away from the two creatures as fast as his bruised leg would carry him. Dormael felt a sudden spike of fear.

"Come on, Jev!" Dormael yelled. "Hurry up!"

The two creatures both stiffened at the sound of his voice, like a pair of hounds with a target. One of them was larger than the other, as if the second one was juvenile. They filled him with the same sort of instinctual revulsion the Taker had.

The things didn't move as Jev scurried away from them, whimpering like a frightened animal. Other things rushed from the shadows behind the two crouching creatures, though, taking to the walkway and leaping over the sides in a mad rush. They disappeared into the shadows under the kettles, and Dormael pulled his Kai awake. He couldn't tell what the things were, but they looked like people—enraged, very quick people.

"Bethany! Shawna!" Dormael screamed, turning his gaze in their direction. *"Run!"*

**

D'Jenn pushed aside a grate and pulled himself up onto the edge of the Bruising Stretch, being careful to keep silent. He crawled like a shadow from the hole and used his magic to put the grate back in place. It went down with a low, metallic clunk.

He could feel the bracer around his arm—the piece of infused armor he'd taken from the dead Cultist in Soirus-Gamerit—sputtering as it resisted the pull of the Mekai's spell. The Mekai's magic came up from the ground like a creeping, whispering haze. The bracer didn't completely shield him from it, but it disrupted the energies enough so D'Jenn could use his own magic to resist it. It made a low, discordant note on the edge of his senses.

The Bruising Stretch was a wide, white space of flat paving stones reflecting the moonlight with cold indifference. It was strange to see it so deserted, though D'Jenn had certainly seen it so before. Perhaps his mood was coloring his sight. His mood clutched his heart, raised the hairs on the back of his neck, and bent his ear to every little sound.

There wasn't a soul in sight.

The walls of the Conclave Proper rose like a monolith into the sky, only a short run from the Bruising Stretch. D'Jenn quested out with his own magical senses, trying to pierce the cloud of magic to spy anyone moving. The bracer on his arm sang its discord into his mind, but D'Jenn was able to see around it. The grounds were deserted.

He turned his eyes on the tower.

The Conclave Proper rose many stories above the ground. The tower had been constructed with both magical and natural techniques, and its style reflected it. There were platforms on the side of the tower attached by impossibly thin branches of stone and steel. In another place, a steel frame flourished from the side of the tower to support a room shaped like a bubble of stone. It was hundreds of links high.

The Deacon's study was at one of the topmost rooms

branching from the tower, held up by one of those flowing steel cages. D'Jenn wished—and not for the first time—that he had Dormael's affinity for flying. A quick slip of the skin and a short flight would be preferable to a long, arduous climb, magic or not.

The gods like to laugh at our misery.

Going into the tower would be folly. The Mekai's spell was an effective one, but even that wouldn't have caught everyone. There would still be people moving around. If another Warlock saw him, he was finished.

If one wasn't watching him at this very moment.

D'Jenn moved the axe to the small of his back and walked down the path toward the Conclave Proper. His back itched for the entire walk, but appearing normal was more important than rolling through the shadows like an amateur. If someone was looking, he was just an ordinary wizard out walking the pathways through the grounds.

D'Jenn encountered no one, even when he got close to the Conclave Proper.

As he reached the base of the tower, he moved along the edge of the wall to the southern face. He could get a great distance up the side of the wall before he needed to scoot his way around, but there was no changing the winding path he would have to take in order to reach Victus's study.

Nobody ever said being a Warlock was easy—another maxim learned from the Deacon.

D'Jenn's hands itched to be around the man's throat.

He whispered a spell onto his hands and feet and started to climb. The wind was cold, and the stone under his hands was still damp from the day's rain. His fingers grew numb, but he split his consciousness and channeled heat to keep them warm. Numb hands were unresponsive hands, and that was the last thing D'Jenn wanted.

He pulled himself up the side of the tower, using his feet to help support his weight. The higher he went, the stronger the wind blew, whipping his *mesavai* around his thighs. The tugging garment pulled at the haft of the axe, and D'Jenn had to reach back on reflex to catch it. He almost fell from the tower, but his magic kept his other hand stuck to the wall.

D'Jenn hugged the wall for a moment, his heart pounding

against his ribcage.

Victus had betrayed them all. D'Jenn replayed the words of Vera's letter until they were burned into his skull. They spun around his head like a miniature whirlwind.

I will always love you, she had said. *He killed some of us already, I'm sure of it.*

Clenching his teeth, D'Jenn continued up the wall.

Vera, Taglion, Kirael and Jastom—all his friends. They had all trained under Victus, had all grown under his tutelage. They had been family to him. D'Jenn had eaten and slept alongside them.

The wind tore at the side of the tower.

Dormael had given Jastom the nickname Three-Fingers on the first day of their training—he'd had two of them bitten off by a dog as a young boy. Kirael had been in love with Taglion all throughout their training, and even after. Taglion, though, had been a complete rake, and never acknowledged her.

D'Jenn chanced a look at the ground, grew dizzy, and kept climbing.

Everyone used to cringe every time Kirael looked longingly across the room at Taglion, and at the way she'd been green with jealousy when Taglion had been partnered with Vera. D'Jenn smiled as he remembered the way Jastom would mime her, fluttering his eyebrows in mockery of her undying love.

They're all dead now.

Vera was dead now.

The one thing D'Jenn had to know above all else was the truth about their deaths. He needed to hear it from Victus himself, listen to the man explain his reasons. Nothing could salve the pain at having lost them—at having lost Vera—but he had to know. The need smoldered in his chest.

The climb seemed to take an eternity. The tower was high, and each stylish platform, hanging room or gigantic window was a hazard for someone trying to remain unseen. After crawling a meandering path up the side of the tower, D'Jenn made the base of the steel beams which cradled Victus's study.

His arms shook from the climb, his legs from anxiety.

Closing his eyes, he listened with his Kai. The bracer continued its discordant warble, and the tower hummed with the Mekai's spell. The steel just above him was cold, and it lacked any sort of magical ward. D'Jenn reached a tentative hand up to touch the cold metal, hoping to the gods he could trust his senses. If a hidden ward gave him an unexpected shock, it wouldn't be good.

A fall from this dizzying height would splatter him like a bug.

His hand rested on the steel, but no hidden spells sprang into action. D'Jenn breathed a sigh of relief and readied himself for the confrontation to come. There could be no room for error—this was the Deacon of the Warlocks he was dealing with, the very man who had trained D'Jenn in the first place. D'Jenn would be surprised if there was nothing nasty lying in wait for potential assassins.

Would he have expected anyone to make this climb, and in the heart of his power?

He hoped it would prove a blind spot in Victus's plan. Doing the unexpected was always the best way to see an operation through, but Victus would know that. Would he anticipate the unanticipated, or would he dismiss the idea as impractical?

I'm too close to worry about it now. Nowhere to go but forward.

D'Jenn clung to the curving steel bars and shimmied into the complicated web of metal branching from the tower. His spell didn't work quite as well as it did against the flat surface of the stone, and D'Jenn had a terrifying moment when one hand slipped on the damp steel and he clambered to hold on. He worked one foot into the web, then the second, and he was suspended from the side of the tower. The flat bottom of the stone room was some distance above him, supported by a network of flowing steel bars. The wind howled, tugging at his clothing again.

Are the gods trying to taunt me now?

D'Jenn reached back to check the axe Allen had given him and started a slow, arduous crawl through the web of curving steel. He could see the Bruising Stretch from where he was, just a white square smaller than his palm. Moonlight sparkled on the surface of the river. The distance to the ground yawned beneath him, but it was his anger making his legs shake.

He kept telling himself that.

D'Jenn worked his way to the top of the cage, crawling to where it fell away into open air. It supported the huge stone room with delicate swirls of metal, as if the block was being carried upon a gust of wind. D'Jenn had to hold on to those curving, slippery metal rails and pull himself out to the edge of the study. There was nowhere to rest his feet, so he had to hook his legs over the rails and hug them as tightly as he could while stretching outward to get a hand flat on the stone.

For one dizzying second, he hung over the open air below, muscles spasming with tension.

His hand stuck to the stone, and he crawled around the bottom edge of the study like a spider. He let out a huge breath in relief and clutched to the side of the room, letting his face rest against the cold, damp stone. He gave his legs a few moments to calm themselves.

There was a single square window that opened into the study. It was large enough for two people to stand upright and looked out over the river. In the morning, the shadow of the tower stretched over the river and through the valley. The view from Victus's window was one of the best in the Conclave. From his desk, he could see the river and the city splayed out beneath him. The window was shuttered against the cold night air. Candlelight shone from the edges of the shutters, orange peeking through in straight, orderly lines.

D'Jenn delved the room with his Kai and found Victus inside, bent over a scroll at his desk. There was a ward around the edge of the room, but only a general ward against magical intrusion. D'Jenn listened to the Mekai's spell slipping off the edge of Victus's ward, its effects nullified. The man was wide awake and probably didn't realize there was magic at work outside the door.

He always works late into the night.

D'Jenn sidled across the stone, working his way toward the window. Victus was alone in his office, his Kai as silent as a sleeping babe. D'Jenn gathered his power, drawing energy from the ether.

Summoning his anger, he slammed his Kai into the window.

Glass shattered inward, blasting the wooden shutters into the room. Victus made a startled noise and cringed away from the flying debris, yelling a loud curse. Victus's song blared into the ether, uttering an angry, startled melody.

D'Jenn punched once again into the room, sending a wave of pure force rushing across the floor. The spell took Victus from his feet and slid his furniture to the wall with a clamor. D'Jenn slipped through the shattered window and hopped into the room.

Victus brushed broken glass from the folds of his robe and regarded D'Jenn with a stare that could have melted steel. His hair was as wild as ever, his eyes alight with rage. D'Jenn's skin crawled as Victus's magic thrashed about in indignation—his body's reaction to the Deacon's song. Victus planted a meaty hand on the floor and pushed himself to his feet.

He paused when D'Jenn whipped the axe from his belt.

"You climbed all the way up the tower?"

"I did." D'Jenn nodded.

"That's a bastard of a climb, D'Jenn."

"I was motivated."

"Obviously."

"I need to know a few things, Deacon. I came to have a talk."

Victus's face deepened into a scowl. "You could have walked to my gods-damned door and *knocked*, you bloody fool."

"We both know it's not that kind of talk."

D'Jenn could feel the wood of the axe beneath his grip and realized how hard he was squeezing the haft. The blade twitched eagerly in the air, drawing Victus's eyes. D'Jenn clenched his jaw, trying to rein in the storm of rage in his chest.

"You need to put that bloody axe down, boy," Victus snarled. "You don't know what you're doing. You're confused."

"I *am* confused," D'Jenn agreed. "You're right. I'm confused about a lot of things, Deacon."

"Just put the weapon down, and let's get this furniture put to rights. We'll smoke a bit of the Leaf, and I'll answer whatever questions you wish," Victus said. He sighed as if D'Jenn were an errant child making some endearing mistake. "I can't believe you actually climbed the bloody tower. Might be the first time that's been done. Here, give me a hand with—"

"We're not going to touch the gods-damned furniture!"

D'Jenn surprised himself with the vehemence in his tone. Victus froze, eyes regarding D'Jenn like a wild animal. The head of the axe twitched with his anger.

"D'Jenn, do you forget to whom you're talking, boy?" Victus asked. "I'm still the Deacon of this Order, and—"

"Would you stop with the facade, Deacon?" D'Jenn said. "We both know I didn't climb the side of the tower to come have a friendly chat. I want answers."

"I said we'll talk about whatever—"

"Kitamin Jurillic," D'Jenn said. "You had him rescued."

Victus's expression went blank as the mask dropped away. "How do you know about that?"

"I had a chat with his mother," D'Jenn said. "She was under the strong impression you had sent me there to kill her."

"The woman is a fool," Victus said. "I don't need to kill her, boy. She will be deposed by her Clan Leaders, and she's already served her purpose. Frankly, I couldn't care less about the woman or her hand-less shell of a son."

"So you *did* have him rescued."

"Of course I bloody did," Victus growled. "You're not an idiot, D'Jenn—I didn't train you that way."

"Why was instituting that tax so important?"

Victus sighed and gave D'Jenn a withering look.

"D'Jenn, I want you to loosen your gods-damned grip on that axe and think for a moment. Use your mind, boy! Think of what you know about the world, about the threats out there. Think about the damned Galanians, the Dannon, the Rashardians, and now this *vilth*—war is coming to our shores, boy. Whether we want it or not, something bad is going to happen soon. The money is a precaution against that eventuality—a coffer for the Sevenlands to use when the war gets here."

"I didn't realize you'd gotten into soothsaying." D'Jenn tightened his grip on the axe.

Victus's scowl darkened. "Do you know how many children were ripped from their homes and taken into the desert last year?"

"What does that have to do with—"

"One hundred and six," Victus went on, "though that number is a loose estimate. The Mals don't care much about the yearly census. Their kids are taken all the time, marched across the desert and sold into slavery. The ones who survive, anyway. I'm sure there are mountains of little Sevenlander bones under the sand of the Golden Waste."

"What's your bloody point?"

"The Galanian Empire now occupies a strip of some of the most fertile land in Alderak," Victus continued, ignoring D'Jenn's scowl. "Before long, they'll grow fat on the tax revenue from the trade now forced to travel through their lands. With more money will come more troops, and with more troops, more conquest. The march of war brings strife, starvation, rape and the general upending of life for everyone in its path. The last report I received spoke of the success of the Empire's winter campaign against Thardin. If the Emperor conquers the Thardish, no one in Alderak will be able to stand against him."

"Are you drawing to the end of this little tale?"

"This is the tale of the ages, boy—use that mind of yours!"

"Tale of the ages," D'Jenn scoffed. "My curiosity is wearing thin."

"A failing," Victus said, "of your mentor."

Victus held up his hands for peace and stepped to where D'Jenn had tossed his desk—a heavy, dark thing that looked older than the stone. He picked up a pipe and lit it with an errant flick of his magic. Shaking his head, he rested his backside on the desk.

"Do you think allowing the Empire to grow unchecked is a good idea?" Victus asked.

"Deacon, I didn't fucking come here to talk about—"

"Answer the bloody question, boy!" Victus snarled. "If you came here to kill me, you can repay all I've done for you by humoring me first."

D'Jenn's eyes narrowed. "I don't think it's up to us what the bloody Galanian Empire does."

"Shouldn't it be?" Victus asked, taking a long pull from his pipe. "Just think about what they've done in the last season, think about the thing they sought from your friend—that pretty Baroness."

"That's different," D'Jenn said. "That's magic—that *is* our business."

"And why shouldn't we work to prevent the rest of the evils they have committed? Why is it not upon us to prevent the raiders from attacking the Mals, or the families on the southern coast of Soirus-Gamerit? Why is it not our responsibility to protect *those* children? Because their enemies weren't dangerous enough?"

"Because that's what armies are for, what soldiers are for—we're not soldiers!"

"Well maybe we *should* be!" Victus growled. "Maybe we should be."

"What do you mean?"

"For the gods' sakes, D'Jenn—you *know* what I mean." Victus gave him an all-suffering glance and shook his head. "If you walked through the East Market tonight and saw a woman being raped, a child being killed, or a man being beaten—you'd intervene, would you not?"

"Of course I would."

"Of course you would—so why in all the Six bloody Hells does that change when you simply add more children into the mix? Why would you save one but whine about principles when many are dying every day?" Victus shook his head and blew another mouthful of smoke into the room. The tobacco smelled expensive, as if it had been treated with something sweet.

"I don't decide who lives and who dies," D'Jenn said. "I'm not the gods, or fate, or whatever the bloody fuck you want to call it. Don't try to pile their deaths at my feet."

"Not the gods, no," Victus agreed. "But think on this, D'Jenn— why do we call wizards born with the spark 'Blessed'? Do you think it's because it rolls off the tongue easily, or that it's a nice thing to say about them?"

"Of course not—"

"Of *course* not!" Victus yelled. "It's because we're different, D'Jenn—we're better. Some even believe that we are *chosen*."

Cold disgust welled in D'Jenn's belly. Words like 'chosen' only rolled from the tongues of raging zealots. Hearing it come from Victus's mouth was like a slap in the face.

"Chosen?" he asked. "Chosen by whom, Deacon? Fate? The gods?"

"Whatever the bloody fuck you want to call it."

"You're mad," D'Jenn said. "You've been stuck in this tower, neck-deep in tragedy for years, and it's driven you mad."

"D'Jenn, we have the power to change things for the better! We can decapitate the Galanian Empire before it eats everything in Alderak alive! We can fly directly to Sul'Shuram and end the Rashardian slave trade for good! We can destroy anything we wish—we can build a better world!"

"And who gets to decide what sort of world is better?"

Victus raised his chin. "We do."

"Because we're chosen?" D'Jenn grimaced down at the head of

the axe.

"Because we can, D'Jenn—and we should!"

"What did the others say when you sold them this little story?"

"Ask them," Victus said, gesturing toward the door to the Conclave Proper. "Any of them will tell you. They've all known my heart since this began."

The head of the axe came up so fast that it made a swishing sound in the air. Victus started back from it, but D'Jenn had only pointed it at his face. The blade gleamed between the two of them like an accusation made of steel.

"What about Vera?" D'Jenn asked. "What did Vera say? And Taglion?"

Victus's eyes went flat. "Vera went down in the—"

"—Sea of Storms," D'Jenn finished. "Her ship lost at sea, correct?"

"Correct."

Victus kept his forehead as smooth as a paving stone, though his eyes tightened with the lie. D'Jenn saw it painted over his expression like a splash of color, and he was seized with the urge to spit. Anger made his hands tremble.

"But she knew—before her accident, I mean?" D'Jenn asked. "You'd spoken to her of your plans. What did she say when you tested her loyalty?"

"I don't see what this—"

"What did she *say*?" D'Jenn shouted, moving a step toward Victus in what nearly turned into a headlong, murderous rush. He drew himself up short after starting forward, but only just. Victus didn't move, but D'Jenn could see the readiness in his stance.

It's only a matter of time now.

"D'Jenn," Victus sighed, blowing another heavy cloud of sweet-smelling smoke into the room, "you need to calm down, son. You need to listen—you're not thinking."

"Here's the thing, Deacon," D'Jenn said, waving his axe blade at Victus's eyes. "Vera would never have signed on to your little cabal—of that, I am completely sure. She was gathering evidence against you—she told me so herself." The letter felt like lead in his pocket. "Taglion wouldn't have done a damned thing Vera didn't tell him to do, and Jastom—Jastom had plans to marry! He had a woman, and he had a child with her. The bastard was going to become a Hedge Wizard and settle down in the country. Told me himself in a letter."

"How bloody adorable," Victus said, his voice devoid of emotion.

"So there's no bloody way Jastom would have decided to join the secret Warlock cabal, either—and that leaves only one explanation, doesn't it? Why don't we drop the bloody charade, Deacon, because we both know I'm not stupid enough to believe your lies. You killed them. Vera, Jastom, Taglion, Kiriael—you had to get them out of the way."

Victus stared at D'Jenn, the space between them charged with energy. D'Jenn stoked the fire of his magic, ignoring the discordant note from the bracer. He divided his consciousness into four segments, one of them ready with a Splinter. He kept the rest ready to counter whatever Victus decided to conjure.

His magic coiled like a scorpion.

"D'Jenn," Victus sighed, "is there any point in moralizing any further here? If you're not going to wake up to the realities of the world, I see no value in trying to wake you."

"You killed my friends," D'Jenn snarled. "I loved them! They were family—*you* said that!"

"They were traitors!" Victus screamed, throwing his pipe against the far wall. It splattered in a shower of ashes and splintered wood. "When it came time, when things got tough, they turned their back on the rest of us, boy—just like you and your cousin are doing!"

"We haven't betrayed anything!"

"Bah! Haven't betrayed anything, eh? What does it mean, D'Jenn, when everyone you know is standing on one side of the line, and you're the only one on the other side?"

"That the rest are either wrong, or cowards," D'Jenn spat. "And that you've killed the ones who would have stood beside me!"

"Will I have to kill you, too, D'Jenn? Make your bloody choice before it's—"

D'Jenn was tired of all the gods-damned talk.

He lashed out with the edge of the axe blade, aiming a quick cut at Victus's eyes. The Deacon slipped out of his range, throwing his head away. D'Jenn's arms and legs itched, and Victus's song rang out. A table lifted from the floor and launched itself at

D'Jenn's head, forcing him to lash out with his own magic to block. The table exploded with a loud clatter, sending splintered bits of wood flying around him.

Victus spun away from D'Jenn and the axe, scooting backward along the edge of the desk. He looked a wild man with his hair and beard sticking out, face twisted into an angry snarl. His eyes, though, were bright and calculating.

D'Jenn brought up a magical shield to catch the brunt of most things Victus could throw at him—force, fire, or lightning. Just as the shield crystallized around him, Victus punched out with a thin stream of fire. It burst in front of D'Jenn's face, blinding him. He growled as spots were burned over his vision.

Victus tried to seize D'Jenn with his Kai, but the shield protected him. D'Jenn slammed a Splinter into Victus's power, bursting his spell like a bubble. Light skittered over the floor in incandescent sparks, leaving tiny burn marks on the stone as Victus's magic spiraled out of control. The Deacon reeled back, and D'Jenn advanced.

D'Jenn took three quick swings—over, left, then over again—but he wasn't used to the feel of the Orrisan axe in his hand. It was a great deal lighter than his mace, and he over-judged his swings. Victus threw himself to the side and came to his feet with a long dagger in his hands.

D'Jenn punched the man with his magic, throwing him into the far wall. Victus fell behind the piled furniture, coughing with pain. D'Jenn shook his head at his mentor. In a fight between wizards, the first mistake was most often the last.

D'Jenn gestured to the side, moving the furniture away from Victus's prostrate form. He lay on the stones, spitting blood onto the floor. The room was quiet in the wake of the quick, nasty fight.

I should kill him quickly. Get it over with while he's on his heels.

How could he kill the man who had trained him? Breaking his neck was too barbaric. Burning him alive was too excessive, too sadistic.

The last thing D'Jenn could give Victus was dignity—he would offer him that much. D'Jenn reached out with his Kai and pulled Victus upright, positioning the man on his knees. Victus hissed with pain and cackled as blood ran into his beard.

"Whatever your last words, don't make them something

insane," D'Jenn said. "I don't want to remember you spouting some nonsense about being chosen by the gods."

Victus spat on the floor and sneered up at D'Jenn.

"The arrogance simply astounds me, boy," Victus laughed. "Last words, indeed. You're not going to kill me."

D'Jenn put the axe blade under Victus's chin and lifted the man's eyes to his own.

"I am."

Victus smiled and made to speak again but broke into wracking coughs. He got over his fit and spat on the stones a second time. He smiled at D'Jenn with bloody teeth.

"Does this please you, boy? To see me on my knees? Your enemy, humbled before you?"

"No," D'Jenn said. "I didn't want you for an enemy, Victus. Make your peace with the gods. I'll make things quick."

D'Jenn readied his magic to stop the man's heart.

"You're not going to kill me, D'Jenn."

"Those are the words you want uttered at your funeral? 'You're not going to kill me, D'Jenn'? You could have done better than that." D'Jenn shook his head and tensed his magic.

Victus favored him with another bloody smile.

"Don't be a woman about it, D'Jenn—give me a warrior's death," he cackled. "Go ahead."

"Victus—"

"Your friends," he coughed, spitting another wad of blood to the side, "oh...how they *screamed*. Fire does that, you know."

"I think I'll change my mind after all," D'Jenn snarled.

Victus's eyes grew wide.

D'Jenn screamed and brought the axe down into Victus's skull, piercing the bone with a metallic *clunk*. He yanked it free to bring it down again, but started back as sand exploded from the wound. Victus smiled as his body disintegrated, whispering into a pile of sand.

D'Jenn felt a sudden moment of panic and dove to the side on instinct.

Something cracked through the space he'd just occupied and put a sharp burn across the back of his leg. D'Jenn hissed in pain as he rolled to his feet, trying to ignore the numb feeling creeping through his thigh. A twisting burn mark was painted on the wall—

evidence of the lightning that had nearly killed him. The axe was still tight in his hand, and his Kai sang a tense, angry melody.

"The arrogance simply astounds me," Victus's voice said.

D'Jenn looked around the room, but the Deacon was nowhere to be seen. He cast about with his senses, but he was met with a cloying fog where clarity had been moments before. Something in the room was interfering with his magic, and he was blind to Victus's position.

The fucking tobacco smoke! How could I have been such a bloody fool?

"Don't be a coward," D'Jenn said. "Show yourself!"

"Show yourself," Victus's disembodied voice repeated, laughing under its breath. "The universal rallying cry for those who are about to die."

D'Jenn poured power into his magical shield and hardened it against attack. He spun around, flicking his eyes in every direction. Dread reached cold fingers up his spine, and he felt the hair on the back of his neck stand on end. Air whipped by the open window, making a low whine.

"I find it a bit odd, in any case, that you would throw such a demand at me," Victus said, "after climbing the tower, blowing a hole in my study, and attacking me at my desk. Show yourself, indeed."

D'Jenn felt the attack coming in the split second before it hit.

He turned, hardening his magical shield as a blow hit him like a charging bull. He slid backwards over the stone, heels scraping as he held himself on his feet with the force of his own power. His shield came to rest against disturbed furniture, and a lightning bolt slammed against it, leaving a bright scar across his vision. It arced all over the room as D'Jenn deflected it, igniting several flammable things.

D'Jenn lashed out with a Splinter, but Victus's power was already quiet, and the man was nowhere to be seen. How was he hiding himself?

A vicious spike of power pierced his Kai, and his magic violently unraveled. He stumbled back as his arms and legs went numb, his mind momentarily stunned. D'Jenn reached for his magic, clawed at his Kai, but it would not respond.

Victus had Splintered him.

The energies D'Jenn had gathered rushed into the room, seeping into the floor. The stones under his feet crumbled, eaten away by the random expulsion of magic. D'Jenn had a moment to despair over his numb arms and legs—there would be no way to hold to the steel cage beneath the study. He tried to scream as he scrambled at the crumbling stones beneath him, but nothing would come out.

The stones under him gave way, and he fell through the opening.

Victus's magic squeezed down on his chest, cutting off his air and arresting his fall. His legs dangled over the yawning hole in the floor, the shadows of the steel webbing just visible against the moonlit stone. D'Jenn tried to suck in a breath, but Victus was squeezing too hard on his torso. He could barely hold in the air he already had.

"D'Jenn," Victus said, "did you really think it would be so damned easy to kill me, boy?"

D'Jenn let out something close to an *urk*.

"Climb right up the tower, slip in through the window, and end me—easy as you please." Victus materialized from the air, as if he was just coming into focus. He smiled at D'Jenn as he walked around the edge of the hole, shooting irritated glances to the ground below. "It will be an entire year before that's fixed. I love this bloody view, boy—you've ruined that for me."

D'Jenn wanted to retort, but he couldn't breathe.

"The others—well, most of them just tried to run, after all. None of them actually thought they could kill me," Victus laughed. He shook his head and smiled, as if D'Jenn had done something endearing. "I would have thought you were smarter than this. Dormael would do this. He's always been hot-headed, impulsive—but not you, D'Jenn."

D'Jenn gave him as baleful a stare as he could manage.

"Oh, don't look at me like that," Victus said. "You know very well *why* they had to die, boy. I couldn't leave them out there to gather strength against me. I didn't want to do it, D'Jenn, but I had to. I *had* to."

"Keep...telling yourself...that," D'Jenn squeezed out. The use of air made him light-headed.

Victus turned an angry stare on him.

"I was hoping to the gods that you and your cousin would join me, D'Jenn," Victus said. "Hells, I even said a prayer—me! A prayer, can you believe it? I even left an offering at the temple for good fortune, a lot of gods-damned good that did me. You were my best tactician, D'Jenn, the most shrewd of my students. I would have made you my right hand, your cousin my left. The two of you...you're like sons to me."

D'Jenn felt like vomiting. He would have, could he summon the air to do it.

"You know I can't let you live. Not after this."

D'Jenn was jerked out through the open window, and his groin tightened in terror as the night air embraced him. Victus held him out in the air, hanging in the cold wind. D'Jenn struggled to reach his magic, but it still wouldn't respond. He could barely move his arms and legs, and his chest was still crushed. Spots appeared over his sight.

Come on! Keep talking for a bit longer, let me regain my strength!

"I wish I could tell you how I did all of that back there," Victus said, gesturing over his shoulder at the ruins of his study. "You, most of us all, would have loved it. Now, though...well...what can one do? Make your peace with the gods, son. I suppose this means your cousin will come after me. I promise to make it quick on him, D'Jenn. Despite what you may believe, I am honored to have known you. Luck, on your trip through the Void."

D'Jenn had a panicked moment to pull his arms over his body, then something white and painful hit him square in the chest. The lights of the city spun around him—orange trails burned through silver and shadow. The smell of charred fabric and burnt hair filled his nose. Wind rushed through his beard.

Allen's going to be angry I lost his axe.

A sudden, frigid darkness embraced him, and the world faded to a cold shadow.

**

"Bethany! Shawna! *Run!*"

Bethany turned at hearing Dormael call her name, the fear in his voice tightening her muscles with alarm. Bethany had heard the scream—a blood-curdling howl from some unknown creature.

She shuffled back and forth, trying to get a look at what was happening, but everyone was standing in her way. Fat Lilliane, bull-chested Torins, ice-lady Lacelle, and Shawna—all of them were blocking Bethany's view of what lay in Dormael's direction.

In my father's direction.

Bethany skipped forward, dodging around Lilliane's blubbery arms as the woman tried to grab her cloak. Adults were always so slow and unwieldy, like bears in dancing dresses. Torins stood frozen in fear, and he didn't even see as she rushed past. Lacelle turned an alarmed gaze at her and hissed something as Bethany ran by, but it was lost to her as she saw what was happening. She had already stopped when she felt Shawna's hand clench the clothing at her shoulder.

Dormael and Allen stood with their weapons leveled at a pair of dark forms with burning eyes. Other things—people, Bethany thought—were running into the boiling room, disappearing into the gloom beneath the kettles. The drop from the walkway was enough to hurt someone, but these people made the jump without a noise of exertion or cry of pain. They ran in complete silence.

Something tightened in Bethany's stomach, and she summoned her magic.

"Jev!" Lacelle called, coming up behind Bethany and Shawna. "Where is—oh...oh, no!"

Allen had moved forward to engage one of the running men, and Dormael had taken another with magic, but there were three more rushing out of the shadows toward them, and Jev was still limping on his injured leg. Bethany watched in horror as the things caught up to him.

"*Jev!*" Lacelle screamed.

Jev uttered a surprised scream of terror as one of them grabbed him. He was jerked violently to the ground, and the other two things fell on him, limbs rising and falling. Jev let out pained, gurgling cries as the crazed men tore him apart in complete silence. When they were done, they tore down the walkway toward Allen and Dormael.

"Lady Baroness!" Lacelle hissed. "Lady, what do we—"

"Aren't you bloody wizards, for the gods' sake?" Shawna said, her swords ringing as she slid them from their sheaths. "Do some magic!"

"More of those fucking things in the dark!" Lilliane said.

"Gods of the sky, gods of the Void, protect these poor souls—" Torins intoned, his eyes shut against the dark. Bethany watched the three wizards in complete astonishment. These three were nothing like Dormael and D'Jenn.

"This is no time for prayer, you drooling idiot!" Lilliane hissed.

Lacelle clenched her jaw and gave a sharp nod, looking around at everyone standing on the walkway.

"Right! Everyone, gather in the middle of the path! Now!" she said, the fear gone from her voice. Torins and Lilliane rushed to her side, and Shawna nudged Bethany toward them.

"Go on, kid," Shawna said, hefting her swords. "I'm going to need room to swing these."

Bethany wanted to stay and help, but she'd only get in the way. She scurried over to the three Philosophers. Torins and Lilliane kept shooting fearful glances at the darkness under the boiling globes, but Lacelle got their attention with snapping fingers.

"We're going to link," she said. "We may not be trained to fight, but we *can* provide some safety for the rest of our people to run to. Open your Kais, and I will take control of the link."

"Safety," Lilliane said, a haunted look in her eyes. "Not for Jev, no safety for Jev. Oh, gods, it was my fault! Jev died, and it was my fault!"

"Focus!" Lacelle snapped. "Clear your heads and open your Kais, or do you need to be instructed like children?"

Lilliane nodded, a sour look on her face. Bethany felt Lilliane's song eke into the world, sharp and fearful, like the woman herself. Torins opened his own Kai and joined it to hers. Lacelle reached out and took control of the other two, and the three songs joined to make a new melody.

"I'm going to create a ward!" Lacelle shouted, directing her voice up the walkway. "A shielded area that won't allow anyone past!"

"Will I be able to get in and out?" Shawna asked, eyes still trained on the surrounding darkness.

"I'll let you in, Baroness."

"Good," Shawna said. "Keep everyone on the inside of your...whatever you called it."

Lacelle nodded and went to work with her students' combined powers. She gestured to the stone of the path and dust rose from its surface as symbols were cut into its face with her power. Bethany shuffled back, trying to make sure she didn't step on anything. Once all her symbols were cut onto the floor, Lacelle did something else with her power Bethany couldn't follow. Her ears gave a low pop, and the three of them were standing inside a bubble of blue werelight. Their surroundings were visible through the wall, but tinged in hues of blue, purple and black.

"That will hold out anything that wants to get in," Lacelle said. "This is one of my personal little tricks. We shouldn't have anything to worry about."

"Poor Jev," Lilliane said, sniffing as tears came to her eyes. "I didn't want him to die, not really. Not really. I didn't mean it. Not really."

"It wasn't your fault, Lilliane," Lacelle said. "Tell her, Torins. Tell her."

Torins only stared at them in turn, the blue light reflecting the sweat on his brow. His eyes were wild, and Bethany had seen that look plenty of times before—he was desperate. His big bull-chest was heaving up and down with short breaths, and his jaw was clenched. Bethany shuffled closer to Lacelle. She wasn't going to be near that big, dumb animal when he spooked.

"Torins," Lacelle said, trying to break through his fugue. "Torins, it's going to be alright."

"It's not, though," he rumbled in reply. "It's not."

"Yes, it will. Lilliane, pull yourself together and stop blubbering, for the gods—"

"Incoming!" Shawna called. Everyone turned their eyes in her direction.

Something rushed out of the blue-tinged darkness, eyes locked on Shawna. She quick-stepped to the side and cut a long gash into the thing's neck as it ran past. It slammed into Lacelle's ward with a sharp crack, the bones in its nose shattering as it ran into the wall of magical force. Bethany stared in horror as the thing's dead eyes tried to roll backward to turn toward Shawna, and it pushed itself off the ward without changing its expression. A silvery swipe took the thing's head from its shoulders. It dropped to the walkway, its head tumbling into the shadows below.

"What the fuck...what the *fuck* was that?!" Lilliane screamed.

Shawna was already fighting another, having to dance backwards and plant a sword through the thing's throat to bring it down. The creatures—corpses, Bethany realized with a chill—fought with a level of vicious abandon that chilled the blood in her veins.

"You have to let her back in!" Bethany said, tugging on Lacelle's sleeve. "Tell her to come back in!"

"Give me a moment, child," Lacelle said, eyes darting around.

"There's more of them in the shadows! You have to let her back in!" Bethany said.

"Lady Baroness!" Lacelle called.

"I'm going for Dormael and Allen! Stay there!" Shawna yelled back. Another corpse came out the darkness, and she was fighting again. Bethany watched in terror as more of the things scrambled over the side of the walkway.

"Tell her to come back in!" Bethany said. "Shawna!"

"Be quiet, child!" Lacelle hissed. "Please!"

"Torins! Torins, what are you—*ack*!" Lilliane screamed.

Bethany and Lacelle turned back to find the hulking Torins with one meaty hand wrapped in Lilliane's hair and the other holding a knife to her throat. He stared at Lacelle with crazed eyes. Lilliane grappled with his wrists, trying to stay on her feet as he manhandled her across the stone floor.

"Torins? *Torins*!" Lacelle snapped. "Torins, what are you doing?!"

"You don't understand," Torins said. "None of you understand! He...this must be part of his plan, right? It *must* be!"

"Whose plan, Torins?"

"Victus's plan, for the gods' sake—you *know* what I'm talking about!"

"I don't, but if you calm down and tell me, talk to me like a sane person—"

"He's not bloody sane," Lilliane snarled through her teeth. "The idiot has finally gone soft in the—"

"I don't want to kill you, Lilliane, but I *will*," Torins snarled. "I will!"

Bethany looked back to where Shawna fought, now dancing between two of the corpses. She held her own, felling them both, but Bethany could see more of them coming in the distance. There was no way she could hold off so many.

"You will do no such thing, Torins! What has bloody gotten into you?" Lacelle hissed. "Put her down!"

"Gotten to me?" Torins said. A look came over his face like a dark cloud, and his shoulders slumped the slightest amount. Lilliane struggled, but she was no match for his strength. "He's had something on me for a long time. He...he wanted someone in your camp, someone—"

"Someone to keep watch on me," Lacelle said, eyes widening. "To spy on me."

"Yes," Torins rumbled. "I didn't want to, I didn't...but he knew something about me. He knows something."

"What?"

A sick smile came over Torins's face.

"Lirium," he said. "I've been on Lirium for a long time."

"You fool," Lacelle said, shaking her head in dismay. "You poor, bloody fool."

"I never wanted any of this!" Torins growled, shaking Lilliane by the hair. "It was always just information! Just harmless stuff, nothing important."

"Nothing that *seemed* important, you fool!" Lilliane hissed.

"You shut up!" Torins snarled, pressing the point of his knife into the fat of her throat. "Just be quiet!"

"It's alright, Torins," Lacelle said, trying to keep her tone even. "You're free of him, now. It doesn't matter now if he tells anyone."

"It's not just the Lirium anymore," Torins said, grimacing. "I just...I can't let you leave. I can't."

"You must!"

"I *can't.*"

Bethany's eyes went again to Shawna. The woman cut down creatures whenever they got too close and kept them at bay by dancing out of their range and changing direction. It was a losing game, though. Three of them were after her, and more were in the shadows beyond. Bethany clenched her teeth.

"Torins, look around you—this isn't Victus's work! This is necromancy! You're not privy to all the information, you don't know everything! Think!" Lacelle said, desperation in her voice.

"I just can't let you leave," Torins said. "He wouldn't excuse it.

He wouldn't. He would do something...something terrible."

"We're all going to be ripped apart, you stupid bastard!" Lilliane screamed.

"We have to go back," Torins said, shaking Lilliane to shut her up. "We're going to turn around now. We're going back!"

"That's not going to happen," Lacelle said, holding up her hands for peace. "Why don't you just let Lilliane go, and you can leave? You can go back. Alright? Just let her go."

"I can't!" Torins growled. "I just can't! If you don't come now, I'll kill her. I'll cut her throat right here."

"Torins!" Lacelle hissed. "Torins, I don't want to hurt you!"

"You've got three seconds," Torins replied. He pressed the knife into Lilliane's throat, making the girl stand on the tips of her toes. "Three seconds, then she dies. I'm sorry."

"Torins!"

"One!"

"*Torins!*"

"Two!"

I've had enough.

Bethany reached out with her magic and gripped Torins the same way she had gripped the rock in Gameritus. The man gave a surprised cry of pain as she clamped down on him, and both Lacelle and Lilliane started back in surprise. Bethany took a deep breath, trying to still the wild fright that fueled her spell, and turned her eyes in Shawna's direction.

Three more corpses lay dead around her, and she was in process of killing two more. Three others were running in her direction from farther down the walkway. Bethany judged the distance, narrowed her eyes.

"Pirate-Queen of the Seas!"

She tossed Torins out of the safety of the ward, sending him flying into the group of corpses pursuing Shawna. His body slammed into them with bone-crushing force, bringing the whole group to a chaotic, tumbling halt. Apparently the ward could only keep things out, because Torins had passed through from this side like a knife through hot butter. Shawna took the head off the last corpse fighting her and turned to sprint for the safety of Lacelle's ward.

"Let her in!" Bethany said. *For the tenth time, already!*

Lacelle gestured at the ward, and her song played a sharp melody. The blue light parted, and Shawna came through the hole an instant later, skidding to a halt near the center. She was covered in gore and gasping for breath from the effort of the fight. The light reformed around them, and a moment of tense silence passed.

"What...what happened in here?" Shawna asked between gasps of breath.

Lilliane and Lacelle glanced at each other and regarded Bethany with stunned expressions.

Bethany shrugged. "Flying Rock."

Torins started screaming, and everyone turned their gazes in his direction. Shawna reached out to squeeze Bethany's shoulder. Bethany patted her hand and decided not to make a big deal about saving her life.

Pirate-Queen of the bloody Seas!

**

By the time Dormael turned back to Jev, it was already too late.

Three of the things had him on the ground, pounding him into the stone with bloodthirsty abandon. Jev screamed in wild terror, but his screams soon turned to gurgles as the things cracked his head open with their mad attack. They ripped the little man apart.

Dormael was so shocked by the sight of it that it took him a moment to recover.

"What are those gods-damned things?" Allen asked through clenched teeth.

"No idea," Dormael said.

The things rose from Jev's broken corpse and ran in Dormael and Allen's direction.

"They're coming this way!" Allen said. He hefted his long, curving saber and pulled a spiked buckler into place on his forearm. "I'm not dying like that! Not like that!"

"Nor I," Dormael growled, readying his magic. "Watch your eyes!"

"My eyes?"

Dormael cracked out with his magic, sending a white-hot bolt of lightning at the three silent men. Two of them were blown off the walkway, flying into the shadows below without a sound. The third was lifted from its feet and tossed back toward the two creatures who still crouched in the doorway. Smoke rose from its chest, and Dormael readied a spell for the two creatures behind it.

He nearly fell on his arse when the thing got up.

Nothing should have been able to survive that! He watched in horror as it climbed to its feet, eyes still locked on Dormael and his brother. Smoke was still rising from it—and, in fact, a small fire was burning over its clothing—but the thing didn't even notice.

"What, in the name of the gods, is that thing?" Allen asked.

"I don't know."

"Isn't this supposed to be your sphere?" Allen said. "You're supposed to know these things."

"Not *these* things," Dormael said. "Nor those things behind it. I've never seen their like."

"Beautiful," Allen grumbled. "Bloody beautiful."

Dormael reached out and gripped the burning creature in his Kai, bringing it up from the stone of the walkway. Even suspended in the air, it fought to get to him, kicking its legs in a vain attempt to struggle in his direction. Dormael twisted the thing into a wrecked ball of flesh and tossed it into the shadows.

The two creatures stared at Dormael and Allen, swaying like a pair of poisonous snakes entranced by a charmer's song. The other things—the silent berserkers—had disappeared into the surrounding shadows. The swaying creatures let out a strange series of kettle-like noises and crouched like cats on the prowl.

"I think they're coming this way," Allen said. "They look hungry."

"Let's see if they're like the other things," Dormael said. "Watch—"

"—my eyes? Got it."

Dormael lashed out with his magic, sending a searing bolt of energy cracking across the distance. The smaller of the two was struck, and it uttered a strange cry in what Dormael thought was pain. He could feel, though, an odd sensation as the bolt connected. His magic slid away from the creatures like oil over the surface of water. His lightning hit the thing, but the power of the strike was toothless, diminished. The strange creature shook itself free of the arcing electricity and continued to prowl toward them.

"Evmir's bloody hammer," Allen said. "Can we even kill these things?"

"We have to try!" Dormael hefted his spear.

The first of the creatures—the largest—broke into a lithe, liquid sprint. It had long, thin claws on its hands that made scraping noises across the stone. It uttered a cry, like a hound on the hunt. Allen held up the buckler—which seemed a pitifully small shield in the face of the large, hellish creature—and held his long saber aloft. He crouched, ready to meet the thing's charge.

The second one also tore down the walkway in their direction, vaulting Jev's corpse without looking down. Dormael readied his spear, crouching as if he was about to meet the charge of a wild boar, and clenched his teeth. He reached deep into his being and pulled more power from his Kai, bringing his magic to a single, powerful point.

As the thing rushed him, he lashed out with his magic, trying to knock the creature from the walkway. He hit it with enough force to have shattered a boulder, but his magic again slid away—however, he had poured enough power into the attack to have some effect. The creature tumbled away into the darkness to their left, though it didn't go as far as it should have.

So it does work, though not as well as it should.

Allen screamed in fury and rushed the other creature, meeting its charge head on. His saber whipped in vicious arcs as he advanced, forcing the creature to duck away. Allen scored a slash on its long, distended forearm, and the monster hissed in rage as it rolled away from him. It came back up to a fighting crouch, shooting its glowing eyes between Dormael and Allen.

Dormael reached out and tried to grip the thing in his Kai, but it again resisted his power. His magic flowed away from it, as if its skin was anathema to its touch. It rose from the walkway for the space of a small moment, struggling against Dormael's magic with its arms and legs. Allen moved in and made a swipe at the creature, but its claws deflected his saber with a tense, metallic note. Dormael made a few quick thrusts at its face with his spear, but its claws flicked his attacks aside as well, and he had to let his spell go as a waste.

Allen moved in as the thing's feet hit the walkway, driving it back with cuts aimed at its glowing eyes. Dormael moved in to support him on the other side, threatening it with his spear when it tried to slip aside from his brother. For a brief, glorious moment, Dormael thought they had the creature pinned down.

With an angry cry, it suddenly went on the offensive.

It swiped Allen's saber aside with the flick of one of its claws and wrapped the other around his buckler. Allen gave a cry of rage as the creature jerked him aside by the shield, flinging him down the walkway. He tumbled away, his weapons clinking on the stone.

Dormael stabbed the monster through the side with his spear when it turned its attention away, but the creature paid the wound little mind as it turned back to him. It swiped a long set of claws at Dormael's face, and the only thing that saved him from being maimed was the fact that his heel had slipped on the stone, and he was already falling.

The creature jerked his spear out of its side and dropped it on the stone. It made an odd screeching noise and reached down to wrap a hand around Dormael's throat. A spike of fear stabbed into his heart, and he kicked at the creatures knees, trying to scramble away. His feet connected, bringing the cloth-wrapped thing down on top of him.

It smelled like an open grave.

Dormael reached to his side and whipped a dagger from his belt, punching it into the creature's ribs as he tried to scramble free. It gave little physical reaction as the knife sank in. It raised itself from Dormael's body and looked down at him, shining red pin-points narrowing. It turned its head to the side and sniffled like a dog about to chomp down on a meal. The hand around Dormael's throat tightened, and he was filled with the sudden, sickening fear that he was going to be eaten.

Allen's saber chopped down into the creature's shoulder with a fleshy thump, and it uttered a kettle-like screech of pain. It arched its back, trying to reach behind and pull the saber out of its collarbone. Allen let out another scream of rage and chopped through the creature's leg with one of his short swords, having abandoned the saber in its shoulder. It squealed in rage as it buckled to the stone, and black mist leaked from the severed stump. When the leg hit the walkway, it crackled, hissed, and dissolved into a thick, gray salt.

What are these gods-damned things?!

Dormael scrambled out of the way and lashed out with his

magic, putting every bit of power he could muster against the creature that was even now trying to rise. He held it to the stone, though it struggled to get up and attack him. Dormael felt his magic sliding away from the thing, threatening to give way at any moment.

"Get it!" Dormael screamed. "Kill the fucking thing!"

Allen chopped down with his thick-bladed short sword, severing the creature's head in a series of brutal cuts. It screamed with every blow, clawed hands pawing at the air but unable to block. Once the head came off, its body crackled and disintegrated.

A mournful croon came from the shadows under the kettles.

"I forgot about the other one," Allen said, grimacing as he wiped the salty substance from his hand. He helped Dormael to his feet and went to retrieve his weapons. Dormael picked up his spear and shoved the dagger back into its sheath.

"We need a better way to do this," Dormael said, eyes darting through the darkness. The creature hadn't shown itself. "That one almost got me."

"You're welcome, by the way," Allen said. "If I hadn't been there, you'd have been skewered."

"My magic doesn't work on them," Dormael said. "At least, not as well as it should."

"I noticed," Allen said. "Maybe if we—"

A loud, metallic clang cut off Allen's words, and the brothers turned to see the second, smaller creature leaping down on them from one of the bronze globes. Dormael moved away from his brother just as Allen leapt in the other direction, and the monster landed on the walkway where they had been standing, claws digging furrows into the stone. It keened in rage.

Allen attacked it from behind, saber cutting quick, circular arcs through the air. The creature slipped aside, moving like an eel as it dodged around the saber in a contemptuous dance. It was unclear if the things had intelligence, but it almost looked as if it was taunting his brother.

It's too damned fast! Dormael moved in with his spear, threatening the creature as it tried to dodge his brother's swipes with the curved sword. He sliced at the monster's legs, trying his best to trip the thing up.

The thing moved with an alien, unnatural grace. Allen's saber cut a deadly arc at its eyes, while Dormael's spear descended on an ankle. The creature swayed just out of reach of the saber while slipping its leg wide of Dormael's spear simultaneously. No matter what they did, it stayed one step ahead of them—a breath away from being cut, but dancing along that edge with a cold, contemptuous air.

It snatched the haft of Dormael's spear, moving so fast he had no time to react. It jerked the weapon out of his hands and shoved it back into his chest cross-wise, knocking the breath from Dormael's chest. His feet left the stone as he flew backwards, spear tumbling through the air with him. His head struck the walkway hard enough to jam his teeth down on his tongue. He tasted blood in his mouth, and stars appeared before his eyes.

Another huddled, stinking form appeared above him, and hands clamped around his throat. Dead, milky eyes and rotting flesh filled Dormael's sight. He tossed his arm up in an instinctual motion, throwing his shoulder over the thing's arm and rolling away. He was able to break its choke, but the thing continued to come at him, clawing at his clothing for purchase. Dormael scrambled away in terror, swatting its hands as he tried to get to his feet.

Two more sets of hands grabbed him by the shoulders of his *mesavai*, dragging him back to the stone. More hands, ripping at his right arm. Dormael kicked his feet, panic rising in his chest. The sight of Jev came once again to his memory, ripped apart by those creatures.

Corpses—animated corpses!

Screaming, he lashed out with his Kai. A wave of violent force swept out from him, pushing everything away. Dormael scrambled to his feet and summoned a ball of flame, super-heating the air with a muted *thump.* The light illuminated the slack faces of corpses all around him, the ones on their feet running toward him at full speed.

Dormael swept out with the flame, pouring magic out in wide, sweeping arcs. The liquid fire stuck to every corpse it touched, burning through flesh, bone, and cloth with supernatural speed. Those who made it close enough were crushed to the walkway, Dormael's magic coming down on them like the heel of a giant boot. He yelled something unintelligible, rage and fear powering his magic as he laid about with the fire. Before long, all the corpses he could see were burning.

Dormael gestured, bringing his spear back to his hands, and turned back to help his brother.

Allen spun with the red-eyed creature, dancing an intricate, brutal series of steps. Claws slashed the air, drawing sparks from Allen's saber as he turned them aside. Allen knocked other swipes away from him with his buckler, staying just ahead of the thing's claws at every turn. Dormael would never have been able to move that fast. His brother couldn't keep it up forever, though—of that, Dormael was sure.

He hefted his spear and sprinted back toward the action, splitting his consciousness as he ran. He reached the fight and waded in, scoring a glancing slice on the creature's shoulder while its back was turned. It uttered a high-pitched growl and made to slash at him, but was forced to turn and defend itself from Allen instead. The creature prowled aside from them, disengaging to regard them both with its head cocked to the side. Allen took the opportunity to abandon his buckler.

"Damned thing was getting in my way," he growled, holding his saber out at the prowling, swaying creature. "Any idea how to kill this thing?"

"I need you stick something in it," Dormael said.

"That's the way you kill lots of things, brother," Allen said. "I was hoping for more."

"I mean you need to get something stuck in it—like in its breastbone, or its skull. Somewhere it will *stick*," Dormael clarified.

Allen nodded and flourished his sword. "I'll put something right through the bastard's eye, if that's what it takes."

"Good," Dormael nodded. "Because until you do—"

"Incoming!" Allen hissed.

Dormael crouched, hefting his spear to meet the creature's charge. It darted toward them, trying to get them to separate and break apart. Dormael and Allen, though, kept their backs to where Shawna and Bethany crouched with the Philosophers. They met the monster's attacks, just able to keep it at bay as they backpedaled. It advanced on them with renewed ferocity, its attacks coming too fast by half.

Dormael had an idea, though. Part of his epiphany was thanks to D'Jenn, who had saved his life from the Cultist in that dark, rainy alleyway in Gameritus. His words were ringing through Dormael's head.

If you can't use magic on them, just throw things at them.

If he couldn't cast magic *on* the creature, perhaps he could just cast magic *at* it.

Dormael whispered his power around the thing, thickening the air through which it moved. The creature snarled in outrage as it struggled against the air's heightened resistance. The fight became less desperate, and hope kindled to life in Dormael's chest. Allen snarled in excitement as the rhythm of the fight shifted, and his blade licked out with renewed purpose. His saber scored a glancing cut along the side of the creature's thigh, then another on its ankle when it tried to slip out of range. The monster screamed in indignation.

Dormael snarled and waded further into the fight, thrusting at the creature to drive it toward his brother's whirling saber attacks. The thickened air slowed its reactions by just enough to make the fight winnable, but the thing still possessed unnatural speed and agility. It moved in amazing, disgusting ways.

The creature turned its full attention on Dormael, slashing at his throat with a long, delicate claw. Dormael threw himself backwards, whipping out a circular parry with his spear. The attack, though, had been a feint, and the parry met nothing but air. Dormael slipped as he backpedaled, his balance wavering. The creature let out a triumphant screech and pounced.

The damned thing feinted!

Dormael threw up his hands and poured more power into the air-thickening spell, but it was no use. The creature crashed into him, driving him down to the stone. Dormael panicked, pushing against the monster as hard as he could with his Kai, which raised its body into the air. Dormael brought up a quick shield which saved his life as the creature's claws glanced from it. It slashed at his throat, trying to bash through his shield with its magic-resistant claws. Dormael's magic pushed upward, his power sliding off the thing's skin like water around a boulder.

Allen's arm snaked around the thin neck of the creature, wrenching back on its head. It screamed and thrashed about, but Allen had mounted its back, and the strange shape of its body wouldn't allow for it to reach him. With his other hand, Allen shoved a long dagger into its eye socket, burying it to the hilt. The monster screeched in agony.

"*Now!*" Allen screamed, leaping away from the creature and rolling clear.

Dormael smiled and seized the dagger in his Kai.

The beast howled in rage as Dormael lifted it from the walkway by the dagger stuck in its skull. Dormael used his magic to shove it even deeper, eliciting another pained screech from the creature. It kicked its feet and thrashed with its arms. It clawed at the dagger, but its fingers were too deformed to find purchase on the hilt. It fought so hard that Dormael thought it would rip its own head to pieces.

"What are you waiting for?" Allen asked. "Kill it!"

Dormael pushed against the dagger with all his magical might and slammed the creature into the nearest boiling kettle. It hit hard enough to dent the shell, and Dormael pushed down on the globe and crushed it around the beast, trapping it in a prison of warped bronze. The metal squealed as Dormael manipulated it, and water poured from the cracks. The sounds of thumping claws against the metal cut off as Dormael crushed the globe into the creature's body.

Summoning a chestful of power, Dormael pounded the globe with lightning.

The electricity struck with a violent crack and hummed as it jumped between the globes in the boiling room, lighting the entire scene in bright, white flashes. Dormael hit the globe again and again, pouring all the power he could into each bolt. The room flashed, sparks flew from the boilers, and magic hummed around him. When it was over, the only sound was the water pouring from the crack in the damaged globe.

Dormael watched for signs of movement, but the globe was silent.

Allen came up beside him, saber held at the ready. They both stared at the crushed kettle, waiting for something to happen. Moments passed in silence.

"I told you," Allen finally said, letting the tip of his saber relax.

"Told me what?"

"That I would stick something in that bastard's eye." Allen

smiled. "I told you I'd do it, and I did it. I just wanted to point that out."

"I guess you did, at that. What do you want, a medal?"

"From you?" Allen said. "Worthless. Maybe you can buy me a drink at the next pub."

"I fried the bloody thing with lightning," Dormael said. "How about you buy *me* a drink?"

"Right, but you didn't have to get close to do that," Allen said, gesturing at the ruined globe. "I had to climb on that thing's back. Do you think it smelled any better up close?"

"It's not my fault you can't use magic."

"It's your fault you're not as good a warrior as me—that's what I'm trying to say. You owe me a drink."

"No."

"You can't argue."

"I am."

"You can't."

"Seems like I'm doing it."

"What were those things?" Shawna said, coming up behind them.

Dormael turned, feeling a load of relief at the sight of Bethany. She ran up and wrapped his waist in a fierce hug which he returned. He pushed her hair out of her face, looking her up and down until he was satisfied she wasn't hurt.

"I don't know," Dormael said, looking back to Shawna. "I've never seen them before."

"They were dead bodies," Bethany said. "I saw them. Dead as rocks. Dead as dirt."

"The work of a *vilth*," Lacelle said, gliding up to join them. Lilliane came huffing in her wake, but Dormael didn't see Torins. When no one offered any information, Dormael chose not to ask.

"The two big ones—they were corpses, too, I think," Allen said. "Certainly smelled like it."

Dormael turned to Lacelle. "Do you know anything about *vilthinum*?"

She shook her head. "I've only read a few stories, and I don't remember much. It's not exactly my area of expertise."

"I don't care to stick around here and learn more about them," Shawna said. "We should keep moving, get to the surface before more of those things show up."

"I agree," Allen said.

"Let's get moving, then," Dormael said. "Find the next turn and let's leave this place behind."

Everyone nodded and gathered their things. The remains of Jev and Torins—what little was left—were laid out on the stone, stripped of anything useful, and piled as neatly as possible. Even for Dormael, it was a sickening sight. Lacelle left a pair of copper marks over each of their eyes before turning to follow everyone deeper into the sewers, once again holding her magical light aloft.

Dormael watched her go, offering a tight-lipped smile as she passed by. He waited for a few moments, watching the dark opening leading back toward the Conclave. It yawned before him, offering nothing but silence and shadow. He gritted his teeth and put his spear over his shoulder.

He'll catch up. He always does.

Turning, he left the boiling room in shadow and followed his friends out of the tunnels.

Epilogue

"If you're sleep-deprived, can you still use your magic?" Shawna whispered.

Dormael almost jumped out of his skin. He'd been staring off in the direction of the river, listening for any sounds other than the distant gurgle of water and the swish of wind through the grass. There had been nothing but the darkness and the wind.

"I should go back," Dormael said. "Look for him. He'd look for me."

"Maybe," Shawna said, coming up to sit beside him. She let out a long breath and settled against his shoulder. "You know what he'd *tell* you to do, though."

"Not to look for him."

"And he'd be right."

"I know."

"You should rest."

"I know."

"Then why aren't you?"

"I don't know."

"Don't be a fool, Dormael," Shawna sighed, pushing his shoulder to emphasize her words. "Staring into the darkness until your eyes fall out won't change anything. D'Jenn will be fine."

"Do you really believe that?" Dormael asked, turning his eyes on her. Her own eyes were liquid and opaque, though her silence said enough. "I'll sleep soon."

"The sky is turning blue, Dormael," Shawna said. "And your restlessness is keeping *me* awake. Can you just lie down, already?"

Dormael forced himself to turn away from the river.

"Alright. You're right."

"Yes, I am," she said, softening her words with a smile. "Come on—if you need to get some of your nerves out, you can talk me to sleep."

He followed her to the camp, dodging the lumps of their friends' sleeping forms. Lacelle and Lilliane were huddled on one side of the circle, though there had been no fire around which to huddle. Bethany, for once, slept alone, huddled into her cloak. The girl had fallen asleep with a fierce smile on her face, though Dormael had no idea where she'd found such emotional resilience. Allen snored, but his hand hovered ever near his weapons—only because he had so many of the things that it didn't matter where his hand rested at any given time.

Shawna laid down on her blankets and gestured for Dormael to lay his own out beside her. He obliged her, and soon the two of them were lying side-by-side, if not touching. The stars were starting to wash out from the rising sun, but some of them still shone, defiant through the gloom.

"What happens next?" Shawna asked.

"Orm," Dormael said. "We go to the cursed temple and see what we can dig up about the Nar'doroc."

"How long until Victus comes after us?"

"I'm not sure," Dormael admitted. "He'll send someone—I'm sure of that much. He'll also have a lot of trouble here to take care of, so it might be awhile before we have to worry much about him." Thoughts of Victus brought thoughts of D'Jenn, and fresh worry twisted in Dormael's guts. "If he killed my cousin, by the gods, I'll rip his still-beating heart from his chest."

A moment of silence passed in the wake of his comment.

"I'll help you, if you want," Shawna said.

"You will?"

"Of course I will," she whispered back through a yawn. "We're friends, Dormael. I've met your family. D'Jenn was my friend, too."

"You're right, I'm sorry. Shouldn't have questioned your fidelity." He yawned on reflex, his jaw cracking with the effort.

"You helped me with my revenge—or to start it, anyway,"

Shawna said, another yawn mangling her words until they were barely intelligible. "I should help you back."

"If he's dead," Dormael said around another yawn of his own.

"If he's dead," Shawna agreed.

Dormael closed his eyes for a moment, just to rest them. The sky was turning to a predawn gloom, and it was bothering him. So many things were bothering him.

"Shawna?"

"Mmm?"

"Do you remember visiting my homestead?"

"Mmm."

"Do you remember what happened?"

Silence.

Dormael looked over and found Shawna's eyes closed, her mouth hanging open. Dormael let out a long sigh and turned back over. He would have been irritated, but that sky was so damned bright.

He closed his eyes—just for a moment, of course.

**

Maarkov was watching the light turn from deep blue to predawn purple when the Hunter came limping back into camp. The thing was burnt, slashed, beat up, and missing one of its glowing eyes. Maarkov couldn't help but feel a small amount of respect for their quarry. If Maarkov had been gambling, he would have bet on the Hunters without a second thought.

It appeared that he would have been wrong.

Maaz was not happy, to say the least. He scowled at the Hunter for a long moment before hissing at it in that ugly language. Maarkov couldn't speak the first word of it, but he knew an argument when he heard one. The Hunter was getting the sharp side of Maaz's tongue.

"Brother!" Maarkov called, packing some tobacco into his pipe. "Is everything alright?" He favored Maaz with a toothy grin, pouring a challenge into the smile.

Maaz glowered and went back to bickering with the Hunter.

Maarkov sighed and returned to staring over the valley. The sky deepened to pink as the Hunter argued with his brother. By the time Maarkov watched the sunlight chase the shadow across the valley floor, Maaz appeared at his side.

"Our quarry has eluded us," he said.

"Eluded *you*," Maarkov pointed out. "I'm just along for the ride or the occasional killing."

"As you wish," Maaz said. "Regardless, we must adapt."

"And how do we adapt, brother? I imagine the process involves more riding. More time spent in your company."

Maaz gave him a long, dangerous look.

There were times when Maarkov mocked his brother and almost thought the bastard would finally end it. Maybe he would snap and burn Maarkov where he stood. Maybe he would break his neck or rip his head from his shoulders. Whichever way he might get it done, Maarkov longed for it. He savored those murderous glances like precious gemstones.

"It's no serious feat to track your prey if you know where it's going," Maaz said. "The Hunter has the wizard's scent. It can follow him no matter where he runs, no matter where he hides. Even that, though, is more than we need."

"More than we need?"

"Yes," Maaz said. "I already know where they're going, and nothing could be better for us."

"Why?" Maarkov asked, taking another pull from his pipe.

"They've been hiding in the city up to this point, huddled in the center of the one place I cannot chase them," Maaz said. "There's only one other place on this continent old enough to hold any answers for them, and it's an ancient ruin in the middle of nowhere. They'll have nowhere to run this time, no city full of wizards to protect them. Out in the grasslands, they will be helpless to the full might of my power."

Maaz reached into his robe and pulled out the book he always carried with him—the ancient tome from which he drew his knowledge. It had started everything, had sent them on this mad quest spanning so many years. Maarkov rarely caught sight of it, but when he did, Maaz caressed it like a pet. It gave Maarkov chills.

"Is that in your little book, then? That's how you know about this old ruin?"

Maaz gave him a disdainful look and shoved the book back out of sight. Maarkov waited for an answer, but one never came. His brother was tight-lipped about the damned book.

Maarkov sighed and stared back over the valley. "So, where in the Six Hells are we going now?"

"North, to the ancient ruins of Orm." Maaz smiled. "The Place Where the Gods Listen."

"The Place That Can Kiss My Bloody Arse," Maarkov intoned.

"Laugh all you want," Maaz sighed. "Be in your saddle by midmorning, or stay here and wither."

Maarkov scowled at his brother's departing back. He was struck by the memory of the last time he'd stabbed his brother, of the way his steel tugged ever so slightly as it entered through the fleshy split between Maaz's ribs. He was struck with a sudden fit of blinding rage, a pure instant of white-hot anger that compelled him to move.

Then it was over, and Maarkov persisted.

Maarkov always bloody persisted—whether he wanted to or not.

**

Victus Tiranan stood in his window, staring out over the dark expanse of the river.

So many things had gone wrong. He had thought Dormael and D'Jenn would join him—surely they would have been able to see his logic, had he the proper chance to explain it to them. It angered him to think about the mistakes that led to tonight's folly.

"Why did you try it, boy?" he said aloud for the hundredth time. "Why in the gods' name did you try it?"

No one answered him, of course. The dead never answered, though they were the ones from whom answers were most needed. The only answer came from the wind—the same accusing howl it had given him all night. Sighing, Victus turned away from the window and walked back to his chair.

This little attempt on his life meant several things. One—Dormael would be gone, having taken all his friends and the armlet with him. Two—the Mekai knew something, which confirmed suspicions he'd held for quite some time. Three—he had to make his move soon or risk losing everything he had prepared.

A change in the balance of power was always a delicate thing.

He had been polishing these plans for years, gathering his power, laying out the foundations for something great. Under him, the Warlocks had become deadly, and now they would use that power for good in the world—real good, not just protecting people from harmful magic. They could affect change all over Eldath. They had the power to see their will done—to see *his* will done—and finally, the conviction to see it through to its inevitable conclusion.

The powerful ruled the weak—such was the truth throughout nature. The lion takes the hart whenever it wishes. The wolf doesn't ask the elk for permission before it culls from the herd—it takes. Such had been the truth for human beings since the beginning of time. The strong ruled the weak, raped the weak, enslaved the weak, murdered the weak indiscriminately. The world was full of wolves.

Eldath was full of people who fancied themselves wolves but had never met a real wolf. Amongst humans, wizards were special, and they had the power to do amazing things. Amongst wizards, Warlocks were a breed apart—trained to fight and kill with magic, and under Victus, so much more. Soon, the wolves would meet the Warlocks, and the wolves would learn their new place in the circle of life.

Dormael was now rogue and in control of a magical item more powerful than anything Victus had ever seen. The artifact was the one thing Victus hadn't anticipated. In the hands of a Warlock like Dormael, the threat the artifact posed was too serious to ignore.

Its mystery was confounding. It would be nothing to get his hands on the research the Mekai had been conducting. Lacelle's people had as many secrets as anyone else, and anyone with a secret was a potential asset. Victus had many assets.

He'd have to send someone to kill Dormael and his friends. As much as he hated to do it, the one thing he could trust was that Dormael would make an attempt on his life at some point in the future. He wouldn't stand for the death of his cousin. Victus hated to lose two talented Warlocks—he'd hated losing all the ones who had betrayed him—but there was nothing for it.

Victus lit a pipe and started planning.

**

It had been a shit night for fishing.

"Who do you think he was, Torbi?" Berbin asked, bending over to peer at the dead man. "Do you think he fell out of the sky?"

Torbi and Berbin had been fishing on the river, hoping to pull in something to take home to their Ma. The dead man had splashed into the water somewhere nearby, which had nearly capsized their canoe. When they found the man in the water, Berbin had been sure he had fallen from some great height.

Berbin was dumb as dog shit.

"Don't be stupid," Torbi said, slapping his little brother across the back of the head. "Things don't just fall out of the sky, dolt."

"I'm not a dolt! Don't call me that!"

"Dolt," Torbi said again. "Dolt, dolt, dolt, *fucking* dolt!"

"If Ma knows you said that, she'll whip you into next season!"

"Said what?" Torbi smiled. "Fucking? Do you know what it is, Berbin? Do you know what fucking is?"

"What?"

"It's what Old Jorban does to Willi Thames' mother in the back of his shop," Torbi snickered. "Right up the skirts!"

"I don't get it," Berbin said.

"Of course you don't, you idiot," Torbi sighed. Berbin was only ten, after all. Torbi, though, was thirteen. He'd seen tits and everything—he'd paid one of the girls in the East Market to let him kiss hers. He could never tell his Ma that, though. She really would beat him into next season if she heard that.

"Do you think he's rich?" Berbin asked. "He's wearing nice clothes."

"He's not anything anymore, little brother," Torbi said. "That's the way of the world. He's dead now, see? He don't have no need for all that stuff. We can take it."

"We can?"

"Aye, the gods won't mind. Ma will thank us, too, if we come home with something nice."

"You really think so?"

"I know so." Torbi smiled. "It's the way of the world."

"Where did you hear about the way of the world?" Berbin asked. "Is there somewhere you can go to hear it? Like to the temple?"

"It's not like going to the temple, you idiot," Torbi said. "It's just something you learn. One day you'll get it."

"If you say so."

"I do. Now—look in his purse."

"What? Me?" Berbin asked. He looked terrified.

"Yes, *you*," Torbi said. "I'm the oldest. You have to do what I say."

"Do not!"

"Do so! Besides, it's high time you touched your first dead body."

"You've touched a body before, have you?"

"I have!" Torbi nodded. He hadn't, but Berbin didn't need to know that. "I do it all the time out here. Where do you think the street boys dump their victims, eh? Plop!—right in the river. I see them all the time."

"Then how come I never see them when we go together?"

"Because you're a dolt, Berbin," Torbi said. "A fucking dolt. Now—look in his purse."

"Alright," Berbin said. "But don't tell Ma I touched it."

"Why not?"

"Because she'll make me go say a prayer at the temple, and I don't want to say a stupid prayer!"

"Alright, alright," Torbi said, holding his hands up for peace. "I won't tell. This is our secret."

"A brother secret?"

"A brother secret." Torbi nodded and clasped forearms with his brother. "Now—look in the purse!"

"Fine," Berbin said.

He bent down in the mud of the embankment and poked at the body, shying back with each poke as if the dead man was going to jump up from the mud and eat him. Torbi rolled his eyes and gestured for Berbin to get on with it. Berbin stuck out his tongue and reached for the dead man's purse.

"*Berbin!*" Torbi screamed, jumping at the boy.

Berbin squealed and scrambled through the mud, trying to get away from the corpse. Torbi broke out in a fit of laughter, unable to hold it in. Berbin stared daggers at him, growing so red in the face that his ears shone in the predawn light.

"You nearly pissed yourself!" Torbi laughed.

"Did not!"

"Did so! And you screamed like a girl!"

"Take that back!"

"Or what?"

"Or I'll hit you—that's what!"

"You won't." Torbi grinned. "You're too sissy for that."

"Am not," Berbin said. "I'm the one who was going for the purse. Why don't *you* go for it? Let's see how big and tough *you* are!"

"I'd get that purse any day," Torbi said. "Don't be stupid."

"Get it, then," Berbin said, raising his chin. "I dare you."

"You can't dare me, I'm older than you," Torbi said with a sneer. "Don't you know anything, you dolt?"

"If I'm a dolt, then you're a sissy," Berbin said. "A sissy who won't even take a purse from a dead body."

Torbi raised his chin, echoing his brother's stance. Nobody called Torbi Numarian a sissy—not even his own brother! He thought about punching Berbin in the face, but he'd have to explain that one to his Ma, too. He'd just have to show his brother what was what.

"A sissy, eh?" Torbi asked. "Would a sissy do this?"

Torbi bent down and wrapped his hands around the corpse's belt, trying to rip the man's purse from it. It didn't come free right away, and the cold leather was slippery in his hands. He clenched his teeth and worked at the buckles with his fingers, but he couldn't get it loose.

The corpse seized his wrists in wet, cold hands.

Torbi screamed, petrified with fear. The corpse let go, and he scrambled away, gathering Berbin close. He dug his fingers into his brother's shoulders and shoved Berbin behind him. The man—who wasn't dead—retched and turned to the side, coughing into the mud. He spat a bellyful of the river onto the embankment. Berbin stood transfixed, mouth agape. Torbi was right on the verge of telling his brother to run.

The man looked around, wiping the wetness from his beard. He tossed his long, wet hair out of his eyes and squinted at the two boys, then at the canoe. The man grimaced.

"Is that yours?" he asked, gesturing at the canoe. His voice was a throaty growl, but anyone who had swallowed that much of the river was lucky to have a voice at all.

"It is," Torbi said, holding Berbin behind him.

The man gave Torbi a sour look. He grimaced and sat up, looking over his shoulder at the city in the distance. Looking down,

364

he yanked the purse from his belt and held it out to Torbi.

"It's yours, kid, if you take me up the river."

Torbi shared a suspicious glance with his brother.

"How do I know you're not going to kill us or do something weird to us?"

The man scowled at him.

"I'm not going to hurt you, kid. Here, look," he said. He opened the purse and spilled the contents onto his hand—a pile of silver the likes of which Torbi had never seen. Berbin let out an awed sigh as the money tumbled into the man's palm, and Torbi couldn't help but feel the same. That was more silver than Torbi thought he would ever see. The man tried to smile, though it looked forced.

"One canoe trip, kid. No weird stuff, I promise."

Torbi favored the man with a long, pondering look. His Ma always told him not to talk to strangers, that strangers made off with children and did all manner of things with them. This one didn't strike Torbi as the weird sort, but he had to be dangerous. Nobody who was pulled out of the river with that much money in their purse could be harmless.

"Fine," Torbi said. "But if you hurt my brother, you'll have to answer to me."

The man surprised him with a laugh.

"Deal, kid," he said. "It's a deal. Here." He replaced the coins in the purse and tossed it over. Torbi caught it in his hands, terrified the money would tumble into the mud and be lost forever. He clutched it with reverence. How was he supposed to carry so much money?

"Oh—wait," the man said. "You can have all of those except one."

He gestured, and the purse floated up from Torbi's hands and hovered in midair. Torbi froze, but Berbin let out another awed sigh and clapped his hands. Berbin had never seen a wizard before.

Neither had Torbi, but Berbin didn't need to know that.

The wizard gestured, and a single copper mark leapt from the purse and floated to his palm. He snatched it out of the air and dropped the purse back into Torbi's open hands.

"Not this one," the wizard said. "I need this one."

The canoe was large enough for the three of them, even with

the wizard lying down in the stern. The man slept so hard that Torbi had to check and see if he'd died after all. Every time he got close, the man opened a baleful eye. Torbi decided to leave him be.

Ma would be so proud with all the money. They could finally move out of the Market and into the countryside like she wanted. Maybe Pa would come back. Regardless, his family wouldn't have to worry about money for a long time. For that, he'd row the wizard all the way to Orris if he wanted.

It had been a fine night for fishing, after all.

THE END
of
BOOK TWO
of
THE SEVEN SIGNS

A Note from the Author

I'm stoked you've decided to come this far on our little journey. The series is only getting started, and there's much more to come. I might have said somewhere before that I've got plans.

Nothing helps a book gain recognition more than customer reviews. If you've enjoyed my work, please consider leaving it an honest review at your favorite retailer. It would mean the world.

If you're enjoying my work so far, consider joining the Conclave, the official D.W. Hawkins mailing list. I'll give you a free book if you do. A free Seven Signs book, even.

You can do that on my website.

Thanks for everything, and I hope to see you in book three.

About the Author

D.W. Hawkins lives in southern Arizona.

You can find out more about him at www.dwhawkins.com
You can also look him up on Facebook and follow him on Twitter
@authordwhawkins

He hopes you enjoy reading his work as much as he does writing
it.

More from D.W. Hawkins
The Seven Signs
Child of the Flames
The Knife in the Dark
The Old Man of the Temple
The City Under the Mountain
The Oath of the Blade
The Heart of the Wasteland*

*Coming soon

WANT A FREE FANTASY BOOK?

Join the Conclave and get *The Killings at Rockman's Ford: A Seven Signs Novella* for **FREE**

You'll also get members-only promotions and updates right from the author's desk.

What are you waiting for?

JOIN TODAY *and* **GET YOUR FREE BOOK**

www.dwhawkins.com/the-conclave

Made in the USA
Monee, IL
24 June 2025

19934341R10218